Housewarming

A Novel

Jennifer Bowen

Published in the United States by Rosefall Publications, June 2019

ISBN: 978-0-9990117-2-0

Cover design: Christopher Bowen
Cover image: Amanda Carden/Shutterstock.com

For Mom and Dad

Prologue

Hands held her down, forcing her just below the water's surface. If she could just roll over and push up a few inches, she'd be able to breathe. But the hands were too strong. When she was first shoved downward, she had flipped right-side up and almost saw the face. But the water rippled each time she jerked against those hands, so she could never see it clearly.

Let me go! she screamed, the cry a gurgle letting water in, filling her mouth and throat.

She struggled, but she was growing weak. Her heavy eyelids drooped, pushing against the water as they started to close, exhaustion overtaking her. She stopped the fight and stilled, her hair fanning out around her. The hands relented too, easing their grip until they finally released. Her body drifted, sinking, close to the sandy bottom. She gasped, but there was no more oxygen left.

Her eye wiggled at something black ahead. She watched it stupidly. The blob rolled in the water, lolling along the steadying waves. It neared her pallid face and then shot suddenly for a brief moment before dying there in front of her wiggling eye. She saw what it was.

Feeling returned to her limbs then and she jerked away, screaming.

"Mommy!" she cried, tearing her eyes open. The little girl sat up, flinging her legs over the side of the bed.

Chapter One

"Grace Township," Desmond Howard nodded, clearing his throat for the tenth time in the last three minutes. "It's a beauty of a town. The simple life, that's what you've found." He cleared his throat again, making Kara Tameson grumble inwardly, *If this guy doesn't stop doing that...*

As he paused to wipe sweat from his forehead with a tissue, Kara glanced at her husband, John. But John's focus was on the printout in front of him: a black-and-white photograph of the house they were buying with its property description and a crude drawing of the boundary map below.

"I like to encourage folks to buy when the opportunity presents itself. Owning property has been the American dream since America began." Desmond's wormy lips curled before he cleared his throat again.

Eleven, Kara counted, trying to keep her smile in place.

Desmond continued, his voice too loud for the boxy conference room, "I could go into facts about why purchasing is wiser than renting, but now, ahem, that you've settled on the house on Seter Lane..." He wadded up the tissue and dropped it onto the table, his eyes on John. "You know how unstable the housing market has been."

Glancing up at Kara, John said, "A little. I'm just happy we were able to get approved. The reason why we're interested in this—"

"In this house?" Desmond cut him off, straightening in his chair.

"Yeah. The house is great, but I've—we've—been looking for some acreage."

Nodding, the real estate agent reached across the table and shook their hands. "You've found a wonderful property." He backed up his chair, an ear-splitting sound as it screeched over the floor, and stood up. He placed two fingers on the printout John had been looking at and dragged it away, then put it into a fat folder that displayed the agency's logo.

"What's the next step?" John asked.

"Well, the bank has approved your offer, so next is inspection. I'll set it up. I recommend an inspection for all houses, especially a bank-owned property like this one." Desmond backed out of the room, telling them he'd be back with a copy of the paperwork.

"Looks like we're getting a house," John said, tilting his head toward Kara.

She grinned. "It does." Her eyes drifted over the walls, sliding over a watercolor of pansies before settling on the black-and-white photograph of a nineteenth-century farmhouse. It was hard to tell because of the shading, but after studying it for a moment, she saw roses spiraled up the white façade. *That's the type of house I thought I wanted,* she mused.

There were plenty of older homes in downtown Cosgrove, Ohio where Kara and John presently lived with their young children, but they were either in great disrepair or beyond their price range. John was the only one working, and although he had recently been promoted to I.T. manager, Severs, Ltd. was a small company and his salary had hardly increased. They both carried student and car loan debt and had a couple high-balance credit cards. Their financial portfolio wasn't quite brag-worthy.

But over the last year, the economy had taken a nosedive and, with it, housing prices had dropped. Suddenly, owning a house was a reality. After having browsed a handful of real estate websites in search of an agent, they had settled on Desmond. There was no reason behind choosing him other than his site was just the first polished one they saw. Their house search began downtown near Severs and then in surrounding suburbs. Living in Cosgrove meant an easy commute for John and an area they knew well, but they soon realized prices near the city were too high.

"You know," John said one day, "we may be able to find something out in the country we can afford."

"The country?" Kara had her reservations. What did she know about cows, wells, and leach fields?

"You'd get used to it pretty quick."

But before they had really discussed it, Desmond had called, offering to show them a new-on-the-market, turn-of-the-century American craftsman close to Severs and in their price range. Touring it, they thought it could be The One. It was adorable. The yard was modest, but it was green space the kids didn't have in the apartment. Kara and John practically bounced on the eight-by-ten patio, not minding the tall blades of grass sprouting through cracked concrete. But then Desmond warned them an older home needed constant upkeep. Using his fingers as counters, he proceeded to list all of the ailments a house more than a hundred years old could have: black mold, lead-based paint, outdated plumbing, no central air conditioning...

Kara zoned him out when he turned to his second hand to rattle off more potential problems. She no longer admired the lilac bushes lining the white picket fence; the beauty of old-time elegance had already wafted away. They went home crestfallen. Ironically, six months earlier, they had been complacent living in cramped quarters above a parking garage, but it was all somehow different now, as if they had always planned on buying a house.

They had continued searching, but there was always an issue: this house had an iffy foundation; that one was in a rough neighborhood; this one was too close to railroad tracks...

Eventually, John called Desmond, telling him they were pausing the hunt; they'd try again in a couple months.

Desmond interrupted, however, apprising him of a pocket listing. "It's a bank-owned property, not yet advertised for sale. Ever hear of Grace Township? Something special is coming on the market."

That was the day they saw their dream home.

Grace Township, a place John and Kara had never heard of, was an hour southeast of Cosgrove. It was charming with its small community of shops, churches, and schools. Just a mile from the town square, on a tree-lined road, was the house Desmond was anxious to show them. The French country two-story sat at the summit of a hill. The property was seven acres, surrounded by woods on three sides. It was only a year old and had never been lived in. Desmond explained the house wasn't perfect: the builder had been foreclosed on before completing all of the rooms. It was because the bonus room and den were down to their studs that the house was being priced far below fair market value.

"Better act now. A deal like this won't last," Desmond had warned.

There was nothing to discuss. John's commute to work would take nearly an hour, but he said he wouldn't mind—not if he could have this much acreage. The trade-off was worth it.

Presently, in the stuffy conference room, Kara traced a finger over an elm towering in the foreground of the framed photograph. There were trees like those on her new property. She smiled, envisioning nine-year-old Jack and four-year-old Lilah climbing them. Maybe they'd even build a tree-house.

"Ahem!" Desmond popped into the room, handing John a folder. "Your copy of your financial statements. I'll be in touch about the inspection. If all goes well, you should close in a few weeks."

"Hey, John—" A car honked, making Kara flinch. Reflexively, she grabbed the already-unstable lotion bottle that had been balancing on the mattress before it could spill. The noise had jolted her, but she was used to the sounds of traffic rising up to the apartment a floor above. It would only get worse as the night progressed. "Where's the packet from Desmond? Have you looked at it yet?"

John sat beside her on the edge of the bed and grabbed the opposite leg of the one she lathered. "Need any help?"

"Already did that one," she laughed, pulling away.

He went to the bedroom window and twisted open the blinds, looking out. Vehicles in the parking lot below pulled in and out, moving as if they had choreographed their turns. It was Friday night and downtown was bustling, but inside the two-bedroom apartment, the whir of the pedestal fan covered much of the city nightlife.

"John?"

He turned away from the window and went into the bathroom, flipping on the light and starting the shower. Popping his head out, he said, "I think the packet's on the nightstand. It has coupons, stuff about the town. There's a school enrollment packet. You'll be very interested in that, I'm sure."

He wiggled his eyebrows as she sarcastically replied, "Great."

"Oh, and there's a brochure or something about the strip club in town. Maybe for date night?"

Kara rolled her eyes, setting the lotion on her nightstand. "What a quaint town."

He laughed, closing the bathroom door.

She crawled to his side of the bed, plucked up the folder, and scooted back, resting against the body pillow that served as a headboard. As she flipped open the folder, she reflected on seeing the new house for the first time.

"I love how it's tucked back from the road," John had said to her in a hushed, almost reverent, tone. Desmond had stood back, letting them wander on their own. The house felt enormous, wide and towering. They were ridiculously giddy walking through it.

It's perfect, Kara thought, smiling, paging through blank school registration forms.

But perfect harmony was rudely broken.

"Mommy!" The cry penetrated through the paper-thin wall.

Kara groaned. Lilah's nightmare phase had been going strong for the last couple weeks. The child called out nightly and usually, her yelps woke her brother, who shared her bedroom.

Kara hurried into the bedroom next-door, hoping Lilah hadn't wakened him.

"Mom, she won't shut up," Jack muttered, clamping a pillow over his head.

She whispered, although now there was no need to, "I know, Jack. Go back to sleep."

Lilah clung onto her mother as Kara carried her into the master bedroom. "What's wrong, Lilahbean?"

"Bad dream," she replied babyishly, pressing her face against Kara's neck.

Kara, her arms wrapped around the child, sat down on the bed and leaned against the pillowed wall. "Aw, honey, what're we gonna do about your dreams?"

"I dunno," Lilah whimpered.

Kara rested her cheek against Lilah's dark, knotted hair. "You're okay now," she soothed. She pulled the covers over them before reaching for the nightstand to turn off the lamp. "Did you have fun with Tracy today?" She was thankful her friend, Tracy Poresky, had stepped in to babysit, as she had done several times during their house hunt.

"Uh-huh," Lilah mumbled, already starting to doze.

Kara snuggled with her, closing her eyes, relieved Lilah's breathing had slowed. Calming her down after a nightmare wasn't always so simple. John was better at it. He usually asked for details, somehow making it seem less frightening. However, oftentimes, Kara disappeared into another room to bide her time just so she couldn't hear. It was as if the recounted nightmare would infiltrate her dreams. She blamed her imagination for that, seeing or hearing things that weren't always there.

After his shower, John climbed into his side of the bed. When he noticed the small lump beside him, he asked, "Nightmare?"

"Yes," Kara replied, quietly.

"Was it the same dream?"

"Don't!"

He chuckled as she admitted, "I didn't ask. If we were good parents, we'd probably take her to a specialist."

"Not for a kid's nightmares. She doesn't have much interaction with kids her age. It might be a good idea to get her into a playgroup once we're settled in the new place."

"What's that have to do with it?"

He yawned. "Stress? It can't hurt."

She let the thought stew for a moment. Lilah didn't have any real friends; she'd made no long-term bonds playing with random kids at the playground. Pre-K was probably something they needed to start anyway. Kara was about to tell John she agreed, but he had fallen asleep.

She listened to the traffic and voices outside. After a while, she sat up, her eyes finding the sealed cardboard boxes beneath the open window. She had already started to pack, labeling them, "knickknacks," "photos," "blankets"…

Even though she only saw a partial outline of the dresser, she located the top drawer, visualizing the white box inside. Her thoughts scattered immediately when a car emitted a series of short honks, pulling her back to the present. She went to the window, peering out. Vehicles drove in and out of the well-lit parking lot and every so often, people walked past as couples or groups. She imagined John had once been part of that nightlife, living in the same apartment they now shared as a family, before he had met her anyway. She had been a single mom with toddler Jack when they had started dating; there had been little time for clubbing then.

She closed the window and returned to bed, her movements making John shift to his back. Lilah didn't move, her relaxed face aimed at the ceiling.

Chapter Two

"I don't know why you decided to move all the way to Grace Township," Margaret Sadler said, haughtily. "He did it on purpose, you know."

Kara sighed, readjusting her grip on the cellphone as she maneuvered the ageing sedan onto the freeway. Following the rented moving truck that carried John and Jack, speaking with her mother wasn't how she wanted to kick off moving day. But she knew by answering the call, she'd be met with her familiar tone. Margaret never sugar-coated anything; she was no-nonsense, always had been. Kara assumed it was a defense mechanism her mother employed, started when her father skipped town so long ago Kara had no memory of him. Growing up a latchkey kid, Kara had spent most of her childhood alone at home, while her mother had worked to make ends meet. But even when Margaret had been home, she hadn't been one for coddling. She had always been matter-of-fact, even to the point of harshness, and there had certainly been few terms of endearment.

"Did what on purpose, Mom?" Kara asked, glancing at Lilah in the rearview mirror. The four-year-old's head bobbed as she rifled through toys in her tote bag.

"He wanted to get you all away from me."

"Yeah, John's master plan finally worked."

"Here we go again."

To Margaret, no man was good enough. Even though John had never let Kara down, there was apparently nothing he could do to boost his rating on Margaret's invisible scale. It didn't help matters that Kara's ex had abandoned her when she was five months pregnant with Jack. That had been a college romance gone wrong—he decided not to come home one day and Kara hadn't seen him since. Margaret must've thought the pattern was inevitable: men always skipped out on family. And maybe that was Margaret's truth, because that's what the immediate three that came to mind had done: David, Kara's father, her grandfather—all of them had abandoned the family one day without warning.

"How am I supposed to see my grandchildren…and you, if you leave? All I'll have left is Tracy, but she won't have any excuse to visit me anymore with you gone."

Kara didn't indulge the statement, because she knew it wasn't true. As long as Tracy lived in the same apartment building as Margaret, they'd stay friendly, much to Kara's displeasure. Tracy was generally a good friend, but she had a habit of keeping Margaret up-to-date on Kara's goings-on; as a result, Kara had learned not to divulge too much information to her. Censoring herself was annoying, but Margaret didn't need to know everything.

"What's wrong with Cosgrove?" her mother asked. "There are plenty of good schools and neighborhoods here."

"We tried. It doesn't matter. It's not like Grace Township is on the other side of the state. Mom, I've gotta go. I'm literally moving right now."

"Grace Township! I've never even heard of it!"

"I'll call you when we're settled." Kara hung up. "Oh my goodness, Lilahbean," she said, glancing in the rearview mirror. Lilah leaned back in her booster seat, her face turned to the window.

Kara asked her, "Are you excited?"

Lilah didn't reply, her eyelids lowering. She would be asleep soon.

Kara refocused on the road, the moving truck always in her line of sight.

Forty minutes later, they pulled off the interstate, driving deeper into the hills. Easing off the accelerator, she enjoyed the early afternoon. The sun's rays filtered through the shimmering leaves, and the constant green of the stationed spruces dotted the roads they steadied past.

She mimicked John's turn onto another road and passed a boulder with an affixed plaque reading, "Grace Town." She smiled. The moving truck double-honked and John waved his arm out the window. Kara double-honked back. He turned right, but she got stuck at a red light, the only traffic signal in town. She turned off the air conditioning and rolled down the windows, watching the postcard town in action. The bells of a Roman Catholic church chimed, "Come All Ye Faithful," marking the one o'clock hour at the same time laughter erupted from the sidewalk across the street. She watched the group, chatting and laughing intermittently, until the light blinked to green.

She turned onto Main Street, the main strip in town and passed the brick, nineteenth-century library and an equally-ancient, white-washed Presbyterian church towering close to the street. She drifted by an ice cream shop and outdoor café, bursting with customers of all ages. On the sidewalk was a folded sign reading, "Happy Cones" in swirled green letters.

A grand Federalist-period house stood on the other side of the road, instantly capturing her attention. It was coated in red brick and set back from the street, with a hip roof topped with a white balustrade. White pillars proudly held up the covered wraparound porch. Black, wrought iron fencing separated the property from the sidewalk. A plaque set into the gate read, "Private Residence" in bronze letters. She noticed two urns filled with pink and white roses on both sides of the double doors before she obeyed the posted speed limit, which commanded she increase her speed by ten more miles per hour.

She hummed, not realizing it was a melody her mother had sung to her when she was a little girl, and passed a hobby shop and perfumery store before turning left onto Seter Lane. Instantly, charming town life morphed into country living. Even the dilapidated weathered barn at the corner added to the scenery. Her eyes flitted over it as she passed and then she glanced over the houses that led the way to hers. The trees broke away on the left and she slowed, turning into their opening, which was the start of her gravel driveway. Steering carefully up the hill, not used to the incline, she pulled in beside the moving truck where the driveway spilled into a pool of gravel to the left of the garage. John and Jack waited at the rear of the truck.

"You made it," John said when she stepped out of the car.

She smiled at him before gazing at the house. Her eyes trailed down, over the front sidewalk, and down to limestone tiles scattered in the grass, connecting the lawn to the driveway. She turned to Jack, noticing the medium-sized box he held. "Is that heavy?"

"No." He scowled. "Can we go in now?"

John peered inside the sedan's backseat at Lilah. "Is she still sleeping?"

Kara replied, "You guys go on in. Jack wants to see his new room."

"I'll show him the woods first," John suggested. "That way we can all go in together. Jack, go ahead and put the box down."

"Okay, we'll meet you on the porch." Kara unbelted Lilah, who had woken up and was looking out her window. Kara followed her gaze to the yellow, two-story colonial next door, peeping through the trees. An old-school antenna stood crookedly from the roof of the screened-in porch that jutted out from the front of the house.

Kara returned her attention to Lilah. "You awake?"

In her stupor, Lilah continued staring at the yellow house.

Following her gaze again, Kara squinted, seeing nobody. "We'll meet the neighbors soon." She tugged on Lilah's foot, then backed up.

Lilah finally blinked, then yawned, and a moment later they were walking hand-in-hand at low speed over the gravel.

"Rabbit," Lilah said, rubbing her eye with her free fist. They stopped. A brown rabbit, a yard from them, nibbled on grass, eyeing them.

"Oh, wow! I bet we'll see lots of animals." As if on cue, a fawn darted out from the rear of the house, escaping through the yellow house's front yard. "Did you see that?"

"What?" Lilah jerked her head, stealing away toward where Kara pointed.

"A deer. You didn't see it?"

Lilah shook her head.

"That's alright. You'll see plenty more."

"When?"

"Just keep your eyes open." Someplace in the woods a chorus of birds chirped, their ruckus making them glance over as they neared the front porch.

"Hey, Mom!" Jack called, running ahead of John as they came into the front yard. "Can we go swimming?"

"Swimming?" Kara wrinkled her nose. "We're moving in today."

"Come on! I've never had a pool."

"What?"

"Dad said maybe today."

Kara turned to John. "What?"

John tilted his head and whistled, looking skyward.

"Jack, what are you talking about?" she asked.

"Come on!" Jack took off around the house. "See?" he called when Kara appeared in the backyard.

"What in the world?" She approached the above ground pool that hadn't been there the last time she had toured the property, and dipped her hand into the water.

John laughed as he and Lilah neared. "It was installed last week. Thought the kids would like it. Do you like it, guys?"

Lilah hopped from one foot to the other, alert now. "Yeah!" John lifted her up to see the water.

Jack nodded, pushing his arms over the pool's edge, his fingertips just barely touching the water.

13

"How deep is it?" Kara asked.

"Four feet," John replied. "I thought we could eventually extend the deck to reach it."

Kara walked to the deck steps and stopped, laying a hand on the railing. "Wait. Was the deck finished? The last time I was here there was no railing."

"Maybe I enlisted somebody's help and maybe we got said deck completed...just not extended to the pool." He cleared his throat. "Yet."

Kara asked amazed, "When did you do that?"

"I gave Dolph a day off and let him work half days in the office so we could finish it. Most of the deck was here already. We just needed to add railings and stairs."

"You guys did a great job!"

"It's alright, needs to be bigger." He slapped the railing. The deck was modest in comparison to the width of the house, but it could easily fit a small gathering.

"Can we go swimming today?" Jack asked.

Kara shook her head. "Not today. We have a lot to do."

He flicked the water. "Tomorrow?"

"Maybe."

"Who wants to see their room first?" John called.

Everyone hollered, "Me!"

They went back to the front porch and John unlocked the rounded front door. Kara slid a hand down the bumpy stone façade before following the family over the threshold. She looked up and scowled at the brass chandelier dangling from the foyer's two-story ceiling. One of the projects she hoped they'd work on soon, the rounded and obnoxious light fixture hung just a couple of feet above John's head reminding her of a giant's teat. Why would anybody select that style? It didn't go well with the rest of the house at all.

She glanced into the office that would be John's and then turned around to the mouth of the staircase off the entry. The bare walnut treads stopped halfway at a landing before twisting and going up the rest of the way to the second floor.

John bent toward the kids. "Your bedrooms are upstairs." Jack took off up the staircase and Lilah trotted behind, holding onto the railing as she went.

Kara turned to her left, looking down the narrow hallway leading to the garage. She glanced at the powder room off the foyer and then moved down the main hallway that ended in the breakfast nook at the back of the house. She surveyed the adjoining great room and the closed door to the unfinished playroom, which anchored the eastern side of the house. On the other side of the breakfast nook were the kitchen, dining room, and spacious master bedroom.

John followed her into their bedroom. On the far side were three side-by-side windows with a bare MDF window bench below. Tucked partially behind the garage and jutting out just beyond to the side of it was the master bathroom and through there, the closet.

Kara went into the bathroom, giving it an approving once-over. The white porcelain of the corner soaking tub shone magnificently under the skylight, a five-pointed star with rounded edges—another unique choice of the builder's. Her only regret with the other bathroom window, set a few feet above the edge of the tub, was it didn't open. It would've been nice to take a hot bath with it open to an outside breeze.

"Now that's what I can't wait to do," Kara said, running a hand over the tub's edge.

"I can't wait."

"Yeah, yeah," she said, poking John's side. "Maybe not now. I have a feeling this moving situation is going to be exhausting."

"Well, it's half over. Maybe if we tried running, it'd go quicker…" He raised his eyebrows, trying to appear serious.

"Brilliant idea."

"You think so? Yeah, I have my moments."

She laughed, wrapping her arms around his neck. "This place is perfect."

15

"See?"

"Well, I *am* farther from my mom, you know. That's the real bonus."

"No Daughter-of-the-Year Award for you this year."

"I guess not." She would've loved to have had a normal mother-daughter relationship, but there was nothing she could do with the hand she'd been dealt. Besides, it was how her mother had raised her. The estrangement wasn't all Kara's fault.

"That's okay. You win the Wife-and-Mother-of-the-Year Award," John said, kissing her.

They broke the embrace and Kara opened the door to the walk-in closet. She flipped on the light, then halted. "What's that?" There was a pile of green fabric on the far side of the otherwise empty closet. She picked it up. "Whose blanket?"

"Maybe it's Dolph's."

She turned it over, finding streaks of red paint on the wool fabric. "Does he want it back?"

"I doubt it. You don't want it?"

"No, it's scratchy. It's got paint or something on it anyway."

"Throw it away. He probably left it behind as trash."

"Why's it in here?" She looked at the white walls. "Did you guys paint?"

"No. Maybe he thought we'd be painting. He was probably wandering around and just left it."

They corralled the kids back outside and Kara dropped the blanket in the garage, the first item in the trash heap. "Is the truck close enough to the house?"

John scratched his head. "I could probably get it closer. The ground's flatter in front of the garage."

"So now you're telling me the house isn't on a flat surface."

He looked at her with a raised eyebrow and she laughed. "Keep the kids with you." He hopped into the truck and they watched him quickly reverse to the front sidewalk. He

16

jumped out and slid open the rear door of the truck. "Okay, the smallest boxes and bags are in front of the big stuff. Jack, you can help with that. Kara, you can start pulling out the small stuff too. Lilah, you'll need to stay out of the way."

Kara told him they'd get her some toys from the car and sit her in the grass while they worked. She led Lilah toward the sedan. Kara squeezed her hand and said, "Come on, Sophie." Kara dropped Lilah's hand and double-blinked, stopping short.

Sophie.

It was like being stung, feeling the name drop from her lips, and hearing it. Confused by it, Kara tried to swallow as her thoughts raced, but failed, the back of her throat putting on the brakes. Suddenly, she had been struck deaf. She grounded her feet in the gravel, straining to hear the rocks clatter. She heard the pounding of her heart, but that was of little encouragement. She forced herself to try swallowing again to pop her ears, but she couldn't. It was as if the name had poisoned her throat.

She pressed the small flap of cartilage on her ears. There, she could hear a distinct rustling. Her eyes searched for what made the noise, moving over trees beyond the driveway's turn-around. Was it a bird or squirrel?

A blue jay screeched, making her jump, and just like that, the outside sounds returned. She took quick breaths, clearing away the strange feeling, and looked over at John. Had he heard her flub?

Sophie.

It didn't look like he had. He was hauling a large box out of the back of the moving truck, concentrating on the task at hand. She looked at Lilah, who made careful steps down the driveway. She hadn't noticed either. Deliberately, Kara made her way to her. She wondered at her error, stealing a glance at John and Jack, who busily stacked boxes in the garage. The slip-up was bizarre, but she pushed it away, forgetting it.

Dinner was a hodge-podge of snacks left over from the apartment, as no one felt like finding a restaurant or grocery store at the end of the first day in the new house. After they ate, the Tamesons made ready for bed. The kids, excited to have bedrooms of their own, were tucked in on hastily-dressed mattresses. Both had a bedspread and pillow, which thankfully, hadn't been hard to locate.

Kara closed the door to the master bathroom, refraining from turning on the light. Moonlight streaming in from the skylight guided her as she gave the bathtub a quick rinse. She undressed and stepped in, pausing to peer out the other window. The lamppost stood at the edge of the driveway's turn-around, situated where the side lawn began, illuminating the gravel and the start of the lawn. The woods bordering were just darkness; not even moonlight touched the trees.

When water had risen above her ankles, she sank into the tub and closed her eyes. John's movements on the other side as he pushed boxes along the carpeted floor were the only sounds in the house. After a while, Kara opened her eyes, lazily capturing the bathroom. She couldn't believe she was a homeowner and the fact that their first house was their dream home was unreal. She turned off the faucet and slid down, luxuriating in how the water warmed her. Her eyes moved across the room to the custom two-person shower stall, cast in shadow. It was a dream shower with four shower heads, surrounded in Tuscan tile.

She rolled her head back and looked up at the skylight directly above. She wasn't sure if she liked the star-shaped window. Was it charming or gaudy? She gazed through it, presently charmed by starlight dotting the night sky. She closed her eyes again, sinking further into the tub, a head poking out of a pool of ecstasy. After a moment, she stretched her limbs, looking up again. She frowned. Was the ceiling darker at two of the rounded star points?

She studied them, but couldn't tell, so she begrudgingly got out of the tub. She dried off, pulled on a nightshirt, and flipped on the light. She squinted at the ceiling, seeing tan stains touched two edges of the star. She opened the door. John was dragging a sheet over the mattress. The bed frame, in pieces near the far wall, hadn't been assembled yet.

She asked, "Did the inspector mention a skylight leak in his report?"

"Hmm?"

"There's a leak in the bathroom ceiling."

He tossed pillows on the mattress and followed her into the bathroom. "Hmm…I don't remember if he pointed that out."

"Could he have missed something like that? Is it bad?"

"I don't know. The stains look faded. I guess we really won't know if it's an issue until it rains. I'll check it out."

They went into the bedroom and he flipped off the light.

"Well, we moved," Kara said, when they settled onto the mattress.

He placed a hand on her arm. "Yep. How do you like it?"

"So far so good."

He kissed her, then rolled to his side, facing away from her. "Goodnight."

"Goodnight." She closed her eyes and started to drift to sleep until an image of Lilah crying flashed in the dark. Kara blinked her eyes open. "Do you think the kids are alright upstairs?" Jack and Lilah were on the other side of the house, a floor away. Would she hear them if they needed her?

"John?"

He didn't respond.

She propped herself up on her elbow and, peering over his shoulder, saw he was already asleep. She shifted away and looked at the dark doorway, listening. The house was silent. Was she too far away to hear?

She waited another minute before getting up. They had kept the light in the foyer on and Kara passed under it, squinting. Met by Jack's snoring on the second floor, she bypassed his bedroom and went to Lilah's.

She had just stepped into her room when Lilah cried, "Mommy!"

"I'm here," Kara whispered. "Bad dream?"

She whimpered, "Uh-huh."

"I'll lay down with you."

"Mommy, don't go!"

"I won't. I'm right here. Scooch over." It was a tight fit, but Kara managed to squeeze in beside her on the twin-size mattress. She pulled the blanket over them and sang a lullaby until Lilah fell asleep.

Chapter Three

Kara woke up the next morning, stiff. She rolled off Lilah's mattress, careful not to wake her. Downstairs, she stretched her arms and rolled her shoulders, then flipped off the foyer light. The house was still asleep, but outside a morning dove cooed. Grabbing her cellphone, she crept out the front door. It was early, but the sun had been up for at least an hour.

Kara clicked on her phone, seeing immediately no one had called. She also noticed she had no cell reception. She waved the phone around, then walked around the yard, willing a cell tower to find her. After a few minutes, she gave up and returned to the porch. Sitting on the top step, she leaned back, resting on the palms of her hands, and gazed at the hills, taking in the countryside. Because of the sweeping trees edging the front border of the property, she could only catch glimpses of the road where the driveway bottomed out and then again where the lane reappeared as it rounded the bend, curving farther away from town.

Frogs from a nearby spring croaked, locusts clacked, and a woodpecker had joined in with the morning dove. Kara leaned forward, noticing two cows grazing in the distance on a steep hill. She had never been neighbors with cows and found it both fascinating and slightly worrisome at the same time. Did cows stink? Were there bulls around? If so, should she avoid wearing red outside? She chuckled at her last thought.

When she turned to look at her driveway, her breath caught. She was surprised to see someone walking up. The stranger was probably in her sixties, her face tan and her short hair a mix of light brown and gray. Her stride was steady, revealing her good physical shape. She glanced up at

Kara, flicking her bangs to the side, and raised a hand. Kara, returning the wave, met her on the driveway.

"Good morning!" the woman called, her voice loud and raspy. "I'm Diane Foreman."

"Good morning! I'm Kara Tameson."

Diane's smile thinned as she dragged a dirty gardening glove from her pocket and pulled it onto her hand. "I own the property to the east of you, the lemon house. We're neighbors."

"Oh," Kara nodded, glancing at the house next door. "My daughter and I noticed the beautiful color of your house."

"Stands out, I suppose." Diane sounded regretful. "So, it's just you, your husband, and your daughter that's moved in then?"

"And our son."

Diane frowned, looking toward Kara's front porch. "I missed him."

"Yep, there's four of us."

Diane turned her muddy brown eyes on Kara and smiled stonily. "Gonna be a hot day. Got to get the gardening done before the heat sets in. Do you garden?"

"Not re—" Kara flinched, catching sight of something black swooping low from overhead. She covered her head even though the bird was already rising, moving away. She had glimpsed its ugly, withered face before the black-feathered creature swept up high in the sky.

"Turkey vulture," Diane replied in disgust.

"Do they usually come so close?"

"If you have any small dogs, keep an eye on 'em when they're out. Turkey vultures will scoop 'em up real quick." The bird circled them for a moment before moving off toward the treetops at the edge of the woods.

Kara watched, waiting for it to swoop down again, and said distractedly, "We don't have any pets. I've never actually had any. That's probably a little embarrassing to admit." She broke her gaze from the sky, chuckling as she looked at Diane, but Diane didn't smile.

"Just make sure you don't get a small animal, not like it'll matter anyhow. Marvin, my husband, and I had a schipperke. The dog was small, only a couple years old. Never saw anything like it. It was a long time ago. We let Blacky out as you do. We thought nothing of it. Schipperke's a small dog, but a sheep dog can normally take care of itself. After a while, I went to let him back in. At first, I thought, him not being a fixed dog, that he was nosin' around. But, then, as I walked into the backyard, the woods there..." She gestured toward the trees behind her house. "I saw what had happened..."

"He was killed?" Kara was horrified. Her eyes flitted over the trees. There was no sign of the vulture now and everything was oddly still; even the birds had stopped, making the yard feel strangely muted.

Diane rubbed her nose with the back of her forearm. "Just be careful if you let any pets loose. If I were you, I'd stay with them when they go outside."

Kara nodded as if they had made a pact. "If we get a pet, I'll make sure we stay with it." Her promise sounded hollow even to her. But how could she make a promise for something that didn't exist? None of them, not even the kids, had expressed a desire to have a pet.

"Good." Diane's eyes combed over the front of the Tamesons' house. "Pretty house you have here. I hope you enjoy it."

"Thank you, I'm sure we will."

Diane pulled on the other gardening glove and turned away, starting her descent down the driveway. When she had made it halfway down, she took the stepping stones and detoured onto the grass, crossing through the lawn until she eventually disappeared through the tree-line to her property.

Kara looked up at the empty sky, then directed her gaze again at Diane's house, feeling awkward. Wondering what words of wisdom her other neighbors would share with her, she turned back to her house. As she stepped onto the porch, her cellphone trilled.

Looking down, she smiled, seeing Tracy's number displayed on the screen. "Hey, Tracy! I have a signal, after all!" She sat on the top step.

"Hey, stranger. So, what's going on? Friends call friends."

Kara laughed, hearing the smile in Tracy's voice. "I know, I'm sorry. I was going to call today."

"I figured you've been busy. How's country living?"

"I don't know yet." Kara glanced at the yellow house. "We still have to unpack and return the moving truck."

Tracy groaned. "I hate moving."

Kara stretched out her legs. "Are you checking up on me to give my mom a full report?"

"She cares about you."

"You can tell her we moved in. Nobody died, no one was hurt."

"Oh, that's a relief!" Tracy laughed. When Kara didn't comment, Tracy said, "I'll just tell her you guys made it safely...I wasn't just asking for her, you know."

"We're fine. I even met a neighbor."

"Ah, replacing me already!" They laughed, both satisfied they wouldn't end on a sour note. "Well, I'll leave you to the unpacking."

After they said goodbye, Kara hesitated, then scrolled through her phone's contact list, stopping on her mother's name. Sighing, she tapped it and sent a quick text:

Made it to the new house. Still unpacking.

Kara went inside, not noticing her text had failed and the cellphone screen displayed, "No service."

Nobody went inside the old apartment when they returned to the familiar building. None of the Tamesons sensed nostalgia for the worn-down building they had called home for several years. John and the kids waited in the moving truck, while Kara hopped into his parked car. They followed her to the rental facility, turned in the truck, and then they all rode together in his car back to the new house. It was a long, boring drive, but Lilah napped through most of it and Jack played a handheld video game.

When they returned home, John and Kara assembled beds, suggesting the kids go outside. The idea was something of a novelty. They were used to playing indoors, with the occasional trip to the nearest playground. Notorious for dirty syringes and strewn garbage, the kids hadn't gone often, nor had other children.

The summer sun glimmered through the leaves and the temperature had risen, but Jack and Lilah didn't mind the heat. They wandered through the backyard woods, weaving around trees.

"Where're we going?" Lilah asked, her stubby legs finding it an effort to keep up with Jack.

He grunted noncommittally.

"Will we see rabbits, Jack?" she asked, recalling the one she had seen the day before.

"Maybe. There's the neighbors' house." Jack stopped and pointed straight ahead, glimpsing the yellow house through the trees. Sunlight struck the upstairs corner of the two-story, making it beam glaringly white.

"Does that house glow in the dark?" Lilah asked, awed.

"No."

Assuming they had reached the eastern boundary of their yard, Jack turned and started heading west. Lilah, however, stayed put. Through the trees, she could see flowerbeds and a vegetable garden running from the edge of the woods to the Foremans' rear sun porch. The flowers reminded her of the gardens fairies lived in, as depicted in her favorite picture book.

"Come on, Lilah!"

"Oh!" She jumped and hurried to Jack's side.

They saw nothing extraordinary at first. The only animals they came across were birds, but there was nothing interesting about that. Jack had hoped to at least run into a squirrel or, better yet, a snake.

"What's that? A truck?" Lilah stopped a few yards behind him.

He stopped, his eyes following the angle to where she pointed at the woods ahead, the side yard nearest town.

From his angle, he couldn't see what she saw. "What do you mean, a truck? On the street?" But the trees were too dense to see the road.

"Huh-uh. A truck in the woods."

He backed up until he was standing beside her. Squatting down at her level, he studied the trees. It took him a moment to see it.

"What's that?" Through his partially-obstructed view, he saw something light-colored. It *did* look like a small truck. "Is that a truck?"

"I dunno." Lilah shrugged awkwardly.

"C'mon." Jack headed purposefully to the woods. Lilah hobbled behind. After passing through a row of trees and sidling carefully past the brush, Jack feasted his eyes on it. There was, in fact, a small pop-up camper in the woods.

"A truck!" Lilah exclaimed, working her way through a narrow opening, impressively avoiding the xanthiums' burrs.

The camper had seen better days. Its ivory exterior was dirty from exposure to outside elements and splattered mud. Splashes of rust-orange paint coated its sides, and the fabric pop-up was shredded, its canvas sides hanging down in crude strips. Jack crept up to the partially-open metal door. It was missing a screen and dented as if it had been kicked shut several times. He pulled it open. Debris covered the floor and countertop; paper plates, patio chair cushions, a fire extinguisher, and a pair of bleach-stained jeans lay among the mess. Jack pocketed a toy metal star from the heap.

"Let me see in, Jack!" Lilah shoved his back.

He shrugged her off easily. "It's just a mess. There's nothing to see."

"I wanna see!"

He backed away. "It's a mess, Lilah. You'll get hurt hanging around here." He used words his mom would say just to get her to back off. He, however, pictured this as an awesome place for further exploration. He didn't need Lilah nosing around.

As if he had channeled her, Kara called them to lunch. Jack peered through the trees, seeing her on the deck. She called again, scanning the yard, but he stayed still until she went back inside.

"Come on," he said to Lilah, stepping out of the woods and crossing the lawn, putting distance between the camper and him. When he got to the deck, he waited. Lilah passed the swimming pool, combing her hand over its plastic side, her head not even close to clearing its height. He blurted, "You can't tell Mom and Dad anything about the truck, okay?"

"Why?"

"Because they'll say we can't play in it and you know how cool it is, right?" That was true; they'd never let them play in it, especially not in its current state. "I'm gonna clean it up first and then we'll surprise them."

"Okay, I won't say anything."

"You promise?"

"Uh-huh. I promise."

Kara was at the kitchen sink when they tromped inside. "There you are. See anything interesting outside?"

"Not really," Jack replied. He stole a glance at Lilah, but she had wandered down the hallway. Noticing the food on the L-shaped kitchen counter, her asked, "What're we eating?"

"We have carrots, chips and macaroni and cheese. Wash your hands first."

Jack took off for the powder room.

"Mommy, where's the mac and cheese?" Lilah whined from the hallway. She made her way back to the kitchen, as if she had been lost.

"It's on the kitchen counter. Where did you go off to?" Kara asked with a laugh.

"I'm hungry." Lilah started to reach for the tub of noodles, but Kara stopped her, foreseeing a gooey mess on the ceramic tiled floor. She handed it to John, who had just walked into the room.

"It's 'hungry,' " Kara corrected. "Wash your hands and then you can eat." John plopped food onto their plates while Kara got them water. She set the cups on the table before surveying the adjoining great room. Seeing familiar furniture throughout the house made it feel more like home. Some of the pieces had been purchased used and all of it was cheap. They didn't fit the expansive room perfectly, but they made it home, and in time, they'd be able to fill the rooms with proper chairs, sofas and ottomans.

When her family was seated, Kara held up her cellphone and snapped a photo of Jack and John chatting as Lilah looked down, selecting a chip.

"Okay, this time, everybody look at me," Kara chuckled. The three heads turned. "Smile!" They grinned and she took the photo, capturing shared excitement on their faces.

"That was a good one." She looked up from the phone, her eyes glimpsing the great room again. She frowned, noticing the door to the unfinished playroom was open halfway.

"Who opened that door?" She crossed the room and shut it. "Don't open this door until we've fixed the room."

John turned around to look as she returned to the kitchen. "Oh, yeah. Guys, you can't go in there. That room still needs to be finished."

"It's dangerous," Kara told the kids. "There are nails and wood on the floor. Okay?"

"Okay," Jack said.

"Okay," Lilah echoed.

"You can get hurt. That room is off limits." Kara looked at them pointedly.

John asked with a mouthful of food, "So, what's the plan for tomorrow?"

"More unpacking." Kara swallowed a bite of macaroni. "Why? What did you have in mind?"

He shrugged. "I guess the same."

"What do you mean? We have a lot more to do."

"Well…" He gave her a mischievous smile.

"John."

"What're we doing tomorrow?" Jack asked with interest.

John baited him, "What do you want to do?"

"What're we doin'?" Lilah asked.

"John," Kara said.

John laughed. "I was thinking we could explore a little. See the town."

"Not tomorrow. You go back to work soon and I need help."

"We'll have time to finish unpacking this weekend. I have a few more days until I have to go back. We can even run errands, like grocery shopping, mailing stuff at the post office…"

"The post office?" Kara wrinkled her brow.

He continued, "See where Jack's new school is…"

Jack scowled at that.

"Check out preschools…"

"Preschools?" Jack was aghast.

"For Lilah," Kara explained.

John asked, "Wouldn't you rather go to preschool than regular school? It's all coloring and naptime."

Kara shook her head, chewing a chip. "We can go grocery shopping tomorrow, because that can't wait. I don't see why we can't dedicate one more day getting things set up before becoming full-fledged members of the community."

"I don't want to wait," Jack moaned.

"Don't start." Kara brought her cup to her lips just as the doorbell chimed.

"Is that the doorbell?" Jack jumped up from the table.

"Jack, wait for Dad!" Kara called.

"Let's see who it is," John said, following him to the front door.

"Me too!" Lilah ran after them.

Kara stayed seated, suddenly anxious it was her mother popping in on them. Tense, Kara told herself that would be out of character.

"Huh," she heard John say.

She hesitated before joining the family at the door. "Who is it?"

"I don't know." John stepped onto the porch, his eyes drawing in the yard. "Apparently nobody."

She stepped out behind him, just clearing the entryway, and looked out over the lawn. No one huddled, hiding, in the wide oak dead-ahead; nobody ran down the road, laughing they had gotten away. "Is the doorbell broken?"

John pressed the button, hearing it chime, and looked at it briefly.

"Who was it?" Jack asked.

"We don't know," Kara said, looking down the vacant road again before going back inside. The others followed and they sat down at the kitchen table. After a couple minutes, the doorbell chimed again. Kara set down her water. "Okay, this is getting annoying."

John hurried to the front door, intent on catching the culprit. The kids ran after him.

This time someone had materialized at the door. An unfamiliar male voice carried into the kitchen. Kara heard them, but couldn't make out what anyone was saying until she heard John say, "Come on in."

Heavy footsteps came down the hallway as John, the kids, and an elderly man holding a shoebox entered the kitchen.

"How do, ma'am." He was thin, apple-cheeked, and clean-shaven. "I didn't mean to interrupt your meal. I just thought I'd swing by and say hello. I live in the lemon house next door. Marvin Foreman."

"Oh!" Kara smiled. "I met Diane this morning."

Marvin's lips parted and then he nodded. "Oh."

Kara pictured the turkey vulture circling and resisted the urge to ask about his dog. She shook his calloused hand. "I'm Kara."

"Did you ring the doorbell earlier?" Jack asked, steering formalities to the present mystery at hand.

Marvin glanced at the front door before looking gravely at him. "When I just came over I did, young man. Did you hear the bell?"

Kara laughed nervously, hoping he didn't notice Jack's tone of accusation. "Either somebody rang the doorbell earlier or there's something wrong with it."

"Probably some kids playing Ding-dong Ditch," John said.

"What's that?" Jack asked.

John replied, "Nothing, Jack."

"Ah, well." Marvin tugged at the waistband of his jeans, once black, now a faded gray. "I've never heard of a doorbell just ringing on its own, but I also don't know about any pranksters around here." He gave Kara a reassuring smile and said, "I wouldn't worry about it. I brought you some fresh eggs." With a flourish, he withdrew the lid and handed the shoebox to Kara. They all peered in, finding it filled with brown eggs. "They're from my chickens."

"Oh, do you have a farm?" Kara asked, remembering the cows across the road.

"Just a small chicken coop."

"Thanks! We're starving."

Marvin squinted and blinked. "How's that?"

John cleared his throat and asked, "Anything we should know about in Grace Township? We're from Cosgrove."

31

"The only thing you need to know is that it's mighty quiet. Coming from Cosgrove, that'll be a big change, I'm sure. This town is a nice place to grow up in. Say, Jack, what grade are you going to be in?"

"Fourth."

"Good year. I don't suppose you're in school yet, are you?" Marvin asked Lilah.

Kara spoke up, "Lilah will be going to pre-kindergarten. Our real estate agent gave us an application for Grace School. Do you know anything about them?"

"I'm afraid I don't, but if it's in town, I'm sure it's a fine place. Well, I'd better get out of your hair."

John and Kara walked him to the door and said goodbye. Once the door closed, Kara spun around. "Want an omelet?"

"That sounds good," John replied. "Got cheese, onion, and peppers?"

She scowled. "We really need to go to the store." She set the eggs on the kitchen counter and they returned to the table. "He was nice."

"Yeah," John said, tipping back his water. He gestured to his empty plate. "It's really good."

"Yeah, I slaved away all day. Speaking of which, do you know where the grocery store is?"

"I guess it would've been smart if we had looked into things like that before we moved. Did you know there are no gas stations in Grace Township?"

"Then where do people get gas? They don't have their own oil refinery, do they?" she joked.

He pulled his cellphone from the pocket of his cargo shorts and tapped on its screen. "I looked up the nearest gas station this morning. It's in Harper. It's close. Don't worry, they have more than one gas station. And..." He slid his finger across the screen. "They have a grocery store. Yeah, looks like they have fast-food restaurants, car dealerships. You know, civilization like we're used to."

"How far?"

"Not far, like eight miles." The phone pinged then and he read the text. "Crap."

"What?"

He replied to her as he texted back, "I've got to do some work tonight. Drummond's coming in tomorrow. He's going to want to see the project list and all the deadlines."

"Drummond?"

"The CEO."

She asked, disappointed, "You're going back to work tomorrow?"

"No, I shouldn't have to, but it does mean we should get all the unpacking done before Monday. This project's starting soon and he's gonna want us to get started right away."

"Lovely."

Kara clicked off the TV and turned off the light in the great room. The house was quiet; the kids had been in bed for over an hour. She popped her head in the office, telling John she was going to bed.

"I'm ready. I'm done for the night," he said, turning off the computer. "If they don't like what I have, they can wait 'til Monday."

"You don't have to go in tomorrow?" They left the foyer light on and headed to the master bedroom.

"No, I just emailed the project list." He pulled off his shirt and crawled into bed. "Still happy?"

"Mm-hmm," she murmured, changing into her nightshirt in the dark room.

"Okay, just checking," he said, a smile in his voice.

"Are you still happy here?" she asked, sliding under the bed covers.

"Oh, yeah. I love it out here."

She smiled and laid a hand on his chest. "It is pretty nice." She moved in to kiss him just as Lilah screamed from upstairs. Kara moaned, rolling away and collapsing exaggeratedly on her side of the bed.

"Great," John sighed. When he felt Kara getting up, he said, "Let her cry. She needs to learn to get over it on her own."

"It's not like letting a baby cry."

"Why not? Maybe it is," he countered.

"She's scared."

"Maybe we shouldn't go to her every night."

"She's going to wake up Jack." Kara left the room and hurried up the staircase, whispering Lilah's name when she got to her bedroom.

Lilah was sitting, her outline highlighted by the nightlight plugged into the wall. Kara eased her back down, saying her name again, "Lilah."

Lilah closed her mouth, cutting off her next scream, realizing it was her mother beside her. She sniffled.

Kara went to wipe Lilah's cheeks, but there were no tears. Her hand hesitated, cutting through the nightlight's beam, before lowering Lilah with her so they were now lying down. "You're alright. It was a bad dream, just a dream."

"A bad dream," Lilah whimpered, pushing against her mother so they were practically one.

Kara chewed her lip a moment before asking, no matter how much she didn't want to ask, "Do you want to tell me about it?" *You're such a scaredy cat,* she scolded herself. *How can a child's dream scare you?*

Lilah shook her head, Kara's sudden sensation of relief making her also feel cowardly. "Don't leave, Mommy."

"Okay." Kara kissed the top of Lilah's head and stayed on her side. She didn't pull her arm back from under Lilah until the girl was asleep, nor did she shift away and get up until she had been steadily breathing for a while.

Kara watched her from the doorway for a moment, glad Lilah's face had relaxed and looked peaceful. But Kara frowned. How would they get her to overcome this phase?

And what a strange phase it was. Kara didn't remember having gone through this as a child; Jack hadn't. Was is stress from moving that caused them? Could it be stress from the move? The dreams *had* started around the time they started discussing moving. Maybe once they were settled and Lilah started pre-K, the nightmares would go away. If they didn't…Well, then Kara supposed she'd have to consult a pediatrician.

Kara sighed, leaving the room, and stopped at the open bonus room at the top of the stairs. It was currently a pre-construction zone; the door hadn't been hung yet, its entryway opened to a room of unfinished walls, wooden beams, and plywood flooring. Unlike the curved dormer windows in Jack and Lilah's bedrooms facing the front yard, the bonus room had a row of four plain windows lining the eastern side of the house, facing the Foremans' property. From the squat hallway, she saw the hint of lighting coming from the neighbors' porch. As Kara walked toward the light, her bare foot stepped down on something small and hard, making her stumble.

She cursed. She bent to retrieve the tiny ball from the floor, holding it up in the weak lighting the Foremans' house provided. It was heavy and weighted, most likely a marble from one of Jack's games. She closed her fist around it and moved toward the windows, noticing John had stacked cardboard boxes against the lower half of the row of them. They were boxes of miscellanea: holiday decorations, photo albums, wedding memorabilia, winter clothes…

They'd probably stay untouched for years, save the box with decorations. She toed the largest box. It sagged under the weight of the smaller ones sitting on it. She cursed again, recognizing the artificial Christmas tree inside. They hadn't packed it away properly.

She removed the smaller boxes, setting them on the floor, and pulled back the cardboard flaps on the last one she lowered. Right on top was the baby monitor and receiver they had used when Lilah was an infant. She let the marble roll out of her hand into the box, and pulled out the parent unit. She twisted the dial and the green light turned on. Having a eureka moment, she wondered if it might be useful for their current nightmare issue.

She inspected the freed Christmas tree, checking branches. Satisfied there didn't appear to be any damage, she closed the box and dragged it to the far side of the room. She restacked the other boxes and pushed them back against the windows.

Quietly, she padded out of the unfinished room and returned to Lilah's bedroom. She set the monitor on the dresser and turned it on. She turned to look at Lilah. The child's face was still content and her breathing even.

Kara returned to her bedroom, setting the parental unit on her nightstand, clicking it on.

John asked, his voice heavy, fighting sleep, "What's that?"

Sliding into bed, Kara said, "It's just for the time being. If Lilah wakes up, I want to make sure we hear her."

"Ahh." He pulled the covers up over his shoulder. "I haven't seen that for a while."

"I'll feel better knowing how often she wakes up."

Chapter Four

Saturday was mild. Windows were open, the kitchen curtains fluttering in the breeze. Kara had spent a good portion of the morning in the kitchen, leafing through paperwork, while half-listening to the kids' voices filtering in from the backyard. Lilah sat on a quilt, stretched out over the grass, playing with her dolls, while Jack kicked around an oversized ball.

After a while, Kara went out to the deck. She leaned on the railing, watching Jack before settling on Lilah. For a girl who was yanked from sleep every night, she seemed to function quite normally during the day. However small it may be, it was a small win, at least to Kara. Kara's eyes moved to the trees; the way the sunlight filtered through them made a pretty picture. She spotted the red of a cardinal and watched it before it flew away. She looked over her shoulder and flinched, catching movement. Something hobbled behind the tree-line. She narrowed her eyes just as the bobbing figure emerged, making her stand straight. It took her a moment to recognize Marvin.

"Hi there!" he called, waving.

Lilah and Jack flinched.

Kara forced a smile. "Hello!"

"Thought I might see how the new neighbors were faring," he said, approaching the deck.

Kara collected herself and replied, "We're doing good. Still getting settled."

"Yup, that'll take some doin'. How're you kids doin'?"

Jack hesitated before saying, "Fine." He wrapped his arms around the ball. Lilah walked her doll around on the quilt, her eyes fixed on Marvin.

Marvin said to Kara, "Nice to see a family finally moved in." He chuckled. "We were beginning to think the place was cursed or something."

"Cursed?" Kara asked.

"This land's been vacant all these years. The man who built it cleared all the trees. We're standing in the woods!"

"Oh. Did you know the man who built the house?"

"Not that I can say. I seen guys out here a few times building, but never came over. So, I can't say I knew them at all. Guess I didn't pay much attention. But I'm real happy you all moved in."

She looked up at the back of her house. Even as a joke, telling someone their house was cursed was an odd thing to say. She glanced at the yellow house peeking through the trees. "Tell Diane I said hello."

He followed her gaze and started to say something when Kara made a sound. Her eyes followed a hawk circling above the trees. Predators snatching prey came to mind and she said, "Diane told me about your dog...about the vulture...taking him."

Marvin's lips twitched, noticing the hawk too. "Diane told you that?"

Kara nodded.

He scratched the back of his neck, glanced at the kids who had resumed playing, and lowered his voice so only she could hear. "Between you and me, it was no turkey vulture that killed Blacky."

"Oh?"

"He was in the woods alright, but no bird killed him. Vultures don't attack living creatures. They're looking for fresh animal carcasses. Newly dead."

The hawk was drifting away. "Was it another animal?"

He shook his head slowly.

"Well, how do you know?"

He grunted, then said, "Animals generally can't tie things to trees, especially knots around necks."

Kara narrowed her eyes, then covered her mouth when she comprehended. "Somebody killed your dog?"

"Yep. Diane didn't see the dog until I let him loose. She walked up on me as soon as he dropped to the ground. Sad thing."

"That's terrible." There was unexplainable cruelty in the world, and for it to have happened in Kara's backyard was unsettling. She didn't ask where exactly Blacky had been found; she didn't want to know. "Do you know who did it?"

"Nope, probably some teenage prank. It was a long time ago." He brightened, saying reassuringly, "Seter Lane's really quiet. We don't get any trouble. Like I said, a very long time ago."

"Oh," she replied, the word trailing from her parted lips as she eyed the trees on the north side of the yard.

Marvin looked over her shoulder to the backdoor. "There's John. How do?"

Kara turned around to see John closing the door behind him.

"I'm doing good. How about yourself?"

"All's good here. I thought I'd drop by to be neighborly. You folks still settling in?"

"Yeah. Well, everything's unpacked pretty much. Now we have renovations to tackle. I was just taking a look at the skylight in the master bathroom. Looks like we might have a leak. I thought I might be able to pry some of the caulking down, thinking it just needs a fresh coat. You happen to know anything about skylights?"

"Nope, but I could take a look."

"Any help would be awesome."

"Got a honey-do, eh?"

Kara laughed. "I'll help where I can, but I think some of these jobs are going to have to be done by a professional."

John said, "We have a load of projects. Two rooms are down to the studs, we need new lighting, and possibly need to repair that skylight."

Marvin whistled. "That's a shame you bought this beautiful home and got left holding the bag."

John wasn't familiar with the etymology, but murmured his agreement. "Well, that's what you get with a bank-owned property, I guess."

"I s'pose so."

"I'm not really handy with tools. I'm a computer guy, spend most of my time on my butt." John laughed.

"Well, I'm glad to help out where I can. I'm always working on some project or another."

"That'd be great."

"For the bigger projects, you can probably find somebody in town."

"Do you have any recommendations? Someone who can do a good job for a good price?"

"Low price doesn't mean fair price. Not always."

"Yeah, I know what you mean. But, I'm not rich, you know."

Marvin's cool blue eyes met John's. "No? This big house and you're not well-off?" He clucked. "Now John, you're not house-poor, are you?" The wispy, white hair curling over his forehead hid deep wrinkles Kara knew were there. For a moment, she envisioned what he had looked like many years ago as a young man with dark hair and smooth skin.

"We get by," John finally said.

Marvin slapped him on the back, chortling. "Good answer, good answer."

Kara worked a smile on her face. She looked at the kids, seeing they were still playing, then turned back, noticing a track of crumbled dirt and stray pebbles on the floor. They led from the stairs to Marvin. His work boots were caked in dried mud. She asked, "Do you work outside often?"

"Always," Marvin replied. He tapped one boot against the other, but no dirt fell. "I'm retired officially, but I'm always getting into some project. Speaking of which…" He said to John, "I'd better get going. You let me know when you want to work on that skylight."

"Will do."

Marvin winked at Kara and called goodbye to the kids. The Tamesons watched him move, quite spritely, across the yard and through the woods toward his house.

Chapter Five

Kara sat at the only available table in Garden Café. There were four circular tables, positioned in the center of the room, with the back and side walls bordered by booths. Up front was the counter, and behind its wall was the hidden kitchen. Two busy teens took orders from the counter and a middle-aged man manned the cash register. It was just after noon and the lunch rush was in full swing.

From her purse, she fished out her phone and opened an odd jobs app. It was to pass the time while she waited for her order to be ready, but she wanted to check the entry she had posted earlier that morning.

Handyman Wanted:
Family needs renovations done
Please call for details

It was short and to the point, but she wondered if she should add more. She had never posted online before, so was unsure what people usually wrote. She was looking through ads like hers when a woman asked, "Excuse me, do you mind if I sit here for a second?"

Kara looked up, seeing a blonde about her age.

"Or, are you waiting for someone?" The woman smiled pleasantly, sliding her sunglasses up onto the crown of her short hair. She swung slightly forward the bulging tote bag that was over her other shoulder. "This is really heavy and I don't have much room to set it down." She glanced around the room, indicating it was packed and the chances of having her property trampled was highly probable.

"Oh, sure," Kara replied, pulling her purse to her side of the table. "I'm just waiting for my order."

The woman looked relieved, sinking onto a chair and sitting her bag on the one beside her. "I should've thought better about coming at this time."

Kara laughed. "Oh, I know. This is my first time here, but I should've known coming here on a Saturday at lunchtime was a mistake."

"Oh? Are you visiting, or did you just move here?"

"We just moved here, this week, actually. My husband and our two kids."

"Oh, cool. Welcome. I'm Shannon Smith."

"Hi. Kara Tameson."

"How are you liking Gracie Town so far?"

"Gracie Town? Is that what you call it?"

"Well, it separates the tourists from the locals, I guess," Shannon chuckled. "If you call it Grace Township, it's a dead giveaway you're not from around here."

"Gracie Town. That's really cute."

"So, whereabouts do you live? Are you in town?"

"We're on Seter Lane."

"Seter?" Shannon pulled her head back in thought.

"Do you know it? It's up the street and around the corner."

"Oh, okay, yeah, I know Seter. It's a long country road, right?"

"Yeah, that's it."

"It's pretty out there. You really see the hills going that way."

"Do you live in town?"

"I'm on the opposite side, just inside town limits. I've lived here all my life. A lot of the people who live here work in Cosgrove, but I was lucky to get a job at a small accounting firm in town. I could literally walk to work if I wanted to." Shannon laughed. "But I don't want to. The firm is so close to here too, it's embarrassing I still drive on lunch breaks."

"We came from Cosgrove. I've lived there all my life."

"Ah, so this is a change for you, small town living."

"Yeah. I don't even think I've *been* to a small town. But I like it so far."

"Good. Did you guys go all out then? Did you buy a farmhouse?"

"No, no. That would be crazy. No, we're in a new-build. I wouldn't be able to live on a farm. No thanks."

"A new-build, nice. I didn't think Seter had anything new out there. I just remember it being older homes and farmland."

"That's how most of it is. We might have the only new-build."

"That's smart. Saves you money in the long run with not having to worry about things breaking down for years."

"Oh, I wish." Kara laughed. "Actually, I'm literally sitting here posting a want ad for a handyman. The house it new, but it's not completely finished. There are a couple rooms that weren't fully built. So, with having gotten the house for a reasonable deal, we ended up having an immediate renovation on our hands."

"Wow. So, you're looking for someone?" Shannon asked with some excitement. "My boyfriend, Tom, is in construction. He'll need something for when he's between jobs."

"Really? Let me give you my husband, John's cell number. He can give Tom all the details." A teen at the counter called Kara's name then. "My order's ready. I'll see you later. It was nice meeting you."

"See you." Shannon grinned. "Welcome to Gracie Town."

While Lilah napped, the other Tamesons ate the takeout Kara had brought home from the café. Lunch was quick, with John anxious to continue yardwork. Jack moped around the house, complaining of boredom, so after a while, Kara sent him outside to help his father. In the great room, she dropped displaced toys into a laundry basket. She scooped up another armful of stuffed animals and released them into the basket, then bent to retrieve a stray action figure from behind the couch. Coming back up, her eyes caught movement out the window, something dark shifting out of view.

She knelt on the couch, looking, but saw nothing, just an empty backyard. She heard the buzz of the weed trimmer, knowing it was John out there working. *It must've been him passing into the side yard*, she thought, dropping the toy man into the basket.

"Mommy?"

She turned around to find Lilah standing in the kitchen, rubbing her eyes. Kara asked, "Hey, Lilahbean! Sleep good?"

"Uh-huh."

"Good." The nightmares only seemed to haunt her at night, a small reprieve. Kara gestured to the toys in the laundry basket. "Look at this mess, Lilah."

"Mommy, I'm hungry."

" 'Hungry'."

"Hungry."

"If you take toys out of your room, you need to put them back as soon as you're done playing. Okay?"

"Okay."

Kara sighed. "Okay, let's get you lunch."

Lilah hopped onto a chair at the kitchen table.

Kara pushed the laundry basket against the cushions and straightened. She halted, her eyes having landed on the playroom door. Sunlight spilled through the doorway, which was exposed a few inches.

"Who opened that door?" She pushed the door open. "Did you come in here?" She stepped over the plywood threshold and surveyed the drywall and wood planks, propped against the framed walls. Nails were scattered everywhere. Sawdust coated much of the floor.

"No. Not me."

"Did Jack? Did you see him come in here?" How had she not noticed earlier the door was open? She looked out the three bare windows that gaped at the woods and the Foremans' tree-nestled sun porch.

"No."

"No one goes in this room, okay? It's dangerous."

Lilah nodded vigorously, understanding.

Her eyes on the trees, Kara noticed something white waving in the woods. She leaned closer, but before she could make sense of what she saw, a blue jay came into view, stealing her attention. She watched it hop along the ground for a moment before it fluttered to a branch and then finally flew away. She pressed her face close to the window pane, looking for it, scanning the trees and what of the ground she could make out. Her eyes flicked over branches, but the bird was gone. She took in the same area again slowly, one last time. Nothing stirred; even the leaves had drooped, coming to a stand-still. She wrinkled her brow and left the room, shutting the door.

John moved to the backyard, the sun beating down on him; there was no breeze to speak of and the air was sticky. He worked the electric string trimmer, cutting neglected weeds along the perimeter of the house, alternating swipes at the sweat tickling his brow.

It wasn't like he wasn't used to yardwork. Apartment living had softened him and had given him more time to do things he enjoyed, but he really didn't mind getting his hands dirty. He had grown up in rural Iowa where country roads and fields dotted with animals was the normal scenery. Not for the first time, he thought about the new house with pride. He released the trimmer's trigger and leaned back to gaze up at the stucco exterior and over the rear rounded windows that, like the front of the house, were edged in uneven, decorative brick. That and the chocolate shutters gave the house a sense of old-world charm. Grace Township was quite an upgrade from his childhood town, but that *feeling* of country living he had felt as a kid hovered here too. He hadn't realized before he had missed it.

He pushed back his damp hair and toed the stubborn weeds sprouting around the rear corner of the house. He made to push down on the trigger again when he heard scuffling. It came from the woods. His eyes darted over the trees, his finger straying from the trigger. He skimmed the trees until he spotted something white. It looked like a flag, which stirred his curiosity. The little breeze shifted, stalling out completely, as he stepped into the contrasting coolness of the woods. He held the trimmer ahead of him like a shield. He moved deeper, engulfed by alders, ashes, and maples that were spaced just far enough apart to allow him room to pass unscathed by thorny berry bushes sprouting haphazardly all around.

Twenty feet in, he was at the white banner that had lured him. Up close, he saw it was just a strip of white fabric, the length of a typical scarf, tied tightly around one of the lower branches of an ash. He stroked the dingy material, his fingers trailing to its frayed edges. He looked up at the towering tree, thirty feet from roots to canopy. A bird from a neighboring ash chirped and nearby, a squirrel tussled with a pile of dried leaves left behind from last autumn.

John's eyes drifted back to the scarf; he wondered if it was a boundary marker. The Foremans' property line started somewhere close to where he was, so that was possible. Or, he supposed, it could've been something mindless, someone simply tying a length of fabric around a tree. Looking at it closer, he saw it was held by a simple knot; a child could've tied it. As he reached out to touch it, something smacked the trees above.

Thwack!

He squatted, holding the trimmer in front of his face.
Thwack! Thwack! Thwack!

Dark wings and a round, feathered body skirted down to the ground with a thump.

John jumped away. It took him a moment to realize it was a turkey vulture. Twigs and leaves pooled around it on the ground. If John hadn't known any better, he could've sworn it had shaken its withered head in bewilderment. He watched in stunned silence as it got up and waddled out of the congestion of trees. Seconds later, the vulture found enough open ground and took off, soaring until it disappeared beyond the treetops.

Jack brooded. He sat hunched-over on the top step of the deck. It was hot as heck, and there he was, being forced to do yardwork. He had looked for his dad in the front yard, but he hadn't seen him. The last thing he wanted to do was pull weeds. He watched the pool water ripple steadily, wishing he could go swimming instead.

After a while, he felt eyes on him. His skin prickled with gooseflesh.

Something stared at him.

He rolled his eyes to the right, and his body jerked when he saw her. A doe stood at the edge of the woods, her ears standing at attention, her almond-shaped eyes focused on him. Jack couldn't remember seeing a deer in person. He rose slowly and stepped down from the stairs, his eyes locked on hers. Stealthily, he moved over the grass, heading for her. She eyed him a few more seconds before leaping away.

"Darn!" He watched her prance to the opposite side of the yard, quickly vanishing into the woods.

"Jack?" His dad appeared then, staggering out of the trees, a few yards from where the doe had escaped to. John held the trimmer ahead of him with one hand lowered like it was a leashed dog. He shook his head, as if clearing it. "Are you here to help?"

"Dad! You just missed a deer!"

"Oh yeah? Where was it?"

Jack pointed to where they now stood. "He was right here and he was watching me. But then it ran off over that way."

"Wow, that's cool. I just saw a big bird in the woods." John grimaced, seeing in his mind the turkey vulture that had rattled him just moments before. Forcing away the image, he said, "Come on, I need your help bagging weeds."

Jack scowled, following him to the front yard. He watched John shake open a large paper bag. "Why are we throwing away weeds?"

John stood the bag up near the corner of the house and handed Jack a pair of oversized work gloves. "Because if you keep the weeds on the grass, you'll end up with more weeds. The weeds' seeds—"

"Weeds' seeds," Jack chuckled.

"—will make more weeds and then you won't have any grass…" John's words drifted, his eyes going to the sky. The clouds had thickened and were darkening to the west. He looked back at his scowling step-son and said, "Okay, have at it. Just grab what you can and toss it in the bag. The goal is to get all the cut weeds off the ground."

"What about the bushes?"

John glanced at the wiry thornbushes he hadn't yet yanked. They sprouted at the far corner of the house and near the front sidewalk. Not knowing why the builder hadn't ripped them out, he wondered if they flowered in the fall.

"Just be careful if you pick any weeds by them…Never mind, I'll get the ones near them. You get the other ones."

Jack made a face and squatted down, doing as instructed. His work gloves were too big, so dirt and pebbles snaked in, crumbling down into his palms. The work wasn't hard, but he felt suddenly uncomfortable; the temperature had dipped and mugginess still clung to the air. The wind had picked up and flicked his hair.

This sucks is what Jack wanted to say, but he didn't because he knew his parents didn't like that word. They told him it was the same as cussing, even though kids at his old school had said it all the time. They had even said it in front of the playground monitors and never got in trouble.

Suck.

So far there weren't many plusses living in the country, not if it meant spending the end of summer break doing yardwork in some boring small town where the only neighbors were the old people next door. It sucked.

John spotted a clump of weeds he had missed and picked up the trimmer. He aimed it at the spiky beasts and pressed the trigger, but it was silent; the battery was dead. He grabbed a shovel and dug into the ground, unearthing the leafy mess. After tossing a few shovelfuls into the communal paper bag, he dragged an arm across his sweaty forehead. A chorus of birds chattered somewhere nearby. He paused, his eyes going to the trees lining the driveway. The birds changed tone as if they were agitated, bickering. A gust of wind rushed over John and a shadow draped over the lawn, making him look up. The sky was night to the west.

He quickened his pace. "How's it going, Jack?"

"Fine."

John gathered handfuls of weedy stalks around the thornbush nearest the sidewalk and looked over at him. The boy slumped nearby, picking up a single stalk. "Jack, hurry it up. There's a storm coming."

Jack picked up pace—slightly—and plucked another stalk, which he dropped casually into the bag. Distant thunder rolled.

"Okay, let's do one more handful before we start cleaning up," John said, grabbing two more bunches. He watched as Jack dropped another stalk into the bag, losing some of its leaves where they slipped down onto the grass. Sighing, John told him he could go inside. Jack sprinted through the front door, the wind helping him slam it behind him.

Thunder rumbled closer. John folded the top of the bag and picked up the shovel. He stepped onto the sidewalk, spotting a family of weeds growing mercilessly below another thornbush. He set down the bag and awkwardly dug, trying to wedge the shovel in under the stubborn branches. Juice sprayed as he hacked into them, splintering the stalks, but their roots were strong. He pulled out the shovel and pressed it in at a new angle, jumping onto its step. The roots didn't break.

Thunder cracked long and slow, ominous, as he turned over the shovel and scraped at the dirt. He dropped the shovel, ignoring the raindrop that plopped onto the nape of his neck. Kneeling on the ground, leaning close to the bush, he smoothed a gloved hand over the root. Thunder growled, making him look up at the sky; darkness blanketed over him. He made to go, giving one last pat on the thick root when he noticed a length of ivory uncovered beside it. Intrigued, he ignored the thornbush as it scratched his arms as he dug his fingers into the ground, uncovering the cylindrical object. Unlike the roots beside it, he was able to unearth it easily. He wiped away some of the dirt.

He sat back on his knees and unwound the fabric that covered it, shaking away dirt. It was a lump of clay, some sort of statue, about fifteen inches long. The fabric had been poor at protecting it, as the statue was caked in dirt as well. Thunder cracked again overhead and lightning zig-zagged across the sky. Raindrops were multiplying; soon, he would be caught in a rainstorm. He tucked the statue under his arm, grabbed the fabric, paper bag, and shovel, and hurried to store them near the stained, woolen blanket in the garage.

Kara looked up when John walked into the master bedroom. She sat cross-legged on the bed, folding laundry. She watched him push back the curtains, looking out at the rocking storm. Lightning flashed mercilessly, thunder cracked over them, and rain drove wildly down the window panes.

John released the curtains and sat on the MDF window bench. With the statue on his lap, he worked his thumbs and fingers, carefully massaging away the dirt.

Kara asked, "What's that?"

He didn't hear her and got up abruptly, going into the bathroom. He returned to the window bench with a wet washcloth. Carefully, he worked the cloth over the statue's grooves. "Oh," he said finally, sitting back and holding it out.

It was girl and a frog, grinning, their color a dingy, yellowish ivory. The girl, standing, held a folded umbrella, its tip touching the round base, and the frog squatted beside her.

The baby receiver on the nightstand beside Kara crackled, startling John and her. They stared at the plastic box. The green "on" light flickered and when the static died seconds later, the light glowed steady again.

"What's that, Daddy?"

Kara flinched, but recovered, seeing it was Lilah who had materialized at the door, the page from a coloring book trailing from her hand.

John replied, "I found it outside, Lilah."

Kara and Lilah came up to him.

"Isn't that cool, Sophie?" Kara murmured.

John's eyes flashed. " 'Sophie'?" He looked at Kara's downturned face.

Kara hadn't noticed. She was looking at the statue, sensing an air of creepiness in the plastered jovial faces. "Where'd you get it?" she asked.

"You called her Sophie," John prompted, nodding at Lilah. "Didn't you notice?"

Kara's eyes shot up, meeting his. "No, I didn't." Had she?

"Daddy, is that a dolly?" Lilah bounced up and down, oblivious to the worried faces exchanged above her.

John cleared his throat, discarding the slip-up. "It's a statue I found outside, buried like treasure. I just cleaned it up a little."

Kara stepped back. Had she really called Lilah "Sophie?" John must not have heard right, because Sophie wasn't even on her mind. Her thoughts went to the day they moved in when she had caught herself calling Lilah that as she stood on the driveway. Why had she said it again?

"You said you found that outside?" Kara asked, pushing away the slip-up he had noticed.

He seemed to ignore it too as he replied, "It was buried in the front yard under a thornbush."

"That's weird. It's not like it could've been there for very long, right?"

"Maybe it was buried before the house was built."

"I wonder how old it is." Kara peered closer. To her unexperienced eye, however, it could've been an antique or a new statue from a garden center.

"I don't know," he said, turning it over in his hands.

Lilah hopped around. "Daddy, let me see!"

Kara held out her hand. "Can I see it?" John gave it to Kara, who saw it wasn't chipped, but felt how rough the material was. Kara studied the clay girl's face; she had been sculpted to be pretty, but the eyes ruined the effect. It was as if they had been made too wide or the pupils too small in contrast. Hair had been carved, long grooves giving the impression of it falling just past her shoulders. A bonnet rested on her back. She wore a simple dress and gripped a closed umbrella in her clasped hands. Kara frowned at the frog beside the girl. Its hunch was lopsided and it too grinned with curved, wide lips carved below large, buggy eyes. Kara turned the statue upside-down to see if there was a maker's mark, but there wasn't.

"Can I see it now, Mommy?"

"Yes, I guess you can." Kara placed it carefully in Lilah's hands. She asked John, "Disappointed?"

He shrugged. "Nah, I have plenty of ground here to find real buried treasure." His eyes twinkled. "We need a metal detector now," he commented before leaving the room.

Kara peered out the window. The rain had slowed to a steady sprinkle and the sky had lightened to gray-green. "Looks like we survived our first storm in Gracie Town."

"Mommy, is she mine?" Lilah asked.

"I guess, but you have to be extra careful with her. She'll break if you drop her. Daddy found her in the ground."

"I know." Lilah combed a finger over the ridges of the umbrella. "The lady told me too."

"What lady?" When Lilah didn't respond right away, engrossed with stroking the humps of the frog's eyes, Kara asked again, "What lady, Lilah?"

Her eyes rolled up, connecting with Kara's. "The lady with the yellow hair like the dolly used to have." She rubbed the palm of her hand over the statue girl's carved hair. "The lady in the woods."

"Did you see someone in the woods?" Had the movement Kara had caught from the great room windows been the lady? "Was it a lady visiting next door...with Marvin?"

"Maybe."

Kara wrinkled her brow. "But, Lilah, that doesn't make sense. How can a lady in the woods have known about a statue buried in our yard? When did you see her?"

Lilah shrugged.

"Maybe you had a dream about a lady and a doll?" Kara suggested. Lilah had to be confused, or maybe even making it up.

"Maybe."

"You know you aren't supposed to talk to strangers, right?"

"Yeah." Lilah cradled the statue in her arms and headed to the doorway.

"Lilah, look at me."

The bluest full moons looked up at Kara.

"I don't care if you think someone is friends with next-door. You don't speak to them unless someone you know really well, like me, Daddy, or Jack is with you. I don't want you going into the woods without one of us."

"Why not?" She narrowed the moons to slits. "Jack goes by himself."

"Because Jack is a lot older than you and he knows better what to do if something happens. Okay?" But did he? Had she taught him well not to talk to strangers?

Lilah hesitated before finally nodding.

"Say 'okay' so I know you understand, because there will be consequences. Do you remember what consequences are?"

Lilah shook her head, her eyes back on the statue. She wriggled, the talk never-ending. Kara was losing her fast.

"Consequences are a punishment for when you do something bad. Like we take away the dolly for a week. Got it?"

"Yeah."

Kara relented with the lesson on stranger danger. "Come on, let's go to the kitchen and I can fix her up for you."

Lilah plopped down on a chair at the table as Kara rifled around in the junk drawer. Finding masking tape, she said, "Here, give me the doll. I don't like how rough she is. You don't want to get scratched or cut."

Kara wrapped tape around the statue girl's mid-section. She did a crude job and the tape hid a good chunk of the dress, but you could still see all of the frog and the upper and lower parts of the girl.

"When you hold her, only hold onto the taped part. When you put her down, put her down gently."

"Okay." Lilah pulled the statue from her mother's grasp and ran from the room.

Kara turned to the playroom door, satisfied it was still closed, then went out the backdoor. She walked to the end of the deck and leaned on the railing, looking out at the trees, as if she'd spot a blonde passing through. The sun hid behind clouds, darkening the woods. Even with straining her eyes, she couldn't see beyond the cluster of overgrowth crowding the trees. She hadn't thought to ask the Foremans if they had children; perhaps, the blonde was a relative of theirs.

Kara went back inside and found Jack lying on his bed, leafing through a comic book. "Lilah told me she was approached by a lady in the woods. Were you there?"

"No."

"You didn't see a lady outside? A blonde?"

"No."

"You know how you're not supposed to talk to strangers?"

"Yeah."

"You and Lilah are not to talk to anyone your dad and I don't know. Okay? That includes anyone you see with Marvin next door."

"I can't talk to him?"

"You can talk to him. We know him. You just can't talk to strangers, even if they're in his yard. Okay?"

"Um, alright. But won't it be weird if I'm talking to him and someone's with him and they say something to me, but I don't answer back?"

Kara thought for a moment. Okay, maybe that sounded strange. But, no matter, you never knew who people really were, and especially meeting a stranger in the woods...

"I don't care if they think you're weird. Don't talk to anyone your dad and I don't know. Okay?"

"Yeah, okay."

"You're sure you didn't see Lilah talking to a blonde lady?"

"No. She probably made it up."

Kara nodded, wondering the same. She sighed, combing her hand over his cowlick. "And stay out of the unfinished room downstairs."

"Okay. I don't go in there anyway."

"I found the door open today."

"I didn't open it."

She believed him. Maybe it had been John. "Alright, good." She left his room and paused in the hallway, looking into Lilah's bedroom. Lilah sat on her bed, balancing the statue on her stretched-out legs, moving her hands over it.

Kara walked away without a word and returned to the kitchen. Like a magnet, her eyes were drawn to the playroom. The door was open a crack, a band of sunlight framing the edge of the doorway.

"What in the world?" She looked in the room and saw no one was inside. She closed the door and waited, watching it. After a short moment, the door creaked, opening an inch. She pushed it open the rest of the way and looked around the room, seeing nothing aside from the wood planks leaning against the walls and the nails scattered on the floor. She closed it again, pulling tightly on the doorknob, and waited…five…fifteen seconds. It didn't open.

She backed away, zeroing in on the door. It stayed shut. Mentally, she added the shoddy doorjamb to the repair list.

"So, the skylight has a leak, after all," Kara said later that night, flipping off the bathroom light and crawling into bed beside John. "The corner of the window is a little wet."

"Okay," John replied with a yawn, turning to his side. "I'll figure out what we need to do to fix it. Hopefully, it doesn't rain in the meantime."

"Do you think Marvin will help, or have you talked to Tom yet about it?"

"Tom?"

"Shannon, who I met today at the café, her boyfriend."

John yawned again. "Oh, no, I haven't talked to him yet. But yeah, either way, it'll get fixed."

The kids had been in bed for a couple hours. From the silence of the baby monitor on the nightstand, Lilah was still sleeping well. After Kara and John had been quiet for several minutes, Kara started to wonder if he had fallen asleep. But then she felt him adjust and readjust his position.

Lying in the dark, her thoughts shifted, taking root in what he had said earlier. She hadn't heard the flub earlier that day (*Sophie*), but she believed him. Finally, after he had been still for a few minutes, she approached the subject with caution, asking quietly, "Why did I say it, John?" The air conditioning cycle ended with a click, making the room feel terribly intimate.

The crickets outside the closed windows mocked her. *He's not going to answer you*, they chided. Kara almost said his name to make sure he'd heard her when he finally spoke.

"I don't know," he replied. He was on his side, his tee-shirt-covered back to her.

She hesitated. "Have you ever heard me call Lilah that?" She refrained from mentioning the *other* name.

"No."

She was quick with a reply, "Good," because the moment was awkward and it was a subject they didn't discuss. They said nothing else. She closed her eyes, but instead of seeing a blank canvas on the backs of her eyelids, she saw a pale face and blue lips.

Her eyes flipped open.

She stared at John's back for a long time. Eventually, she saw the rhythmic rise and fall of it as he slept. She turned to her side, facing away from him. She didn't dare shut her eyes for a long time, not until she was fairly certain she wouldn't see Sophie's slack face.

Chapter Six

The screeching end of the scream woke Kara.

Lilah.

Kara's eyes flipped open, but she closed them again just as quickly. Her bedroom was far too bright. The curtains looked like they would burst into flames for all the brilliance the morning sun offered.

She rolled to her side. John was not beside her. She glanced at the clock and widened her eyes. It was nearly ten. She couldn't remember the last time she had slept in so late, even though she didn't feel like she had slept at all. She was groggy and her eyes burned. What was it she had dreamed? She couldn't remember.

She sat up as realization came to her: she hadn't heard Lilah during the night. She looked at the nightstand, seeing the baby monitor's green "on" light glowed. She trained her ears, but all she heard was the hollow knocking of a woodpecker outside.

She padded through the kitchen, calling, "Hello?"

"Hello?" John called back.

She found him in his office. He sat at the scuffed, walnut desk they had purchased a few years ago second-hand. "I overslept," she told him. "Did Lilah wake up last night?"

"She was fine at breakfast an hour ago." He glanced up and smiled. "I guess no nightmares last night."

"Really?" The nightmares had become the norm for the last several weeks. She smiled wearily. "I can't believe I slept in so late. You shouldn't have let me."

"Why?" He had returned his attention to his computer screen and was typing.

"Are you working today?"

"Just a little. I want to get something done before tomorrow."

She started to leave, but remembered the unused pool in their backyard. "I think we've tortured the kids enough. Any chance of opening the pool today?"

"This brilliant guy here was smart enough to dump in chemicals yesterday. It's all set."

"Ah, now we just have to make sure we have swimsuits."

"If not, who cares? Our pool, our rules," he joked as he typed.

"Still, I'm gonna check to make sure I have suits for everybody. Jack and Sophie are gonna be over the moon."

They both heard it this time.

"Sophie," he repeated her slip-up, no longer typing. The name hung there, naked.

Her hands covered her burning cheeks. "Did I say it?" She knew she had.

He nodded, his face serious.

"Oh."

"Have you been thinking about her lately?" he asked quietly.

"I don't know. No more than usual." Her answer sounded stupid. *Had* she been thinking more about her? Was there a place somewhere deep down inside her where she harbored something unexpressed? She and John hadn't discussed Sophie for years, and to be honest, Kara hadn't thought there had been a need to. She had accepted the loss long ago. Hadn't she?

He turned slightly toward her in his chair, but didn't fully face her. His expression pained, he asked carefully, "Do you want to talk about it?"

She replied, the words rushing out, "No, I'm alright. It was just an accident."

"It's alright. We can talk about her if you need to."

She picked up on it, the singularity of the situation: if *I* need to.

It was clear. He didn't need to; he didn't want to discuss his first legitimate child with her. Did she need to talk about her? *Should* they feel *something* after so much time had passed?

"It was just a slip-up. I'm fine." She turned to go.

"Have you found a place for the memory box?"

She shook her head, picturing the white box packed away in one of the cardboard boxes in the bonus room amid the clutter. "Probably in our room. I haven't gotten around to it yet."

His voice low, he suggested, "You might feel better if you did."

The statement sounded absurd. She might feel better? Well, I'm glad he's over it and has moved on, she thought sardonically. But she had moved on too…hadn't she? She had grieved years ago. That was over and done with.

"I'm going to look for swimsuits." Soberly, she left the room. She packed away the slip-up, blocking it from her thoughts. She wasn't going to go back to that place, not now.

On Wednesday morning, Kara, Jack, and Lilah climbed the wide, concrete steps that led to the front door of Grace School, a white clapboard nineteenth-century two-story. Opening the door, their noses were struck by a mixture of pine and mothballs. The entrance hall opened up to a polished wood staircase, their treads covered in worn floral carpeting. Kara had just turned to look into the adjoining room when the director, Joyce Chandler, joined them.

Unsmiling, the middle-aged woman jumped right into it after Kara introduced themselves. "The official school season starts in two weeks. That's when you'll see Grace School functioning at full capacity. Not only do we offer pre-kindergarten preparation, but we also have a number of before and after-school programs. We've been operating as a school for over seventy years. We're an institution to Grace Township. Are you originally from here?"

"No, we just moved in from Cosgrove."

The woman gave Kara a once-over and nodded curtly. "Unfortunately, I'm pressed for time. My staff is here, however. They'll give you a tour."

Kara watched her take to the stairs, gliding up as if she were an old Hollywood glam star, until three female teachers, all looking to be college age, came around the corner. By contrast, they were all smiles as they led the Tamesons through the building, explaining they were normally closed during the summer, except for random special events. The group tromped through classrooms, the musty smell of the remains of the house's library, dining room and living room hardly subtle under pine air fresheners, their sneakered feet rough and loud on original hardwood floors. Lining the walls hung student drawings and colored pages torn from coloring books. Lilah's face lit up and even Jack seemed curious about the different play stations that were filled with beads, blocks, and puzzles.

"Can I see your doll?" They were at the end of the tour and Miss Fiona was bending toward Lilah. "I had a huge collection of them growing up. I had rag dolls, porcelain dolls, plastic dolls, paper dolls…"

Lilah met the ponytailed teacher's eyes, hugging her new statue tighter. They all waited while she mulled the idea over, her hesitation so long it hinged on awkwardness. Just as Kara was about to prompt her to show the teacher, Lilah swiftly turned the statue around, revealing the faces of the grinning clay girl and frog.

"Oh," Miss Fiona said, her smile lessening. She gave the other teachers a look before straightening and took a step back. Recovering, she said with a smile, "How sweet."

Kara looked down at the statue, which Lilah had flipped around again. She suspected Fiona thought it was ugly like she did, or perhaps, she found it strange a child carried around a statue.

Miss Jill squatted in front of Lilah, saying kindly, "We hope to see you again."

Miss Lisa said with a perky smile, "We have lots of dolls here you can play with too."

Outside, the Tamesons crossed through the blacktopped parking lot. Immediately forgetting the awkwardness of their goodbyes with the staff, Kara's attention turned to the residence next door. As pretty as Grace School was, it was dwarfed by the grand, two-story brick American Federalist-period house that was set further back from the street. Kara's eyes ran past the surrounding iron fencing, drifting over the wraparound porch and the dentil molding peppering the upper perimeter of the second floor. She was gazing at the upstairs windows when the lacy curtain twitched and a face appeared.

Startled, she turned her back on it. "Come on, guys."

"I'm hungry," Jack whined.

Kara looked down the road. A handful of people walked by, enjoying the mild day. "Okay, let's get something to eat." She steered them across the street to Happy Cones. The air-conditioned diner was snug, offering a long bar, four square, black-and white checkered tables that took up much of the floor space, and booths lining the perimeter. Sitting at a corner booth, eating sandwiches and fries, Kara read over the headlines of the old newspapers plastered to the walls that stretched to the ceiling, as Jack and Lilah blew straw wrappers at each other.

She craned her neck, reading a page stretched along the wall behind the kids. "Grace Township Hero Home from Overseas," the headline read. A yellowed image of a smiling young man in Navy service dress shook hands with a man in horn-rimmed glasses, wearing a business suit. The caption read, "Mayor Snell welcomes hero home." She skimmed over the article and read a few others before turning to the wall beside her. Looking up, she squinted at the top headline, barely making out some of the words, "Museum Suspects Drowning in Centuries Old Mystery."

Jack interrupted her reading by asking for ice cream.

"Sure," Kara replied, turning to her wallet and handing him cash. "You can order it at the front counter."

The kids took off. Kara was piling discarded wrappers onto a plate when the bell over the door tinkled. She and Shannon, the blonde she had met at Garden Cafe, spotted each other at the same time.

"Hi!" Shannon said, approaching.

"Hi, how are you?"

Shannon smoothed her hands down the sides of her pencil skirt. "I'm good. I just came to grab lunch."

Kara laughed, asking, "Did you walk here?"

"I work close to town, a couple blocks from here."

"I know. I remember you saying you can walk, but would rather drive."

Remembering their earlier conversation, Shannon nodded and chuckled. "Believe it or not, I drove. I know, I know. I need to walk more." Still smiling, Shannon pointed at the counter to where Jack and Lilah sat on stools. "Are those your kids?"

"Yeah, Jack and Lilah."

"Oh, nice."

"Do you have kids?"

"No. I think Tom and I'll get married soon, but I don't know if we're the parent type. But you never know. Maybe someday."

"You still have time to decide." Kara grabbed her purse, standing.

"Have you guys started working on repairs yet?"

"It's slow-going. Did Tom call John?" If he had, John hadn't told her, but she hadn't seen much of him the past few nights. He had returned to work, but headed in much earlier now that they lived farther away, and came home later too. He also spent the evenings working in his home office directly after dinner.

"I think so. Tom's wrapping up the job he's been on, but he's anxious to have another lined up."

Kara saw something, perhaps worry, pass over Shannon's face, but it was quick and Shannon was smiling again. "I'll give Tom a friendly reminder to call if he hasn't." She picked up her ordered lunch, said hello to Jack and Lilah, and with a wave, left the parlor.

After ice cream, the Tamesons returned to their car, theirs now the only one parked in Grace School's lot. Kara opened the driver's side door, pausing to look up at the brick house next door. Her eyes drifted to the upstairs windows, as if challenging the person from before to reappear. But the lacy curtains were lifeless. She glanced at the windows on the first floor and then the double doors, but spied no one.

When they got home, the kids changed into swimsuits and got into the pool. Kara relaxed on the deck, easing back onto the chaise lounge.

"We need to get you swimming lessons, Lilah," she called, but Lilah, floating contentedly in the inner tube, didn't hear.

Kara turned her attention to beach towels piled on the floor beside her. She reached over to unfurl the heap, but as she did so, something fell from it with a thump. Twisting downward, she saw Lilah's statue teetered from the fall. She frowned, looking at the carved eyes, bulging from their clay sockets. The girl and frog were ugly. She wondered if she would've been fond of it when she was a little girl, seen something lovely in it. Children saw things differently.

Looking at the adjoined frog, a cold sensation crept into her. It was as if it stared at her, saw her. Repulsion came over her; she didn't want to look at the statue anymore, didn't want to touch it. She laid it face-down again on the floor, dropping the towel back over it.

Goggles clamped over his eyes, Jack swam underwater toward Lilah's dangling legs. Pretending he was a shark, he pulled on one of them, making her squeal and kick violently at him. He swam away as fast as he could before popping above the surface.

"Jack, leave your sister alone!" Kara hollered.

He plunged down again, staying at the far end of the pool. He came up for air and went under again, trying to sit on the floor. Bobbing right back up, he broke through the water, hearing Lilah singing a song from the radio, most of the words nonsensical. He went under again. He didn't stay down for long, because water had seeped into the plastic lining of the goggles, shooting into his nose and eyes. He jumped up, coughing, dragging the face mask off.

"Are you alright?" Kara called.

"Yeah." He laid the goggles on the pool's ledge. He squeezed his nose with his thumb and index finger, swimming underwater again, back toward Lilah's lax legs. At the last second, he swooped sideways, narrowly passing her. He bobbed up and gulped air, then sank down. Underwater again, he passed her, swimming nearly to the far end.

He hopped up again, took in a deep breath, and was under again. This time, he spotted something stringy and yellow. He jerked his head back, trying to avoid the loose tentacles coming toward him. The water had turned murky and he could no longer find his way to his sister's legs. He saw the affronting yellow strands, though, inches from his face.

Was it string?

He paddled his arm in front of him, knocking it away. When he came up for air, he saw Lilah was still singing.

His mom was reaching over the pool ladder, ushering the inner tube toward her. "Lilah's getting out," she said, noticing him.

"Do I need to get out too?"

"We'll sit out to dry, so you can swim for about ten more minutes."

He swam around, but accidentally kicked the side of the pool, knocking his goggles in. As they sank, he tried to get a hold of the plastic head strap, but he was too slow and they dropped to the floor. He gulped in air and went under, into the murky water again. Chlorine stung his eyes. His vision limited, he felt along the floor for the goggles and when he started to buoy up, he forced himself down. His fingers wiggled until they struck something smooth. He closed his hands over the solid object. Automatically, he registered this wasn't the plastic texture of his goggles.

The water pushed against his eyes as he widened them to glimpse what he had found. He pulled on the rounded object as the back of his head crashed up through the water's surface. The object, peachy and large, moved under his grip. He held tight for a moment, until he recognized what it was; he wasn't alone in the pool. The rounded object was someone's shoulder…and it wasn't his mom or his sister's.

Blonde wisps of hair billowed toward him. He gasped, releasing his grip and jumped up.

"All done?" Kara asked, her voice mixing with frantic bird chirping. It sounded like a pet shop or the bird exhibit at the zoo. His eyes went to the white sky, his shoulders near his ears, as if expecting a murder of crows to descend upon him. But he saw none, just heard chaos ensuing from the trees.

He ignored his mother, hustling instead to the ladder. He grasped onto a rung, and then with all of the courage he could muster, plunged his head back down into the water. It was too hazy to see beyond a few feet ahead of him. Holding his breath for as long as he could, he looked around, not daring to let go of the ladder.

But there was nothing, just water. Nothing floated near him. Nothing came for him. Even the blonde strands were gone.

He straightened and climbed out. His voice quiet, he explained, "I dropped my goggles in the water."

"That's okay." Kara replied. "They'll be fine."

He stepped up onto the deck, looking over the surface of the blue pool, the ripples already slowing. He saw nothing in the water; even his goggles hid.

Kara wrapped a towel around his shoulders. He pulled it tight, shivering. He wasn't sure, and he definitely wasn't going to get closer to see better, but he thought he saw strands of blonde hair caught in the top screw of the ladder, waving in the breeze.

John came home that evening as Kara was clearing dishes from the kitchen table. He dropped his keys on the counter, but his laptop bag remained slung over his shoulder.

"Well, hello there," she said, setting the dirty plates beside the discarded keys. "You just missed dinner."

"I didn't realize how late it was."

"How was the drive?" she asked, glancing at the microwave clock.

"It wasn't that bad. I had to stay a little late."

"Are you hungry? We had chicken."

"That sounds good. I'm going to eat in the office. I need to finish something for work." He made himself a plate of leftovers and left the room as she loaded the dishwasher.

When she was done in the kitchen, she grabbed a can of cola and went into the office, setting the pop on John's desk. She asked without preamble, "Do we have a plan of action for these renovations?" Every day she passed under the brass chandelier, ignored the unusable rooms, and scowled at the stained ceiling in her bathroom. She was anxious to be fully settled. "We ran into Shannon today. Her boyfriend will be ready to start work soon. John?"

"One sec. I just need to finish one thing." He was typing something on the computer keyboard.

She sat in the chair opposite his desk and waited, looking around. The white walls were still bare and there were two half-filled cardboard boxes sitting in the far corner of the room next to a clunky, gray filing cabinet that was missing two drawer faces. She had thought they were going to toss it. Although John tended to work easily in messes, she planned to keep the rest of the house tidy.

"Are you ready to get your hands dirty on some repairs?" he asked when he was done, easing back in his chair.

"I'm ready to hire somebody. Did anyone call you?"

"Nope. You posted an ad online, right?"

"Yeah, it's been a few days. Tom is supposed to call you, Shannon's boyfriend."

"Oh, wait. He did call."

"John!"

"Sorry, I forgot. We're going to set up a time when he can come out for a quote."

"Can you remember now if anyone else called?" she asked, mockingly.

He shook his head. "Just the one so far. But that's okay. I can do some of the work on the weekends. The easier stuff." His eyes twinkled.

"Like replacing light bulbs?"

"Mm-hmm." His computer beeped then, stealing his attention.

"Where is it?" The woman's voice from the shadows was soft and pleading.

"Why do you want it?" The man, also hidden, asked. His tone was gentle as he reasoned, "It's nothing, a lump of stone."

Kara was surrounded by a gray mist, but she might as well have been in a black hole for all she could see.

"Please. It's mine," the invisible woman said. "It reminds me of her."

After a moment, the man said, with obvious distaste, "I always loathed that thing."

Kara woke up.

Chapter Seven

Two weeks passed and with it John's work hours steadily increased, taking away any available time to meet with Tom. One afternoon, Kara searched DIY how-tos online, keen on attacking *something*, no matter how small the project, but it was done in vain. She eventually gave up, not having the experience or confidence to attempt any projects on her own.

She had adapted to avoiding the empty rooms and pretending the tacky chandelier didn't exist. Instead, she spent the weeks preparing the kids for school. She thought Jack seemed apprehensive, but he didn't admit to it. Lilah seemed oblivious she'd be spending Monday through Friday mornings in pre-K, away from her family. Kara stayed positive on the surface, shopping with them for new clothes and school supplies, but she had butterflies in her stomach, absorbing the stress she imagined they kept hidden.

When Jack's first day of school arrived, Kara, a bundle of nerves, observed him as he brushed his teeth and got ready, searching for any hint of anxiety. He shrugged off all of her words of encouragement. No, he didn't need help picking out clothes; no, he didn't want anything special for breakfast; no, he didn't need her to walk him down the driveway to wait for the bus.

He let her take a picture of him at the front door and she watched from the office window as he made his way down the driveway. He waved at her when he was at the bottom of the hill. Her stomach in knots, Kara was glad that at least he didn't have to wait long for the bus to arrive.

She still had one child at home, since Lilah started pre-K the next day. The house already seemed empty and Kara wished Lilah hadn't chosen that day to sleep in later than normal. She forced herself not to wake her.

Restless, Kara sat in the great room and pulled out her cellphone. Her mother had texted her sometime within the last twelve hours.

Kara, call me.

She tapped her mother's name, calling her. When it went straight to voicemail, Kara texted, *What's up?*

She waited for her message to go through, but the status bar on the phone's window showed the message had stopped. A moment later, she got a message telling her the text had failed to send. She tried to resend it, but got the same error.

"Hi, Mommy," Lilah appeared in the room, cradling the statue in her arms.

"Well, good morning there, Lilahbean," Kara said, a little too cheerfully. She set down her phone, asking, "Do you want eggs? Jack started school today." She threw in the last bit as a reminder, but judging by her response, Lilah didn't seem fazed by it.

"Cereal." Lilah plopped down onto a kitchen chair, standing the statue on the table.

Kara went into the kitchen. "So, what do you want to do today? It's just you and me. If it's hot today, we can go swimming."

"Okay." Lilah tipped back the statue, looking it over.

Kara frowned. Was it awful she found Lilah's attachment to it irritating? "Have you given it...her...a name?" Kara asked, setting down a bowl of cereal and a glass of milk.

Lilah stood the statue upright and picked up her spoon. "I dunno."

"You don't know if you've given her a name?" Kara chuckled, not really feeling any humor in it. "You either have or you haven't."

"No." Lilah took a bite of the frosted Os.

"That's okay. I didn't name all my dolls growing up either," Kara replied, good-naturedly, even if she was pretty sure that wasn't true. But, she allowed herself, it was

71

probably best Lilah hadn't named it; maybe that would mean less of an attachment, and that would make it easier to throw away...

It's just because you know the statue isn't a plaything, Kara made the excuse in her head. *It's not supposed to be a toy.*

But, if anything, it was teaching Lilah how to take care of something, and she took very good care of it.

After breakfast, Kara watched Lilah ride her tricycle up and down the front sidewalk for a while before they moved to the lawn to blow bubbles. At lunchtime, Kara laid out a quilt on the deck for a picnic.

"Do you want to swim?" Kara asked when they had finished eating. The last two weeks had been cool, so the pool had been forgotten. But summer had made a comeback that August afternoon; the temperature was quickly rising into the upper eighties.

"Okay," Lilah said, yawning.

"Or maybe a nap is a better idea. We can swim when Jack gets home."

"I don't want a nap!" Lilah picked up her spoon and dropped it into a bowl of barely-touched pudding. Chocolate sprayed on her clothes and cheek.

"Whoa!" Kara stood up, pulling Lilah to her feet. "It's definitely naptime."

"I'm not tired!" Lilah tugged against Kara's grip until she had freed her arm. As she snatched the statue, the ends of her hair dipped into the pudding.

"Lilah!" Kara grabbed Lilah's hand and led her inside the house. "Now you're taking a bath and *then* going to sleep."

Lilah didn't protest, following Kara's lead upstairs.

"You can't act like this, especially after the nice day we had," Kara said, turning on the tub faucet.

Lilah set the statue carefully on the sink counter and undressed. She climbed into the tub and turned her eyes upward on Kara. The little girl asked, a soft lilt to her voice, "No Sophie?"

Sophie.

Kara snatched her hand from the faucet, as if she'd been burned.

"Mommy?"

Kara demanded, as if her daughter had sworn at her, "What did you say?"

"No Sophie? In the bath?"

Uncomprehending, Kara glanced down at the clear water and back at the innocent face looking up at her. "No…" Kara shook her head slowly and then forced herself to repeat it, "Sophie?" Had she heard right?

"Sophie! Sophie water! I want bubbles! Can't I have bubbles, Mommy?"

"Bubbles?" Kara mumbled. She mulled it over, her head spinning. She sat down on the toilet lid, seeing a pale face with blue lips.

"Mommy?" Lilah asked with a whine. "Why not? Bubbles!"

Kara double-blinked. "You want bubbles?" Her mind was clearing. "Do you mean you want the water to be soapy?"

Not Sophie. *Soapy.*

"Soapy water. Can't I have a bubble bath?"

Kara exhaled, covering her face with her hands.

"Mommy?"

"Yes, Lilah." Kara straightened and, with jittery hands, pulled out the bottle of bubble bath from under the sink.

After putting Lilah to bed, Kara found herself in the bonus room, a barren shell filled with nothing but cardboard boxes, partially blocking the windows. How could she not think of Sophie after a scene like that?

She sat on the plywood floor, careful of splinters, and reached out to tug on the nearest stack of boxes. She stopped herself. She couldn't do it. She pulled her knees to her chest and pressed her forehead against them.

I'm so sorry. I can't.

Sighing, she got to her feet and wandered outside to the deck. She looked at the trees, trying to clear her whirling thoughts. Why was her mind going back there after all this time?

Her eyes snaked over the woods, until she glimpsed something white mingling with the leaves. Her thoughts twisted then as she remembered the tale of Blacky, the dog hanging in the woods. Her woods.

Would she always think of that damn dog every time she looked at the trees?

She stepped off the deck and walked around the house, stopping on the gravel driveway. Two cars passed by on the road below. Cows grazed on the hill beyond.

Sophie crept into her thoughts again. The white box she pictured packed away in the bonus room wasn't her; it was just a symbol of her, a reminder. John had suggested she take it out. Why did that seem like a terrible idea?

She looked down at the driveway. Grass sprouted through the gravel. She squatted, pulled the tufts out, and threw them into the yard. She went into the garage to get grass killer, but didn't find any.

She spotted the forgotten woolen blanket she had discovered the day they had moved in. She turned it over in her hands, touching the dried orange paint, and dropped it into the plastic garbage bin, which she wheeled to the end of the driveway. She looked down the empty road, knowing Jack wasn't due home for another two hours. She climbed up the driveway, her eyes finding the yellow colonial peeking through the tree-line. The thought of the blonde woman fluttered into her mind, but was forgotten when she went inside her house.

John arrived home in time for dinner. Jack did the most talking as they ate. He had already made a friend and liked his teacher. Kara was glad for his chatter. She made no mention of her confusion from earlier in the bathroom and

Lilah seemed oblivious it had happened. There was no point in Kara bringing it up to John. It would only make him uncomfortable and maybe even lend to his recommendation that she seek professional counseling. If it kept happening, he'd have to suggest she get help, wouldn't he?

She received a text from her mom after dinner, *Are you all moved in?*

Kara texted back, *Just about. It's been busy. How are you?*

When Margaret didn't immediately respond, Kara checked to make sure her text had gone through. It had. She monitored her phone throughout the evening, but didn't receive any more messages.

She crawled into bed that night alone. John was in his office. The kids had gone to bed hours earlier. She willed sleep to come, but her thoughts wandered to Sophie.

She turned on her side, shifting the pillows. She inhaled deeply and let out a shaky breath, trying to relax. In the dark, she gazed at the unwavering green glow of the baby receiver. Lilah hadn't had a nightmare for weeks now. It was like the monitor was a talisman, warding off night terrors. Or maybe the statue was the charm. Kara visualized the crude, grinning faces. She fought to will away the image, as it made her skin crawl.

She concentrated on her breathing, emptying her thoughts, and eventually, fell asleep…

She was standing on a dirt path, surrounded by mist. Gnarled trees encroached, their knotted roots making the ground bumpy. On wobbly legs, she followed the road, clumsily stepping along. She moved so slowly; it took all of her strength just to go forward.

Up ahead, she sensed eyes on her; she knew the watcher waited on the other side of the fog. They wanted something from her and she wanted to give it to them, if only to get them to leave her alone. She forced her hands into her pockets, searching for it. She fought the fabric. Her pockets weren't deep, but still, her fingers rooted around for it, as if it were hidden in a secret lining. Where was it? If she gave it back, they'd leave her alone. Of course, she had it!

But she didn't.

Chapter Eight

"No toys. That includes your dolly," Kara said, opening the car's backdoor.

Lilah's forehead wrinkled. "But she has to stay with me."

"Sorry, she's not allowed." Kara softened, explaining, "It's a school rule." She wasn't sure if that was true or not, but thought that it very well could be. Besides, if it wasn't a rule, she worried the statue could be a distraction from learning. The statue seemed to distract her from playing with her other toys lately, anyway: another thing Kara had noticed and had wondered why it bothered her.

Making no further argument, Lilah climbed out of the car and opened the door to the front passenger side. She propped the statue against the vinyl seatback and patted the frog's head before closing the door. Kara noticed she didn't kiss her beloved dolly and was inexplicably glad.

It was Lilah's first day of school and she bubbled with excitement, immediately seeming as if she had instantly forgotten the ugly statue. When they located the classroom Lilah would be spending most of her day in, the little girl let go of Kara's hand and scrambled to the floor beside a girl stacking blocks. Lilah got to work building her own tower. Kara smiled at their turned-away faces, but they didn't look her way. Other children in the room glanced at her, curiously, and she smiled politely on her way into the hallway.

Miss Fiona smiled pleasantly, passing Kara. "We'll see you in a few hours for pick-up."

Kara returned to her car in the half-filled parking lot. She started the engine, but left it idling when something swept over her, tickling her. She twisted her arm, but saw nothing, and looked at her lap to see if a bug had crawled on her. But she didn't see one. Excusing it as a phantom itch, she scratched her arm, then placed her hand on the gear selector. She paused again.

She felt eyes on her.

She looked out the windshield and through the side windows, but saw nobody in the lot. The cars surrounding her were empty. She looked at Grace School, but the blinds were shut. Turning, her gaze crossed the parking lot to the Federalist house next door.

The curtains on the third floor were drawn, as were the ones on the second floor, but the first...

She flinched, seeing movement cross one of the side windows. Had they been watching her?

Her stared, willing them to come back past the window. But no one did.

She glanced away, looking down at the passenger seat. The statue leaned on its side, facing her the clay girl and frog staring at her.

She leaned over—careful to grasp onto the masking taped mid-section—and laid the statue face-down on the floor mat. She looked at the house again. The sensation of being watched was gone.

She headed home, her eyes drawing in the weathered barn at the corner of Seter Lane as she drifted by under plumed trees lining the road. Turning onto her driveway, she drove up the incline. She waited as the garage door opened, her eyes going to the front porch. Something was on the doorstep, but from there she couldn't make it out.

She parked the car in the garage and walked up the sidewalk, her keys jangling in her hand. She approached the front steps, slowing down as she neared, comprehending what her package was. She halted, then did a half-jump back, crying out. It was an animal, unmoving, slumped at the front door.

Covering her mouth, she forced herself to look at the opossum, its ugly open snout revealing sharp teeth it didn't need anymore. She shuddered, unwillingly committing to memory its rat tail and light gray fur before running into the garage and into the house through the mudroom. She called John, but got voicemail. She texted him to call ASAP, then peered out the front door sidelight before shrinking away. She didn't know what to do; she certainly wasn't going to touch it. She wondered if finding a dead animal on your porch normal in the country.

Dismayed John didn't sense her panic, she paced around the foyer, avoiding the sidelight. After a dozen back-and-forths, she went into the kitchen and stopped at the table: she felt the sensation of being watched again.

Slowly, she turned toward the great room. It was mostly dark because the drapes hadn't yet been drawn. Her eyes went straight to the only source of light: the playroom door was open a few inches, a rectangular streak of light cutting through the opening.

Kara shoved the door closed and leaned against it, closing her eyes. She sighed heavily, releasing some of the agitation. She eventually moved to the couch, then gradually made her way into the laundry room.

When she was done putting clean clothes away, she pulled out her cellphone to try John again. She saw she had no phone signal and her earlier text to John had failed.

"Dammit," she muttered. She went outside through the garage and wandered around the front yard, holding out her cellphone, trying for a signal. After five minutes of walking aimlessly around, she wanted to toss the phone. She groaned, giving up, looking across the road. No cows were out; no cars paddled down the road. She felt absolutely alone.

She was turning back to the house when she heard a screen door slam shut. She followed the sound with her eyes to the yellow house behind the trees. She wasn't alone, after all.

She didn't look toward her porch as she passed by and crossed the lawn. She rapped on the screen door of the Foremans' screened porch.

"Kara," Diane said, moving through the shaded enclosure.

"Hi! I was just in the neighborhood and thought I'd drop in," Kara joked, her voice higher than normal.

Diane didn't laugh, but opened the door. "Want to come in?"

"Thanks."

"I was about to have a glass of iced tea. You can join me if you like." Clandestinely, there was a half-full pitcher and two empty glasses sitting on a wicker table. "Unless this is a quick visit and you need to get back to the little ones?"

"They're in school, so I'm alone for at least another hour."

"They're both in school? I hope you don't mind sugar in your tea." Diane had already started to fill the glasses.

"Sugar's fine. Yeah, Jack's at the elementary school and today's Lilah's first day at Grace School." Kara accepted the glass and took a drink. It was more sugar than she was used to, but she drank it gladly. She hadn't realized how thirsty she was.

"That's beside the Collumber house, isn't it?" Diane eased into a white, wicker rocking chair, settling back against a cream-colored pillow, cross-stitched with a trio of violets.

"The Collumber house?"

"The three-story brick house on Main Street. I'm sure you haven't missed it."

"The Federalist-style house with the black fencing?" It had a name; it deserved a name: Collumber house.

"That's the one. Next door to Grace School. Both houses are almost as old as the American Revolution."

"I love that house!" Kara admitted, "There's something about it."

Diane gestured toward her house, connected to the porch. "This house came almost a hundred years later. This is a new-build in comparison." She sipped her tea. "Grace

School is a good school. Marvin went there and so did Matthew."

Matthew? Kara wrinkled her brow and parted her lips.

Diane continued, "I suppose you're anxious being alone in your house. You're not used to the children being gone." She leaned back, regarding Kara. "Why a large house for such a small family?"

Kara held the glass with both hands, feeling the slick coolness seep into her skin. "We lucked into it. I don't think we really wanted a large house when we started looking."

"You're not sure?"

"The idea of getting a house sort of just sprang up on us. John grew up in the country and when this house became available, well, we were lucky we got it."

Diane curled her upper lip, her eyelids heavy. "You said that already, that you were lucky." The conversation halted in the suddenly too-small enclosed porch.

Kara laughed nervously. "Yes, well, I guess we were doubly lucky."

Diane's laugh was husky. "You have a beautiful home. If Marvin hadn't been willed his family's house, I would've looked for something new as well. He wouldn't let us leave this place."

Kara's eyes scanned over the antique contents of the porch. Even the patio furniture was ancient. The wicker chair she sat on was faded and splintered and the tan-and-lavender striped cushion squeezed wilted cotton through its ripped seams. "Your house is great. Older homes are so stately and their history is so fascinating."

Diane looked pointedly at the termite-infested window sill. "Not every old house is 'stately,' and not every old house has a 'fascinating' history. Marvin's family was full of cold, inconsiderate bastards. Some actually *were* bastards, now that I think about it!" Her laughter was coarse.

Kara laughed half-heartedly, unsettled, and blurted, "Is Matthew your son?"

81

Diane's eyes flashed, but her face turned grave. "Yes." She wrinkled her brow, selecting her words carefully, "He's had a troubled life. Things have always come to him with difficulty, you know, like with school. He's a grown man now and sometimes he stays with us weeks at a time. But he has his own place in Taylortown. He manages, but sometimes it gets too hectic and he comes home to relax."

"It's always nice to be able to come home," Kara replied stupidly, not knowing what to say. Remembering suddenly the blonde Lilah had mentioned to her, she blurted again, "Is the blonde your daughter?"

Diane furrowed her brow and stopped rocking. She looked out the screen for an awkward moment before settling her gaze on Kara. "I don't have a daughter."

"Oh, she must've been someone else."

"I haven't seen a blonde." Diane's expression was stony.

"Oh. Lilah thought she saw someone...I guess she was mistaken." She sipped her tea and changed the subject. "John told me Marvin will be helping us with some repairs around the house."

"You need repairs? It's a new house."

"Apparently, newer than we'd like. It's not a lot," Kara reassured her. "Two rooms and some minor cosmetic projects. We'll pay Marvin, of course. We're hiring a contractor for the bigger jobs."

"Marvin likes to keep busy. He needs to keep busy." Diane looked out the screen again.

"Well, we'll have him busy soon!" Kara laughed. She set her mostly-filled glass on the table and stood. "I should get going. I left my cellphone at home and who knows if the kids' schools have been trying to get a hold of me," she lied. She didn't mind returning home to the dead opossum. Her body urged her to exit the stifling porch.

Diane opened the door for her.

"Thank you for the tea." Kara stepped onto the grass.

Diane nodded, her lips curving up slightly.

When Kara had crossed the tree-line into her yard, the screen door banged abruptly, startling her. She turned around, seeing Diane's shadowed form return to sit in her chair and start rocking.

Chapter Nine

The shuffling along the roof irritated Kara more than the banging. It sounded like a hunchback slinking across the shingles, slithering like a monster up and down and side-to-side, pausing here and there and then moving again, scraping along. More than anything, it was probably the start and stop of the noise that irked her. She moved from her bedroom into the great room, trying to ignore the commotion John and Marvin made that Saturday afternoon. Normally, she would've been excited that John had a sudden lull at work and was using his downtime to tackle the first of their many renovations, but her headache made that impossible.

She closed the windows, even though it was cool outside and turned on the air conditioner to try and block out the sounds. She lay on the couch with her eyes closed, but couldn't nap like she wanted to. She had taken ibuprofen every few hours for the last two days, but it hadn't helped.

She blamed the headache on lack of sleep. Lilah's nightmares had seemingly vanished, but now Kara was having trouble sleeping. She slept some through the night, but her troubling dreams kept her up.

She sighed, finally giving up on the nap, and slipped into her flats. She stepped outside, grateful John had power-washed the remnants of the opossum away. He had tossed the rodent in the trash and the garbage truck had taken it away the day before.

She moved down into the lawn and turned to look up at the roof. John and Marvin knelt there. "How's it going?" she called.

Marvin stopped hammering the metal flashing, calling down a hello, and John hollered, "Skylight's almost done!" He picked up a drill and pressed the trigger, making it zip for emphasis.

"I don't know if I like you doing renovation work. Construction makes you cockier than normal," she joked. "And why is Marvin doing all the work?"

Marvin grunted through his hammering blows. "Ah! Got it!" He reached for a shingle, which John promptly handed over.

"Hey, when you guys are done, do you think you can get the playroom door to stop popping open?" she asked.

"I can take a look at it after this," John said.

She gave a little cheer before calling, "Okay, I'll leave you guys to it." A motor rumbled, making her turn around. An SUV drove leisurely past on the road, taking a peaceful country drive, no doubt. Kara stepped back and looked at her house. She, too, admired the ivory stucco and the brick accents creeping along the windows. The second-floor dormer windows were adorable, and the porch was inviting, the swing they had recently purchased tucked under the eaves. The lawn was less whimsical, bare except for the center oak and the trees that bordered the yard. Next spring, she'd plant lilacs, hydrangea bushes, and lilies. That would make the house look even more like a storybook cottage.

She followed the sound of the kids' voices to the backyard. They played catch with an oversized ball near the woods. She called hello and told them to stay together.

Jack twisted around. "Alright!"

"Okay, Mommy!" Lilah called back.

Automatically, Kara sought out the statue. Had Lilah left it in her room? There was a spark of hope, until she caught sight of it in the grass, not far from Lilah's sneakered feet.

Kara turned away, rubbing her temples. She retraced her footsteps, walking around the house, and nearly tripped over the tangled garden hose. Regaining her balance, she dragged the hose to its rack, but she didn't fuss with it for long. Her head was pounding and it was just too much to bear right now. The hammering had started again...and then the scraping.

She wiped her hands on the back of her shorts and turned toward the woods. A hint of gray slipped through the trees. It was the barn at the end of Seter Road that she had spotted. Curious, she made her way down the gravel driveway, telling no one her travel plans. There wasn't a sidewalk, so she took to the edge of the quiet road.

Moving through tree shade to a soundtrack of rustling leaves and birdsong, she noticed the sweetness of the air, wondering if it was hay she smelled. She couldn't place the relaxing scent; it was new to her, reminiscent of honey. Seemingly, the elixir relieved the pressure in her temples.

As she moved up a slight incline, the trees edging the road parted so she could glimpse a ranch-style house on her right. The garage was open, displaying two cars. Finely-trimmed shrubs flanked both sides of the house and rosebushes filled the area in-between. A two-story farmhouse with green shutters was on her left. An SUV was in its driveway, the garage closed. Its front yard was also well-kept.

The treed border appeared again as the road dipped, but then it parted soon after as she came upon a weathered farmhouse, set back from the road. Its white paint was faded and chipped and the large shutters that had once been black had turned gray. The lawn lacked flowers, but full trees and shrubs zigzagged throughout the front yard and continued into the back. The gravel driveway lay to the right of the house and disappeared within the sheltering grandfather trees, their boughs of full green foliage shading its final destination. Drapes were drawn closed on the windows and the house was silent, exuding emptiness. She noticed the birdsong had ceased and the leaves had stilled. She was alone in the world.

She stepped onto the shoulder of the road and continued onward another fifty yards, stopping when she came to the barn. Set much closer to the road than the farmhouse, it sagged on its rear haunches, displaying its interior like a can-

can girl lifting the skirt of her dress. Strategically-placed posts and a jumble of wooden beams held it up.

Kara had been in a barn only once, and that had been at a municipal park. Re-enactors had worked the fields, giving modern-day suburbanites an idea of what it would've been like to raise pigs and chickens in the late 1880s. The farmhouse had been bright red and safe enough to let the general public mosey in and out of, poking around at farm tools and the animals inside.

The barn she gazed at now was well-used. As she came closer, she saw seated at its rear, peeping just so, was a silo. She hadn't noticed it before on any of her car rides. She assumed grain was housed in the cylindrical building; her imagination and lack of farming experience prevented her from making any other guesses as to what else could be inside.

She glanced at the unassuming farmhouse next door and, feeling confident she hadn't been noticed, inched closer to the barn. Her sightline of the silo was dashed out. She could see how truly dilapidated the barn was; the wooden posts holding it up were rotted, infested with termites. Some of the posts did better than others, but from what her untrained eye could see, most of them were one strong wind-gust away from crumbling into splinters. It was a shame. She felt sorry for the barn, silly really to feel something emotional for a building, especially one she had no previous attachment to.

Because of the apparent safety issue, she was consciously wary of entering it. But, even so, Kara moved to the farthest front corner and took a brave step inside. Her feet moved over sandy soil, thinly covered in matted straw. Rays of light shooting in through slits in the roof lit portions of the straw, revealing much of it was moldy. She wrinkled her nose at the rancid odor. Bird droppings coated the beams overhead and the flapping of wings and stirring from someplace above told her birds and rodents had been calling the place home for quite some time.

She walked further. A thick rope knotted into a hangman's noose hung from a spike set in the wall; four bales of hay sat near it, so nibbled on that they were hardly square; and a stack of sacks was piled at the foot of a ladder. The ladder, looking structurally sound from where she stood, leaned against the opening of the loft that stretched over the rear of the barn.

Kara moved to it now, her steps making crunching noises, passing through a ray of sunlight. She was fascinated to discover what was in the loft. What were they storing, or hiding, up there?

Suddenly, a shadow draped over her.

Climb up and see...

The shadow clung, beckoning her to come further.

She slid her tongue over her lips, wetting them. She had forgotten the worry of the barn's weakened condition; she didn't care about being caught trespassing. She needed to see what was in the loft.

Come and see.

She started to climb the ladder.

It's here.

She stepped up another rung. She looked up at the wood-slatted edge and felt dizzy. The loft above started vibrating, tilting sideways. She shut her eyes, feeling sick.

"She's gone!" a man's voice, sounding so far away and yet inside her own head was shouting. "...Left a letter..."

Kara opened her eyes, wondering vaguely if she was falling sleep, caught, faintly now, "with child...must find..." She heard thumping—galloping—in the distance until it muted completely.

She twisted around. The barn was empty.

Come see!

The voice was urgent, pressing her to continue. Looking up again, the loft no longer titled; the dizziness had passed. Kara advanced another step. Something scrambled on the floor above, but she didn't think of mice. She took another step; she was so close now. She lifted her foot to step again when a sudden commotion below halted her.

She scrambled down the ladder and spun around, the haze lifting, the spell broken just like that. Her hand went to her chest and her eyes darted around the room, a bright stream of sunlight hanging over her. She had been caught.

She heard the whistling before she saw them. Jack was musical one approaching the barn, Lilah just behind him. They didn't see Kara at first, which was fine because it took her a moment to slow her heart.

When she regained her composure, she met them as they started for the interior, demanding, "What are you two doing here?"

Jack jumped. His head whipped back. Surprise was on both of their faces.

When he recognized his mother, he stammered, "Uh, w-we were just, uh playing."

"I see that. Do you think you should be playing in here?" She pretended to herself it wasn't a double-standard that they had caught her there.

Jack and Lilah shook their heads solemnly.

"This is not a playground and it's definitely not safe. Not only could the barn come crashing down on you, but you could also get bitten by a raccoon or even a snake!"

"I'm sorry, Mom," Jack replied, guilt readable on his down-turned face.

"A snake?" Lilah murmured, looking down at the ground around her.

"Let's get out of here," Kara said. "We're not safe in here."

Because the barn can fall apart at any moment, or because you don't know what drew you here? Kara ushered them outside, ignoring the mocking question. "Why were you in there anyway?"

"We were just exploring," Jack replied. He didn't mention the urge that had drawn him to it. He wouldn't have been able to explain it anyway.

"Exploring? You couldn't find enough to do at home? Come on. Let's leave before someone sees us trespassing. Lilah, give me your hand. We have to be very careful walking on the side of the road."

Why *had* she gone in there? She knew better than to trespass. It was just that the barn looked abandoned, she supposed. It had been forgotten, taken for granted maybe. Surely, she hadn't disturbed anything inside. But even in her thoughts, she couldn't accept those as reasons to wander onto property that wasn't hers.

"Why don't we just go through the woods?" Jack asked, pointing to somewhere behind the farmhouse.

"Is that how you got here?"

He nodded.

"It probably *is* quicker," she murmured. She glanced back at the road again, and as if on cue, a furniture truck sped by. How quickly the scenery had changed and now the road seemed dangerous. "Alright, show me how you guys got here."

Following Jack, Kara repeatedly glanced at the still farmhouse as they progressed behind it and stepped into the woods, holding onto Lilah's hand. She was aware people who lived in the country were no strangers to protecting their property, taking stock in their right to bear arms. It was probably a very big mistake to have let Jack take them back this way, as it could be construed as encouraging her children to trespass if it meant involving a shortcut. She said nothing, however, and was relieved to see a decent path had been worn into this side of the woods. The trees were dense and at night she was sure it had to be pitch-black, but soon she was able to catch glimpses of the ranch as the trees thinned closer to home.

They crossed their driveway and Kara saw John and Marvin packing up their tools. She said to the kids, "You're not to take that path again and you're not to go to that barn again. Alright?"

They agreed they wouldn't and took off toward the house, both spent on exploring for the day.

As the evening sun set, John and Kara took advantage of the porch swing, rocking as they gazed out over the yard.

"How's your headache?" John asked.

"It's gone now that that hammering is over," Kara replied. After a beat, she laughed. "You guys did a great job today. I'm excited we got something off our to-do list."

"Yeah." John ran a hand over the armrest, looking out at the evergreens where the road curved and climbed again uphill. "It's a nice night."

"Yeah." She looked at the doorway and said, "Thank you, by the way, for getting rid of it."

He followed her gaze before looking out at the trees ahead of them. "You get strange stuff like that when you live in the country. Wild animals are all around." He widened his eyes and looked at her. "Watching us. Now."

She slapped his arm and relaxed on the swing. "Don't try to scare me." She glanced surreptitiously out at the shadowed yard and then laughed.

He laughed too and rested an arm behind them on the backrest.

"So, we've been here for a little while now," she said. "What do you think about having a housewarming party?"

"That sounds good. I mean, the house isn't a disaster or anything."

"Yeah, far from perfect."

His eyes twinkled and he tilted his head back. "I'm glad you agree."

"You did a really good job today," she said again, leaning her head on his shoulder.

91

"Marvin's pretty cool. You should've seen him climb up on the roof. I think he's in better shape than me."

Kara leaned forward to look at the Foremans' house. Their houselights were on, highlighting yellow siding behind shadowy trees. "His wife is a little intense."

"Oh, yeah?"

"She's alright. She just gives off a vibe." She pictured the older woman with the direct gaze.

He kicked his foot out, gently rocking the swing back and forth. They rocked a while, neither one saying a word. The last birds chirped from their nests in the ashes and oaks that threaded along the property line.

Finally, Kara broke the quietude. "When do we want to have the party? I haven't seen Tracy in forever and I know she'd love to see the house."

"Up to you. If you're alright with short notice, how about Saturday? That'd actually be good. Work's about to get even busier, so the sooner we throw this shindig the better. This is the calm before the storm."

"What's going on?"

"We're transitioning to a new database. It's a big deal. I'll probably have to work late nights and weekends."

Kara scowled, looking out over the darkening yard. The sun had dipped low, making the porch light responsible for most of the light cast around them.

"Would it be weird if I invited Shannon and Tom to the party?"

"That'd actually be a good way to meet Tom. Give him a good ol' interview."

"Oh, no," she groaned. "You're not going to interview him, are you?"

"Well, probably not an all-out interview. But I think I need to ask him about his experience, don't I?"

"Just like you asked our neighbor?"

"That's different."

"Okay. Yeah. Not really."

He looked at her slyly. "Just invite them. Oh, yeah, and while you're at it, you can take charge and invite *all* the guests."

She slapped his thigh and he grabbed her offending hand and held it. She didn't upset the moment by bringing up Sophie or the incident in the barn. It had been a while since she had felt this at-ease; it was nice. They rocked in silence for a while longer until the sun vanished completely into the night sky.

Chapter Ten

Screaming had erupted around her.

The pitch varied—high, low, and in between—an anguished chorus of cries.

She pressed her hands over her ears. The gesture altered the noise, twisting the screams into a bleating. It wasn't much of an improvement.

She squeezed her eyes shut, whimpering inwardly, *please stop, please stop…*

And just like that, it stopped.

Kara rolled to her side, opening her eyes to silence. Breaking free of the nightmare, the contrast was jarring. Seeing nothing but white was unsettling too.

She blinked a few times, erasing the nightmare, and realized it was the blank bedroom wall she faced.

"Awake?" John came around to her side of the bed. "I'm leaving now." He kissed her briefly, unaware of her stupor. "Have a good day." He left the bedroom as she managed to say goodbye.

Another night, another nightmare.

She groaned, craning her neck to see the clock. It was time to get the kids ready for school. They followed their usual morning routine: Kara watched from John's office as Jack climbed onto the bus; she walked Lilah to her pre-K classroom; and she sat in the car for a moment, staring at the Collumber house. Without fail, she glanced at the house in her rearview mirror just before she steered out of Grace School's parking lot. She ignored the statue rolling on the passenger side floormat as she slowed down to peer at the rundown barn on Seter Lane, her eyes combing over its shadowed interior.

She glanced at the front porch of her house as she pulled up the driveway, making sure no animal had decided to die there that day. Inside the house, she sat at the kitchen table with a cup of tea. She sipped it, trying to absorb what caffeine she could get from it as she stared at the wall calendar. It took her a moment to break her trance and remember what she was supposed to be doing. Saturday was starred: the date of the party.

Acting on adrenaline, she texted Tracy the details, apologizing for the short notice. Everyone she invited got the same apologetic invite: *Hope you can make it! Sorry for the short notice!*

The party wouldn't be big, they didn't know that many people. It'd just be a few guys from John's work, Marvin and Diane, Tracy, Shannon and Tom.

When she was done, she sat for a moment, running through the names of the people she had texted. Her mind was clouded (she was so *tired*), so she didn't dive deep thinking beyond the names of the people she'd already contacted. She looked through the contacts in her cellphone and stopped on her mother's name. It was the longest they had gone without speaking. Honestly, Kara wasn't trying to make a point, even though it probably looked like she was. She just hadn't been in the mood to talk to her generally-disapproving mother. Time had lapsed naturally and she had just been so busy...

Her thoughts drifted to the memory of her wedding day. She supposed most people would've completely cut their mother off if the same had happened to them. And maybe, she should've. Margaret had actually tried to stop the wedding. Kara, a beautiful courthouse bride, dressed in a white blouse and a navy blue broom skirt, had stood hand-in-hand with John, handsome in his dark suit and navy blue-and-cream necktie. To make it a bona fide elopement, Tracy had stayed home, volunteering to babysit Jack.

John and Kara were waiting outside the courtroom when her tipped-off mother approached them from behind. Tracy admitted to Kara later that she had shared the secret news with Margaret.

Margaret dropped her hand on Kara's shoulder and tugged. "Not today, Kara. Not to him. It's a mistake. You don't want to ruin your life." She turned to John, her words cold, "Walk away, John. Don't do an idiot move and marry someone who's already got a kid. You don't want that kind of baggage."

Kara felt Margaret hadn't liked John from the start, simply just because. There was no reason for her to not like him. Margaret had only seen him a few times and on each occasion, he had somehow offended her. He said the wrong thing, he did the wrong thing, *he* was the wrong thing. She pulled him apart any chance she got.

John's face had gone white as he struggled to bottle up his fury in the courthouse.

"Let me go," Kara hissed, breaking free of Margaret's hold.

People passed by. Some stared.

"Go away," John growled.

Margaret jerked her head toward Kara, demanding, "Is this what you want? Do you think you're making the right choice?"

How dare she, mother or not, forcefully try to stop their wedding? John had never been anything but supportive to Kara and Jack. Why did Margaret want her to be unhappy like her?

The courtroom door opened and the bailiff waved them in. The couple entered the room, leaving Margaret alone in the hallway.

They hadn't completely shut her out of their lives; they joined Margaret every year for Christmas lunch, no matter how awkward it was, and Kara still spoke with her every so often.

There was no fixing their relationship. Kara certainly didn't have to invite her to the housewarming party. She set down her phone and looked out the backdoor. Spotting the hawk circling low over the trees reminded her of Blacky, the dog she wished she'd never heard of. She shivered, noticing now there were two turkey vultures circling. Imagine if she had discovered them on her porch devouring the opossum?

She frowned, troubled. How much longer would she have had to wait to see them on her front porch, digging into the wretched, deceased creature? She was thankful the kids hadn't seen the opossum. She had made sure they hadn't used the front door that day.

Chapter Eleven

"It's beautiful, Kara. When do I get to move in?" was Tracy's greeting when Kara opened the front door on Saturday.

"I guess we can put you in the bonus room. You've got to bring a bed, though. Oh, and your hammer and probably some walls. Oh, and did I mention that it's more of a storage room than a guestroom? Well, more of a construction site."

"Sounds like my kinda place!" Tracy laughed as Kara led her inside the house. "You definitely have the perfect place for a party."

"I love it. It's just so peaceful out here. It even smells different."

"Like what? Manure? I think I could pass on living in the country if I had to smell cow poop all day."

"No, not that. There's a farm across the road, but I haven't even smelled anything like that. Maybe we're upwind." As they crossed the foyer, Kara explained, "It's like a sweet smell. I don't remember smelling it when we lived in the city. It's just different. You'd have to smell it."

Kara led her through the kitchen. "I hope you don't mind going back outside. I promised John we'd relieve him. The kids are swimming." She introduced Tracy to the small group chatting in the great room before they went outside to the deck.

Tracy said hi to John, who was leaning against the railing, and joked, "I see you've brainwashed Kara into being a country girl. A month in and she's already picking her teeth with hay."

"Straw," John corrected with a smile.

"Oh, sorry. Straw. We city girls don't know any better."

"We'll forgive you this time."

"And we say 'gal' out in these parts," Kara quipped before telling John he could go inside.

"You sure?" he asked.

"Yeah, go ahead. One of the hosts should be mingling with the guests."

"These kids have it nice," Tracy commented when he had gone inside. "Big house, a pool, deck…"

"It's not what I had growing up," Kara replied, seeing Lilah drifting lazily over the water in her inner tube. Jack, in dry swimming trunks, was perched on the deck steps, staring at the water. "Jack, why aren't you swimming?"

"I don't feel like it."

Tracy combed her fingers through her auburn bangs. "Are there many kids in the neighborhood?"

"I haven't seen any kids on our road, but Jack's got a new friend at school. He wasn't able to come."

"None of the guests brought kids?"

"They don't have any!"

"Oh," Tracy laughed. "You started young. I'm sure pretty soon they'll start having them."

"But by then, mine will be adults!"

"They'll be the ones wishing they'd started sooner, because you'll have the rest of your lives to do what you want."

"That's true, except then we'll be dealing with grandchildren."

"I hear that's the best part of having kids. You only see the grandkids for a day, spoil them, and then ship them back home." Tracy looked out over the yard. "Is all of this yours, Kara?"

"Yeah. Who would've thought a year ago I'd be living here?"

"I'm jealous. Do you own the woods too?"

"Some of it. There are boundary pins somewhere in the woods marking the property line. They're probably in nondescript tree trunks somewhere." They looked out to the wooded area to the west and gazed for a moment in quietude. Lilah's splashing mingled with the hum of buzzing locusts.

"Have you met your neighbors yet?" Tracy asked after a short while.

"Just the older couple next door. Marvin's here today. His wife couldn't come." Marvin had excused Diane, telling Kara and John she was feeling ill and thought it best to stay home. Kara was disappointed John wouldn't be meeting her. She was curious if Diane acted with the same air of suspicion toward him as she did with her. Or, if it wasn't suspicion, whether the older woman would make him feel awkward like Kara had felt around her.

Kara adjusted the angle of her patio chair. "I didn't think it'd be so hot today." The sun was high overhead and there wasn't a cloud in the sky. She wiped her brow, watching Lilah, whose face was turned upward. Strands of her dark hair draped into the water.

Tracy murmured, "Ooh, a fire pit."

Kara reached over and touched the steel cauldron by their feet. "We might make s'mores tonight."

"Nice." Tracy eased onto a chaise lounge, pulling a beer from the cooler beside them. She looked down at the floor. "What's this? A garden statue?" She picked up Lilah's masking tape-wrapped doll, which had been peeking out from under a beach towel. "She's kinda spooky."

"You think? Lilah loves that statue. John dug it up in the front yard."

Setting it down and covering it with the towel entirely, Tracy said, frowning, "There was probably a reason why it was buried…"

Kara shifted in her seat, wondering why Jack was now standing, arrow-straight, staring at the water.

"Have you heard from your mom?" Tracy asked, breaking into her thoughts.

"Next question."

"Has she been to the house yet?"

"Not yet."

"When my mom's in town, we hang out, go sightseeing. I don't know if it'd be different if she lived closer to me. Maybe I'd be irritated by the things she did or said. Maybe that's why I don't mind your mom, like I'm just tolerating Margaret, trying to make up for missing mine."

Kara scoffed. "You don't just tolerate her. You're BFFs."

Tracy crossed her arms. "We're definitely not BFFs. I don't know. I kind of feel sorry for her. But I hate saying that because I really don't mind spending time with her. Your relationship with your mom is nothing like mine. We never really get into it."

"Yeah, it's different."

Tracy was saying, "I don't want to meddle, but I—" when screaming erupted from the pool. She and Kara jumped to their feet, seeing Lilah's arms wrapped around the inside pool ladder. The inner tube had floated away.

Kara scrambled to pull her out. "Lilah, what happened?"

Sobbing, Lilah clung onto Kara.

Kara tried to pull her away to check for injuries, but Lilah held tight. "Are you hurt?"

"Where's Jack?" Tracy asked.

Kara turned around and scanned the pool, then the yard. He was gone.

"Lilah, where'd Jack go?" Tracy asked urgently.

Lilah buried her face into Kara's neck.

"Kara?" Tracy prompted.

Kara pulled back Lilah's hair to see the side of her face. "Lilah, where did Jack go?"

Lilah sniffed, her sobbing ceasing.

"Hey, there you are!"

Kara and Tracy whirled around. It was Shannon, huge sunglasses covering half of her face, walking from the side of the house toward them.

"I thought I heard voices back here," Shannon said, smiling.

"Hi, Shannon," Kara said breathlessly. "We've had a bit of a crisis. We don't know where Jack is."

"He's over there with the hose."

"What?" Tracy jumped off the deck and jogged past her.

Kara shifted Lilah in her arms. She whispered, "What's the matter, Lilah?"

"He's over here!" They heard Tracy call from out of sight.

"Oh! Thanks, Tracy! Crisis averted!" Kara rested her head against Lilah's, whispering, "Jack's okay, Sophie. Is that what scared you?" Kara didn't notice she had used the wrong name. Lilah tightened her hold on Kara.

Tracy called over, "Jack and I are going in to get some food!"

"Okay, we'll be in soon!" Kara called back.

Shannon asked, "Is everything okay?"

Kara nodded. "Have a seat. We just had some confusion."

"Oh, yeah?" Shannon looked at Lilah sympathetically as she stepped onto the deck.

Kara asked, "Lilah, did you fall in the water?"

Lilah flipped her head the other way and stared at Shannon.

"Are you tired?" Shannon asked her, but Lilah didn't respond. "I think this one's all tuckered out for the day, mama."

"That makes both of us. I don't know what happened. You missed the whole thing. She was floating in the pool and then the next thing we know she's screaming her head off and Jack's missing."

"Maybe she should take a nap."

"Yeah, you're right." Kara sighed.

"She just closed her eyes," Shannon whispered. "I'll join the others while you put her to bed."

"Okay, I'll see you in a bit. Is Tom here?"

"Yeah. He's inside fending for himself."

"Okay, so I won't call the police if I see some strange dude walking through my house."

Shannon laughed, going in through the backdoor.

Kara leaned down carefully, cradling Lilah against her, and picked up the statue, an item she would've rather have kept baking in the sun. She handed it to Lilah and straightened, turning toward the house. She hesitated when she caught a face looking back from the closed kitchen window. The reflection of the trees over the pane distorted the image, making it unclear who it was. She could just make out blonde hair, but it seemed yellower than Shannon's and was parted down the middle, unlike anyone else's at the party.

Kara went inside, her eyes on the kitchen. No one was there. She glanced in the great room. The guests, all of them invited people she recognized, were laughing, their faces turned to the TV screen. She moved into the dining room and then her bedroom and bathroom, but didn't turn up anyone. She went down the hallway and into the foyer. No stranger with blonde hair anywhere.

The lady with the yellow hair like the dolly used to have.

Kara looked over her shoulder as she climbed the stairs, and looked in the rooms upstairs. She frowned.

"Mommy," Lilah whined, pulling away.

Kara eased her into bed, watching as Lilah rolled to her side, smothering the crude faces of the statue against her. A chill coursed through Kara, sudden and quick. Something crackled, making her turn around, her eyes zeroing in on the baby monitor. Its green "on" light blinked and the crackling stopped abruptly. The bedroom returned to quiet. She stood for several seconds staring at the steady light before leaving the room.

She returned downstairs, remembering the face in the kitchen window. Had she truly seen someone? Had it been a trick of the sunlight?

The lady in the woods.

Kara walked into the kitchen, expecting to see her. She stopped short. Someone was at the window.

But it wasn't a blonde.

It took her a second to realize it was Jack. He looked up at her, turning off the faucet. She glanced at the great room—no blonde there—and crossed her arms, changing course. "What happened in the pool?" she asked him.

"I dunno."

"Did you push Lilah off her innertube?"

"No."

"Did you?"

"No!"

"Why weren't you swimming?"

He broke eye contact to look at his feet. "I just didn't want to. Lilah's boring in the pool."

Kara looked past him out the window; the water rippled slightly because of the filtration system.

"Can I have ice cream?" he asked.

She sighed, frustrated. "Sure, but you have to make your own bowl." She turned to the great room, ignoring the murmur of the room.

"Did you hear there's wine that tastes like coffee?"

"Ugh. No thanks."

"It's not bad actually."

"Did you hear there's an apple that tastes like a tomato?"

"Ugh. No thanks."

"What?"

There was laughter as Kara joined the guests, who spoke gibberish. She sank onto the armrest of the couch, perching beside John, who sat next to Marvin and Dolph on the couch.

"I'm losing my mind," she told John.

"What's up?"

"I'm just seeing people who aren't there…"

"Okay…" He raised an eyebrow and looked around the room.

She laughed. "It was the sun's reflection, I'm sure."

"Okay…Yeah, happens *all* the time." He made a face, teasing her.

"I'm serious. I thought I saw someone with blonde hair looking out the kitchen window."

He glanced around the room and nodded toward Shannon. "Was it her?"

Kara shook her head. "It was the sun." Time had passed and she was beginning to believe that's what it had been. "I must've hallucinated it."

"Well." He leaned back, crossing his legs. "That settles it, Sherlock Jones. We're all here and accounted for. No one at the window. Hallucination confirmed."

"Yup, me and those hallucinations," she said sarcastically. She slapped his hand. "Who's Sherlock Jones?"

A smile twitched at the corner of his mouth. "What? What's his name?"

"Holmes!"

They laughed, grabbing Marvin's attention.

"Whatcha been up to?"

"Dealing with kids," she sighed. She gave him a tired smile. "I just took Lilah to bed. She had a scare in the pool and went right to sleep."

"What happened?" John asked.

"She fell out of her inner tube. It was nothing. She's fine." The image of Jack watching her in the water fluttered into her thoughts.

"Gotta get her some swimming lessons," Dolph said before downing the rest of his beer.

"Yeah, probably need to do that…" Suddenly remembering, she asked John's co-worker, "Hey, I hope you didn't want your blanket back. I threw it away."

Dolph's expression went blank. "Blanket?"

"You helped John with the deck before we moved in."

Laughing he said, "I don't know about 'helping.' I think I did pretty much all of it."

John jumped in, "I think you've got something wrong with your brain there. I remember you drinking and sitting on your butt most of the time."

"Oh, that's right!" Dolph drained his beer and grinned, displaying crooked teeth.

"Well, anyway," Kara continued, "John said to throw it out. I hope you didn't want it back."

Dolph's smile lessened a degree. "I don't know what blanket you mean."

"You didn't bring a blanket as a drop cloth or something? It was a green, wool blanket with orange paint splotches on it."

Dolph flexed his jaw and shook his head. "I didn't drink *that* much. I think I would've remembered bringing my blankie. I just brought beer that day."

She looked questioningly at John, but he just raised his eyebrows and said, "I don't know then. I thought it was Dolph's."

She couldn't dwell on it, though, because Shannon and a bearded guy approached them. "Kara, this is Tom. We met John while you were tucking Lilah in."

"Hey, how are you?" Tom shook Kara's hand. "I'm sorry I haven't been able to come out sooner. The job I've been on went longer than expected, but it's just about to wrap up. Shannon said you've got a few different jobs that need done."

"We have a few things," John spoke up. "The house is new, but there are a couple rooms that need to be completed. It was a foreclosure. I guess the builder ran out of money."

Tom gazed around the room, surveying the custom fireplace and wainscoting. "You get a good deal on this place? Gracie Town's not real cheap and with a nice place like this, and on wooded acreage…"

John replied vaguely, "We came out alright."

Tom smiled good-naturedly. "Well, man, let me know when you need me to start. My prices are fair and I do a damn fine job. Got references too, if you need 'em."

"Okay, great. Marvin's been helping me out too."

Marvin barked, "It's a lot of work, but I'm sure we'll manage. I'm used to getting my hands dirty." His cool blue eyes met Tom's green ones in what Kara read as a silent challenge.

"John and Marvin fixed the playroom door," Kara said, gesturing. Her arm faltered, seeing the door was open slightly. "I thought it was fixed."

"Me too." John got up and closed it, opened and closed it again. It stayed shut.

"Could be the frame," Tom said. "How'd you fix it?"

John replied, "I tightened the hinge screws. They were loose, so I thought that was the issue."

Tom nodded. "I don't mind taking a look. Seriously, any job, big or small."

Shannon turned to Kara, "He's basically freelance. He goes from job to job."

John told Tom, "We have two rooms that need work. They're down to the studs. I'll show you."

After a while, Kara slipped away to check on Lilah, still in bed, her blanket covering her legs. She faced the wall, snoring lightly. Kara sought out the baby monitor. It was silent, but its green light quivered. As she reached for it, Lilah whimpered, making her draw her arm back.

Peering over here, Kara saw her eyes were closed. Lilah whimpered again, but cut off mid-cry. Kara's eyes drifted downward: the clay girl and frog grinned at her. Repulsion creeping over her, Kara dropped the end of the blanket over it. She started to turn away, but Lilah giggled, stopping her.

Lilah was pranking her.

Smiling, Kara pulled back the covers. "Hey..." She stopped halfway, her smile falling.

Lilah was still asleep.

The statue was uncovered again, two faces grinning at Kara. She covered it again, hating it. As she backed away, the giggling erupted again, making the hairs on the back of her neck stand. She froze, staring at Lilah's back as it pulsated. The giggle drew on for a long moment until finally it trailed to a sigh, ceasing.

Kara watched for several seconds, silence settling in the room, until the snoring returned. "Lilah?" she whispered.

The only response was the continued snoring. Finally, Kara turned to go. She turned around in the hallway, her eyes locating the baby monitor sitting on the dresser. It blinked, winking at her, then steadied again. Chilled, she left the room, ignoring the dark bonus room at the end of the hall, and rejoined the party.

When the last of the guests were leaving, Kara was spent. Her mind remained on Lilah, still in bed, asleep. She told herself Lilah had just overexcited herself in the pool, or she was coming down with something. But that didn't explain the eerie feeling she had had in her bedroom or the woman's face she had seen earlier in the window—the trick of the light.

Kara tried to dash away her thoughts as she walked Tracy to her SUV, not finding the energy to muster up a smile.

"I had a good time," Tracy said. "It's weird not being able to just meet for a walk or to go shopping."

"Yeah."

"I wish we had been able to do the fire pit."

"With Lilah not feeling well, I didn't want to exclude her. We'll do it next time."

"Poor baby." Tracy started the engine, hesitated, then said, "Don't forget about your mom."

There it was, the dig. Kara blinked. "We're not getting into that again."

"I won't tell her about the party. She knows where you live, though, right?" Tracy chuckled, but Kara didn't smile.

"Yes, she knows where we moved to. I haven't totally shut her out. I still talk to her. Don't worry about it." *It's not your business*, she wanted to say.

"She misses you."

Kara asked, doubtfully, "Did she say that?"

Shannon's voice carried over from the porch, startling them, "Tracy, are you leaving?"

Tracy called back, "Yes! It was nice meeting you!"

"You too!"

They watched Shannon sit down on the swing before Tracy said to Kara, "I won't tell her I came over."

"Alright," Kara replied, her lips pursed. It wasn't the best scenario to have her friend as the go-between, but Kara knew there was nothing she could do about it. She wanted Margaret to have friends, but Tracy didn't have to be one of them.

They said goodnight and Tracy drove away.

"Tracy seems nice," Shannon said, stopping the swing when Kara approached. "Have you been friends for a long time?"

"Yeah, a while," Kara replied, sitting beside her. "We worked together in retail when Jack was a baby."

"That's cool."

"It was okay. She's a district manager now. We were just salesclerks when I worked there."

"Oh, so you would've moved up in the company if you'd stayed."

"Nah. Tracy's more ambitious. It was just a job to me. I would've worked anywhere. She knew me before I met John. He rescued me from the chaos."

"Chaos?"

"That's the wrong word. It was tough, though. My mom and I have never been close and well, it was hard living with her, her negativity...When John came along, it was like I was going to be okay. I wasn't going to be...like her. It was a fear of mine. I didn't want to be alone."

"Well, you had Jack. You wouldn't have been alone."

"That's true. But I don't want to be like her. She's bitter and vindictive, and then I met John and he was great. I thought maybe I wouldn't be like her after all…I don't want to waste my energy talking about her."

"Sorry. I didn't mean to get you upset."

"No, I'm the one who's unloading on you. Sorry, Tracy just mentions her and it gets me started." Kara laughed half-heartedly. "So, how's your job?"

"Accounting's alright, but if I had it my way, I'd be a stay-at-home mom too. If we ever have kids we'll probably be living hand-to-mouth, though. Tom likes what he does, but it doesn't pay much, not unless he starts his own contractor business."

"You never know. Maybe he will."

"I doubt it. I'm the one who has to light the fire under his butt to get him motivated. Do you like being at home with the kids?"

"I love it." She hadn't minded working, but when she had married John and they had realized they could survive on his salary alone, she jumped at the chance to be home with her children. Every so often she felt a pang of guilt, knowing her mother had never had that opportunity. She had wondered more than once if their relationship would've been different if Margaret had been able to be around more when she was growing up.

"You really lucked out. Supportive husband, good kids, awesome house."

They rocked for a few minutes in silence, looking into the night. Headlights flashed and a car glided by. Kara's eyes followed its red taillights, the only lights on the road, until it disappeared around a bend and was swallowed by a galaxy of trees. Her eyes drifted over the Foremans' lit house next door. A hanging lamp burned in the enclosed porch. She stared until a shadow passed by, dashing it out briefly.

"Oh!" Kara slid back in her seat.

"What is it? What did you see?" Shannon asked, sitting up.

Kara didn't answer at first, her eyes moving over the darkness shrouding the property line. "I don't know," she said finally.

"What happened?"

"The light next door just flickered. It went out for a second. Probably a dying light bulb." A flickering, or somebody walking by?

"I don't know of a time when a light bulb made me jump!" Shannon joked.

Maybe it had been Marvin or Diane passing through to lock the porch door. Or Matthew.

"Did the kids go to bed?" Shannon asked.

"Jack's watching TV. Lilah's still conked out. I'm hoping she sleeps through the night. I hope she's not sick."

"Poor thing. You're probably done with the day too. We'll be leaving soon. Tom was inside talking to John about construction again."

Kara nodded, but didn't say anything.

They rocked and were quiet again until Shannon broke the silence. "I noticed that sometimes you call Lilah 'Sophie'."

Kara's stomach flip-flopped. She had? When had she noticed that? She licked her lips and swallowed. Trying to be nonchalant, she said, "Oh, you caught that, huh?"

"A couple times. I wasn't sure who you meant at first. Is it Lilah's middle name?"

Kara touched her hair where it lay limp over her shoulders. She swallowed. Her voice quiet, she said, "It's not her middle name…Sophie was Lilah's sister." The words were naked, suspended in the humid night. The subject was stilted enough with John, and now to be talking about it with someone she had recently met…It was surreal.

" 'Was'? Oh, honey, I'm so sorry." Shannon touched Kara's shoulder and stopped swinging. "I'm so sorry about your loss."

"We don't need to talk about it." It had happened so long ago. She was over it…or was supposed to be over it anyway.

"If you ever want to talk about her…Seriously, I'm here."

"Thanks." Kara started swinging.

Sophie. She had said the name again without even being aware and now Shannon had heard her.

"I'm a good listener," Shannon prompted.

Kara didn't answer at first, but then from somewhere deep inside, she said, "She didn't live very long. John considers her our stillborn, but she wasn't stillborn. Sophie lived for three minutes. It wasn't for long, but she did live." The first six months after had been the hardest. During those long days, Kara had relived the birth and death nearly every day.

The hospital had given them a white memory box. It didn't hold much, just Sophie's swaddling blanket, the gown and cap she had worn, and an index card noting her date of birth. Kara had returned to it every now and again to reflect, as if a part of her thought she'd forget. In the apartment, she had kept the box in her nightstand, but here, it remained in the bonus room. She was sad, picturing it packed away in storage.

"Wow, Kara, I don't even know how you can manage being in that situation."

"Some people have funerals and others memorials. Some even refuse to remember they were preparing for a baby. We ended up having a small funeral, barely anybody was there. Sophie was buried at St. Michael's in Cosgrove. Jack was a toddler. She was John's first child."

"John's not Jack's father?" Shannon's outburst was loud and obtrusive to Kara's ears.

"N-no, he's not." Kara's mind was halfway in the memory of that heartbreaking time six years ago and halfway on the porch swing. She mumbled, "Jack's father, David, didn't even stick around for his birth. He doesn't even know we had a boy."

"Wow…I'm sorry."

The swinging made Kara dizzy; the scent of the countryside she normally adored was too sweet and the air was stifling. She dragged her feet against concrete, causing them to come to a jolting halt. "I'm tired. It's been a long day." She stood. "I hope everyone had a good time."

Shannon reassured her, "We all had fun."

Tom stepped out the front door then. "Ready to go?"

"Yes," Shannon said. She leaned near Kara. "Thanks for having us."

Kara led them to Shannon's jeep parked in the driveway turnaround where the lamppost cast it in light.

"Kara," Shannon said, opening the driver's side door, "Take a long bath tonight, then stay in bed tomorrow and relax." Tom slid into the passenger side as she said, "Hey, let's go shopping in town Monday. I have the day off."

"John works and I have the kids…"

"We'll go when they're at school."

Kara didn't have an excuse not to go, other than to curl up in bed, feeling sorry for herself. "…Okay, sure, that'd be nice."

She said goodbye and went inside the house, feeling vulnerable. She peeped in John's office, finding him at his computer. "Are the kids sleeping?"

"Yeah. Jack just went to bed. Lilah's still out."

Kara nodded, saying as she walked away, "I'm going to bed."

"Okay. I'll be there soon."

She climbed into bed and closed her eyes. She willed herself to fall asleep, but all she saw was Sophie.

Kara didn't sleep well. What she had managed had been dreamless, but that was better than the strange dreams that had become the norm. Sitting up in bed the next morning, she saw it was just after six, not an indecent hour to get up.

In the kitchen, she leaned against the sink, nursing a cup of tea. She gazed out the window, remembering the blonde apparition from the day before; there was no face in the window now. The kitchen was just the kitchen. She poured another cup, watching the sun rise. Really, there was only one thing she thought about. She set the cup on the counter and went into the foyer. She started up the staircase.

It was time.

She moved with purpose and entered the bonus room, a room she had avoided the last few weeks. Immediately, her eyes located the cardboard box marked, "Personal." She looked away, taking in the rest of the room as a whole. It was dim, the sunrise shedding just enough light for her to see her way around. She stalled a moment, restacking a pile of boxes she imagined was lopsided. Her stomach churned.

Finally, she squatted down and opened the intended cardboard box. Why was it so hard? She had gotten over this, hadn't she? It had been years since she had felt this way.

Gingerly, she pulled out the white memory box, and carrying it in both hands, feeling the weight of it, she took it to her bedroom and placed it on her dresser. John was still asleep. She stood for a moment, running her hands over the glossy lid. She was aware of the weight lifting off her shoulders, as if Sophie had just been scolding her for hiding her away. But Kara was doing the right thing now, she could sense it. Yes, it felt good bringing Sophie back into the fold.

Chapter Twelve

"Eat some of these." Kara pushed the plate of carrot sticks toward Lilah.

"Gross." Lilah wiggled in her kitchen chair.

Jack rolled his eyes. "They can't be gross. They don't have any taste." He grabbed one and chomped down to prove his point. "See, they taste like water, just crunchy."

"They're not like celery," Kara told her, picking one up. "Have at least one."

"They're good, Lilah," Jack said.

"You're not leaving the table until this one's gone." Kara set the carrot on Lilah's plate next to her grilled cheese sandwich.

Lilah wiggled her head and squirmed in her seat nonchalantly, pointing at her sandwich. "I have to eat this anyway."

"Yeah, but you can't leave until the carrot's gone," Jack explained. "So, even if it's the last thing on your plate, you can't leave 'til it's gone."

Lilah took a bite of her sandwich, still wiggling as she chewed.

Kara sank into a chair across from the kids and rubbed her temples, watching Lilah, but already, her mind was somewhere else. She had stayed away from her bedroom all morning, keeping busy in other rooms of the house. She had unpacked the memory box and had put it on her dresser that morning, but she had slipped almost as quickly away, without looking back. It was there in the open, but so far it felt more frightening to her than consoling, and that confused her.

Maybe if she and John talked about it…maybe that was the antidote she needed to be able to sleep again. But talk about what exactly? Did she mean to rehash Sophie's birth and immediate death? Why would she even need to go back there? That had been six years ago. They had already grieved her death.

Or instead of discussing the pained topic with him, maybe she needed to open the white box, slide it back on its hinges and pull out the white notecard that had Sophie's name, date of birth, height, and weight written in loopy letters. Maybe she needed to smell the red-and-blue striped blanket that was inside to see if it still smelled of baby powder, or maybe she needed to trace the outline of the stamped infant footprint.

But that meant she'd have to return to her bedroom and open the memory box.

She bit into her turkey sandwich, looking out the window at the pool. John, having already eaten a quick lunch, was presently tossing a scoopful of clarifier into the water. Lilah's inner tube had been set on the pool ledge. "Lilah, what happened in the pool yesterday?" Kara asked. She turned from the window and looked at her daughter.

Lilah swallowed her mouthful and then drank from her juice box.

Kara prompted, "What made you upset?"

Lilah pulled her mouth off the straw. "I wanted out."

"Nothing upset you? You screamed because you wanted to get out?"

"Uh-huh."

"I don't think that's why." Kara turned to Jack and asked, "Do you know what happened?"

He chewed a carrot, not meeting her eyes. "No."

"Are you sure?"

He started to shake his head, but then said, "Because she fell in the water."

"Is that why, Lilah? You fell in and got scared?"

"Not-uh!" Lilah puffed back. She distracted herself then when the straw she pushed into her juice box emitted an annoying squeak. She giggled, pulling it and out and pushing it back in, recreating the sound.

"It's okay to have been scared when you fell in the water," Kara said.

"I didn't fall."

"Stop doing that."

Lilah did it once more before meet Kara's gaze. Her laughter had faded. "I didn't fall in! Jack pushed me!"

"Jack wasn't by the pool when you fell in."

Lilah widened her eyes. "He did it!"

"I didn't!" Jack exclaimed.

Kara held up her hands. "Okay, guys, enough! Soph—" She stopped herself, closed her eyes briefly, then shook her head before opening them again. "I would've been scared too."

Lilah whined, "I didn't fall."

Kara sighed. "Eat your lunch."

Jack had lost his appetite and drank his water to refrain from having to admit what had really happened in the pool. The truth was he knew why Lilah had screamed. It was because the blonde lady had pulled her in. He had seen her in the water again, well, he had seen the back of her head. The long yellow hair had floated just under the surface of the water, spreading out as she had drifted from the middle of the pool, edging close to Lilah and then away again. He had watched, promising himself he'd act if the lady had tried something. And she had tried something, hadn't she? But he hadn't been there when she had made her move. He had taken off, suddenly nauseous, feeling a dark cloud hovering over him. The feeling had vanished once he had distanced himself from the pool. But although he could breathe comfortably again, his sister had been in danger: she had been pulled in. He hadn't been able to protect her, after all.

He took another gulp of water, grateful his mother seemed to have dropped the subject and Lilah seemed alright. Nothing truly bad had happened.

Kara's eyes lowered on the nameless statue standing on the table. The uncanny grins faced Lilah, making Kara's view of the ivory girl and frog's backs unidentifiable shapes of conjoined clay. Kara frowned as she recalled the unsettling feeling she had had the day before as she listened to Lilah giggling in her sleep. She didn't mention it, didn't ask her daughter what she had dreamed, hoping they had been truly good dreams. After all, why would they have not been?

Kara turned back to the window, listening to the crunch of Lilah's teeth as she ate the carrots on her plate. She saw John walk away from the pool, disappearing out of view. She took in the pool again and watched the water ripple from the rhythm of the filtration system as it stirred in the powder he had just poured in.

"I'm done!" Lilah announced a moment later.

Kara looked over and, seeing her plate was empty, told her she had done good and that she could place her plate in the sink. When Lilah had done so and had taken off with her statue, Kara noticed Jack had moved to the backdoor and was looking out.

Just as she was going to ask him if he was going outside, he made a face and asked, "Mom, what's that smell?"

"What smell?"

"That bad smell. Don't you smell it?"

Kara stood next to him. "Is it you?" she asked, sniffing near him jokingly.

He said with seriousness, "No. It's something outside I think."

Kara's smile fell and she sniffed. "I don't smell anything. What's it smell like?"

"It's nasty"

She reached past him and opened the door. The smell hit her, strong and heavy. "Ugh! It smells like a skunk sprayed!"

He followed her outside, him pinching his nose as she crossed the deck to the steps. She looked out over the yard, hoping not to see a skunk lying in wait to spray again. But then she wondered suddenly if it was hiding under the deck and so hurried back up the steps.

"Looks like he's gone," she said, not really knowing if that was true. She noticed the cooler, still sitting near the fire pit, left out overnight after the party, and went to pick it up. "Come on, let's go in. The smell will go away eventually."

She started to follow Jack inside, but the glint from the sunlight on the steel body of the fire pit caught her attention. She turned around and advanced on it, stopping when she had neared enough to see something was inside the basin. It was something round and dark.

When she made sense of what she was looking at, she gasped, nearly dropping the cooler. An animal lay dead inside.

Road kill. That was the smell.

It wasn't a skunk, but a raccoon, folded over so its furry, striped tail touched its opened paws.

Kara cried out, backing away, the stench seemingly more potent than before, filling her insides with the sickeningly heady stuff.

"John!" she hollered, hoping he was still outside somewhere. "John!"

He came hurrying around from the side of the house. "What happened?"

"There's a dead raccoon in the fire pit!"

"What?" He jogged up the deck steps and looked down into the fire pit. He made a disgusted sound and stepped back.

Kara's newly-found instinct made her look up at the sky. Were the black birds waiting to descend? She scoped out the cloudy sky and saw nothing hovered in the air. She didn't know how long it normally took, but imagined vultures would soon catch the scent of the fresh corpse. She pictured the opossum on the front porch who hadn't been touched, but then imagined Blacky, swinging from a tree. Had the vultures eventually gotten him?

The image frightened her, revealing itself in her loud, high-pitched voice, "We need to get it out of here before the vultures come."

"Do you see any?" he asked, looking at the trees.

"Not yet. Can you get it out of here before they come?" She remembered Marvin had said vultures dined on fresh animal carcasses.

"Yeah, let me get a bag." He turned away, saying as she followed him through the backdoor, "It must've climbed in, looking for food."

He yanked a trash bag out from under the sink and returned outside. She watched from inside as he squatted, inspecting the creature. He prodded it with his bag-covered hand, looking it over, then plucked it from the fire pit and dropped it into the bag. He disappeared around the side of the house.

"It's at the curb," he said when he came inside. He opened his hand, revealing a nail. "I found this laying on the driveway by the garage. From what I could see, it stepped or rolled onto some loose nails. One was in its foot, in its neck and in its stomach, from what I could see."

She asked, horrified, "What?"

"I think he must've worked his way to the backyard and just died."

"Does that just happen? Why are there nails...the skylight?"

"Probably. I'll take a look at the driveway to see if there are any more nails laying around. Just be careful when you're out there. I thought we did a pretty good job of cleaning up."

"That's horrible."

"Yeah." He pocketed the nail.

As with the discovered opossum, John and Kara didn't tell the kids about the ill-fated raccoon. Kara wondered, however, if either child wondered why she told then more than once to stay in the house that day. She hadn't even offered an excuse. Lilah had been content to play in her room and Jack had been fine hanging out in the great room, mostly watching TV, while playing with his hand-held video game. Of course, he probably assumed it was the trail of skunk smell Kara was keeping them from. Regardless, neither child questioned her and she was glad for that. Kara refrained from looking out the window and pretended she didn't still smell the remains of the dead raccoon.

When she prepared for bed that night, she passed her dresser without a glance, not risking a glimpse at the memory box sitting on top, and went directly into the bathroom. As she brushed her teeth, she looked in the mirror at her worn reflection. She was only in her early thirties, but there were shadows below her eyes and her cheeks looked sunken, easily making her look fifteen years older. Her lips were pale in color and chapped, her eyes were darker than normal because her pupils were dilated, and her hair, messy, was in need of a cut. Surely, this would all be remedied by a good night of sleep or so she hoped for vanity's sake alone. Finally, she turned away from the image and spit out toothpaste in the sink.

She turned off the bedroom light, passed the dresser again without looking at it, and climbed under the bedcovers. She rolled over to her stomach and placed a pillow over her out-turned ear, wanting to smother out the sounds of the settling house, along with her thoughts. Finally, sensing John had entered the bedroom, she fell away from the present and sank into a black pit, the dream taking her wholly.

Chapter Thirteen

"Mom, wake up!"

Kara blinked her eyes open. Jack was looking down at her to where she still lay in bed.

"Mom, I'm going to be late," he said, backing away to the doorway.

"Hmm…?" She stretched, a fog of the dream lifting entirely away, forgotten the instant she saw the time. She sat up. They were running late.

She hurried, successfully getting Jack ready and out to the bus stop (admittedly, he did most of the work), and got Lilah to pre-K on time. She was able to finally slow down, her morning having started as a scattered mess. She was walking down the front steps of Grace School when she heard her name called.

She turned toward the parking lot and saw Shannon crossing it her way. She had forgotten they had planned to meet up. She groaned inwardly, preferring to go back to bed, if only to lie there.

Shannon waved, grinning as she approached. "It's so weird to be in town on a Monday morning."

Kara smiled, her mood lightening despite herself. Shannon looked so happy. "Oh, yeah?"

Weekends were clearly the busy days for Gracie Town. Saturdays and Sundays brought both townspeople and tourists out for afternoon strolls, bicycling, and shopping. Weekdays were when it resumed its sleepy small-town ways. That day, traffic was dwindling as the last of the working residents drove down Main Street, most probably headed to jobs in Cosgrove.

"Let's go this way," Shannon suggested, steering them down the sidewalk away from the town square.

"So how did you get today off?" Kara asked, matching Shannon's leisurely pace.

"If my boss takes a day off, he closes the office. It doesn't happen often, though. Benefit of working for a small company."

"That's awesome."

"I'm really glad you were able to come out with me. I get to show you all my favorites."

Kara's cellphone dinged. She reached into her purse for it without slowing. Her mother had texted. She didn't bother reading the message, though, sliding the phone back into her purse. Tracy had probably told her about the party, after all, and Margaret was upset. Kara wasn't going to confirm that suspicion now. "Okay, so where to?" she asked Shannon. "Is the antique shop down here?"

"No, that's on the opposite side of town on Channing, off Main. It's closed on Mondays. We'll go another day. You'll love it. They have the cutest stuff, things you wouldn't find anywhere else. So, this—" Shannon stopped abruptly and spread out her arms. "—is a cool boutique. Everything is Ohio-made." After twenty minutes, they walked out, Kara with a bag of candy and Shannon had a candle.

They visited every shop on one side of the street, a handful of businesses that took up residence in brightly-colored converted colonials and two Victorians. Neither made additional purchases, but Kara found the shops adorable and marveled at the thought of earlier generations calling the buildings home.

"These shops are so cute," Kara commented as Shannon steered them across the street and turned them back toward town. They walked onward until Kara stopped again, looking pointedly at the Collumber house across the street. "There's something about this house…"

She looked beyond the iron fence to the finely manicured lawn before resting her eyes on the wraparound porch. "This is where I would've lived back in the day." She laughed, amending, "If I had been wealthy anyway."

Whistling, Shannon nodded. "That house is ancient, built in the 17-or-1800s. Collumber was already rich when he joined the American Revolutionary War and apparently, came out even richer. The estate used to be larger. They had a farm and stable, I think." She tilted her head, admiring the square lines of the Federalist architecture.

Kara's eyes moved over the windows, finding the downstairs curtains open. She stared, unable to see inside.

"There was some tragic story about him and his wife," Shannon continued. "I don't remember all the details, but she died from illness, or was killed. Something really sad. She was known for her long hair. That's all I really remember about her. There was a poem we learned in school about her. 'Yellow hair, gold hair, dressed in bands, met a fair man on unfound lands.' That's all I got. You'd think I'd remember the rest since we had to memorize that damn thing!"

"That's funny," Kara murmured. Her eyes moved to the front door and then back to the yard. "So, they lived there?" The romantic in her pictured a dashing colonial and his bride, stepping out of a horse carriage and crossing the front walk to the door.

"I think so. I'm sure they have more about them in the museum. It's been years since I've gone."

Kara's eyes combed the brick house, taking in the porch, the long windows, the side yard...

She flinched. Someone had appeared from around the house. The man in the suit moved toward the sidewalk, carrying something large and square. Both women watched from across the street as he up-righted the sign.

" 'For sale'?" Shannon was the first to read it as he forced the sign into the ground. "Well, now's your chance to buy it, Kara!"

"Ha! Yeah..."

As they walked to the Garden Café, moving away from the Collumber house, something akin to sadness or jealousy hovered around Kara. It was as if the very real opportunity of living there was there for the taking, but ultimately, not hers to take. It was a strange sensation, especially since she loved her new house, one that was very much to be pleased with, but still, the dark cloud surrounded her. They ordered brunch and, before the food came, Shannon excused herself to go to the restroom. While she was gone, Kara started to unwrap her straw when her cellphone chimed. It was a reminder ding that her mother's text had gone unread. Sighing, she fished the phone out of her purse.

Kara, David contacted me.

Kara's heart stopped for one breadth of a second as she stared at her mother's words, texted in black Helvetica. His face—David's—appeared as a ghost in her mind: fresh-faced, slightly muscular build, blond.

Releasing the breath she had been holding, she tapped her mother's name, opening the message. Margaret had texted a follow-up, *Hello?*

Kara glanced around the café, seeing a handful of faces she didn't recognize before hesitantly texting back, *David Reynolds?*

Jack's biological father, the man who abandoned them, deadbeat dad.

Shannon returned, sitting down with a grin. Leaning forward, she said, "You have to check out the bathroom. I forgot how retro it is. They have this faded pink floral wallpaper…in the stalls! It's got to be original to the building. I think 'retro' may be too cool a word for it, though…" She noticed Kara's grim expression then. "Are you okay?"

Kara looked up. David wasn't a subject she normally discussed. She had all but forgotten him. Looking now at Shannon sitting across from her as the waitress dropped off their garden salads and walked away, Kara saw her genuine concern. There was something about her that just felt easy; unlike Tracy, with Shannon, there wasn't the worry of her running to Margaret and reporting details of any conversations they had.

"Did something happen?" Shannon asked.

Kara glanced down at her cellphone; there was no reply yet. She clicked it off, but kept it face-up on the table beside her plate. "Do you remember David, Jack's dad?"

"Yes."

"He contacted my mom."

"What?"

"Yeah. She just texted me that he reached out to her."

"Wow. What do you think he wants?"

"I don't know. I texted her back, but she hasn't said anything else. My mom's not the most forthcoming person."

"You haven't seen him since Jack was born?"

"No, I haven't seen him since *before* Jack was born."

"Are you worried?"

Kara shrugged. *Should* she be worried? She mulled it over. It wasn't like he had ever hurt her, not physically anyway. "David is just someone I don't ever want to see again. He's the past, he's been the past for ten years." She spilled it, telling Shannon about him, her relationship with a preppy guy that started and ended in college; he had been attractive and funny, someone everyone liked to be around. But something happened to him a few months into their relationship.

She noticed the change soon after a simple pink stick confirmed the hard nose of reality. Barely in her twenties, in a relationship she was still breaking-in, Kara found herself pregnant. Scared, she tried to make an unstable relationship mature. But she failed. As her belly swelled, David started staying out later than usual at night, hanging out with friends—his friends, people he had never introduced her to. He stopped attending classes and had no desire to find a job.

Margaret's sage advice was for Kara not to come across as too needy. "The last thing you need is for David to leave you when you're four months pregnant."

So even when he started pulling money out of Kara's savings account (how he got her PIN, she never knew), she didn't make any fuss. She only asked that he let her know when he needed cash instead of taking it out himself. He acquiesced, but that turned into him asking for money all the time. She finally told him she wasn't giving him another penny unless he proved he was earnestly trying to get a job. But he never proved that and, as her pregnancy advanced, he took to staying out all night, sometimes not even seeing her for a couple days at a time. Eventually, he just stopped returning.

She came home one day after class and found a scrawled note on the coffee table beside a glass, dirtied with a milk ring. David wasn't coming back.

"I barely knew him," Kara said, moving the lettuce leaves around on her plate. She had never truly thought that and saying it now, she wasn't so sure that was entirely the truth. She tried to forget the twenty-year-old who had approached her in psychology class a decade ago. She had tried not to dwell on the moment she had literally felt her heart beat faster and the blood rush to her face when she looked up to see the dirty blond with the tanned skin. He had smiled at her, revealing an orphaned dimple in one cheek, asking if the seat beside her was taken. She pushed away the image now, taking another bite of salad.

"Try not to worry too much about it yet. I know that probably sounds like crap advice from an outsider, but just wait and see what else your mom says."

Kara sipped her iced tea and nodded. "No, you're right. I'm not going to worry about it. That's really funny coming from me. I worry about everything. But I know what you mean."

"Have you had a chance to tell Tracy?"

127

Kara chuckled mirthlessly. "Funny."

"What?"

"I'm going to stay away from her on this topic, I think. She didn't know David anyway. But then again, my mom would probably tell her what's up with him before she'd tell me. Unfortunately going to her is like going directly to my mom. Tracy's known to report on me to my mom."

"Really? That's not cool."

"Yeah. Tracy and I were good until she moved into the same building as my mom. It's just an awkward situation. She feels obligated to both of us on a friendship level. It's weird." Kara chewed, her eyes on the black cellphone screen.

"The distance of being out here might help you guys then."

"Yeah."

"Maybe David just wanted to say hi. It might not be bad."

Kara slid her cellphone into her purse, realizing her mother was done texting for the moment. There was nothing she could glean from the text anyway, so there was no point in worrying. Margaret could've just seen him somewhere, or who even knew if it was David Reynolds she meant? She thought for a moment, thinking of how many different Davids she knew. Nobody else came to mind, but that didn't mean it wasn't a different David her mother knew.

Kara watched a mother burping an infant at the next table, bringing to mind another delicate subject. "You're probably thinking I'm a mess. Sophie's memory box," she began, stirring leaves of lettuce around with her fork, feeling the confession come bubbling out. "In the apartment, I kept it on the dresser in my bedroom. It's nothing fancy, just a plain white box. Inside are a few items like her receiving blanket. She was wrapped in it and…I swear, I can still smell her when I pull it out."

"Oh, Kara."

"I've always thought about Sophie. I mean, I've never forgotten her, but I had thought of her from time to time, and it had always been more of thinking about her in passing. I had never gotten below the surface in thinking of her, if that makes sense. I mean, I had a daughter, she died, and that was that. I hadn't actually sat and *meditated* or whatever. I hadn't dwelled on her, on actually *her*, not since after she...But, I don't know, maybe it was the move, but it took me a long time to unpack her box after we got here. I finally did. I thought it would make me feel better. It's now on my dresser."

"You've been busy."

"You know how you heard me call Lilah 'Sophie'? I don't remember ever doing that before we moved here. Even right after Lilah was born, I never messed up and called her the wrong name."

"Moving's stressful," Shannon murmured.

"I haven't been sleeping well either. I've been having these bizarre dreams..." She was confessing secrets John didn't even know.

"I've never lost anyone close. I can't imagine losing a child. If there's anything I can do to help, let me know."

"Thanks." Kara's heart was heavy, but she felt a sense of relief wash over her. Finally, she had told someone and there wasn't any worry that she'd be deemed crazy. She sipped her tea and admitted, "John doesn't like to talk about Sophie."

"You can always talk to me. If you ever want someone to go to the cemetery with you..."

The modern cemetery, not the historical tourist attraction, Kara thought rigidly. "Thanks." Was it terrible she hadn't gone back since the funeral? She chewed on lettuce leaves and was relieved when Shannon changed subjects, lightening the conversation, making them laugh at an embarrassing moment she had at work a year before.

After their meal, they crossed the street so they could walk past the Collumber house. They stopped at its iron gate, centered with the front double doors. The man who placed the For Sale sign was gone. Feeling brave now that she knew it was a property on the market, Kara pushed the gate; it didn't budge. Then she saw it was padlocked. For sale, but not ready for public viewing.

She abandoned the fantasy of touring the house and walked with Shannon to Grace School where they parted ways. Kara picked up Lilah from pre-K and as they drove past the wilting barn, Kara's eyes glided over it as normal. The slight tug was there (*Come and see*) and shadows twitched inside, but she pretended not to notice.

"Mommy, look!" Lilah exclaimed when they had nearly reached the top of their driveway.

Kara followed her gesture to the front porch, her jaw clenching. Oh Lord, what was there now? But looking over, there was no dead animal. In its place, were flowers.

Kara parked in the garage and followed Lilah to the porch. Yellow mums puffed out from a terra cotta pot, set in front of the door. Kara pressed through the blooms and checked the planter, but found no card. "I don't know who they're from, but they're pretty. Let's leave them here as decoration."

Kara made Lilah lunch and then called John to see if he sent the flowers, but she got his voicemail. She hung up, then sought out Margaret's text, *David contacted me.*

She slipped into the office and sat down, not wanting to continue wondering about her mother's message, but found herself trying to get into the computer to do some research. She wiggled the mouse and saw the computer was locked. After trying a handful of possible passwords, she gave up and turned to her cellphone. Leaning against the chair's webbed backrest, she opened her phone's Internet browser and typed in the name that felt strange to be entering, "David Reynolds." She added "Cosgrove, Ohio" and searched. There was a couple dozen hits. Scanning the returned listings and webpages didn't immediately point to him, though. She narrowed the search to include his age, but that didn't yield any reliable results. She scrolled through images of Davids and men related to Davids, and when she stumbled onto a photograph of the statue *David*, she ended her search.

Was it good or bad she hadn't found anything on him? She texted her mother, *Any news on David?*

She hoped that would prompt a reply. But there was no response. Her thoughts drifting, she opened a real estate app and, not knowing the exact address, typed in "Main Street, Grace Township." She only had to scroll through a handful of properties before she saw the familiar house she laid her eyes upon every school day.

"Circa 1790's historical Collumber House for sale. Original hardwood floors and hand-hewn wood built-ins in this charming estate make you feel as if you've stepped back in time. Six bedrooms, five baths, library, and solarium make this home perfect for a large family or business…"

Kara tapped the digital image of the house, trying to expand it, but it wouldn't enlarge. She scrolled past the property description for additional photos, but was disappointed when she saw the agency hadn't included more. She scrolled down and saw the familiar face of the agent who had sold them their house smiling back. Her finger hovered over the hyperlinked phone number for Desmond Howard.

Impulsively, she tapped the hyperlink. *I'll just ask if he's having any open houses*, she thought. She would love to tour the three-story and peek inside those elegant rooms. It wasn't odd to be curious about a historical house in virtually her neighborhood…right?

Her phone immediately dialed and she hunched over it, staring at the screen. But after the second ring, she tapped End, her self-talk reasoning with her, *it's nuts; he'll know you can't buy the house. You just bought one and besides, he's seen your financial records and knows you can't afford it.*

She scrolled back up, looked at the price and laughed. Not quite in her price range. She tapped on the photo again. The blurred image had been taken from across the road; it didn't quite capture the beauty of the house, but its stateliness was apparent. She studied the picture a moment longer before clicking off the phone.

Chapter Fourteen

On Tuesday morning, as routine, Kara watched Jack get on the bus, dropped Lilah off at school, gazed at the Collumber house, drove past the barn slowly, and went about the house doing housework. After loading the dishwasher, she poured a cup of tea. She regarded the brown swill and wondered if she should limit her caffeine intake until her sleep had normalized. Stretching, she yawned, then wandered into her bedroom. She didn't lie down, though. She was too wound up to sleep. Thank the tea for that?

She made her bed and fussed with the tail of the comforter, patting down stubborn wrinkles. When she turned around, her eyes located the white memory box immediately. It sat on the dresser, prominently displayed in front of a bottle of lotion and a paperback. She had purposely made the effort to keep it out; look: no hiding here, no secrets to keep.

She picked it up and sat on the window bench, twisting around to open the windows behind her. A breeze came in, moving the back of her hair gently. She turned back around, settling, and opened the familiar box balanced on her lap. She pulled out the receiving blanket, touching it like it would disintegrate from the slightest mishandling. She lifted it close to her face, but kept it inches away from her nose so she could inhale Sophie's scent without possibly marring the material. Imagining the breeze flowing in enhanced it, she closed her eyes. She was sinking into the ground, softly moving into a pillowed floor that enveloped her and covered her wholly as if she were encased in a comforting womb. She sank further and further, releasing herself to it.

She saw toddler Jack in the haze. He was waddling to where she sat on the couch. "Mommy, what is that?"

She took his pudgy hand and pressed his pointed finger lightly against her swollen belly. Months earlier, she and John had told him in vague terms she was pregnant and he'd have a sister before the year was over, but he hadn't commented nor shown any interest in the miracle of life happening before their eyes. But now, finally, he had noticed.

"That's baby Sophie."

"Baby Sophie?" he asked uncertainly, careful he said the name correctly.

"Yes. Your sister is in there."

He flattened his hand against Kara's cotton shirt. "Baby Sophie is in there?"

"Uh-huh."

"When she coming out?"

"Oh, in about two more months. Do you want to meet her?"

"Uh-huh," he murmured, then jumped onto the couch beside her, the memory turning blurry.

She sat at the bedroom windows, time getting away from her, her memories drifting until she just sat in the stillness, her mind blank. She had been sitting like that for a while when there was a bang-bang-bang at the door, snapping her back to reality. It took her a moment to realize what had disrupted the peace. When she had gathered her wits, she closed the box, set it back on the dresser, and hurried to the front door. She pulled back the toile curtain covering the sidelight, but couldn't see who had knocked.

She unlocked and opened the door, but there was no one there. She looked around, over the porch and front yard. She stepped down to the sidewalk, looking at the driveway, but it was empty. Her thoughts went to that second day in the house: Ding-dong Ditch. Someone had played a prank on them; maybe this was more of the same. But then she remembered kids who were old enough to play pranks were still in school.

She turned back and started up the porch steps, looking to her right, seeing clear to the Foremans' house. At the final step, she looked ahead at her front door and stopped short.

Taped to the face of the hardwood was a sheet of torn notebook paper written in red marker:

LEAVE!!!

She whipped around. Her eyes darted over the yard again and this time to the top eaves of the trees. But she saw no one.

David? The name sprang to her mind.

Kara tore down the paper and hurried inside, slamming the door. She peeked out the office window, trying to hide from whomever might be watching. She looked again at the yard, the trees, the road.

But the road was empty. A cardinal fluttered for a moment to the oak, but was gone seconds later. She sat down, gripping the paper, and studied the sharp letters and three exclamation points. What kind of prank was this? Was her family just chosen randomly to receive it? Or did someone really want them to go?

She called John, but it went straight to voicemail. She texted him to call her. Would he think it was a joke? What if it was David..? Was that dumb? Why would he want them to leave? It didn't make sense.

She left the paper on the desk and started to leave the room, but went back to flip it over, not wanting to see it. She jogged upstairs and looked out the kids' bedroom windows and then through the windows in the bonus room in the off-chance of catching the culprit, even though several minutes had already gone by. She saw no one.

She scrolled through the names in her cellphone. *It's not David, that's dumb,* she thought again as she tapped her mother's name. She left a voicemail asking her to call.

By the time the bus dropped off Jack on Seter Lane, he was itching to get to his secret camper. The afternoon had dragged by, all thanks to his new friend, Alan, who had spent the lunch period telling the boys at the table about the awesome fort his dad had built for him. Jack had thought it

135

was cool for the first five minutes as Alan had described it. The fort was built in a tree and you couldn't be afraid of heights if you wanted to see it. It had a ladder, but Alan's rule was you could only exit by sliding down the fireman pole. He had a cooler for drinks and snacks and a shelf for "important stuff." As Alan droned on, Jack wanted to jump in and tell the guys about the camper. But Alan had just kept on and actually, the more Jack heard about the fort, the more he thought the camper was unready for people to see anyway.

When he got home, he dumped his book bag in the foyer. He ran out the backdoor, calling to his mom that he'd be outside. He heard her answer back from somewhere upstairs, but her voice was muffled and he was already closing the door. His sneakered feet thundered over the deck. He veered away from the swimming pool, sure not to look at it in case…(in case he saw something? In case something grabbed him?) and ran through the copse of trees on the western side of the yard.

He slipped through the bracken, watching out for thornbushes, and was soon within reach of the camper. Sunlight filtered through the trees, making the grimy vehicle dazzle. He pushed the dented door, opening it halfway where it stopped in a pile of jeans and white rags. He squeezed inside and looked around. An opaque window ran nearly the full width of the side of the truck, just above a pulled-out table that was flanked on both sides by ugly brown, cushioned seats. He wrinkled his nose at the rotting stench; it was *just* bearable to be inside.

Bending down, he tugged the jeans material. When he saw it was a dark blue denim jacket, he tossed it aside and picked up the white cloth beside it. It was dirty from the filthy vinyl floor. He stood, spreading it out to its full length, seeing it was nothing more than an old table cloth, one of its ends frayed where it had been torn. Splatters of orange paint were on the back side. He dropped it onto one of the seats and shoved his sneaker around in the debris covering the floor.

It was all junk. Empty plastic bottles, a flattened tennis ball, unused napkins, crinkled newspapers, an unwound wire coat hanger… He plucked a smashed plastic milk container, its top sawed off, and went outside. He pushed the door closed.

Breathing in clean air, Jack scrutinized the container. But there was nothing interesting about it; it was ordinary white plastic with the remains of its mostly stripped blue label. He tossed it back inside. He looked through the door, seeing a fire extinguisher propped up on a ledge near the ceiling. It would be interesting to check that out, see if it still had foam.

But there was just so much trash everywhere. His eyes ran over the wall. He noticed a red ring of linked measuring spoons hanging from the other side of the window, but he wouldn't need those.

Well, one thing was for sure. Nobody would want to spend the night there anytime soon. He'd have to clean it up and somehow get rid of that awful smell. He could barely spend five minutes inside as it was.

He walked around the camper, his eyes moving over the grimy windows. He had been standing there for just a moment when a stick broke from somewhere behind, making him turn around.

Where the trees thinned behind, he could just make out the roofline of the gray barn on the corner of Seter Lane. A few birds dropped to rest on its peak, settling their wings post-flight. Jack edged into the woods, discarding the camper. Weaving in between trees, he looked around for one with branches low enough to climb, but most were thin with branches out of reach.

He looked up at the sky, suddenly becoming aware of the blackbirds circling the trees in the distance. The cawing he heard didn't come from them, however. The screeching cries coming louder and louder were directly overhead. Four, large birds were so close he could make out the detail of their black, glossy feathers. It was amazing how close they circled him. He couldn't remember wild birds ever coming so near. When he looked into one of their eyes…that's when he started to feel uncomfortable. Surely, they posed no threat to him. He was larger than them; he was the human.

But staring back into those blank, black eyes, he started to feel confused, as if he were lost in the middle of a vast forest and not really in his backyard. Perhaps here, *he* was the wild one. The bird he eyed opened its beak to caw again, making Jack back away, grateful the trees were too housed together for one of the strange predators to swoop closer to him; at least he thought that was what kept them just above the full height of the shortest tree.

He backed up until he was beside the camper again. His eyes stayed on them. He was relieved they hadn't moved closer now that he was unprotected. Maybe they had realized he wasn't an animal, and were just curious. He wasn't going to wonder anymore, though. He went home.

"What do you mean you're not coming home tonight?" Kara dropped the folded towel onto her bed.

"We have to make some headway on this project," John replied over speakerphone. "The guys can do an all-nighter. I can't say that I can't."

"Why not? You can't. You have a family."

"I'm sure they have families too. How would it look if the project manager went home but the other guys stayed in the office?" His tone was neutral as he attempted not to bicker with her.

"They'd get over it. And isn't that the benefit of being the boss?"

John laughed. "It isn't like at home where you can boss the kids around."

"Don't act like what I do isn't work. Taking care of the kids, cooking, cleaning…it's a full-time job. Don't minimalize what I do."

"I didn't say anything against what you do." He lowered his voice as if others in the office could hear him. "Why are we even arguing about this?"

"Don't they think it's unreasonable to stay all night at the office?" Kara crumpled one of his tee-shirts before tossing it on the bed.

"It's just this one time."

"Did you see my text from earlier? I wanted to talk to you." She thought, *I wanted to tell you about the note I found* (LEAVE!!!). What if she told him she thought David was back?

"Sorry. I just saw it. What's up?"

She sighed. As more time had passed, she was more convinced it was another prank. Telling him now wouldn't persuade him to come home anyway. "I'll show you later. When will you be home?" She didn't bother asking him about the mums she had found on the front porch earlier that day. He could bring it up if it was his idea of a pre-emptive peace offering for his latest change in work shift.

"Tomorrow morning. I'm not working a full day tomorrow, though." His tone shifted and she heard the smile in it. "What do you want to do with our time off?"

She didn't take the bait, but made an effort to soften her tone. "Okay, well, it's six-thirty, so I'd better let you get back to work."

After they hung up, she looked at his crumpled tee-shirt. John hadn't really done anything wrong; she was so tightly wound, she could feel the stress in her shoulders. She flattened the shirt, smoothing it with both hands. She was just overly tired and she never had liked being home alone at night.

Sunlight brightened the bedroom, but the house was quiet. The kids were quiet; the birds were silent. The room felt empty and she realized that already, the house felt lonely without John. The fact that he would positively not be home until the next day meant the night would drag by. She was starting to see what it was like having the morning hours alone to herself and that hadn't been so bad. But nighttime was different. Even with children in the house, she'd feel alone. Apparently, watching scary movies as an adolescent had screwed up her imagination for the rest of her life.

Tracy and John were an hour away; they might as well be ten hours away. And besides, she wasn't sure if she felt like speaking with Tracy at that moment, not after wondering if she had something to do with her mother's cryptic texts about David. But really, Kara felt like she and the kids were practically isolated; it would take too long for them to reach them if there was an emergency. The only people she knew in the neighborhood were the Foremans and then there was Shannon on the other side of town...

There was nothing she could do about her misgivings, but she found herself springing to her feet and knocking on Jack's open bedroom door. He sat on the floor playing with toy trucks. She watched him, looking for some resemblance to David. Jack shared Kara's dark hair and his facial features were similar to hers. Physically, there was absolutely no reminder of her ex and she was grateful for that.

If David sought visitation rights, would Jack want that? Jack knew John was his step-father and they had encouraged him to ask questions about David if he ever had them (very unlike Kara and Margaret's own relationship, as Margaret kept the past forever closed), but Jack didn't seem curious. Maybe that would change if he learned David had returned. If Jack did want to see David, would Kara's relationship with him change? How would their family dynamic be altered?

Kara cleared her throat and leaned against the door frame, pushing away her thoughts. "Hey, want to have a sleepover?"

"With who? Can I invite Alan?"

"No. With me and Lilah. It's a school night." It was a ruse to keep her loneliness at bay. She imagined the sun sinking quickly and thought of how truly alone they were in the countryside.

"You and Lilah wouldn't be a sleepover," Jack grumbled.

"Come on, Jack, it'll be fun. We'll watch TV, eat popcorn, and then we can all sleep in my great big bed. We can even tell stories."

She saw the scowl on his down-turned face. "Ghost stories?"

Absolutely not. "Not ghosts. I was thinking more like adventure stories."

"When's dad coming home?"

"Not 'til tomorrow morning."

He looked up at her, studying her. Finally, he said, sounding resigned, "Okay, we can have a sleepover."

After dinner, Jack sat down at the kitchen table with his math workbook and Lilah lay on the floor in front of the TV. As Kara turned to the dishwasher, her cellphone chimed, making her jerk. Her nerves bunching up, she slid in a chair across from Jack and looked down at the phone screen.

He didn't look good.

There was a hitch in her breathing. The text was from Margaret and even though she knew who she meant, Kara texted back, *David?*

Yes. He looked wild.

Wild? Kara pictured the clean-cut David she had known: always in nice clothes, well-groomed, smelled good...What did she mean by wild?

Kara texted, *What did he want?*

There was no immediate response and as she waited for a reply, she glanced at Jack, whose head was bent over his homework, unaware she was texting about his biological father. She returned to her phone, staring at the words, waiting for Margaret to give her the reason for his contact.

But the minutes ticked by and after several more had passed, Kara prompted, *What did he want?*

She waited a beat, then called her. She was sent straight to voicemail. "Mom, what did David want? Call me back." She hung up, laying the phone face-up on the table.

Jack piped up, "Mom, can you help me with this?"

The next two hours dragged by. Margaret didn't call or text again, making Kara more exasperated than concerned. Was she playing games? Was this because she was irritated they hadn't talked recently?

After Kara had put the kids to bed, she went into the great room to watch TV. Twenty minutes into the program, she started to feel sleepy, but then the show broke for commercial and her thoughts drifted back to her mother's text messages, so vague and incomplete she didn't know what to make of them. Cool, calm David…She wondered how he really was now.

He looked wild.

She crossed her arms over her chest. Who cared how he looked? She didn't want anything to do with him. He was the past. She had cursed his name throughout the pregnancy and had hated him as she started to mirror what her mother's life must have been like as a single parent. But then she had met John and the cycle had been broken. Thank God for John, a father who cared.

Without warning, Kara's thoughts flipped and Sophie appeared. She didn't have to close her eyes to see her. Kara's gaze was to the right of the TV, her eyes fixed on the wall. Projected there was Sophie, lying still as always, in the bassinette that had waited at the apartment for her. Of course, in reality, Sophie had never lain in that bassinette. She had never felt comfort in their home. Kara's pupils grew larger, taking in the infant's eyes. They opened for the first time, glowing electric blue, an unnatural hue. They didn't blink, the relaxed mouth didn't twitch, and there was no flush to those sunken cheeks.

Kara blinked and the trance was broken; she'd never seen Sophie's eyes. She felt a numbness come over her and realized the great room had turned chilly. She covered herself with a throw blanket, pushing away the image of her daughter and turned her eyes to the TV. A sitcom was on, but she couldn't follow the storyline. She found herself looking into the shadowed kitchen. The outside lantern and foyer chandelier added light to the otherwise dark house. Besides the TV, it was quiet.

Her eyes drifted again, over the playroom door. It was closed. She returned her gaze to the screen again, but she had lost all meaning to the episode. She turned off the TV and picked up her cellphone. She scrolled over the few texts between her and Margaret. She couldn't read between the lines; there wasn't enough content. Giving up, she skimmed articles online instead. After a while, she went back to her contacts list, scrolling through names, looking briefly at John's before clicking off the phone.

She headed to bed, but stopped to peek out the dining room curtain. She didn't know what she expected to see, and as it turned out, there wasn't much to see, since the deck light didn't reach that far. She hardly saw the outline of the pool. She released the curtain and stepped into her bedroom, pulling the door closed and locking it. She used the toilet, then flipped off the light and peeked out the bathroom window. The lamppost at the edge of the driveway poured a ring of light all around it, but only reached so far. There was blackness beyond.

She closed the curtain and looking up at the star-shaped skylight, she saw a smattering of stars thousands of miles away. Her eyes drifted and she noticed a shadow draped over three of the window points. It didn't waver as it darkened half the outline of the window. Perhaps, it was the effect of moonlight bending over the trees. She rubbed her eyes and looked up again. The shadow was gone; perhaps, the moon's angle had shifted. Perhaps, Kara had caught the change by chance.

She climbed into bed, lying down between Jack and Lilah, who both slept. Kara closed her eyes. Minutes quickly turned into an hour as she worked at ignoring the sounds of the house settling. But her ears were trained, listening for any sounds that didn't belong.

The floorboards creaked and her eyes opened, darting to the closed door. Were those footsteps?

Her fingers tightened around her cellphone and she listened intently, pushing the blanket down, as if the cotton impeded her hearing. Jack on her right started snoring. She was glancing at him when something thumped against the floor, nearby.

Kara sat at attention, her heart in her throat and her eyes back on the closed door. She couldn't hear beyond her racing heart and Jack's steady snore. Her thumb poised to dial 911 on her cellphone, she slid to the end of the bed, not breathing as the sound of the blankets and sheets rubbed against her. She waited a few seconds, then got up, rounding the bed slowly to Lilah's side from where the noise had come. She moved closer to Lilah, whose face was turned to the ceiling. Hovering close to the cool wall, Kara clicked on her cellphone's flashlight and aimed it at the floor.

Finding Lilah's statue there, Kara's head came slightly back, stunned to see it, before she swiftly got to her knees and aimed the light under the bed. Nobody there. She trained her ears, but heard nothing besides Jack's steady snore. She scowled at the statue. The clay girl's head was hidden beneath the bed, looking eerily lopped off, but the frog was in the open, grinning at Kara, as if laughing at her. She picked it up and shoved it under the blanket beside Lilah.

Wide awake now, Kara rechecked doors in the house, ensuring they were still locked, then walked around, identifying the refrigerator made the hum in the kitchen, John's computer whirred in the office, and the buzzing came from the baby monitor on Lilah's dresser. She picked up the monitor. The green light burned steadily and the buzzing chirped intermittently. How in the world did Lilah sleep through that? Kara turned it off. The house was even quieter than before.

She aimed the cellphone's flashlight at the bonus room, the familiar boxes unmoved. She went downstairs, passed under the harsh foyer light, peeked in the powder room, and went into the great room. Greeted again by the refrigerator's hum, she rechecked the backdoor and peeked outside. Nothing stirred within eyeshot. She turned back to the great room. It was dark, but she saw the outline of the playroom door.

It wasn't closed.

Hairs standing on her arms, Kara held out the cellphone, its flashlight extending a few feet ahead of her. Her steps were quick; one would've mistaken it for bravery, but it was more an adrenaline rush, like ripping off a Band-Aid: get to that door quickly and get it over with.

The beam of light fell on the open door, ajar a few inches. She stretched her arm out as far as possible through the doorway, illuminating boxes of nails, drywall, and wood planks. No monsters lay in wait.

Entering the room, her light reflecting off the naked windows, she felt exposed to the outside world, the world from which she was trying to hide. She ignored her reflection, sensing a pale-faced woman stared wide-eyed. She backed up, glancing out the backdoor as she headed back to bed. She was passing through the dining room when there was an abrupt *Boom!*

She jumped, practically dropping the cellphone.

Crrrrrrrrackkkkk! Booooom!

A flash of light illuminated the closed curtains.

It took her a moment to realize it had started storming. The window flashed again as lightning struck nearby. The sound of a million nails spilling erupted as it started to rain.

She sighed, the storm instantly relieving some of her stress. Who would break in during a thunderstorm?

She returned to her bedroom, locked the door behind her, and climbed into bed, closing her eyes. She ignored the banging, so loud it sounded like somebody was trying to break inside. She ignored the wind howling like an anguished banshee, and pushed away the ugly statue that had edged to her place in the bed.

Chapter Fifteen

Seven the next morning Kara awoke, still sandwiched between Jack and Lilah. She placed a hand on both, rousing them. "Time to wake up, guys." She checked the office and garage for John, tamping down her annoyance that he hadn't returned from work. Following routine, she watched Jack ride away on the bus until it disappeared behind the trees, and dropped Lilah off at school.

She left Lilah, crossed the Grace School parking lot, and sat in her car for a moment. The sun was still rising, casting light on the bottom third of the Collumber house, its remainder in shadow. The windows were dark, the covered porch swept clean, and the For Sale sign in the yard near the locked iron gate. To her, the sign might as well had read, Keep Out.

She drove away, but slowed as she advanced on the weathered barn on Seter Lane. It too was shadowed, but she remembered the hayloft and a smile played on her lips as she imagined it in light with dust motes sparkling in its wake.

Come and see.

The leaves crinkled, whispering in the wind. Her smile fell and her foot pressed hard on the brake, the abrupt stop rocking her harshly forward and backward. Her lips parted as she reached for her seatbelt, her fingers fumbling for the push button.

A car came up behind her then, honking, and her fingers let go and her head snapped to attention. Birds scattered from the trees. Avoiding the rearview mirror, Kara pressed down too firmly on the accelerator, and returned home.

John was not there. As the coffee percolated, she pressed his name on her cellphone. "No service" flashed back. She roamed the front of the house, waiting for bars to appear, but they didn't. She gave up, sinking into the office chair. She played with the phone in her hands, mindlessly scrolling through her contacts list. Her eyes eventually lowered to the desk to the note she had left there.

She flipped it right-side up, looking at the hand-written uppercase word.

LEAVE!!!

It didn't seem so foreboding as it had when she first found it taped to the door. There was no way to tell, but it very well could've been the writing of a teenaged prankster.

Of course, it had to be a kid, she told herself. Who else would've thought that was funny?

A joke. Just like Ding-Dong Ditch.

She looked at her phone again. Still no bars. She clicked back to her text messages from her mother. Kara's thoughts flipping to David, she texted her now, even though there was little chance of the message going through due to poor cell reception.

Hello?

She watched the status bar crawl across the screen, and after a moment, the message sent. She waited, but there was no immediate response.

What did David want? Why was her mother not responding?

Sighing, Kara went down the hallway, glancing at the playroom door. She was glad it was closed. She turned off the coffeemaker, didn't bother to pour a cup, and went into the master bedroom. With sore eyes, she looked at her bed, crumpled sheets and blankets hanging off the edge. It looked inviting and she desperately wanted to catch up on quality sleep, but she went instead to the window, collapsing onto the cushioned bench. She gazed outside for a while, glossing over the surrounding trees that outlined the backyard. She narrowed her eyes, spotting something metallic in the far reaches of the yard. She tried to make out what it was, but was distracted when a buck darted past to the lawn. He paused, looking at the house, perhaps seeing her, before scampering beyond the north end, disappearing again into the woods.

Kara turned back to her room, her eyes locating the white box sitting on her dresser.

Sophie.

Her fingers itching to open the box, she started toward it. But, nearing it, something screeched, high-pitched, from behind her, making her whirl around. She went to the windows, peering out, but couldn't find what it was. Then there was another screech, this one not as jarring, which she recognized as a bird.

Turkey vulture.

She wrinkled her nose, hating the creatures she hadn't even known had existed months ago, and backed away from the windows. Her eyes trailed down the window bench, inviting in the light, spotting two brass hinges beneath the cushion. Remembering what she had stored inside days after they had moved in, she removed the pad and pulled open the seat.

She pulled out the cardboard box and opened it, finding leftover invitations from their wedding, photographs from her last day at work, two baggies holding Jack's and Lilah's first hair clippings, and three photo albums.

She selected an album and closed the bench to sit on it. The first photograph inside the cover was of John and her sitting awkwardly on a park bench. It was from their first date. Their cheesy grins made her smile. She remembered he had asked a passerby to take their photo.

"For prosperity," he had told Kara, jokingly.

Later, he had confessed to her that he had just wanted to capture how beautiful she had looked in the sunlight. She had told him he was full out it, but his words had pleased her and had made her feel loved.

She took her time, flipping through the laminated pages, pausing on various photographs that had captured their lives: John and her as boyfriend/girlfriend, married life, snap-shots of Jack and Lilah as babies, and some professional stills of the kids taken at the mall.

She stared at one of the family portraits, wondering how different it would look if Sophie was there too. Big brother and his two sisters.

Kara closed the album and looked up.

A figure stood in the doorway.

Kara jumped to her feet, dropping the album on the floor. It took her a moment to recognize John.

"Hi," he said.

"Welcome home," she mumbled, bending to pick up the album, the chore an excuse to regain her composure. She straightened and glanced at the clock. It was almost eleven.

"I'm done for the day," he said.

"It's about time," she replied, snidely.

"Well, we got a lot done," he replied, an edge to his voice.

She noticed dark lines under his eyes and softened, realizing he had probably had a rough night too. "Are you working any more overnights?"

He replied, his tone lightening to match hers, "We got a lot accomplished. I'll be happy when this project is over."

"You didn't answer the question," she pointed out. When he didn't say anything, she asked, sighing, "Is there much more to do?"

He nodded, sighing. "Oh, yeah." He gestured his chin toward the bench. "What're you doing?"

She glanced at the white box on her dresser and admitted, "It may sound morbid, but I wish we had taken at least one picture of Sophie."

He looked horrified, instantly causing her to regret her confession. His face hardened. "Why are you suddenly obsessed?"

Her pulse quickened, driving her from zero to eighty. "Obsessed?" Suddenly, the urge to talk openly about it was upon them. *Let's get this over with. I'm tired of agonizing over it*, she thought.

"What's going on?"

She shrugged, glancing back at the box, and then at him. "I don't know." And that was the truth. She was just having these strange dreams, seeing these images of Sophie.

"What happened to get you so…wrapped up in this?"

" 'Wrapped up'?" She guffawed. "I'm not the one trying to forget her." She had stunned herself; she hadn't intended to say it. Is that how she felt? That John was trying forget Sophie? Feeling panic rise inside her, she spun it back on him. "What's your issue?"

"I don't have an issue." His face had changed and the way he looked at her…It unnerved her. He was a stranger eyeing her carefully.

"You've forgotten her," Kara repeated, her eyes challenging his. "You don't want to remember her."

"I've never forgotten her," he said quietly.

"You've moved on."

He shook his head, setting his jaw. "I'm not getting into this. It was a long night. I'm tired."

"You're 'not getting into this'?"

"I'm done. I'll be in my office." He left the room. They had finally discussed Sophie and it was over before it had even begun.

She stared at the empty doorway, hearing his heavy steps, leading him away. There was the squeak of the office chair and the swell of the computer being turned on. She remembered the note laying on his desk (LEAVE!!!). He'd probably think she had written it and had laid it there like a petulant child.

A child who was afraid of the dark.

He didn't say anything else; it was unclear if he had even noticed the note. But, even from the bedroom, she could tell his mind was elsewhere, their moment forgotten.

She slid her cellphone into her jeans pocket and left the house without telling him where she was going. She had time to spare before she'd have to get Lilah. The house was too stuffy and she needed out.

The sky was heavy with clouds. Puffs of white, light grays, and deep charcoals drifted now and again just to show a glimpse of the yellow sliver of sun playing hide-and-seek. Her feet led her blindly down the stepping stones that drew her through the front yard and soon, she was on the road walking with purpose. She walked down its center, empty of traffic, headed toward town. The wind picked up and strands of dark hair stroke her cheeks and dabbed her lips.

After a time, she found herself looking squarely at the gray barn. Crooked, worm-eaten posts tiredly held itself up. The interior was mostly covered in shadow. It was an ugly building, surely a code violation, there was something pitiful about it. The structure drew her in and she couldn't explain why it happened, or what magic it held, but she felt a sense of calm. From a car, you could only take it at face value: an ageing eyesore. But, standing level with it, sharing its breath, truly gazing at it, she felt its warmth. The splintered roof, chipped gray paint blending with decayed wood, bird nests housed under corner eaves, it was a presence that sat behind the dirt carpet that extended from the road.

From the dark recesses of her mind, she recognized the double standard; she had told Jack and Lilah to stay away from the barn. But why hadn't she heeded her own words?

She stayed a while, unmoving, until a truck came bumbling toward her, making her hurry onto the dirt that stretched like a hand, beckoning her toward the barn.

She bent forward, now that she was closer to the structure, gaining a look inside. She was struck with an urge to explore it. There was nothing remarkable about the building that nature alone could raze. She tore her eyes away and glanced at the farmhouse next door. It sat smugly in the backdrop.

You want to go in, don't you, it taunted. *You want to see.*

As always, the curtains over the farmhouse windows were drawn closed, lifeless, no sign of anyone.

Her eyes flicked back to the barn, mere yards from her. She pictured its loft again, wondering what hid there. But the image vanished when a screech trilled in the sky. Her eyes shot skyward. Three large turkey vultures circled above the roof.

Kara stepped back, inching close to the road. Had the sky darkened further? It was a trick, because although the sky there was a mix of charcoal and white, the day was comfortably warm.

The birds landed as one, ruffling black feathers, settling on the roof. Two groomed themselves, but the third watched her, its dead stare dashing out her desire to enter the barn. She backed away, stumbling over the raised surface of the road.

"On your right!" a man's breathless voice called, making her spin around.

She staggered backward to clear the way, catching the side of the jogger's face. Dumbstruck, she watched him as he strode past. She hadn't had a good look at his face, but did his dark blond hair and his build look like…

David?

She stared.

It couldn't be. No. If that were David, he would've stopped; why would he be jogging on her street anyway?

He's looking for you.

She watched him until he disappeared over the crest of the hill. *How random*, she thought, *David wouldn't just be out here jogging. You're losing it, Kara, get it together.* She looked back at the trio of vultures, seeing they all watched her. Chilled, she turned away.

Heading home, her eyes trailing over the empty farmhouse, her cellphone rang. Her fingers fumbled over the phone as she pulled it from her pocket. Was it her mother calling to warn her, "David's in town"?

Seeing Tracy's name on the phone's screen, she swallowed the thought, convinced the jogger hadn't been David. It was just too impossible a thought. It had to be impossible.

"Hey! What're you up to today?" The familiar voice was loud on the otherwise quiet lane.

Kara kept walking, her eyes on the road. "I was just taking a walk." Trying to keep her voice light, she asked, "Hey, did my mom mention David to you?"

"David who?"

"David Reynolds." Saying his name aloud tasted bitter, summoning a creep. "Jack's dad. My mom told me he reached out to her."

"He did? No, she hasn't said anything about it. What did he want?"

"I have no idea. She texted me that he called her, but she hasn't given me any details."

"Do you want me to ask her about it?"

Tracy was already too involved in Kara's drama with Margaret. Kara instantly regretted mentioning it. "No, it's fine. I'll call her later. I was just curious."

"I'd be curious too. You haven't talked to him since you had Jack, right?"

Kara was nearing her driveway and wasn't comfortable talking about a ghost from her past out in the open. "No. Well, I have to get Lilah from school soon."

"I won't keep you. I was just seeing if you wanted to hang out this weekend. You can show me your marvelous town."

Kara was hesitant, not sure how she felt about Tracy these days, but agreed to the idea. "Sure. Shannon told me about an antique shop in town. I haven't gone yet. Want to do that?"

"Saturday?"

"Sure."

"Okay, great!

Kara ended the call, wondering if mentioning David had been a mistake; she had been subconsciously trained to not divulge too much to Tracy, who tended to leak information to Margaret. It was the reason Kara hadn't told her about her recent thoughts (*obsession?*) of Sophie, her strange dreams, and her squabble with John. With Tracy, there was always the risk that anything they discussed would get back to Margaret.

As Kara climbed the driveway, her cellphone rang again. The name, Desmond Howard, her real estate agent, flashed on the screen. She wrinkled her nose, remembering the call she had made about the Collumber house the day before. She thought about letting it go to voicemail, but then after the third ring, decided she should get her embarrassment over with.

"Hello?"

"Hello, this is Desmond Howard from Duchess Real Estate. Is this Kara?"

"Hi, Desmond. This is she."

"Ahem, great! How are you?"

"I'm fine. How are you?"

"Wonderful! Ahem! I see that you called..."

Kara's face grew warm. "Yeah." She let out a short laugh. "Ignore that. I was just looking through listings and saw the one for the Collumber house. I didn't mean to call."

"You were looking through house listings? Is there anything wrong with your house?"

"Oh, no. We love it here. I was just being nosy when I saw it's for sale."

"Ah, yes." He cleared his throat. "It is. Magnificent house."

"Will there be an open house?" She jumped at the idea. Imagine touring the Collumber house, running her hand along the polished wood banister...

"No, no. It's toured by appointment only. Only serious buyers can view it."

She frowned.

"Everything's alright? John and the children are well?"

"Yes. Everyone's doing good."

"Yes?"

"Yep."

"Did you get my housewarming gift?

"Um…"

"I left it on your doorstep."

Her thoughts sifted through what she had found recently at her doorstep: a dead opossum, a threatening note…

"The plant?" he prompted.

Her eyes settled on the mum sitting on the porch. "Oh, yes! It came from you? I wondered who had sent it."

"Yes. A housewarming gift."

"Thanks! I haven't gotten around to planting flowers yet, so they're very appreciated."

"Well, then. I am glad everything is going well for you and your family. Call me if you need anything or have any more questions."

"Okay." She hung up, feeling idiotic. Desmond knew their finances as well as she knew them, and it was obvious they couldn't afford an additional property, especially a large historical house. Well, at least one mystery was solved: he had sent the mum. But who had left the note?

John wasn't far behind when Kara crawled into bed that night. "You're coming to bed early," she commented, feeling him pull the covers. Dinner had passed with practically no words spoken between them, an easy task when your children controlled the tempo of idle conversation. He had spent the day tucked away in his office and she had stayed away, avoiding the room.

He said, sounding like his normal self, "Well, I thought if there was ever a chance to spend alone time with my wife, it'd be now." It was as if they hadn't had words earlier that day, as if he hadn't accused her of being obsessed with their dead child, as if she hadn't pouted about his late hours.

She started to say, sarcastically, they could've had time together that morning, but didn't when he draped a protective leg over hers.

He pulled her in close and kissed her. Nuzzling her neck, he said, "I'm sorry for not coming home last night."

She sighed, interlacing their fingers. "We missed you."

He shifted to his back, releasing her hand, and pulled his arms up under the pillow behind his head. "This project is really important. It's the first big task I've been put in charge of. I don't want to screw it up."

"I know." Keeping her voice steady, she asked, "So you think more overnights?"

"I can't promise there won't be any more, but I'll try. We actually made a lot of headway last night. The project can make or break the company right now. It's that important. I don't like working all the time, but…it'll be over soon."

"Okay, but if it gets out of hand…" she trailed off, then chuckled, flipping to her back.

He took her hand in his again and rested their joined fists in the narrow space between them. "Were you able to sleep last night?"

Ah, she thought, *he does know I'm afraid to be alone at night. 'Fraidy cat.* It really was embarrassing to her.

"A little," she admitted. "I haven't been sleeping very well lately anyway."

"You haven't?"

"No, not really. Have you?" She wanted to ask, *Have you been seeing strange things in your dreams too?* They haunted her nearly every night now. The details were vague, but each morning, a feeling of dread hovered over her.

"Yeah, I sleep great."

"You're probably exhausted by the time you get to bed." She felt him nodding.

157

"That's probably true. I've slept like a baby since we've been here."

"Lucky you."

"Guess you don't need that anymore." He gestured toward the nightstand.

She looked over, knowing he meant the baby monitor, still turned on, tuned to Lilah's bedroom. "I probably don't. Lilah hasn't woken in the middle of the night in weeks. "I'll store it away tomorrow."

After a while, he said, softly, "The house is so quiet out here."

"Except for the crickets and frogs." They could hear them now. The cloudy day had kept the temperature mild and even now at night, the room was comfortable with the windows open.

"That's probably what puts me to sleep."

"Country boy for life."

"Let me turn the fan on. That might help you sleep." He let go of her hand and she watched his silhouette get up and turn on the pedestal fan across the room. He aimed it at the bed and she felt the temperature cool even further. Its hum was soothing. He climbed back into bed and held her hand again.

She pulled the covers over her arms and finding the mood easy, asked, "Did you see the 'leave' note on your desk?"

He shifted, but remained on his side. "No. What is it?"

"Somebody knocked on the door yesterday and left a note that said, 'Leave.' I put it on your desk."

" 'Leave?' " He chuckled.

"Do you think it's a prank?"

"Yeah, a lame prank. Kids do dumb things."

Kara wondered why they were the butt of a joke. Risk of being the new people in town?

John yawned and was soon asleep. Kara turned to her side and reached for her cellphone. Clicking it on, she pulled up her mom's text messages. There was nothing new, Kara's last text being, *Hello?*

She laid the cellphone on the nightstand and settled under the covers. She tried to shut out her thoughts and concentrate on the whir of the fan, but she could still hear the underlying chirp of crickets.

*Go to sleep, go to sleep, go to sleep...*she chanted the mantra, focusing on the words, over and over until, gratefully, her subconscious finally took over and she too, fell asleep...

Just a couple more rungs she'd have to mount and her head would clear the hayloft...if she could make it this time. It wasn't the ladder she climbed that kept her down, though. Made from rough-hewn wood with splintered arms she tried to avoid each time she slid down, it was the invisible force she fought against that knocked her down repeatedly.

Up, up, up, she urged herself not for the first time. She had been pushed down to the straw-covered floor so many times already.

The barn was oddly bright. It felt similar to the gray one she drove by during waking hours; it had the same floorplan, even the location of the hayloft was the same. But still, it wasn't the same, it didn't even smell the same. Kara stole sideway glances, taking stock of the ropes, hoes, shovels, and other tools that kept the barn in working order. She looked up, beyond the loft, and saw a gap in the wooden wall, a makeshift window letting in sunlight. She clung tight to the ladder, willing herself to make it to the top. She was nearly there.

Up, up, up.

Desperate to reach the loft before being sent downward again, she shot out an arm and laid her hand flat on its wide-slatted floor. She wiggled her fingers, feeling the spindly straw. She had never made it this far. With renewed confidence, she lifted one leg, making to step up the next rung.

But her footing was wrong and down she went, both feet striking the golden floor below.

A weight pressed against her, but still, she grabbed hold of the ladder and started to climb again. In no time, she was near the loft again, so close.

But this time, a male voice, called, "Stop! Leave!"

It startled her, making her jump. She lost balance, letting go of the ladder, and fell.

"Ugh!" Kara hit the carpeted floor, hard. Her eyes popped open. It took a moment to realize she was sitting cockeyed on her bedroom floor. The sun filtered in through the drapes and the bed sheet was tangled around her legs. She groaned, feeling like she had busted open her elbow and hip. She looked herself over, finding nothing was bleeding or appeared broken.

"Mommy?"

She looked up, seeing Lilah standing in the doorway. "I'm okay," Kara said, feeling silly being caught falling out of bed.

But Lilah seemed to pay no mind. "I'm hungwy."

Kara pulled away the sheet as she straightened to a sitting position. " 'Hungry'."

"Hungry."

"Alright, I'm getting up." Kara's eyes zeroed in on the statue gripped in her daughter's hands. The frog's grin mocked her as she sat there stupidly. She shook her head, clearing it, and with the dream hazy now (she had been climbing stairs or something…), she got up. John had already left for work and she had little time to get the kids ready for school.

Later that morning, she padded into Lilah's bedroom, baby receiver in hand. She smiled, seeing the bed was made. Lilah had even propped her fairy book against the covers.

The baby monitor was on the dresser as always, with its green "on" light glowing. She reached for it with her free hand, and as her fingers wrapped around the box, it squealed, making her release it as if it had burned her. The monitor struck the floor, instantly killing the noise.

She turned off the parent unit she had been holding and leaned it against the fairy book. She retrieved the monitor from the floor. It was quiet now, but she twisted the knob to shut it off anyway. Static crackled from it as the light dimmed to black and then went silent. She bent to pick up the parent unit from the bed, her fingers brushing the white plastic. Lilah's monitor crackled, startling her.

But it was off.

She twisted the knob on and off; it stayed silent. As she turned away from the bed, the light on the receiver glowed, stopping her.

But it was off.

Frowning, she touched the knob. It was already turned in the off position. She twisted it on and off again, watching the light brighten, dim, and then die out completely. She twisted it again, testing it. The light glowed green when it clicked on and went to black when she clicked off. She waited a moment until she was satisfied the receiver was truly off.

She straightened and headed for the doorway. The parent unit crackled then, making her flinch and toss it back onto the bed. She stood there, openmouthed, watching it as the light clicked green. It glowed steadily for several seconds before it quietly dimmed to black again. She stared at it, waiting for it to turn on again. Several seconds of stillness passed before she picked it up.

She twisted the knob, but it didn't turn on. She turned it again nearly a dozen times and it stayed off. Figuring the batteries had just died, she shook the strange feeling that hugged her and went in the bonus room. She easily found the cardboard box where they'd stored the monitor and receiver, and closed them away. She'd probably never use those again. Why was she keeping them?

Sophie's face, close-eyed and pale, flashed in her mind.

Kara told herself not to conjure up the name, busying herself with pushing one of the smaller stacks closer to the window. Cardboard rubbed against something, making it clink. She looked behind the stack, finding shattered glass scattered over the plywood floor. She looked around the boxes before looking up. A lower window pane was broken.

"Oh, no," she muttered. She dragged boxes out of the way, searching for an obvious culprit: a baseball, a rock, a bird. But she saw none of those things. She restacked the boxes against the window so the room wasn't exposed to the outside. Kara had only blocked one of the windows, but no matter, doing so had dramatically darkened the room.

Still uneasy, she exited the house and eased onto a patio chair on the deck. She faced the tree-line that touched the Foremans' backyard. By rote, her eyes flicked over the tall, swaying trees, wondering about that poor dog, Blacky. He had been dangling, tightened at the neck by a…what, rope?

She swallowed, looking deeper into the woods, wondering where exactly the dog had been found. The Foremans' rear porch peeked at her through the trees as she called John on her cellphone. When he answered, she saw a flash of white fluttering in the breeze. It was a few rows of trees in, a bag or ribbon.

"Know how to fix a window?" she asked him, leaning to the side to see better.

"What happened?"

She stepped into the grass, her eyes trained on the white swatch as she moved around to the side of the house. "It's in the upstairs bonus room, the lower pane of glass is broken. I think a bird crashed into it or something." She gazed up at the broken window, making out its jagged glass, set against brown cardboard.

"Weird."

"I covered it with some stacked boxes for now." She looked down at the grass for glass shards or what had caused the break, but there were no clues. "Should we call Tom?"

Tom showed up later that morning, a duffel bag slung over his shoulder.

"Watch out for glass. I haven't cleaned it up yet," she warned as he helped move boxes away from the broken pane.

"Lots of stuff you have here," he said, setting a box down on the other side of the room.

"Yes, too much." She stood back to let him inspect the damage.

"That's a strange break."

"Yeah...How do you mean?"

He touched the glass remnants clinging to the sash. "Single-paned." He looked briefly at the other windows. "Hmm, they're all single-paned..."

"Is that strange?"

"On a new-build, yes." With his booted foot, he swept the shards closer to the wall. "Just makes you wonder what else the builder skimped on."

"How do you think it broke?"

"I'd say something outside hit it. See how all the glass is inside?" He glanced around the room. "Find any stray baseballs or birds?"

"No. That's what I thought too. Could the heat have done anything like this? We had a storm the other night. Maybe it was from that?"

"I don't think so. This break is almost in the center of the window. To me, it looks like something came through it with some force. Could've been an animal. I don't see feathers or fur, but it's possible."

Kara wrinkled her nose. "Animals seem to be dying all over the place."

"What?"

163

"Nothing. You think you can fix it?"

"You'll want a replacement window, a double-paned one this time. They insulate better and are stronger." He sniffed in a couple times, glancing in between the boxes. "I don't smell anything dead anyway."

"Well, that's a good thing."

"Do you want me to replace the other windows with double-panes?"

"No, not now. It's probably expensive, right?"

He nodded. "Yeah. I think so anyway. At least a thousand."

She laughed. "Um, yeah…Just the one window. We haven't priced any of the other work we want done yet. I don't even want to think about how much all that's gonna cost."

"Let me take some measurements and I can place an order. For now, we can seal the hole with plastic."

Chapter Sixteen

"I'm working late again," John said without preamble on Friday afternoon.

Kara tapped her cellphone to speakerphone and resumed hand-drying dishes the dishwasher hadn't completely dried. She glanced at the microwave clock: 4:52. "When do you think you'll be home?"

She felt his hesitation across the phone line. "I don't think I'll be home tonight."

"John."

"Why don't you invite Tracy or Shannon over?" he suggested, keeping his voice light.

She knew he was trying to distract her already-creeping anxiety with the idea of a grownup sleepover. She simply replied, "Call me later." After they hung up, Kara mulled over his suggestion. Company would be welcome, but she'd see Tracy the next day, so that would be a wasted trip for her. Inviting a local over might be nice, though.

She pressed Shannon's name on her phone, but it went straight to voicemail. She didn't bother leaving a message. Oh well, she had to suck up her courage to be the grownup again. Besides, she didn't want her kids thinking they were unsafe because they're mother was a scaredy-cat. They'd be fine.

She looked through her stored texts, resting on her exchange with her mother. The last message Kara had sent, "Hello?" had been left unanswered. She still had no idea what the David situation was. Should she even be concerned?

She tapped Margaret's name and rested the phone against her ear.

"Hello?"

She blinked, surprised Margaret had actually answered. "Hi, Mom."

Margaret sighed in exasperation. "Kara, I'm in the middle of something. Can I call you back?"

"I just have a quick question."

"Look, I can't right now."

"You never called me back."

"It can wait."

"Can I just ask you—"

"We'll talk later."

"Mom, it's about David. You said he contacted you?...Hello?" Kara pulled the phone away from her ear and saw her mother had already hung up.

Love you too, Mom, she thought with annoyance. She didn't get it. What was Kara supposed to think? Had her mother forgotten about it? Was it a joke?

It was unreal. She had been raised not to depend on her, and here she was, in her thirties, being let down.

She texted Margaret, *I'd appreciate if you told me what David said to you. Thanks*, and slammed the cellphone on the kitchen counter.

Dusk was turning into night, and Jack, who had been watching the sun sink into the woods, spotted the first of the lightning bugs twinkling in the backyard. He twisted around from the great room windows, his knees digging into the couch. "Mom? Can we catch lightning bugs?"

Kara looked out the windows, noticing not for the first time night was coming on fast. She had been dreading it all evening. "Yes, but let's stay close to the house."

"Do we have a jar I can use?" Jack asked when they were outside. He neared the eastern edge of the woods. Three yellow lights blinked sporadically near him, beckoning him closer to the dark trees.

"Jack, stay out of the woods!" Kara called to him from where she and Lilah were, near the swimming pool. "No, I don't have any jars."

"What about a shoebox?" he asked, moving closer to the tree-line.

"No, you're not using a shoebox. I don't want any bugs in the house. Jack, I said stay away from the woods!"

He took a few steps away from the trees, but still hovered close to them.

"Jack, come over here. There are a lot coming out now. See?" Kara gestured to the blinking lights that multiplied every few seconds.

"Mommy, I want to catch it," Lilah announced, reaching her arms out. But every time Lilah was at the brink of catching one of the glowing bugs, its light would blink off, making it disappear. When it beamed again, it was ten feet away and three feet higher, out of reach.

"Mom, they're all coming this way!" Jack called to them, reaching out straight from his chest to several that blinked in front of him.

Kara looked over, seeing he was right. The little bugs seemed drawn to the trees. "Come on, Lilah, let's try to catch them as they head this way." Kara and Lilah moved toward Jack. She willed herself not to visualize Blacky. That happened a long time ago, Marvin had said; the neighborhood was quiet now.

"I got one!" Jack's excitement broke into her trepidation. He cupped his hands together and walked over to them. "See?" He opened his hands so they all could peer at the black bug crawling around his left palm, blinking its light.

"Gross!" Kara laughed. It reminded her why she had outgrown her interest in catching them.

"There are so many of them," Jack murmured.

Kara looked up. All around them teams of lightning bugs flew up and down, their yellow lights disappearing and reappearing. It was amazing seeing so many fairy lights surrounding them.

"Cool," Lilah said, before exclaiming, "I got it!"

"You did?" Kara and Jack asked in unison.

Lilah opened her fist, showing them the bug crawling on her finger. She squealed when it glowed. Swiftly, it took flight again, escaping smoothly out of her reach. Kara watched it float upward and toward the tree-line, following its friends to whatever magic drew them to the woods. She watched it until others drew near it, all of them bouncing up and down, their lights flickering on and off again. *Now you see us, now you don't.*

Kara looked back at the house. She had purposely kept the first-floor lights on, so that the inside glowed from behind the curtained windows. Its contrast to the night was jarring. The single deck light was on, but its light barely covered the small deck, so inadequate it didn't reach the grass.

She turned around, taking in her nearby surroundings. They were much too close to the woods. It was now so dark Kara could only make out the kids' shapes when they were just close enough to the house. She no longer heard the squeals of her children who were catching fireflies at a quicker pace, now that the flashing lights were everywhere. Her ears were wide open to what went on beyond the lawn, hearing the wildlife that had fully awakened within the boundaries of the woods. She heard scampering somewhere near the trees they had gotten too close to. Her eyes were trained on the blackness of the woods now, listening intently to the rustling of the underbrush and the scampering bodies. She heard an animal scream, her cue to go inside.

"We're getting bit by mosquitos now," she said, ushering Jack and Lilah toward the house. "Come on. Now."

Inside, she locked the backdoor and settled the kids in front of the TV. She made them popcorn and hesitated, gripping onto the filled bowl, her back on the French door.

She trained her ears, but didn't look outside. It wasn't that she heard anything concerning, it was just she didn't want to look out at the night. She felt like she had been thrust into a spotlight, on display to whatever lived in the night. She supposed the feeling was silly, part of her natural paranoia, and tried to ignore it as she set the bowl down on the coffee table near the kids. But she didn't glance out the dark windows as she pulled the drapes shut, nor as she passed the backdoor on her way through to the kitchen.

She pulled the kitchen and dining room curtains closed, averting her eyes so that she only looked at the fabric, then headed to her bedroom. She flipped on the light and was grateful she had thought to close the drapes earlier.

Such a scaredy cat, she scolded herself. She stood for a moment, twisting a hand in the other, her thoughts for once not on the memory box on the dresser, a mere five feet from her. She felt restless, uncertain what it was she wanted to do. Ultimately, after some internal debate, she decided on taking a bath. She had lavender bath salt; perhaps, that mixed with warm water could help her relax.

She flipped on the bathroom light and closed the bathroom door. Thinking of the kids, she left the door unlocked, in the event they needed her. She turned on the tub faucet, then opened the door to the closet that was across the room beside the shower stall, and flipped on the light: nobody there. She hadn't thought there would've been someone lurking in there, but checking made her feel better. She undressed and sank into the tub, resting her head against the cool porcelain. Steam from the hot water rose around her. She closed her eyes, promising herself the night would pass quickly and John would be home soon. It was silly to feel that way; she had no justification to be on edge. Her mother had worked late nights throughout her upbringing. Why was she so nervous now?

She opened her eyes and soaped up a washcloth. It wasn't normal for John to spend nights away from home. Her thoughts went dark. What if he wasn't really working? What if he was actually doing something else: having an affair?

She quashed the thought. There were no signs of that. But…would she have thought that if it wasn't true? Was this a hint of woman's intuition?

No.

She was positive he was being honest about work. Why would they have bothered moving to their dream home if he wanted to be away so often?

Unless he wanted to keep her far away.

She thought about that. Is that why they had moved away from the city? But who could he be having an affair with?

The thought made her queasy. Besides, she couldn't imagine him straying. She had never even caught him looking at another woman. He was a devoted husband and father, her ally. Well, she corrected, he hadn't been her ally as of late, not when she mentioned Sophie.

She rinsed her hair, suddenly wondering if this was the conclusion her mother would make if she knew John was out late at night. Her mother, the cynic, of course she'd assume he was cheating. It brought Kara shame, as if she was siding with Margaret over John in her moment of distrust.

John was working, he had a deadline fast approaching. They'd be back to normal soon.

The water was too hot to bear anymore and she was sick of thinking he was someplace other than the office. Kara got out of the tub and wrapped herself in a towel. She turned off the light and opened the door, the light from the master bedroom wrapping a wide band across the tiled bathroom floor. She returned to the tub and sat on its edge, wiping perspiration from her face, relaxing as the bedroom's coolness drifted in.

John's at work; he's a hard worker, give him a break.

She took a deep breath and released it before standing up. She reached toward the counter for her nightshirt, freezing as her fingers touched the fabric, but then she pulled her hand away.

Someone was watching her.

Her eyes darted over the bathroom. The doors to the shower and closet were still closed. But, she realized, she hadn't thought to check the shower earlier. Goosebumps covered her arms.

She snatched the towel without looking and pressed it against her front before approaching the shower door. The glass was clear, but that didn't help in the dark room. Holding her breath, she reached out and, in one swift movement, pulled the shower door open. She jumped back, her wide eyes as she looked in the small space. It was empty.

But still, someone watched.

She stepped into the tub, still draining water. The curtains were closed against the decorative window, but there was a gap between the two panels. Careful not to disturb the material, she peered out.

She gasped. Someone was outside.

The figure, the black shape of a person, stood just beyond the shelter of the tree-line, its dark silhouette outside of the lamppost's beam at the driveway's edge. Kara ducked down. Her heartbeat thundered in her ears; it was all she could hear. She reached out to the countertop and grabbed her nightshirt, quickly pulling it on, then peered outside again. Only her eyes and the top of her head cleared the sill. The figure was gone.

Kara scanned the trees, her eyes wildly searching. But all she saw were trees.

Had she imagined it? Had it been a tree?

She stepped out of the tub and wiped up the water she had dripped onto the floor with her bath towel. She folded the damp towel and draped it over the tub's edge, then climbed back in the basin. She drew in a breath and held it. Slouched, she peered through the curtains again.

The figure had returned.

171

She cried out in surprise. It was in the same spot as before. Did he want her to know he was there? Could he see her staring back?

"Mommy!" The bathroom light snapped on.

Kara's knees gave, bringing her down to a squat below the window sill.

Lilah didn't notice how the color had drained from Kara's face. "Jack ate all the popcorn!"

Kara slipped awkwardly out of the tub, hunched out of sight of the window, and flipped the light off.

"Mommy?"

"Just a second." Kara stepped gingerly into the tub and peered outside again. The figure was gone or had moved out of view. Her eyes searched the darkness, willing it not to show up again. She saw no one in the yard nor driveway. Was he hiding in the woods?

"Mommy?"

Kara left the bathroom and Lilah snatched her statue from the end of the bed. She followed her mother into the foyer. Kara listened for odd noises, ignoring the steady drone of the refrigerator and the chattering TV. She didn't hear a maniac trying to gain entry into their house; she didn't hear the rattling of the doorknob twisting. She crept into the office as Lilah stood at the foot of the stairs, watching questioningly. Kara peered out the curtained window. She couldn't see the side of the house, but she could see the wide expanse of the front lawn and the entire length of the porch. The porch light revealed no movement outside, except for a litter of fluttering moths. Darkness covered the front lawn and Seter Road.

He could be behind the oak, she thought, her eyes analyzing the sides of the tree that stood dead-center with the front door. The light fell short of its trunk.

Her eyes moved over the porch again, the swing, and then back to the oak.

She saw nobody.

Was it another prank?

She closed the curtain, thinking about calling John. But what could he do? She could make a plea for him to come home; but if she did, it would take him at least an hour to get there.

Should she call the police? Would she be able to describe what she saw...or thought she saw? Maybe it really had just a tree.

Or what if it was David?

But why was she thinking of David as the Boogeyman? He had never threatened her....that she knew of anyway.

Kara confirmed the front door was secured by twisting the knob and eyeing the locks before ushering Lilah into the master bedroom. She sat with her on the bed, trying to steady her breathing.

You saw trees, only trees.

"Jack ate all the popcorn?" Kara asked, striving to return to the mundane brightly-lit bedroom.

Lilah held the statue by the girl's head with both hands, rocking it back and forth. "Yeah."

"Aww. I'd make you more, but I think you're tired. Are you sleepy?"

"Yeah," Lilah admitted, then whined, "When's Daddy coming home?"

"He's working late." *Not coming home tonight at all*, she left unspoken. "You can sleep here tonight."

"Okay." Lilah crawled under the covers, tucking the statue completely underneath.

"I'll be right back. Let me see if Jack's ready for bed too." *Tell me if you hear anything*, Kara wanted to say.

Grasping her cellphone, Kara went into the great room. Jack was on the couch sleeping, covered by a throw blanket. Her eyes darted to the playroom door. She was grateful it was closed. She flipped off the TV and decided against waking Jack. This time she looked out the backdoor window, checking for her Boogeyman, if he existed. To her relief, she saw no one passing through the yard nor stationed near what she could see of the woods. She returned to her bedroom, flipped off the light, and hesitated at the foot of the bed. The goosebumps had faded from her arms. Her body was starting to calm down, she was beginning to believe she had imagined it. But still, she went into the bathroom and, leaving the light off, opened the door to the walk-in closet. She flipped on the light and scanned the hanging clothes before looking at the floor beneath them. No one was hiding there.

She turned and started to exit, her hand poised on the light switch, when her eyes went to the mirror on the other side of the bathroom. It wasn't her face she saw.

She inhaled sharply. She saw, for a split-second, another image, the flash of another face, and then it was gone. In its place was her stunned expression. Her heart had struck up its beat again and she stood there, dumbfounded, staring at herself in the mirror.

You're tired, she finally reasoned with herself after she had stood there motionless for several minutes. *You haven't slept well in so long. You're functioning on fumes.*

She accepted that, because what else could she think, and flipped off the light and closed the closet door. She mustered what courage she had left and peeped out the bathroom window. The figure had not returned. The lamppost stood guard over the yard, a beacon of steadfast protection. She stared outside for a long while, trying to hear beyond the crickets who were now chirping.

She went around the house once more, checking locks, and then turned off the great room light for Jack's sake. She kept all the other first floor lights on. The broken window in the bonus room challenged her nerves, but she checked the three layers of plastic Tom had taped over the hole. It would be crazy for someone to climb up to the second floor, wouldn't it? There were no trees that close to the house, so the intruder would have to bring their own ladder to get in. That wouldn't happen, right?

She forced herself to go to bed and not worry about it. Glancing at her cellphone, she was dismayed the "No service" message flashed, but she still kept it by her side. She pulled the blanket up and closed her eyes, waiting for morning.

John came home after 10 a.m. He had also had a sleepless night for much different reasons, and went straight to bed. Three cups of coffee revived Kara enough to visit the lamppost. She didn't know what she was looking for (footprints, binoculars, a cigarette?), but there was nothing out of the ordinary. She changed direction from the driveway and walked to the location of where she had seen him (her?...it?) standing. She eyed the ground where the grass met the gravel and then looked back at the house, using the figure's supposed vantage point. The bathroom curtains were still closed as she had left them the night before.

The house sat at a higher elevation from where she stood, so it was a relief to realize no one could stand at the window and peer in. She paced some more, went to the edge of the woods, looking through the trees and at the ground. Returning to the driveway, she surveyed the gravel, but her untrained eye saw no evidence of a prowler. Eventually, she gave up her search and headed toward the porch. She glanced at the house next door and, glimpsing Diane in an orange top, she changed course and crossed the yard. On hands and knees, the older woman pulled weeds from a flowerbed that bordered her screened porch.

"Good morning!" Kara called as she approached.

Diane looked up and sat back on her heels, wiping her forearm across her nose. "Good morning." Her husky voice was loud and carried well beyond Kara's nearness.

"Those are beautiful."

"Begonias," Diane said, allowing a prideful smile at the delicate blooming pastels.

"I need to get around to planting some flowers myself."

Diane didn't reply, looking expectantly at Kara.

Awkwardly, Kara cleared her throat. "So, the weirdest thing happened last night. I was taking a bath…Well, right after my bath, I looked out the window and I-I think I saw somebody. Someone was in my yard last night."

Diane's eyes narrowed. "How do you mean? Someone was walking through your yard?"

"No, someone was watching me. Well," Kara, blushing, amended, "someone was standing in my yard. I think I was being watched. It was dark, but…"

"Are you sure you saw someone? You don't know who it was?" Diane looked at her critically.

Is this woman doubting me? Kara asked herself. *Am I doubting me?*

Kara stumbled over her words, "Well, I-I saw someone. It was dark. I was just wondering if you saw anything."

"Have I seen any peeping Toms?" Diane tilted her head to peer around Kara, looking out at the Tamesons' yard.

"Yeah. Or have there been any break-ins around here that you've heard of?"

Diane shook her head, frowning. "Seter Lane's always been quiet. Nothing I've noticed as being out of the ordinary. Must've been your imagination. Was it late?"

Kara looked down the road, her eyes moving over houses she could see from there, dotting the neighborhood, as if she'd find some sign of distress. But they were quiet; the hilly countryside was peaceful as a whole, looking as if nothing untoward could happen there. She returned her gaze to Diane's property, her eyes resting on a pair of dirty men's sneakers sitting on the bottom porch step.

Diane followed the gaze. "Those are my Matthew's. He's staying with us for a couple days. Matthew's a little troubled, but I think we've already discussed that." Diane's expression turned serious. "He's harmless. He knows not to bother folks. I'm sure of that." She turned away and resumed work in the flowerbed.

Kara didn't want to sound accusatory, but she also didn't want to be regarded as a pushover that would allow a stranger hanging around her home at night. Delicately, she asked, "Do you think he may have been the one I saw last night?"

Diane, bent over the flowers, twisted her head. Her eyes narrowed. "He was with Marvin and me last night watching television. Matthew doesn't bother anyone."

Kara waited a beat before pressing on, laughing superficially, "Oh, alright. Actually, if it were him last night, I'd feel a lot better. I'd at least know I didn't have some creeper watching me." She knew it sounded bad. Diane turned away and busily patted the soil around her flowers. She was dismissing her.

Kara hadn't meant to offend her, which somehow she had. When she had walked to the edge of the property line, Diane called, not looking over, "Kara?"

Kara turned around.

"Leave my son alone."

Kara watched Diane for a moment before crossing into her yard.

Chapter Seventeen

"Ooh, how cute!" Tracy crooned.

She and Kara took in the wide, first-floor storefront window of Buried Treasures. An aged secretary desk was showcased with worn paperbacks and writing implements on its tabletop, set in front of a faux schoolhouse backdrop. Tracy went to the door as Kara stood back on the sidewalk, gazing up at long, narrow windows set into the second and third floors of the lavender building. She froze when she saw the flag suspended from the second floor. Underneath the store's moniker on it was a whimsical caricature of a frog, squatting with one leg extended to the side and a girl beside it, carrying a parasol.

Tracy pointed at the rusted, brass doorknob that was chest-high. "This is so cute." She pulled the door open. "How could a kid reach this?"

Kara didn't comment, but followed her indoors, pretending the flag wasn't similar to the statue Lilah carried around with her.

Wind chimes over the door tinkled as they entered the store, an open room filled with shelves of miscellanea. Kara looked around, surprised there were no other customers that Saturday afternoon.

"Hi!" They heard the woman before they saw her. Bespectacled, she came out from behind a counter tucked near the back. "Welcome to Buried Treasures. Is there anything I can help you with? I'm running a sale on arrowheads." She smiled pleasantly, clasping her hands together.

"Hi," Kara and Tracy replied.

Kara glanced briefly beyond the clerk, taking in the shelves stacked with pails and oil canvases depicting colonials and Redcoats. Tracy didn't stray far from the entrance, finding interest in a floor-to-ceiling bookcase displaying dolls, dollhouses, and wind-up toy cars.

"We're just looking," Kara replied. Browsing through the front of the store, she stopped short, noticing a tin sign on the wall. It depicted a partially-clothed blonde leaning, grinningly, against the hood of a cherry red 1957 Chevy Bel Air.

"Not everything is to everyone's taste," the clerk chuckled. "But, I assure you, there's something you'll like here."

"This place is so cute." Kara moved on, glancing over a glass case carrying an assortment of thimbles made of brass, porcelain, and what looked to be paper. Her eyes drifted upward toward the ceiling, spotting a chandelier with beige-colored lampshades covering eight sconces. It was understated, but elegant. She knew it'd be perfect in her foyer. "Is that for sale?"

The clerk nodded enthusiastically. "My dear, everything's for sale." She came over and looked for a price tag, but when she saw there wasn't one, she bobbed her head. "I've got everything catalogued in back. If you give me a moment, I'll let you know just how much it is." She went toward the back of the shop and pointed at Tracy on her way. "Your friend also seems to have found something of interest."

Kara looked over, seeing Tracy had moved further into the store, squatting now, moving toy animals around a gray four-foot plastic barn. "Funny how it's gray and not red."

"Hmm?" Kara raised her eyebrows, walking toward her.

Tracy carefully opened and closed a hinged barn window. "When you think of barns don't you always picture them as red?"

Kara shrugged. "I guess." The sagging gray barn on Seter Lane flashed in her mind, but the image was gone as she neared the rear counter. The clerk was moving a thumb down a hardbound, handwritten ledger that took up a quarter of the countertop.

Kara looked about her and noticed a metal shelving unit filled with statues. She glanced over them, wondering if there were any similar to Lilah's. The ones displayed, however, were mostly gnomes. She took a stab, asking the clerk, "I noticed your shop sign outside with the frog and girl on it. Did you, by any chance, sell a statue resembling it?"

The clerk settled her thumb on a line of text and looked up at her. "Like the sign?" She shook her head. "I'm afraid not. Our merchandise is largely one-offs due to the subject matter of the shop. It is a charming sign, isn't it? It was here when I bought the business about five years ago. Are you interested in dolls or frogs in particular? We have dolls, but I don't think I have any frogs right now."

She started to move toward a space behind Tracy, but Kara halted her. "Oh, no. I'm interested in a specific statue that reminds me of the sign, that's all."

"Oh really?"

"Yes. I recently moved to the area and my husband dug up a statue that looks similar to your shop sign."

Her interest in antique toys spent, Tracy joined the ladies.

The clerk fixed her gaze on Kara. "You say you dug up a statue?"

"My husband and son were doing yard work when they came across a statue of a girl with an umbrella and a frog sitting at her feet. It's just like the flag outside."

"Interesting."

"I think it is." *Strange really*, Kara thought.

"I don't know of a statue being modeled off of that image." The clerk raised her eyebrows and admitted, "Or of the sign being modeled off of a statue. But that is something, isn't it?"

"My daughter's been playing with it as a doll, so I haven't analyzed it too closely, but it looks just like it."

Tracy piped up, "I wonder if it's an antique then, the statue Lilah has."

"It could be," the clerk said, glancing at her. "Especially if it was in the ground. How odd. Was it buried deep?"

Kara shook her head. "I don't think so. It couldn't have been if my husband was just weeding around the house when he found it."

"Where's your house? Here in town? I often visit neighbors who have the most interesting antiques they discovered in their attics or cellars. There is a lot of history in Gracie Town."

"I live on Seter Lane, just outside of town."

The clerk smiled. "Oh, that's a lovely road. You're a mile from the bustle, but it feels totally different. Very quiet."

Kara smiled to herself, finding it funny people could refer to Grace Township as bustling. She supposed the clerk's head would spin if she ever visited the Cosgrove Center of Science or tried to find an available parking meter in the city.

"There are some older houses on that street too," the clerk continued. "It wouldn't surprise me if an antique statue decided to unearth itself."

"Actually, Kara lives in a new-build," Tracy disclosed.

"Oh, so you're the new owner of that French country two-story."

"Yes, that's me." Kara's face grew warm at the mention. She hoped the town wasn't gossiping about her family.

"Your house is beautiful."

"Thanks. We haven't been there for long, but we like it."

"So, it doesn't make sense then that your statue would've been buried in the ground," Tracy said.

The clerk moved to the front of the store and opened the door. Kara and Tracy followed her outside where they all looked up at the flag.

"There wasn't anything on your property before they built the house, was there?" the clerk asked.

Kara shook her head. "No, I believe this was the first house built there. If I remember correctly, the deed didn't show anything was there before our house."

"There's a barn not far from you. I haven't been down that road for a while, but I think there's an old gray barn on Seter. Is that right?"

Kara nodded, picturing the barn that haunted her.

"Is the barn yours?"

"No. It's a few doors down from our place. I don't know who owns it."

"I don't know who does either. For what I do for a living, I should really know more about the places around here. Shame on me." She laughed and then pointed up at the sign. "I have a hunch that if your statue is very much like the image on this sign, then they very likely have something to do with each other. It's too coincidental and the fact that it was buried in the ground...Do you know that Seter Lane, and actually much of Grace Township, was grant land paid out to soldiers who fought in the American Revolutionary War? A lot of the land in this region was used to pay eighteenth century veterans for their service. The government needed to entice settlers to move westward to build up America and this wild country was perfect for soldiers who wanted to build westward. Maybe for some, it was to make a new start."

"So, it's possible the statue we found in our yard is as old as the eighteenth century?" Kara's head was spinning, wondering at the possibility of an artifact from hundreds of years ago found on her property. Who knew what else could be buried in the soil?

"Well, I can't say the statue you found is as old as the American Revolution, but it might be an antique. I'd have to have someone analyze it to determine its age. Would you mind bringing it in so I can take a look?"

"Oh, that'd be interesting, Kara," Tracy cooed. "Maybe it's worth something."

Kara replied, "Well, I'd have to see if Lilah would be okay with that first. It's hers."

"Well," the clerk said, "I'd be interested in seeing it. Perhaps, I can get in touch with the former shop owner to find out the story behind the sign, as well as behind your daughter's toy. If they're connected, that is."

Returning inside, the clerk disappeared through the back of the store while Kara and Tracy browsed the salesfloor.

"I can't believe you can cram so much old stuff into one room," Tracy murmured, moving toward the back.

Kara went the other way, her attention caught by a dozen wind chimes suspended from an over-emphasized window casing. She weaved her hand among their metal tubes, making every set spring to life in their unique tones. She was turning over the paper price tag tied around one of the tubes when Tracy's cellphone dinged.

A moment later, Tracy's voice came from somewhere on the other side of a bureau, "Hey, where are you?" She wended through stacks of dusty books and around a rusty tricycle before stopping next to Kara. "Hey, I just got a text from Margaret."

Kara turned to look at her. "My mom?"

"Yeah. I told her I'd be out here with you."

"She's not coming here, is she?"

"She can if you want her to."

"Why would I want that?"

"You guys haven't seen each other for a while, right?"

"We talked recently." Not that it was much of a conversation, given the fact her mother had hung up on her. "I'm surprised she didn't tell you," Kara muttered.

"Oh, really?" Tracy smiled and clapped her hands together, irritating Kara. "That's great! I'm glad you talked. I think it hurt her not being invited to your housewarming party."

Kara threw up her hands. "How did she know I had a party? Didn't we talk about this?"

"Well, I don't really get why you didn't want—" Tracy's phone dinged. Another text message. After Tracy had texted back, she said to Kara, "She wants to go shoe shopping today. Want to come? She can come out here, if you want."

"No thanks." It was weird Tracy and her mother were friends. It was on the verge of disturbing. Apparently, Tracy was the daughter Margaret should've had; at least, as long as Tracy was unmarried anyway.

Tracy looked imploringly at Kara. "You look like hell, if I'm going to be honest with you. Something's off. If you're having any problems right now…If you feel you can't confide in me, then maybe talk to your mom."

Confide in her mom? Was she nuts? They didn't have that sort of relationship, and after thirty-two years, Kara didn't see it changing now. Besides, she was pretty sure telling her mother how she had been feeling would end up with her being reminded again she shouldn't have married John. She'd feel worse.

Kara asked with irritation, "Does she know we're talking about this right now?"

She doesn't, and I didn't promise her anything. I just said maybe we all could get together today."

"Maybe? Really?"

"Will you talk to her?"

Kara's words were stunted, a pause between each word, "I do not want to talk to her." Margaret was still withholding information about David, and Kara was over it.

"See it from her side. You did just up and leave her, not only you, but her grandkids too. She has virtually nobody now. Do you see how crummy that is?"

Kara scowled. "You don't know our history. Just don't get involved."

Tracy crossed her arms over her chest. "You're right. I don't know how it is. Why don't you tell me?"

Kara scoffed. "Has my mom told you anything?" She tried not to think about the lunchtime chats they had behind her back. Any discussion about Kara had to be negative if it came from Margaret.

"No, she doesn't talk either. But you guys should. I hate to say this, but maybe moving away from her wasn't a good idea. You're all she has. Would you ever consider moving back?"

Kara was flabbergasted. What an absurd thing to suggest. Her face was hot. Move so her mother could act as she always had? There was nothing to go back to. She could get that same exchange over the phone.

After a moment, Tracy said, "You really don't look good. You look worn. What's going on?"

"Just stop. I'm done. It's none of your business and I'm just done. You can hang out with my mom, I don't care. When I feel like it and when she feels like it, we'll talk."

Tracy sighed, holding up her cellphone. "What do you want me to tell her?"

"You can tell her the truth, that I don't want to see her today."

"Alright." Tracy dutifully texted Margaret back. There was some back-and-forth texting before Tracy looked up and said, "Okay, I'm going to shop with her when I get back."

"If I want to see her, I'll ask her to come out myself. Did she even want to come?"

"I'm sure she would've come."

"It was your idea, wasn't it?" When Tracy didn't answer right away, Kara said, "Just please don't interfere with our relationship."

Tracy mumbled, "Okay, I won't."

The clerk returned, oblivious to the tense exchange. "I found the price of the chandelier. If you come back with me to the counter, I can ring you up."

Kara followed her, asking, "Can I take it home today?"

"Certainly, but you'll need some help lifting it. It's very heavy."

"I'm sure we can do it." *That's all I'll ever ask of Tracy again*, Kara thought bitterly. It would probably do her well to take a break from her meddling friend, at least until she figured out what her mother's intentions concerning David were.

The clerk opened the ledger to a handwritten page, almost all of its lines filled. "There we are. Just write your name, phone number, and address, and I'll ring you up." She turned the book toward Kara and offered a pen.

Kara had filled in her information and was turning the book back around when her eyes fell on a name written near the top of the page. She laid her finger on the line below Shannon's name.

Kara looked up with a smile, easing the book back toward the clerk. "Sorry, I just noticed the name of someone I know."

Chapter Eighteen

Kara's pace had slowed as the days progressed. Her eyes burned and she saw shadows lurking sometimes—inside the house and outside. She tried not to be alarmed; they always subsided. There had been no more sign of the shadowed figure, which by then, Kara had chalked up as having been part of her imagination.

After she dropped Lilah off at school, Kara went to her bedroom, wanting to do nothing but sleep dreamlessly. She looked at the bed with its crumpled, silky sheets, and knew she'd never sleep, wouldn't be able to relax. Standing there, her ears were tuned to the settling sighs of the house and the hollow knocking of a woodpecker outside.

She turned around and settled a hand on the memory box, pausing a moment before pulling back the lid. She hovered over, close to the neatly-folded, striped receiving blanket, and inhaled its scent. Sophie's baby powder smell lingered. She closed her eyes and was back in the hospital. Instead of the backs of her eyelids, she saw a long corridor with a gray-and-white speckled floor. The nurses' station abutted another hallway that ran perpendicular; wide, brown, numbered doors dotted her peripheral. A sign on the wall read, "Maternity" with an arrow pointing to the left.

She had forgotten her room's number—it didn't matter now anyway. Her room had a window with a view of the roof and the fifth floor of the building next door. Across the way she could see the south wing. Theirs was newer, four floors higher and perched with heart patients who looked upon the drab maternity building where she was housed temporarily.

Her room smelled heavily of disinfectant and there was a TV attached to the wall in the corner. John napped on the couch, which was too narrow for his broad shoulders, while they waited for her to dilate to 10. They had been there for over 18 hours; she, with John by her side, had waddled around the corridor, pushing an IV stand. It felt like their new home, they got so familiar with the patients they passed and the constant noises of the murmuring TVs in other rooms.

Pushing the baby out had been frightening, but exciting. Kara paused and pushed for nearly an hour, her angle of John's face above her changing from excitement to worry to confusion. When she had delivered, the room had grown eerily quiet, and then it was empty of hospital personnel. The nursery warmer and the infant were gone too, no longer in Kara's room.

The doctor told Kara and John that Sophie had lived for three minutes, but there was nothing they could do to keep her heart pumping on its own. Puzzling things like this happened sometimes, unfortunately. In their case, it was a tragedy no one saw coming. When Kara held Sophie after being told the news, she wondered if the doctor was wrong. The infant she cradled in her arms was pink-cheeked. How did she not breathe? Her daughter with fine, blonde wisps of hair, her eyes forever closed, was dead.

A thump brought Kara back to the present where she still stood in her bedroom. She blinked dry eyes and, hearing something tap, closed the memory box. She returned it to the dresser before going down the hallway. She saw movement through toile that covered the sidelight of the front door and cautiously moved to it.

She pulled the fabric back slightly to peek out at the same time a man's face came close to the window. They both jerked back in surprise. He backed up and waved. It took her a moment to recognize him. She waved back, wondering why Desmond Howard was standing on her porch. He wasn't asking her again about the Collumber house, was he? She unlocked the door and he backed down to the sidewalk.

"Hi, Kara!" he said a little too enthusiastically. Smiling, he ran his hand over his mustache and over his jaw, before dropping his arm to his side.

"Hi."

"Ahem! I was just checking in. I see the mum is still in bloom." He gestured to the potted plant beside the door. "Still thinking of moving to a mansion?" He wiggled his eyebrows and chuckled.

She gave a short laugh. "No, that was a mistake to call. I hope you weren't waiting long. I didn't hear the doorbell."

"I knocked." He combed his hand through the side part of his short brown hair and shuffled his feet. He looked over the house and then toward the driveway where his sedan sat, its engine idling. The moment felt awkward to Kara, as she watched him surveying the property. Finally, as if remembering she was standing across from him, he turned back to her, the smile having faded. "I'm happy you're still enjoying the house. You *are* still happy?"

"I...yes. We're still happy here."

"No complaints, hmm?" His smile broadened again, but didn't quite reach his eyes.

Her smile fell. "Everything's fine."

"The Collumber house is still for sale!" he chuckled, then he cleared his throat. "Well, fantastic! You have a great property." He backed down the sidewalk. "Call me if you have any questions or concerns, and feel free to pass my name along to friends and family."

She went back inside, regretting again that she had dialed his phone number, asking about the Collumber house. She hoped this was the last time he'd be checking in. He was an awkward man in general and she could do without the visits.

When John called just after four, she brought him to speed on Desmond, wondering aloud if his coming around was normal.

"I don't know, I've never bought a house before," John replied. "He's probably just looking for referrals. Maybe the housing market is still rough."

"He's just weird."

John laughed. "Yeah, a little."

"So. Why am I the lucky recipient of this afternoon call?" She was suspicious of the reason for the call and he proved her suspicions correct.

"The team came up with a new strategy today. I want to try it…tonight." He explained it'd be another late night and that he'd try to make it home, but he'd call again if it ended up being another overnight.

"You know I don't like being home alone."

"I know."

She confessed, "I thought I saw someone the last time…by the driveway."

"You did?"

"Well, I think I did. I don't know. I'm not sure. But I don't like you being away all night. What if it was someone watching us?"

"What did they look like?"

"I don't know, it was dark. It may have been a tree, okay?" she laughed, but at the back of her mind, she still wondered what she had seen.

"I'll try to come home tonight. You know I'd rather not work this late, but this project—it's the first one I'm leading. I just want it to go alright."

"I know, and it will."

"Call the police if you see someone out there."

After she hung up, Kara checked on the kids. They played in Jack's room. He was at the head of his bed, playing with a building set and Lilah was on the floor nearest the closet, playing with the statue and her stuffed, pink unicorn. It pleased Kara to see she played with something in addition to the statue. It felt healthier for some reason.

"Hey guys, Daddy's working late again tonight."

Jack's head whipped up. "Again?"

"Yeah."

"Why?"

"He's working on a big project."

"Daddy always works late," Lilah said, nonchalantly. Her tiny fingers twisted a lavender ribbon in the unicorn's white yarn mane.

Jack added, "Yeah, since we moved here."

"Daddy doesn't like this house," Lilah said simply.

Kara watched her as she struggled to tie the ribbon, her matter-of-fact statement giving her pause. Was there truth in that? Did John not like the house? "Why do you say that, Lilahbean?"

"What's for dinner?" Jack grumbled.

Lilah shrugged. "What's for dinner?"

Kara watched her for a moment, but saw she wouldn't get anything else out of her. "How does fried chicken sound?"

"Pizza," Jack said.

"Ja-ack," Kara's voice sing-songed. "We've had a lot of pizza lately."

"I want pizza!" Lilah jumped to her feet, the unicorn rolling from her lap onto the floor. The statue remained in her hands.

"Pizza! Pizza! Pizza!" Jack started the chant and Lilah joined in.

"Okay, okay! We'll get pizza!" Kara gave in, backing out of the bedroom. When they followed her, continuing their chant, Kara warned, "If you guys want pizza, you need to stop saying that."

They finally stopped the chant when they entered the kitchen, breaking into laughter. They hovered around until she popped a frozen pepperoni pizza into the oven, as if they needed visual confirmation.

Kara sat at the kitchen table, crossing her arms. "Now what should we do?"

"I'm going outside!" Jack announced, going out the backdoor.

"Only for twenty minutes," Kara called as he closed the door. She noticed Lilah still held tight to the statue. "Can I see your doll?"

Lilah moved away.

"Lilah, why can't I see her?"

"She's mine."

"I just want to see her."

"I want to go play."

Broaching the subject of the antique shop, Kara asked, "Would you mind if I had somebody look at it?"

Lilah's eyes narrowed. "Huh-uh. She's mine."

"I know she's yours, but I know somebody who wants to see her, to see how special she might be."

Lilah hugged to statue to her chest. "No!"

"Lilah."

"I wanna play!" Lilah whined, turning away.

Kara sighed. "Alright." She didn't want to touch it anyway, even though she knew it was strange to feel such abhorrence to a sculpted hunk of clay. There was something about the molded faces, their grins were creepy. She hated the sound of it rolling around on the floor of her car every time she dropped Lilah off at school, as if it was a boulder thumping from side to side. To have to carry it, feeling its surprisingly heavy weight as she touched the rough texture and the contrasting smoothed masking tape that covered its mid-section as she handed it to the shop clerk, gave her the willies.

Her cellphone rang then and seeing the name displayed on the screen made her smile.

"Hey, Shannon!"

"How are you guys?"

"Me and the kids are just hanging out, getting ready for dinner. John's working late tonight."

"Oh, I'm sorry. I don't want to interrupt dinner."

"No, that's alright. It's still in the oven. What's up?"

"Not much. Tom went out with some guys and I'm bored."

"You can come over if you want. I could use some grownup conversation."

"That sounds nice actually. Are you sure?"

Was she sure? She was *relieved*. "Come on over."

"Okay, I'll be there in a little bit. I have wine!"

"Okay, see you soon."

Another grownup in the house. She was such a scaredy cat.

Jack came inside, slamming the backdoor behind him, "Mom? Can Alan come over?"

The more, the merrier, she thought. "Sure, and you guys can go swimming, if you want."

She went to the oven, not noticing Jack shift his weight or move his eyes over the window. "Yeah, maybe."

"Sunscreen, boys," Kara said, tossing the tube to Jack an hour later. "I don't care if the sun will be going down soon, coat yourselves. We'll be watching from the kitchen."

Jack watched her go inside, leaving Alan and him on the deck. He looked over the trees bordering the lawn and stole a glance at the swimming pool. The water rippled leisurely.

Alan dabbed sunscreen over his arms and pulled goggles on and Jack carefully worked the lotion in over his belly. He picked up a scuba diver action figure and held it in both hands, watching Alan climb down into the pool.

"Do you swim underwater?" Alan asked.

Jack crept closer to the edge, eyeing the blue surface. Something had kept him away for weeks. He knew he had seen something; it had touched him and Lilah.

Looking in, he saw only Alan bobbing around. "Yeah," Jack finally replied. He approached the ladder, looking at the screws that fastened it to the pool. There were no strands of hair there. He climbed up, hesitating at the top.

"Are you getting in?" Alan squinted at the sun.

Jack looked over the pool edge and in the water. It was just an ordinary swimming pool. Nobody but Alan floated in the water. Jack nodded, shaking away his misgivings and jumped in. The water lapped around him. He looked over the surface again, seeing it was ordinary water. He was just in the pool in his backyard. He was with Alan and everything was normal.

They swam underwater to prove they could. While Jack swam the left length of the pool, the action figure in his hand, Alan headed to the right. They held their breath for as long as possible, seeing how much distance they could tread. Jack didn't wear goggles and the water was a bit murky, but he relaxed in the coolness wrapping around him. When he got to the end of the pool, he stood up tall, waiting for Alan to come up for air.

When Alan popped up, Jack held the scuba diver over his head. "Okay, I'm going to throw this man into the water and we have to see who can find him first."

"Okay!" Alan called, adjusting his goggles.

"One, two...three!" Jack threw the action figure as far as he could, toward the far edge of the pool. Both boys dove underwater and swam, searching for it.

After several seconds, Alan came up as the victor. "Got it!"

Jack scowled. "Okay, count to three and throw it."

"One...two...three!"

Jack dove into the water, anticipating the diver's descent. But Alan waited an extra moment before throwing it toward the center of the pool. Goggle-less, the water was too cloudy for Jack to see clearly. He pushed leaf bits and dead bugs away from his face, but he had no idea where the toy was. He hadn't taken a deep-enough breath and so came up for air a moment later. He was about to go under again when Alan's head popped up.

Alan shot his arm out, revealing he had the diver. "Want to do it again?"

"No goggles this time," Jack said, chirping off the new rule.

"Why not?"

"Because I don't have any and it's hard to see."

"Oh, okay," Alan said, seeing no problem with making the game fair.

As Alan swam to the ladder to drop off his goggles, Jack stood, his eyes on the shadowed trees. Insects rattled, the noise all at once loud and irritating. The wind had picked up and the topmost branches of the skinnier trees waved to the pull of the breeze, their leaves wiggling. His eyes scanned the offshoots before settling on a white scarf. It was high and it must've weighed more than the leaves, because it didn't move. He wondered for a fleeting moment why it was there.

"Alright, I'm ready," Alan said, grabbing Jack's attention. Alan had moved to the center of the pool.

Jack said, "Okay, count," but part of his mind stayed with the rattling insects.

"One, two…three!" Alan tossed the diver over Jack's head, and both boys dove under, murky to both of them this time.

Jack swam to the bottom, feeling blindly along the floor. He saw Alan swim close to him, moving his hands through the water. Jack turned and swam a yard farther, still holding his breath, searching. He was losing air and soon buoyed up.

He popped out of the water and sucked in air, choking on it when he caught a flash of yellow beyond the tree-line. He looked away while his coughing fit ran its course, then turned back to the woods. The yellow was gone. His eyes combed upward until he spotted the drooping white scarf. He noticed then the insects had silenced.

"Did you find it?" Alan asked, his eyes gliding over Jack.

Jack shook his head no.

Alan dove back down, splashing Jack's face. Jack wiped his chlorine-stung eyes and sank underwater. He swam away from Alan. He didn't think the plastic diver could've slipped this far from the center of the pool, but he swam away anyway. The water was hazy, but the sunlight worked its way to highlight the indigo-and-orange figure the boys sought.

Jack had no other strategy than to move his arms around, hoping to strike something hard and small. Where was it?

He turned and swam in Alan's direction. He could see the outline of his friend's legs, skinny and kicking.

Something tugged on Jack's leg. It couldn't have been Alan, because he was ahead of him. Jack changed direction. It couldn't have been the pool filter. It wasn't that strong and he wasn't anywhere near the far corner where it was. He swam to the ladder, coming up for air. Stepping on the bottom step, he felt something fuzzy wrapped around his toes. He climbed up, pulling his foot out of the water.

"I got it!" Alan shot up, holding up the plastic diver. "What's that?" he asked, looking from the confused expression on Jack's face to the floss the boy pulled from his toes.

Jack held it up and both boys saw they were long strands of blonde hair.

Something shrieked, making Jack scramble to the grass.

"Jack? Why you gettin' out?"

Jack heard Alan's question, but couldn't comprehend him. He hurried to the deck and opened his fist to release the hair. But when he looked, it was gone.

"Jack?" Alan climbed up the ladder.

"D-did you hear that?" Jack whispered, his eyes combing the pool's surface.

"What?"

Jack's eyes went to the trees, but he didn't think it had come from the woods. The sound had come from the water, shooting up from below. It reverberated inside him. "That scream."

"What scream? I didn't hear anything." Alan was looking around now, scanning the trees. "Huh?"

"I don't want to swim anymore."

"That was pretty good pizza, huh, Lilah?" Shannon asked, smiling.

Lilah nodded shyly before whispering to Kara she wanted to play.

"Go ahead," Kara said.

"She's so cute," Shannon said, watching Lilah walk down the hallway, the statue hanging from one hand at her side.

"I think she's in a shy phase right now."

"Is that a phase?"

"Yeah, I think so."

Shannon got up and squatted next to the antique chandelier. It leaned lopsidedly on the tiled floor near the far kitchen wall. "Is this replacing the light in the foyer?" She touched a sconce.

Kara nodded, sipping wine. "Yeah. I actually got that from Buried Treasures last weekend."

"Oh, so you got to check it out. How'd you like it?"

"It's a really cute shop. I can't wait to take down that God-awful teat we have hanging in the foyer!" Kara groaned with a laugh.

"Teat?" Shannon looked down the hallway to glimpse the dangling, brassy chandelier. She broke out in laughter. "I don't think it looks like that! But this is a pretty light."

"It does! It's awful. I can't wait for John to switch it out. Oh! I have to tell you about their sign! Buried Treasures's."

"What about it?"

"You know Lilah's statue?"

Shannon nodded, sitting down at the table.

"This is going to sound bizarre, but I swear her statue has to be connected to the girl and frog on their sign."

"How do you mean?"

"So, we dug up the statue in the yard. It's the creepiest thing, but she loves it. Anyway, when Tracy and I went to Buried Treasures and saw the sign out front, it was so uncanny. The girl and the frog on the sign look just like the statue."

"Really?" Shannon leaned on her elbows. "I haven't noticed. But then again, I haven't gotten a good look at Lilah's statue."

"Lilah won't even let me look at it. The lady at the store wants to see if it's an antique, but I don't think Lilah would ever part with it."

"She knows something about it?"

"She seemed pretty clueless about it. She wants to have somebody look at it, though." Kara sat back and folded her arms. "It's just the weirdest coincidence if there's no connection to their shop sign."

Shannon looked thoughtful, swirling the wine in her glass. "Unless it was some sort of popular image back in the day, copied or something. The story of the princess and the frog maybe."

Kara considered that. The statue girl held an umbrella and the frog sat at her feet. There were no crowns or anything that she could recall that might be a nod to the fairytale, but the connection could be possible.

"When are you putting up the chandelier?" Shannon asked.

"Whenever John's available," Kara sighed. "He's been working late a lot lately, because of this project. He's already had two overnights at the office. This is number three. I hate when he's out. I don't sleep very well," Kara confessed. She had the dark circles under her eyes to prove it. "I think I hear things." She laughed mirthlessly, her thoughts turning to the shadowed figure, purposely omitting, *I see things.*

"If you'd feel more comfortable having another adult around, I don't mind sleeping over. I know Tom wouldn't miss me. He'll be out most of the night anyway."

"That's okay. I've got the kids. We're fine. I'm just a coward."

"I don't mind, really."

Without further prompting, Kara grasped at the straw being handed to her. "If you really don't think Tom would mind..."

"He won't care. I'll call him to break the news to him." Shannon laughed, taking another drink. "Trust me, he won't care."

"Okay, thanks. I can put you in Lilah's room. The kids are used to bunking with me anyway on these kinds of nights."

"Oh, honey, I don't want to mess with her sleep. I'm fine on the couch. It's probably more comfortable than my bed."

"She's gotten used to sleeping in my bed when John's out. You can have her room tonight."

"Okay. So, what are these noises you hear? You don't really hear anything, do you?"

Kara gasped, remembering. "I have to show you something." Remembering the LEAVE!!! note she had found taped to the door, she went into the office. But it wasn't on John's desk. She checked the wastebasket and glanced around the room, but couldn't find it. "He must've thrown it away," she said, sitting back down at the kitchen table.

"What?"

Thinking it silly now, Kara told Shannon about finding the note.

"That's unsettling," Shannon said.

"We think it's a prank."

"Has anything else happened since you moved in? Anything that could be related?"

"What do you mean?"

Shannon leaned forward, looking serious. "I don't want to make you nervous or anything, but has anything else happened that might seem threatening?"

Kara's thoughts drifted again to the shadowed figure. Was it related? Had she really seen someone? "This is all we've received. Oh," she said suddenly, "when we first moved in, someone rang the doorbell and ran away before we opened the door. John said it was probably kids playing Ding-dong Ditch."

"Hmm..."

"What?"

"Nothing. John's probably right. It's a prank. But just be careful." Seeing Kara tense up, Shannon laid a hand on her arm. "I'm not trying to scare you. I just mean in general. Everyone should be careful."

Kara drained her glass. "I hate to mention it, but...You remember how I got that text from my mom about David and how he reached out to her?"

"Yeah. What did he want?"

"I have no idea. She hasn't been forthcoming after dropping that bomb on me. She's making me sweat about it."

"Would she do that?"

"I wouldn't put it past her. Well, I don't know. She's not that vindictive. I don't know why she's not telling me anything."

Shannon's eyes widened. "You don't think there's any connection with him and the note on the door, do you?"

"No. Why would he leave a note telling me to leave?"

"Maybe it was meant for John?"

Kara looked into her empty wineglass. "But that's a bit vague, isn't it? Why wouldn't he have said anything else in the note? And why would he want John to leave?"

Shannon shrugged. "Or it was for the whole family. Maybe he wants you all back in Cosgrove so he can be close to Jack? Is he still living there?"

"I have no idea where he is. I don't think it's from him." She shook her head and said with more conviction, "It wasn't from him." She thought of the figure in the shadows again. "It was just a prank from some kids."

Chapter Nineteen

Saturday morning, Kara woke up groggy and bleary-eyed. She sat up in bed and looked around, finding herself alone. It was just after seven. She scooted off John's side of the bed and groaned.

They must've had a storm, because the windows in the master bedroom and bathroom had rattled so fiercely during the night that she had thought they would blow in. At one point during a lull, she had tiptoed to the bathroom window to spy. Was the shadow watching? The windows had fogged, so hadn't been able to see, and that had meant no one outside could see in. She had resisted the urge to check the other windows. It would've been embarrassing if Shannon had caught her creeping through the house.

Presently, she stood up, light-headed from the movement, and took a step. Her foot struck something hard, startling her more than hurting her. She looked down. It took a moment to register what it was, and when she did, she sank to the floor. What was Sophie's memory box doing on the floor?

Picking it up, she opened it. Carefully, she leafed through its contents, her remembering fingers moving over the receiving blanket before gingerly tucking it back in. Everything was there, safe and sound. She inhaled the powdery scent and closed the box. Her eyes raked over the bedroom before she set it on the dresser. Who had moved it?

She got dressed and found Lilah curled on the couch in the great room, watching TV.

"Were you playing with my white box?" Kara asked without preamble.

"No."

"Lilah, look at me."

Lilah twisted, her movement turning the familiar statue in her lap, so that three faces looked upon Kara.

Kara glanced at the clay faces that forever laughed at her before meeting Lilah's passive gaze. "Do you know the white box I'm talking about?"

"Uh-huh. The one on your dresser."

"I found it on my bedroom floor. Did you put it there?"

"No."

"You're sure?"

"No, Mommy. I want to watch my show."

"Soph—" *Damn.* Emphasizing her name, Kara said, "*Lilah*, this is important."

Lilah's blue eyes widened. "I didn't move it, Mommy."

"You're sure? You won't get in trouble."

"No, I didn't touch it."

Well then. Had Jack moved it?

"If you ever want to see it, tell me and we can look at it together." *And talk about your sister*, Kara didn't say aloud. "Okay?"

"Okay, okay." Lilah wiggled from side-to-side, her eyes drifting back to the TV screen. The statue's dual faces, however, kept its gazes on Kara. Kara turned away to break contact with it just as Shannon rushed in the room, her short blonde hair swept back and wet.

"Good morning! I took a shower, I hope you don't mind."

"Good morning." Kara started toward the sink. "No problem. Coffee?"

"I've got to run. Tom's probably wondering what happened to me. I couldn't reach him on my cell last night or this morning."

"I didn't know you couldn't reach him. My cell service is hit or miss, but we could've tried my phone."

"That's alright." Shannon grabbed her purse and car keys and headed to the front door.

Kara followed. "I wish you had told me."

"It's seriously no problem. Thanks for having me."

"Thanks for coming over. I appreciate the grownup sleepover." It was true. She would've been a wreck without her being there.

Shannon rested her hand on the doorknob, hesitating. "Did you sleep okay?"

Kara wanted to say, *I never do*, but instead said, "Yeah. Did you?"

"Yeah." Shannon pulled her hand back. "I came down in the middle of the night for some water and I heard you." She looked uncomfortable. "I think you were having a nightmare. I thought it was Lilah crying at first."

"Crying?" Had she not awoken to Lilah's nightmare?

"But I went to Lilah's side of the bed and realized it wasn't her. It was you. You stopped when I shook your shoulder. You said 'Sophie' a couple times and then you were quiet. You were clutching onto a box...Was it her memory box?"

Kara's heartbeat quickened and she studied the tiled floor without seeing it. Had she slept with the memory box? Was she the one who had put it on the floor?

"Are you okay?" Shannon asked.

Was she? Was she sleepwalking now? That was worrisome. "I'm fine," she laughed dully. "I wondered how the box got on the floor this morning."

"Want me to stay until John comes home?"

"No. Tom's probably worried about you."

"He's fine." Shannon glanced at her cellphone and showed the screen to Kara. "Look! I have a signal! I can call him and tell him I'll be home later."

"No, seriously, I'm good. I just haven't been sleeping well. I'll take a nap later today after John comes home."

"You'd better."

"I will. Now you'd better go. Tom won't let you come out and play again," Kara joked. "And hey, tell him he still owes me a window."

"Okay. I'll ask him about it. Call me if you need anything." Shannon opened the door, stepping onto the porch. "Tell Lilah and Jack I said goodbye."

"See you later." Kara closed the door, troubled. How strange she couldn't remember climbing into bed with the box. And she had been crying?

She went back to the master bedroom and plopped defeatedly onto the end of the bed, her eyes on the white box. The lid was closed, protecting Sophie's belongings inside. Had she really taken the box to bed? Why couldn't she remember?

She heard the garage door and then the sound of John whistling when he entered the house. Sighing, she got up from the bed and met John in the kitchen.

"Hey, look who's home," she said, giving him a tired smile.

"Hi, Daddy!" Lilah called from the great room.

"Hey, Lilahbean." He squatted by the chandelier and looked up at Kara. "I got a lot done last night. We seem to be on the right path."

"That was the last overnight, right?"

"Should be." He up-righted the chandelier. "Ready to get this sucker up?"

"Now? Aren't you tired?"

"I took a power nap around three this morning, like an hour. I'm good for now, so get all the work you can out of me before I collapse." He laughed, making her feel guilty.

"Well, my intention's not to work you to death."

"It's okay. I'm awake. I stopped and rented a scaffold on my way home. Thought I'd see what my new pal Marvin is doing."

"Oh, you're going to have him help?"

"It's probably a one-man job, but I'll see what he's up to." John grinned, standing.

"Or you can ask Tom. We need him to finish that window in the bonus room anyway."

205

"That's true…"

By kismet, the doorbell rang and John opened the door to Marvin. The older man slapped his hands together when John told him he was installing the light fixture.

"Happy to help," Marvin said. He looked up at the foyer ceiling, judging the height. "Unless you have a really tall ladder, I think we might need some scaffolding for that."

Kara stayed in the foyer as the men hauled pieces of the scaffold into the foyer and watched as they began assembling it, working like two peas in a pod. When she saw they didn't need her help, she returned to her bedroom, going immediately to her dresser. Without dwelling on it, not questioning her actions further, she stowed the memory box away in the top drawer. She couldn't handle it now; there was something about touching it, an energy she didn't want to be part of. There was something off…

She was exhausted, and embarrassed Shannon had seen her crying, curled up with it. She lay on her bed and closed her eyes. Thirty minutes had hardly passed when she heard a loud scuffle. She jumped up and hightailed it to the foyer.

Marvin was alone, near the ceiling, standing on the platform of the scaffold; the metal poles holding it together looked rickety.

"You okay up there?" she asked, her hands hovering near the ladder legs.

He tugged on the brassy chandelier chain, causing it to sway just above her head. "Just gettin' my land legs." Carefully, he let the slack of the chain go, and grunting, bent down to pick up a drill.

She glanced in the office and the mudroom. "Where's John?"

"Around," Marvin said before pressing the drill's trigger.

"John?" she called, going down the hallway toward the kitchen. She heard scraping coming from the unfinished playroom, the door partially open.

"Lilah?" she called, noticing the little girl was no longer watching TV. Kara hustled to the door and pushed it open the rest of the way. She looked ahead to the windows and started to turn toward the wall beside the door.

A tall figure emerged from behind a stack of four-by-ten wood beams propped against it.

Kara's hands went to her chest.

"Oh! I didn't mean to scare you."

It took her a second to recognize Tom. Slowly, she lowered her hands, blinking away the shadowed man who had appeared in her line of sight for a split-second.

Tom looked apologetic. "I was just taking a look in here, assessing for renovation."

She forced a laugh, embarrassed. "I didn't know you were here," she said, steadying her hand on the doorknob.

"I swung by to install the window upstairs. John let me in."

Having regained her composure, she clapped her hands together. "Oh, cool!" She raised her eyebrows and tilted her head. "You know, I wouldn't mind you fixing this door either. It frazzles my nerves whenever it opens. I'm starting to think we have a ghost."

"Not a problem. I can fix it today."

"Thanks. Hey, did Shannon tell you she tried calling you last night?"

"Yeah. You get bad reception, huh?"

"Sometimes. John's seems pretty good, though. Shannon was so sweet to stay with me." She didn't bother explaining she'd needed the adult sleepover due to her fear of being the only grownup home at night.

He shrugged, and at least didn't let on that he thought she was pathetic. "Sure, no problem."

"So, any idea where John is? Why is Marvin the one putting up the chandelier?" They had a man who was well past seventy standing on wobbly scaffolding without supervision. That and John's lack of sleep probably made them the worst candidates to be installing a chandelier two stories high.

Tom lowered his voice, "I can try to get him down if you want. It might hurt his pride, though. Old guys like that get offended real easy if you tell them they can't do something."

He had a point, and besides, she didn't want any more awkwardness between her and Diane in case it got back to her. "No, let him do it. But maybe someone should be out there with him." *In case he trips and falls*, she refrained from saying out loud.

"Sure, no problem."

John was back in the foyer, sitting beside Marvin, his legs dangling from the platform as he straightened the mini lampshades on the antique light fixture.

"You guys are already done?" Kara asked, surprised.

"Just about. Hey, Tom." John nodded. Then, thinking better of the situation, he gave a warning, "Don't flip the light switch until I say."

Marvin sat down, looking down at Kara and Tom, driving home the command, "We'll tell you when to turn on the light."

"While you guys are working on that," Tom said, "I'm gonna take a look at that window upstairs."

Kara waved her hand. "Awesome, thanks. You may see my monster children up there, but they're mostly harmless...mostly."

He laughed, saying, "Thanks for the warning," and jogged upstairs.

Kara had been in the kitchen for a few minutes when she heard Marvin give John the go-ahead to turn on the light. She turned around, but hadn't yet made it to the foyer when she heard a click, fizzle, and then an expletive.

She hurried down the hallway and found Marvin sitting hunched over on the platform and John standing by the light switch. She glanced at their faces, at the unlit chandelier, and then at them again.

"What happened?" she asked.

John replied, "It shorted out."

"The wiring's old," Marvin said, struggling to stand. "I thought it looked a mite frayed."

"I can rewire it for you." Tom had reappeared on the stairs' landing. "It's no big deal."

"You've done that before?" John asked him.

"Maybe we should take it back to the store, see if they'll fix it for free," Kara suggested.

"That's a good idea," John replied.

"It won't be a fire hazard hanging this old light when it's fixed, will it?" Kara asked.

"Not once the wiring is replaced," Tom replied, coming down to the floor.

"Let me pull this baby down then until we get it fixed." John climbed up the scaffold, plucked up his drill and started undoing their work.

Under the whir of the tool, Tom said to her quietly, "I wish I had gotten a look at it before they started installing. An old light like this one should've been inspected..." He shook his head. "I really do know a thing or two about houses."

"Yeah, they weren't thinking." She felt ignorant on behalf of the two men who very well could've set fire to the house. The fact that the kids were upstairs added to her worry of what could've happened. She said quietly to Tom, "I think we'll have you install it next time."

"Sure." He winked conspiratorially. "The window's in my truck. I'm gonna go get it."

Chapter Twenty

Kara dropped Lilah off at Grace School and returned to her car in the half-filled lot. She slid her key into the ignition and looked up at the Collumber house next door. Her feeling of disappointment was inexplicable, but it stayed with her. The house was still for sale, there for the taking, but she didn't have the means to take it. She was aware the feeling was absurd, but she felt it nonetheless. Her hand faltered. Lace curtains had been pulled back on the second and third floors.

Starting the car, she told herself she was ridiculous. She reversed, the statue rocking on the floor of the passenger's side. She looked out again at the house, noticing pumpkins had replaced roses in the planters sitting on the wraparound porch. She popped the car into drive and started to roll away, but as she glanced in the rearview mirror, she saw the front door to the house had opened.

She pressed hard down on the brake. Tires on another car squealed. The other driver honked at her, making her eyes dart to her front windshield, seeing the nose of his car aimed toward her. He waved his hands at her. She realized she had stopped short in front of him while he was pulling into the lot from the street.

Kara, her face burning, steered past the man who was yelling at her from behind his closed window. She pulled into the street, and glimpsed in her rearview mirror. The front door to the Collumber house had closed. She saw no one in the yard, however. She turned her attention to the road, ignoring the mocking grins of the statue girl and frog, rolling around on the floorboard.

Kara slowed dramatically, nearing the barn. She looked over at its shadowed interior, deciphering little from the weak sunlight filtering in through the window over the loft.

She passed the aloof farmhouse that exuded emptiness, as usual. An urge crept over her.

Come and see.

She reversed and parked on the side of the road where it became flat, beside the farmhouse's driveway. She got out of the car and took to the driveway, wondering faintly why she was there. The thought, however, was so far removed, she hardly acknowledged it. She climbed the drive, glancing over the treed yard, and was soon at the front walk, its cement crumbling, speckled with grass that had broken through. Her eyes scanned the curtained windows before she pulled open the screen door and knocked. Birds twittered, but there was no other sound of life. She leaned close to the door, listening. It was dead quiet: no one ran from the room to hide; no one opened the door.

She looked over at the gray barn, finding herself level with the silo behind it, and turned back to knock again, banging harder against painted steel. Nobody home.

She backed up, confident no one was there. As if that meant she had full access to view the property, she went around the house. She passed a padlocked shed, the rear of the empty driveway, and a thicket of trees before turning back toward the yard between the two properties. Beyond the barn and silo, a wide circle of evergreens stood just before the dense woods. She headed toward it, walking airily through the tall grasses, a giveaway the yard hadn't been looked after for quite some time. The evergreens didn't sway, but the ashes at the start of the woods did, their tops moving in the wind that had just picked up.

As Kara neared the circle of evergreens, her steps slowed. Her eyes drifted upward, over the treetops, to the sky. A turkey vulture landed on an ash. She stopped when she noticed a committee of the black-feathered birds had settled on the same tree. They watched her. What was she doing?

She turned away, glancing briefly at the silo and barn, then the farmhouse, all of the buildings feeling a mile away.

She was isolated, out in the open. Turning back to look at the vultures, a gunshot rented through the air. She jumped and started away, the image of the ugly beasts soaring down on her in her thoughts. The shot had been faraway, someone shooting targets from deep in the woods, but it was the shock she needed to get away. Suddenly the fear of the homeowner returning was paramount.

She hurried to her car, slamming the door behind her, and went home. She shook away the memory by urging sunlight into the dark, quiet house. She opened drapes in the great room and the curtains over the kitchen sink, but that did little to dissipate the melancholy that lingered around her. She went about household chores, working on getting her mind on the normalcy of being a wife and stay-at-home mom. She opened the dishwasher and sighed, discovering many of the dishes had water droplets on them. Pulling a towel out from under the sink, she started drying. She fell into a rhythm: grab a plate, dry, put it away.

As she straightened, she looked out at the pool and then the woods, drying a glass in her hands. When it was dry, she put it in the cupboard and bent to grab another. The new glass had some water in it, which she poured down the sink before pushing her hand into it, drying. She snapped the towel out, put away the glass, and reached for another. She was shoving the towel into the next glass when, slowly, she realized what she was doing, or rather, what she had been using to dry.

She set the tip of the glass on the counter; she didn't hear it fall off the edge and crash onto the floor. Instead, she zeroed in on the towel she had been using, thin and striped, red-and-blue. It wasn't a towel, after all.

Kara slowly unfolded it, her breath catching. She didn't breathe. She *couldn't* breathe. She felt sick with the realization that she had been using Sophie's receiving blanket to dry dishes. She flung open the backdoor, not bothering to shut it, and held the blanket open in the breeze, coaxing it to quickly air-dry.

Who had put it in the kitchen drawer? How had she not noticed it before?

Tears spilled down her cheeks, guilt overriding her soul. No one but she ever touched the memory box. She had to have done it. In her sleep, sometime during the fitful night that she couldn't remember, she had brought the memory box to bed with her. She tried to picture herself pulling out the blanket, curling up with it. Maybe the blanket had gotten mixed up with the laundry. She did fold clothes on her bed…

But she had checked the box the other morning. The blanket had been in there.

She went inside when the blanket was dry to return it to the memory box. She had smoothed out the wrinkles with her hands and folded it carefully. She didn't bring it to her nose to make sure it still smelled like baby powder; it would be unbearable if it didn't anymore. She shut the box away in her dresser, then sat on the bed holding her head in her hands. How could she have been so careless?

She sat for a while, breathing deeply, telling herself it was alright, she had taken care of it, the blanket was fine. When she had regained her composure, the guilt was still there but she had come down from most of the shock, she pressed John's name on her cellphone.

When he picked up on the first ring, she shuddered. He had picked up too fast. She couldn't tell him. If she told him, he'd think she was crazy.

"Kara? Are you there?"

She swallowed, nodding for her own benefit, and finally said, "Hi. Yes, I'm here. Sorry, I was…just calling to say hi…Is work busy?"

"Yeah, when is it not?" he sighed. "Accounting's having an issue and they want me to drop everything to fix it."

"Ugh." She cleared her throat, steadying herself. "How long will that take?"

"I'll know in about 10 minutes after the system reboots and reconfigures. I just don't need this right now."

"Yeah, that's crap." Hearing his voice as he went on about work calmed her. Everything would be okay. The blanket hadn't been harmed. She was fine. She would take a deep breath and start over. "Well, I'll let you go then. Try not to work too hard." She didn't want to let him go, though.

"You too."

She hung up and exhaled, staring at the blank cellphone screen.

I made a mistake; it won't happen again. It *can't* happen again.

Kara lay down to a soundtrack of bird chatter coming from the other side of the closed windows.

It was okay, she was okay.

She pulled the cool sheet over her, sinking into the soft mattress. Her eyelids wiggled and she was soon asleep.

She was drenched in blackness. It coated her, heavy like chainmail, forcing her to the ground. It was too thick, too tight, too much. Fear swelled in the blackness and she was afraid to move. Was she alone? Was she the only one blind?

Were her eyes open?

Kara flicked them from side-to-side. She thought they were anyway, but she still couldn't see. Widening them only made the black seep into her eye sockets, filling her head. Her eyes watered. She closed them again, and now she saw color. Thin lines zig-zagged and spiraled on the backs of her eyelids, painting in various shades of greens, blues, oranges, and reds. At first it was an amazing color wheel spectacular, casually gliding across the black page. Then gradually, the colors twisted, gaining speed until they made her dizzy.

There was no escaping the neon colors that slashed by, then spiraled to the right before crossing to the left. They were wild, becoming circles and Xs and blobs until they meshed again, finally bursting with a flash of white and then becoming black again. Before she could get a grip on what was happening, the blackness subsided, turning lighter and then orange.

She blinked her eyes open, finding herself swathed in light. Squinting, she made to shield her eyes with her hand, but she couldn't move. Her arms, legs, hands, and toes betrayed her, refusing to budge; they were comatose. She felt no sense of panic, however; she felt nothing.

She looked up at the ivory, fabric ceiling above. Sunlight filtered in through seams where the material had been threaded together. Sliding her eyes down the plain canvas walls, she realized she was no longer in her bedroom. She was lying down, but her bed was a bleached, linen sack filled with what appeared to be straw.

Was she in a tent?

She drew in the small room, seeing the only other furniture was a small table that had a leather satchel and wooden bucket on it. The floor was simply matted grass that had started to brown from its lack of water and sunlight.

There was a scuffling then, just outside, a few feet to the left of where she lay. Her eyes widened when the tent flap was yanked open, revealing a man in tan calfskin pants and a dirty, blousy shirt. She was alarmed to see he carried a rifle over his shoulder.

"You're awake," he said, from the doorway.

She tried to move her arms, but they couldn't be stirred.

He said, "You took a fall in the woods early this morning when it was still dark, running as if death had its grip on you." He gestured to the outside. "You were knocked senseless and so I...I carried you here to rest."

Kara stared.

"I hope you haven't been hurt too severely," he said with sympathy. He pushed back stray hairs that had fallen loose from his ponytail. He was muscular, wearing clothing that would've been better suited in a historical re-enactment group than here in this...where was she? Here in this...tent.

"Where am I?" The voice was feminine, light.

215

But it wasn't Kara who had spoken.

Kara twisted around and, as she did, she found she was now standing and in the corner of the tent. Feeling had been restored in her limbs. She glanced down, finding she was barefooted. When she looked back up, a woman with tangled, long, blonde hair had replaced her on the makeshift mattress. The woman's face was a blur, however.

Kara rubbed her eyes, but the face remained impossibly hazy. The rest of her, from her hair to her soiled blue gown to her booted feet, was crisp in contrast.

The man replied simply, with no hint of accusation, "You are trespassing on my land. Where are you headed?" He stepped inside, the flap closing, making the space small and intimate.

Kara's eyes flicked from his guarded face to the blonde's misty one.

The blonde looked around, sitting up. She rested a hand on her belly, which Kara could see was swollen. "I don't remember."

"Were you being chased?"

"I'm not sure…I…" The blonde's words trailed off as she looked down. Suddenly, she was panic-stricken. "Where is it?" She scrambled around on the mattress, her fingers rooting for something. "Where is it?" she asked again, urgently.

"What are you looking for?"

"It's not here! Did you take it?" The blonde looked up at him. She raised her voice, asking, "Why would you take it away?"

Looking confused, he squatted, peering at the bedding. "I took nothing, madam. What are you missing?"

"My father made that. It's not yours to take!" The blonde bent over and started sobbing. Kara stepped closer to the mattress and peered down, as if she would be the one who'd find the lost item. The mat was so thin and ragged, however, that she couldn't imagine being able to hide anything of substance.

"What is it you lost?" the man asked gently. He reached down and touched the blonde's shoulder. The woman turned her misty face in Kara's direction and screamed, "Give it to me!"

Kara jumped back, falling to the ground. She wanted to escape, but her limbs had gone numb again. Squeezing her eyes shut, her only protection in the stifling tent, she blocked out the screams.

Her world went black again; she was spinning.

It was the mewling of an animal that baited her to open her eyes. After a time, she did, with caution.

It was evening now and she was no longer in the tent. She was indoors now, in an unfamiliar bedroom with wood-paneled walls. A fire crackled in one of its two fireplaces. The blonde, her face still a blur, lay in a large wood-framed bed, rocking a bundle of blankets in her arms. Kara's eyes trailed around the room, which was filled with heavy pieces of furniture built with fine detail. Rich linens pooled at the foot of the bed, covering the woman at the calves and down. The man was gone.

The blonde spoke up, her head bowed toward the bundle, "He will be here soon. Papa is never late." But while her words were comforting, the manner in which she said them was not. The arms rocking the bunch were jittery and every now and again she flipped her hair. Kara, standing in the center of the room, her bare feet feeling the tight weave of the woven rug beneath her, looked at the door. She hesitated before going to the window behind the bed. She looked out the nearly floor-to-ceiling window made of bubbled glass. However, the glass didn't look out to the outside. Instead, she was looking into a room.

It was hazy, but she recognized the room. Her eyes rolled down, seeing shattered glass from a broken window dotting the plywood floor. Stacked boxes rose opposite her. She looked across the room and saw a dented box, a branch of an artificial Christmas tree poking out. Somehow, as impossible as it was, she realized she was looking through the window into the unfinished bonus room of her own house.

How could that be?

A silver marble rolled across the plywood, making a scraping sound.

LEAVE!!!

The word flashed behind her eyes, striking so suddenly she stepped back.

The mewling started again. Kara turned on the shrouded woman. Confident the blonde was unaware of her, Kara crept closer to the expansive bed, stepping up onto the platform beside it, close enough to look down at the baby she cradled. The crying was a pinched, aggrieved whine, its timbre rising and falling, like a siren. The infant had to be sick. Kara raised her chin and tilted her head to spy the baby enfolded in the blankets, but there were too many folds. Daringly, she turned down the blanket at the head of the bundle. That revealed more blankets. She turned down another layer and another, but still, there was no baby to be seen.

Ignoring the woman's blurred face, mere inches from hers, Kara worked both hands into the fabric, pulling down and unwrapping. She unraveled them until they fell limply onto the woman's chemise-covered lap. Kara scanned the blankets, then looked up at the blurry face, the awful cry continuing. Through the haze, she saw the formation of the woman's mouth open and close, realizing in horror that that was where the terrible cry came from.

Kara stumbled backward, stepping down off the platform and backing to the door. She tried the knob, but it spun in her hand. She frantically banged on the door, not caring the blonde might break out of her trance and notice her.

Please, someone let me out! Please! Kara's mind screamed.

The mewling continued behind her.

Please! Help! She tugged on the knob.

The whine stopped abruptly, and the blonde said simply, "My baby." Sniffling, she repeated, "My baby."

As Kara turned around to face her, the crying started again, but this time it sounded more like an infant's natural wail. It came from the fireplace on the far side of the room. Cautiously, Kara moved to its stone plate set in the wood floor. The crying was louder, locked within the chimney. She knelt down in front of the hearth, ignoring the blonde's cheerful statement of "Yes, there's the baby! The baby's fine. Yes, yes, fine."

Kara looked up into the darkness of the chimney. The cry was urgent, an infant in distress. Black soot broke free, crumbling down onto her face and shoulders. Kara coughed, backing up, but the chimney stones were breaking. They caved in, the force of the blow sending her through the floor.

She spun, rushing downward. Wind whistled through her hair as she shot through the air, eventually plunging down through liquid. She hit the bottom and stayed there, her rear-end scraping along rocks. Images flashed all around her, so quick she barely made sense of them: a group of men passing through woods, pressing their arms through branches as if searching; beams of sunlight filtering through an open, curtain-less window; blurred faces passing in the maelstrom; a baby, wailing in a cradle, and then...Kara bobbed to the surface of the water.

She looked around, dazed. It took a moment to realize she was in a murky pool...no—a pond. Evergreens encircled it, hiding what lay beyond the haven. She spit out filthy water, crawling to the bank. She had just sat down, shivering, when a yell shot through the overcast day. Her head snapped up and turned toward it. It was the man from the tent, pacing twenty yards from her. He yelled again before running into the water. Alarmed, Kara watched him go under.

His head popped up and he swam toward the center of the pond. He yelled again before disappearing underwater. Kara stood on shaky legs, eyes combing the surface. Several seconds later, he came up for air and then was down again. Her eyes darted over the dark surface. It was steady, except for where the water rippled around him. After several more seconds ticked by, she started into the water. When she was a foot deep, he came up. He swam to shore, something floating behind him.

Kara squinted. It took a moment to make it out, but when she saw the long, matted hair, she knew who it was. She felt sick, watching him lift the lifeless woman out of the water and lay her on the grassy shore, her hair draped over her face.

Kara maneuvered over the rocky soil to meet them. It was at her approach that he noticed her; Kara was a ghost no more. With deafening speed, he flicked his face in her direction, opened his mouth wide and screeched. His face, body, and person transformed into a turkey vulture. He took to the sky.

Kara screamed.

She closed her eyes to shut out the monster and was shrouded in darkness.

The calming sound of water, quiet at first, then growing louder, filled her head, drowning her. The blackness spun to red, purple, and then orange until she dared blink her eyes open.

Chapter Twenty-one

Kara opened her eyes, finding her surroundings had changed. Her legs were crossed at the ankles, a sheet wrapped tightly around her, and both arms stretched straight above her head. She blinked rapidly before recognizing she was lying in her bed. Her breathing slowed as she looked around. She wriggled, unable to feel her arms. She rolled to her side and wrestled around until she was able to break an arm free. It took a moment before she was able to use that arm to pull the other one above her head down to her side.

She rubbed her forehead and leaned against the headboard. She sat like that for a long time, steadying her racing heart and massaging the sensation of needles from her limbs. She tried to remember the nightmare, but it was fading fast.

"Mom?"

Kara jumped. Her eyes went to the doorway where Jack stood apprehensively. She cleared her throat, finding her voice didn't sound as shaky as she felt. "Yeah?"

"Are you okay?" He hesitated, one foot over the threshold.

"I was just napping." Trying to be light, she asked, "Why are you home so early?"

He frowned. "It's four. I just got home."

"Four?" She glanced at the clock, panic rising. Where had the day gone?

"Shannon's here," he said.

"Shannon?"

"Hey there!" Shannon materialized beside Jack. "Hey, lady, how are you feeling?"

"Hi, Mommy!" Lilah called from down the hall.

"Hi, Lilah," Kara mumbled.

"I'm going outside," Jack said, leaving.

Shannon crossed the room and sat on the window bench. "Are you alright?"

Kara shook her head slowly, still trying to clear the fog. "I can't believe I overslept. Did you pick up Lilah from school?"

"Yeah, They called John and he called me to see if I could get a hold of you, since he was only getting your voicemail."

Kara picked up her cellphone from the nightstand. She had missed two calls from Grace School, two from John, and three from Shannon. Dread sank into the pit of her belly. "I can't believe I overslept and I didn't even hear the phone ring. That's terrible. And I'm sorry John didn't get her."

"Don't worry about it. He was worried the drive would take too long. I checked up on you, saw you were napping, and told him I'd get her. My boss is really understanding. He let me out early. It was no problem."

"You should've woken me. I can't believe I slept through it all."

"You were out cold. I didn't want to wake you. I know how hard it's been for you to sleep."

"How did you get in the house?" That was another concern. Kara was so careful about locking the doors.

"I lucked out with the backdoor. It was unlocked."

"It was?" Why would she have left the door unlocked? She scrolled through her memory. Had she opened the back..?

Sophie's receiving blanket.

Kara had used it to towel off dishes like an idiot, a reckless move. She had gone outside to dry the blanket after she had come so close to destroying it.

Mistaking her pained expression for worry, Shannon reassured her, "Don't worry about it. Lilah and I went for lunch in town and we popped in a few shops. She had a blast, mama." Shannon smiled. "We went to Buried Treasures."

"You did?"

"We took her statue in. Lilah was a little reluctant, but she let the clerk look at it."

"Oh?" The haze was lifting and Kara was starting to focus.

"I hope you didn't have your hopes up too high. She said the statue is just a garden statue. There's nothing special about it. It's apparently just a coincidence to the picture on the shop sign."

Kara felt a twinge of disappointment. "So, the previous owner didn't have any reason for the sign being so similar?"

"Nope. Apparently, there's no connection. It's just a strange coincidence. Weird." Shannon laughed, making Kara half-smile. Her head was so heavy.

"I just don't understand how I slept for so long...The dream was strange..." The memory of the faceless woman and the man in historical garb was fading fast.

"Your body needed the sleep. Have you been alright since...?"

Kara cringed inwardly, remembering Shannon had found her sleeping with the memory box. Her cellphone rang before she could reply. She answered the call, following Shannon into the foyer.

"Hey." It was John. "Is everything okay? I tried to call you."

"Yeah, we're fine. I overslept. I meant to just take a nap...but I just woke up."

"Really? Are you sick?"

"No...I don't think so. I'm fine. Thank God Shannon was able to pick up Lilah."

"I'm glad she was able to get her. That was awesome. It would've taken me an hour to get there. You're okay?"

Kara rubbed her temple. "I'm fine, just waking up."

"Good...On another note...I have to work late tonight."

Kara's head dropped. "Great. What time are you coming home?"

He sighed. "At least a few more hours."

"I hate this project," she groaned, exchanging glances with Shannon, whose expression was sympathetic.

"I can stay with you until he comes home, if you want," Shannon offered.

Kara lifted her chin away from the phone, grasping on. "Do you mind?"

"Nope, not at all."

When Kara hung up, Shannon said, "He works a lot, huh?"

"It's this project he's been on. He's trying to meet a dead—" Kara cried out, interrupted by three loud bangs on the front door.

They saw movement on the other side of the sidelight. Frowning, Kara opened the door slowly.

"Hi, Kara."

She blinked, stepping back. "Marvin! Hi."

"John home?" He stepped inside. When he noticed Shannon, he nodded.

"Uh, no," Kara replied, ignoring the image of the man who had flashed in her mind. "He's working late."

Marvin whistled, but the high-pitched sound stopped short when he looked up. "I see you still don't have a light up there."

"Not yet. Buried Treasures is rewiring it. I should have it in a week."

"Don't want to leave wires exposed."

"Is that a fire hazard, leaving it like that?"

"Yup. Need a light up there."

"Oh, I had no idea." Kara wrung her hands. Her kids were on the floor directly above the open wire box. "I'll see if John can put the old one back up tomorrow then."

"Are you sure about that?" Shannon asked, glancing up at the box before leveling her eyes on him. "That it's a fire hazard?"

He met her eyes and smiled. "Yup." Looking at Kara again, he said, "No need to wait. I can put it up now."

"Oh, that's alright. We have to rent scaffolding anyway to do it. John returned the one we had."

"I've got a ladder I think'll reach."

Shannon turned to Kara. "I can call Tom to install it."

"No, no. No need." Marvin shook his head. "I can do it. Be right back." He turned around and left before Kara could stop him. "I guess he's installing the light then," she said with a laugh.

"Can he do it on his own?" Shannon asked, both of them looking up at the ceiling. "That's two stories up. Should I call Tom?"

"I don't want to put anybody out. Let's just see if Marvin needs help. I stored the old light in the garage. Let me go get it."

Twenty minutes later, they heard the rumble of a pickup truck coming up the driveway. Marvin had returned. Ignoring Shannon's chuckle, Kara went outside and helped him heave the heavy aluminum A-frame ladder and carry it into the house.

"What do you need me to do?" she asked him when they had positioned it under the chandelier.

He waved her back, his breath labored. He didn't reply until he slid home the locking bolts. "Just hand the light to me when I get up a few rungs."

Kara held up the brass chandelier, the one that looked like a teat, once Marvin had turned toward them from the fourth ladder step. Carefully holding it by the base, he twisted around and climbed up. Both women watched until he made it near the ceiling.

"Do you want me to hold the ladder?" Kara asked, gripping its sides.

"No. I'm fine. It's sturdier than that scaffolding John had me on!" He chuckled, then grunted. "Go about your business. I'm good here."

"Yeah, Kara," Shannon agreed. "He doesn't need an audience."

"Are you sure you're alright?" Kara hesitated, seeing the chandelier was balanced on the top seat of the ladder. Marvin was reaching above into the electrical box, untwisting wires.

"I'm fine."

"Come on, Kara," Shannon prompted. "Let's see what these kids are doing."

With one last wary glance at Marvin, Kara followed Shannon upstairs. They found Lilah sitting on her bedroom floor, looking at a page in her picture book about fairies. She pinched the corner of the page her focus on an illustration of a fairy that sat on a gold-sparkled flower petal. A year before, Lilah had spilled glitter all over the page. However, despite Kara's best efforts, gold crumbs still festered on the petal, over the fairy's bare feet, and on the background trees. It added a shimmer that seemed to make the picture come alive.

"Hey, Lilahbean," Kara said, sitting on the bed.

Shannon sat on the carpeted floor across from Lilah. "Whatcha up to?" She tugged on one of the girl's sock-covered feet.

"Reading my book," Lilah replied, glancing at them before returning her attention to the page.

"Did you have a good day at school?" Kara asked, still feeling guilty for having overslept.

Lilah nodded without looking up.

"I'm sorry I wasn't able to pick you up today. Mommy had a long nap. I was too tired, I guess," Kara said.

"I know," Lilah replied, turning the color-enriched page. Kara's eyes wandered down, catching sight of the clay base of the statue. Its head was hidden beneath Lilah's folded leg.

"I see your doll," Shannon said, as if noticing what had caught Kara's eye.

Lilah met Shannon's eyes and nodded solemnly.

"Can I see her again?"

Lilah studied her for a moment before shaking her head.

"Lilah!" Kara exclaimed. "Let Shannon see your doll. That's not nice. You let her see it earlier."

Lilah shook her head again, pouting out her lower lip.

"That's okay. I know she's a special doll," Shannon said good-naturedly, getting to her feet.

Lilah turned the page.

"Lilah…" Kara started, but let it drop a she watched her daughter turn pages until coming to the end of the book. Lilah paused at the glossy back cover before opening the book again to the first page. Kara watched as she methodically turned pages until Lilah came again to the glitter-covered page. The girl stopped there and traced a finger over the bumpy flower petals.

Shannon spoke up, breaking Kara's trance, "Are you hungry, Lilah?"

Kara asked, "Lilah, pepperoni or cheese pizza?"

Lilah looked up. "Cheese!"

"Okay, cheese for you and pepperoni for Jack." When they had left the room, Kara said to Shannon, "Sorry about that. She's so attached to that statue."

"That's alright. Kids get like that with toys."

"I guess. But that's not even a toy. I really should've never let her play with it."

"She'll outgrow it soon enough. Wait 'til Christmas and replace it with a doll." Shannon jerked a thumb toward the open bonus room. "Is that another bedroom?"

"It's storage for now. It's going to be our future bonus room. Tom fixed the broken window…" Kara's eyes narrowed, spotting a pebble just past the threshold. She bent over and picked it up. Realizing it wasn't a stone after all, she rolled the silver sphere, a half-inch in diameter, in the palm of her hand. It was similar in size to a marble, but not glassy, instead made of a material solid like iron. She glanced around, the room dark although the sun was on their side of the house. A shiver went through her. There was something familiar about the ball, but she couldn't remember when she had come across it. She dropped it into her shorts pocket and led Shannon downstairs.

"Still doing okay?" Shannon called, as they made their way to the foyer.

The sound of the drill was Marvin's reply. He stretched above his head, pushing it against the electrical box, easing away from the chandelier sitting in front of him.

Taking that as their hint to leave him alone, the women continued through to the kitchen.

"Got any wine?" Shannon asked with a crooked smile.

"Sure." Kara pulled the bottle out of the refrigerator and opened it. She poured both of them a glass and hesitated on a third. "Does Marvin drink wine?" She turned around, intending to ask him, but her cellphone dinged, stopping her.

She picked up the phone from the countertop. Her mother had texted.

He won't stop.

Kara's her heart started to kick.

She texted back, *David?*

Yes! He keeps asking me about you. I told him to stop, but he won't.

Kara texted back, *What's he want?*

She leaned against the counter as Shannon, oblivious, filled the glasses with wine.

What do you think?

Kara's mind was scrambling. Before she could muster a thought, Margaret texted again, *He's not acting right.*

Kara glanced at Shannon and didn't reply to her when she asked, "What?" Instead, she texted back, *What's he doing? Do I need to worry?*

Kara stared at the screen, waiting. After a minute of no reply, she pressed her mother's name, calling her. The phone rang three times before going to the generic voicemail recording. Kara left a message, asking her to call her.

"What's going on?" Shannon asked.

Kara texted Margaret, *Hello?*

"Kara?" Shannon prompted. "Is everything okay?"

Without looking up, Kara replied, "Yeah." Her eyes bore into the screen. When several seconds had passed, she scrolled up the messages and re-read their exchange.

"Anything I can do?" Shannon asked.

Kara laid the cellphone face-up on the counter, finally peeling her eyes away. "No." She swallowed a drink of wine, wondering at Margaret's words.

He's not acting right.

What did that mean? What did David want: shared custody of Jack? Why was Margaret leaving these vague messages? Should Kara be worried?

"Kara? The way you're downing that wine, something must be up."

Kara swallowed the last of her alcohol and looked at the black cellphone screen. "My mom just texted me about David again."

"She did? What did she say?"

Kara picked up the phone, scrolled back and read the text messages aloud. Looking up when she was done, she asked, "What do you think?"

"Wow. She didn't say anything else?"

Kara shook her head. "This is my mother. When she wants to, she can be vindictive."

"Really? About this?"

Kara shrugged, setting the phone back on the counter.

"Geez, I don't know. I don't want to scare you, but…"

"Do you think I should call the police? I mean, is there a threat?"

"I don't know. Well, the thing is, it's your mom who's saying he contacted her…but then you don't know what he said to her…Does he know where you live?" Shannon looked out the kitchen window.

Kara thought of the figure in the shadows. Had that been David? Had her mother given him her address? But she didn't think she would've done that, not without Kara's permission.

"No, he hasn't contacted me." She hadn't seen the figure again. Had she hallucinated it? She had been wrong about seeing the blonde woman in the kitchen, after all. That hadn't been real.

Shannon met her eyes, her expression grim. "Just be careful."

"It's pretty sad if it is just my mom playing games." Kara poured another glass of wine. "She can be pretty obnoxious." She hoped that was it, that Margaret was toying with her, because the alternative of David being a very real menace was something she didn't want to realize.

"Whew. Tough mama," Shannon murmured, drinking.

Kara forced a smile. "I'm not thinking anymore about it." She stretched, centering herself and mentally pushing away the drama.

Shannon leaned forward, asking quietly, "Is your neighbor still here?"

Kara trained her ears; the foyer was silent. "I think so. I feel bad Marvin's installing that light. I don't hear anything, though. I wonder if he—"

There was a yelp, followed by a hard crash and two loud thumps. She and Shannon ran to the front of the house. Both women screamed.

Arms splayed out, Marvin lay on the floor, trapped beneath one end of the ladder that had fallen with him. The bulbs of the brass chandelier had broken and shards of glass were scattered across the floor. Kara's hands covered her mouth in horror.

"Mommy?" Lilah's voice was small as she called cautiously from the staircase.

Kara's legs were immobile. She was stunned and couldn't comprehend the gruesome image in front of her. Marvin's eyes were shut, blood trickling from his gaping mouth, and his legs were turned at unnatural angles.

She finally tore her eyes away and yelled, "Lilah, go to your room!"

Shannon raced around his sprawled body and jabbed her cellphone, calling 9-1-1.

The backdoor opened and Jack called, "Mom, what's for dinner?" at the same time Lilah called "Mommy?" from the staircase landing.

Chapter Twenty-two

Diane didn't discuss Marvin's status, aside from letting Kara know he was "still in the hospital." She accepted Kara's sympathies, but told her she wanted to be left alone while she kept vigil at the hospital and at home. Some days, Kara would look out from her front porch and spot movement, picturing Diane in her rocking chair inside the screened front porch, but she kept her promise by not coming over.

One day, Kara swore she heard someone knock at the front door. She went to check, but was met with the empty porch, vacant yard, and quiet street. She turned around quickly to look at the door, and was grateful there was no posted sign this time, no passing-by real estate agent, and most of all, no David.

She considered telling John about Margaret's text messages, but ultimately, she changed her mind. Better to keep it to herself until she got more information. This would only make matters worse between her mother and him.

Her life went on, one day clicking after the other, hoping each day that passed would be the day Marvin would return home, healthy again. But, each day, she ended up disappointed, seeing no sign of his return. She fell into a depression, ignoring voicemails left by Tracy and the clerk from Buried Treasures, who said the antique chandelier was ready. Sensing her sadness, John suggested Kara volunteer at Jack's school, saying that'd keep her occupied. She took his advice and called them, but they didn't need morning helpers. They did, however, ask if she'd chaperone a field trip in a month. She said she would. It was something, but not the distraction she needed presently.

"I don't know what's going on," Kara said to John several days later. They sat on the deck in plastic

Adirondack chairs, watching Jack and Lilah toss an oversized ball to each other. Kara sat forward, fighting the natural gravity of the sloping chair. "Do you think I should check on Diane?" Her eyes spied the lemon house through the trees. No one worked in the garden; the leaves didn't even stir. She caught sight of the white scarf; it too was limp.

"Do you know what hospital Marvin's at?" John asked.

Kara shook her head. "She wouldn't say."

"I know you feel guilty. I feel guilty too, but it was an accident."

Kara studied his face as he looked ahead, his eyes on the kids. Lines she hadn't noticed before were etched in the creases near his eyes and mouth. She wondered if he was having trouble sleeping too. The event had added to her current bag of drama, adding to her sinking dread. She looked at the leaves again, feeling a sense of eeriness, and murmured, "It's so still out today."

John grunted, looking up at the cloudy sky. "Is it supposed to rain?"

Kara looked up. A turkey vulture drifted out from over the woods, a black blight in the white sky. She looked away, her eyes on the Foremans' house again. "I never hear chickens."

"Hmm?"

"When we met Marvin, he said he had chickens. I've never heard them."

John glanced at the yard next door. "Maybe the sound just doesn't carry this far."

"Should I check on them?" Kara didn't wait for an answer. She stepped down off the deck and crossed through a stand of trees. Lilah started to follow, but John called out to her not to.

Kara spotted cucumbers and tomatoes and a flower garden before carefully wending her way around the yard, close to the rear of the house. She looked about, wondering then if the house was truly vacant. She hadn't thought to knock on the door. What if Matthew was home?

She hurried, not feeling welcome, a trespasser whom the homeowner had already told to stay away. She observed as she went, her eyes scouring the area for cages, a dirt run, pellets, some sign of chickens. It was all grass on the other side of the house, and there was no sound of anything, save birdsong and a car cruising down the road. She moved to the front yard, glancing at the curtained windows before approaching the porch and tugging on the screen door.

Locked.

She peered inside, but no one was in the shadowed room. She stepped back from the door and, looking down, saw a pair of worn sneakers propped on the ground beside the porch. Matthew's.

She stepped away from the house, looking up at it, viewing the curtained second floor windows. There was no movement, no noise coming from inside. Evidently, the chickens were gone and nobody was home.

The next day, Kara relented and went into town for the antique chandelier. Enough stalling, she made the trek alone.

Smiling good-naturedly, the clerk said, "You've been a busy lady I see."

Kara attempted to match the smile, but knew hers looked as fake as it felt. "Busy?"

"Didn't you get my messages?"

"Yeah, sorry about that. It's been…hectic."

"That's certainly no problem!" She led Kara to the counter. "I have the chandelier right over here. I'm sorry you had to have it rewired. But I assure you, I tried it myself and it lights like a charm."

There was no enthusiasm as Kara said, "Great."

The clerk looked around. "You didn't bring anybody to help?"

"No."

"The chandelier is very heavy, my dear. We'll try, but I don't know if the two of us can manage."

"My friend and I managed last time," Kara said, remembering Tracy had helped her load it before.

"Well, we can try."

The chandelier was heavy, but the two women managed, heaving it up off the floor and moving slowly to the trunk of Kara's car.

"Thanks," Kara said, this time her smile genuine.

She pulled open the driver's door when the clerk spoke, "Oh, did you bring the statue?" The woman gestured toward the sign hanging from the second floor.

"My friend and daughter brought it in a while ago."

The clerk wrinkled her brow, glanced down at the sidewalk, and then back up at Kara.

"Is there someone else who works here?" Kara prompted.

The clerk thought a moment, then raised a finger, remembering. "I was out of town. It must've been then. I normally close the shop when I vacation, but a friend of mine offered to keep it open, and well, I would've been remiss if I hadn't accepted. I went to another friend's cottage on an island…" She droned on about her vacation and finally trailed to a stop, reading the disinterest on Kara's face. "Did she tell you anything about the statue? My friend's well-versed in antiques and I had given her a heads up about it and the shop sign."

"There's no connection, just a coincidence," Kara replied, shortly. She wasn't in the mood to discuss the origins of antiques. She didn't care anymore. What did it matter?

"Oh, that's a shame. There's something about antiques, though. Much like an older home, they tend to carry the past with them. I may sound rather odd when I say this," She chuckled, pressing a hand to her mouth before continuing, "But I believe that old items—antiques—of any importance find their way into the hands of people who are meant to have them. Now whether they belong to a descendant of the original owner, or the new owner has a connection to the time period or place where the item is discovered…the item belongs somewhere, if that makes any sense. From the look on your face, I can tell you think I'm nuts!" She laughed.

"That isn't odd," Kara said, but she was just being polite. Honestly, she didn't understand what the clerk was getting at, and really, she just wanted to go home. She was tired.

The clerk's expression softened. Clasping her hands together, she asked, "Mind if I swing by sometime to see the statue myself?"

"Maybe," Kara said, sliding into the car, not intending to set up a date.

That evening, John rented a scaffold so that he could install the antique chandelier. Kara stood at the ready, on the floor by its side, fighting the constant memory of Marvin's fallen body, making sure John didn't lose his balance. The broken glass had been swept away and the mangled brass light fixture had been trashed long ago.

Two days later after a rainstorm had passed, Kara crossed the wet lawn to Diane's house. It had been several days, but Diane appeared, leaving the covered porch to meet her.

Diane said blandly, "Marvin's gone. He died three days ago."

Kara's hand went to her mouth, her words a whisper, "Oh, I'm sorry, Diane."

"There won't be a funeral. Marvin was plain in that he didn't want a ceremony or memorial. Please respect my privacy."

"Will Matthew be staying with you?" Kara noticed Diane's head twitch and wondered if she'd be alright. When Diane didn't immediately reply, Kara went on, "Please visit me as soon as you feel up to it. I am so sorry for your loss. We will keep you and Matthew in our prayers."

Diane opened her mouth, but ended up clearing her throat instead of replying. She opened the screen door and closed it behind her, locking it.

Kara returned home, breathing the humid air, feeling light-headed. She closed the front door behind her, purposely not looking up at the foyer light.

"John." She waited for him to look up from his computer. "Marvin died."

"He did?"

She nodded, coming into the office. She pushed on him so that he made room for her to sit on his lap. He wrapped his arms around her and she laid her head against his chest, starting to cry. She felt so horribly guilty. Why had she let Marvin install that light? Had she been responsible for his death?

Chapter Twenty-three

"John! Lilah!" Kara felt the scream tear through her throat, but it came out instead as a hoarse whisper. "Get Lilah!"

The sun was beating down overhead, the heat searing Kara's skull. It was as if somebody was holding her down, forcing a hot fire poker to her crown. She moved her arms, swinging them back and forth. Her legs wouldn't budge.

"Lilah!" She choked on the name. The little dark head disappeared from sight. It sank below, into the oblong pool; the sloshing water slowed.

She's not struggling anymore!

If she wasn't struggling, then that meant she wasn't conscious. And if she wasn't conscious…

"J-j-j-j!" Kara stuttered.

She couldn't tear her eyes away from the pool. They felt glued on it, burning from staring. Why wasn't John coming? Didn't he know Lilah was drowning? Why hadn't he been watching her?

John! She had lost her voice. *John, it's the baby!*

"Help!" Kara cried aloud in the darkness of her bedroom, rocking as she sobbed. She was sitting in bed, cross-legged and bent over, burying her face in the bedspread.

John stirred from his sleep and touched her back. "Kara? What's wrong?"

She opened her eyes and straightened, pulling the blanket over her legs. Awareness came over her: she was in her bedroom, on her bed. "Nightmare," she whispered.

John leaned back against the headboard, propping himself up. "Do you want to talk about it?" *Talk about rainbows and candy shops like he had done when Lilah had had nightmares.*

238

Kara shook her head and shoulders no and lay back, pulling the blanket taut over her. The bedroom window was open, sending in a rush of cool air. Outside, the breeze rubbed against leaves, causing a cacophony of shhhhhhs.

She twisted to her side, folding the pillow in half and resting it under her head. She lay there looking at the blackness beyond the window. Listening to the sound the dancing leaves made, she wiped away her tears and felt how strong her longing had grown. With Marvin's passing, seeing again the very realness of death and how it was so final, her thoughts directed on the passing that had haunted her for so long. There was no uncertainty. She had to return to Cosgrove.

Chapter Twenty-four

"Are you sure about this?" Shannon asked. "I mean, are you sure you want me to come with you?"

It was Saturday morning and even though it was only mid-September, the day was cool and some of the leaves had started to change color.

Kara pulled on a cardigan and replied, "Yeah, I need to do this. Thanks for picking me up at home." She slid into the passenger side of Shannon's jeep. "We won't be long. John has to work later."

Shannon turned the vehicle around at the top of the driveway. "I don't mind. I came out for you. We can stay as long as you need to."

At the cemetery, Kara's thoughts ran, *where Sophie's buried.*

"Does John know where we're going?"

They pulled onto the road and Kara fought the urge to look at the old barn they passed before heading into town. "I didn't want him to know. I don't know how he'd handle it."

"What if he wanted to go with you? Has he been there…since?"

"He wouldn't have wanted to come out, I don't think."

Shannon glanced at Kara, seeing her uncertainty. "If you're not sure, I can turn around. You guys can talk about it and see if you'd feel better doing this together."

"I'm sorry for making you take me, Shannon." Tears welled in Kara's eyes. What was she doing?

"No, I'm fine. I had nothing planned besides watching Tom sit around the house."

"Thanks." Kara wiped her eyes, grateful the tears hadn't fallen.

"Stop thanking me. Tom's no treat when he's between jobs." Shannon's chuckle was hollow.

"His job ended?" It was a personal subject, but nothing more personal than the situation they were driving toward. Selfishly, it was something to get her mind off the journey.

"Yeah." Shannon twisted the radio dial so that rock music played low in the jeep's cabin. They had turned onto the highway. "How's your neighbor doing? Marvin?"

Kara swallowed, looking out the window. "He passed away."

"What?" Shannon's hand went to her face for a moment, her fingers brushing against her eyebrow, her nose. "Wow. I'm so sorry."

Kara nodded and sighed, not noticing the decorative evergreens bordering the highway whip past. "Yeah, it's terrible."

Kara felt like St. Michael's Cemetery had come upon them far too soon. Located on the outskirts of Cosgrove, it was on Route 604, viewable from the highway. She had only been there one time before, but on that day, she had been a sobbing wreck and oblivious. They pulled off the exit ramp and turned immediately right, passing through the gated entrance, open to green grass spotted with stones and flowers. A van and a truck were the only other vehicles in the blacktop lot.

"Are you ready?" Shannon asked, gently.

Kara's nod was barely perceptible. Shannon squeezed her hand before leading her down the walking path. As the pavement curved around a trio of tall trees, Kara noticed daisies and a lone sunflower, as well as colorful pinwheels tucked into the earth, the breeze making them spin and rattle. Clinking wind chimes drew her eyes to a low-drooping bough where they hung, just steps ahead. The long limb was mostly dead. A dozen leaves were strapped to it, but most of the bark had splintered. A few more strong storms and it would be annihilated. Kara forced herself to look below it, knowing where they had come.

The baby graveyard.

"I came out early this morning after you called," Shannon said. "so, it'd be easier for you. I made sure we'd know where to find her."

Her.

We're talking about Sophie now, Kara thought. It was surreal.

I can't do this.

Shannon continued, "I supposed it'd be difficult for you to remember since you've only been here once."

I'm not ready.

Shannon had slowed her pace and was leading her down a gravel trail no wider than the width of her body. It led past tiny grave markers and headstones.

Tiny like a baby, Kara thought wildly.

Some graves were marked with statues: an angel, a lamb, the Virgin Mary. She passed a stone Celtic cross with etched words, reading, "Our beautiful Briana; early, Heaven called our angel home."

"Oh, wow," Shannon murmured beside her. "She was only two."

Kara's eyes flashed, as she realized Shannon had noticed the grave marker of baby Briana too.

Shannon gestured toward the rear row of graves set flat into the grass. "I'll give you time with Sophie."

Kara swallowed hard, hearing her daughter's name. Shannon moved briskly away, down the path, leaving her alone. Kara took her time, walking leadenly past each marker. She purposefully read each stone, not comprehending the meaning of the words. She ignored their names, paid no mind to the various psalms and poetic quotations engraved into some of the slabs of rock. They were meaningless characters. She did notice, however, there were no flowers, no memento, no child's toy to mark the ground where mothers and fathers and grandparents had laid their children to rest. Abandoned children, orphans underground.

She stopped short of the second-to-last headstone. She had stood there six years ago, dressed in a navy blue suit dress her mother had suggested she wear that morning. The weather had been similar to that day: cool and partly cloudy. She had just given birth four short days before and her body had still ached from natural childbirth and an episiotomy.

They had been a small group: Kara, John, her mother, and a reverend the hospital had recommended. Margaret had told her it would be best if Jack wasn't there. He wouldn't understand what was going on and he'd be confused about everyone's raw emotions.

Margaret had warned, "It could be traumatizing and we wouldn't want that."

John was a wreck himself and hadn't been sure what would be the right thing to do. Jack hadn't even seen Sophie. He had known Mommy had had a baby in her tummy and that he was going to be a big brother, but nothing more concrete than that. When Kara and John had come home without a baby and Mommy's tummy was smaller than it was a couple days before, it had been like it was all a dream. He asked once about the baby soon after, but they had just told him she had gone to Heaven. He hadn't asked questions, had accepted that as a logical enough explanation, and had returned to being their only child. For him, nothing had changed, it had all stayed the same.

Kara looked down at the stone.

Sophie Marie Tameson.

Seeing the name carved permanently into gray rock in this public place was devastating. She dropped to her knees, both of her palms opening flat on the grass in front of the marker. She had carried Sophie in her womb for nine months. They had bonded, always together. During the second trimester, Sophie had let Kara know she was there and a force to be acknowledged. Kara had taken pleasure in feeling her daughter's exuberant kicks; she watched her tumble around, sometimes making her belly look something sinister from a science fiction movie. During the last trimester, Kara spent evenings rocking in her glider, singing and talking quietly to Sophie as the sun dropped from the sky and the room grew dark. Theirs would be a true bond, Kara had thought. Nothing like her relationship with her mother. Sophie and she would always be two peas in a pod; nothing would ever tear them apart.

But something had torn them apart. An unexplainable stopped heart. There had been no warning. The doctors could offer no reasoning. A weak heart nobody had known about that had just stopped beating.

Presently, instead of blue eyes that mirrored Lilah's (Kara knew they would've looked just like Lilah's), Kara was looking at cold, unmovable gray rock, set in the hard ground. She didn't fight the tears.

She didn't notice Shannon, who had heard the first outcry. Shannon made her way back to the woman curling her arms around the grave marker, Kara's body now shaped in a crude "S," hiding the stone from the rest of the world.

"Oh, Kara."

Kara couldn't stop the tears. Although they painted her face and her nose ran, she didn't care. Her head throbbed and the air drained from her lungs.

"Let's get you out of here." Shannon wrapped her arms around Kara and tugged, pulling her to her feet.

Kara was being taken away from her daughter's remains, but she wasn't ready to leave. She tried to push Shannon away, but her strength was gone. She ached to see her daughter's name in print again, but through her tear-filled eyes all she saw was misshapen gray. Shannon led her back to the parking lot. Kara struggled at first, but soon fell limp, allowing herself be directed to the jeep.

Shannon helped her inside before sliding into the driver's seat. "Are you okay?"

Kara strained her neck, earnestly trying to find Sophie's spot from there, but it was over a slight rise and yards away. "I'll be fine," she replied, wiping her wet cheeks.

"I think you should lie down when you get home. Will you be alright when I drop you off?"

"I'll be fine. I just need to go home and see the kids."

"You need to go home and take a bath. I'll take care of them. You need to relax." When Kara started to protest, Shannon interrupted. "Listen to me. You just put yourself through heartbreak again. You need time to decompress. I'm starting to wonder if maybe this was a bad idea. I didn't mean to make you so upset."

"You brought me here because I wanted you to. I needed to come. I was tired of pretending it never happened." Kara choked back fresh tears. She sat up and pulled the seatbelt around her. "Let's go."

When they returned to the house, John grabbed his keys and laptop bag. "Hey! I gotta run." He didn't pay attention to the women's somber faces. Shannon's turned to a scowl when he sidestepped them and pulled open the interior garage door open. Kara's face had dried by then. He called over his shoulder, "I'll call you later," before closing the door behind him.

Shannon asked her, "Are you going to tell him where we went?"

Kara walked into the kitchen and called hello to Jack and Lilah. They sat in front of the TV in the great room. Kara turned back to Shannon. "I will. Right now's not the time, obviously." She didn't offer anything else. Honestly, she didn't know if she'd ever tell John she had visited the cemetery. Now wasn't the right time, not when his mind was absorbed with work. He didn't know about any of it, aside from the couple times she had said Sophie's name aloud by mistake in front of him. He had no idea she had tucked away the memory box and that she now avoided that dresser drawer because she was afraid she'd find a wrinkled receiving blanket that didn't smell the same.

"When's he coming back?" Shannon sat down at the kitchen table and started rifling through her handbag.

"I don't know. Hopefully, in a few hours." Kara opened the refrigerator. "Do you want a drink? I have water, pop, wine…"

"I'll take some wine."

"After my breakdown, I could use some too." Kara's laugh was hollow. "But it's probably wise if I stuck with water."

Shannon pulled a small amber bottle from her handbag. "Actually, I have something you may not want to take with wine anyway."

Kara poured her a glass and called over to the kids, "How's it going, guys?"

"Daddy got me fruit snacks." Lilah smiled, waving a snack bag.

"Awesome." Kara caught sight of the statue under Lilah's arm. Abhorrence crept over her as the frog's buggy eyes stared back at her with understanding. Kara murmured, "Lilah, be careful with the statue, okay? I don't want you to get scratched."

Lilah laid it down beside her, shoving a gummy faux cherry into her mouth.

Kara looked at Jack, his full attention on the cartoon flashing on the screen, the statue inches from his leg. She didn't know what it was that alerted her to be watchful of where Lilah had laid it…Sharp edges, that's what bothered her. It really wasn't appropriate Lilah played with it…with any statue…not just *that* one.

Kara pulled her eyes away sat down across from Shannon, setting a wineglass in front of her, forgetting her own glass of water.

"Okay, I have something for you," Shannon said. "Now don't think I'm a drug dealer or anything."

246

"What? What are you talking about?"

Shannon opened her hand, revealing a prescription bottle. "It's an anti-anxiety med. Well, more of a glorified sleeping pill. I don't think it's much different than any cold medicine you could buy off the shelf. Just in case you need something to take the edge off."

Soon after Sophie had died, Kara's family doctor had prescribed her something for anxiety, which she had needed. She didn't know how she would've ever made it through without it. She'd slept a lot, mostly dreamless slumbers that lasted several hours, almost entire days. It had helped heal her. Well, perhaps, looking back on it now, it had been more of a bandage than a cure.

"No thanks," Kara replied. "I'm fine. I wouldn't want to take any of your medications anyway."

"Oh, it's fine. I don't really need it. I just keep refilling my prescription, out of habit, I guess. Doctors don't like it when you stop refilling them," Shannon chuckled.

"I'm feeling alright now. I think I just needed a good cry. Best medicine there is, au naturel."

Shannon sipped her wine. "That's probably true." She swirled the contents of her glass. "This probably has some medicinal value in it too."

"All in moderation."

Shannon popped the lid off the amber bottle and shook out a pale yellow capsule. "I'm going to leave you one at any rate. Just in case. You can look it up online and read all the warnings and side effects if you want." She pushed the pill across the table before closing the bottle and dropping it into her handbag.

"I really am fine."

"I know you are. Don't use it if you don't need it. I take one on the rare occasion when I feel like the walls are closing in. You still look shaky to me. Just put it somewhere for the off-chance you can't sleep or feel overwhelmed. It's just a safety net. I have my days too."

"If you ever want to talk, I'm here. You've definitely seen me at my worst." Kara regretted their friendship seemed one-sided.

"Thanks." Shannon took another drink. "Everyone's on meds these days. Sometimes we just need a little help to cope."

"Well, I don't think I'll need it, but thanks."

"I'm not taking it back. Keep it," Shannon said, and so Kara slipped the pill into her jeans pocket. "Have you heard from your mom?"

Kara shook her head, picking up her cellphone and scrolling through Margaret's texts. "Nothing new."

"Any sign of the ex?"

"Nope." *Not that I've noticed*, Kara thought.

"Relieved?"

Kara laughed. "Yes."

"Good. Just be careful."

Shannon left an hour later with Kara assuring her she was fine, already felt better, and that she intended to turn in early for the night.

"You're sure?" Shannon had asked. "I can stay longer."

"I'm fine. Seriously." Kara had offered a tired smile, ushering the blonde to the door.

After Shannon had been gone for an hour, John called. He was working another all-nighter.

Kara hung up, instantly uneasy, just like that. She had refrained from telling John her energy had been zapped and that she would rather not be alone with the kids overnight. Instead of admitting her current state, she joined the kids in the great room. Her eyes followed the cartoon characters on the TV screen, but her mind was elsewhere. No one was out there trying to get her; there was no proof. It was all that overactive imagination of hers. Surely, she was too mentally exhausted anyway to worry that night, and she would be a grownup: the kids would sleep in their own rooms.

She tucked Lilah in bed first, averting her eyes from the statue laying beside the girl's head, then went to Jack's bedroom. He was already in bed, his light off.

"Goodnight, Jack," she called from the doorway. She paused, waiting for him to say goodnight, but when he didn't respond, she started to pull the door closed.

"Mom?" he said, halting her.

"Yeah?"

He paused before asking, "Do you believe in ghosts?"

Kara froze. "Why?"

Softly, he said, "I do."

"You believe in ghosts?"

"Yeah."

She didn't ask why, but instead assured him, "Nothing will hurt you. Do you know that? Me and Dad are here to protect you always."

But Dad's not here, she bit inwardly.

"I know." He shifted to his stomach, his face turned toward the wall.

She didn't want to ask, not without John there, but she did anyway because this was her son. "Do you want to talk about it?"

There was no hesitation. "No."

She wanted to ask why he was asking, what had prompted him, but she didn't dare. Not tonight when the house was already too quiet and too dark.

"Do you want me to keep the door open?" Kara asked.

"Sure."

"Okay…Goodnight, Jack."

"Goodnight, Mom."

She stepped into the dark hallway, her eyes settling on the bonus room. She strained to see the outline of the door frame. Remembering the small silver ball she had found, she felt her jeans pocket as if it were in there. It wasn't. She couldn't recall where she had placed it. The boxes were still piled in front of the replaced window, a shadowed building blocking a trace of moonlight that barely touched the room. An image of the dream she'd had where she looked from the faceless woman's bedroom back into this room rose in her mind. Her eyes scanned the room, but it was too dark to see beyond that mountain of boxes. But she didn't really want to see. She held her breath and went downstairs, consciously pushing aside Jack's question.

Jack's mom had taken an awful long time to settle down in the great room. That's how Jack felt anyway. It was getting late, but he wasn't tired yet. When he heard the TV channel switch, he flung off his blanket and pulled on his sneakers.

Hearing footsteps, he spun around.

"Where you going?" Lilah stood there, clutching her ugly statue. He didn't care that she carried that thing with her like a security blanket. It was so boring-looking and bland and looked like it was a hundred years old. Of course, he didn't know why girls liked dolls and frilly things anyway, not that this doll was frilly. But it was still a doll, same thing.

"I'm going outside for a minute," he said. "Don't tell Mom."

"Where? The truck?"

"Shhh!"

"I want to go too!" Her voice was low, but hardly a whisper.

"You can't. I'm not going to the camper. I'm just going out for a minute." The thing was, he didn't know where he was going; he just knew he had to go outside. Not to the pool, though. Something itched at him to come out.

Come and see!

"Jack!" she hissed.

He mulled it over, however, not taking long to concede. There might be wild dogs outside, definitely raccoons. It couldn't hurt to have somebody with him.

"Okay," he relented, his voice conspiratorially low. "We're just going out for a little bit. We can catch lightning bugs."

"I know where we can go," Lilah said a little too loud.

"Be quiet!" he hissed. "Mom can't know."

"Why?" she whispered.

The question gave him pause. Why did he need to go out? He couldn't give her a reason, but something urged him to come and see, and he was too restless to lie in bed, dwelling over things he didn't understand.

"I know where we can go," Lilah said again. She held up her statue, the ugly one Jack frowned at now. "She likes it there."

"Sure," he said, just to get her to stop talking. He helped Lilah put on her rain boots, the only shoes in her closet.

They crept down the staircase and paused, hearing the TV channel switch again. Jack nodded his head, signaling it was time to make a break for it. He carefully unlocked the front door and without looking back, they slipped outside.

Chapter Twenty-five

A bang, like an explosion going off in her head, caused Kara to sit up straight, flinging her legs from the couch onto the floor in one fluid motion. Canned laughter came from the TV. Her glazed eyes combed over the great room.

Where is everybody?

Her head was so heavy. The room was dark, the only light in the house coming from the foyer. Something had woken her. She stood, the sudden movement making her dizzy. Her heart thumped faster and off-rhythm, knocking within the confines of her chest. The room was spinning; even the kitchen was set on a rotating tilt.

She stretched her arms out and closed her eyes, trying to steady herself, but that just made her feel nauseous. She opened her eyes and as she lowered her arms, she felt as if she was moving them down through molasses. She was in slow motion, looking around the room.

"John?" she called. But then remembered he was working through the night. That was tonight, right? And the kids…they were in bed.

She lumbered to the switch plate beside the backdoor and flipped on the light. She moved slowly through the bright hallway and up the staircase, forcing her leaden legs up the steps. She stumbled over one, so reached for the railing, her fingers barely skimming it, until she was in the hallway.

She flipped on the hall light and popped her head in Jack's bedroom before entering. His bed was empty, his blankets shoved to the footboard. She glanced around and, seeing he was not there, went to the hall bathroom and flipped on the light. Nobody there.

She looked in Lilah's bedroom, finding crumpled blankets at the foot of her bed. Kara turned on the light and flung open the closet door. Her eyes ran over the floor, the bed, and the dresser. The room was empty and the statue was gone.

Her heart raced. Leaving the light on and moving a tenth of the speed she wanted to go, she returned to Jack's room and looked in his closet and under his bed. He wasn't there. She staggered back to the hallway, paused to look in the bonus room, but it was spinning and the floor rippled beneath her feet. She covered her mouth with her hand in case she got sick and dragged her other arm along the wall as she trudged downstairs. She looked in the garage, finding only her car. She checked her bedroom and bathroom, pausing to look up at the skylight. She was struck still, mesmerized by the moonlight, solid white light beaming down onto the tiled floor. She toed the light with her bare feet, flexing them in the spotlight before looking up again and noticing a ring circling the five points of the skylight: had the leak returned?

Her head flinched back as if someone had yanked on her hair, returning her to the crisis at hand: where were the kids?

She moved like a buffalo into the kitchen. The clinking of the backdoor's bolt sounded like a faraway echo; she wasn't even sure it had been her fingers turning the lock.

"Jack? Lilah?" she called, desperately. Escaping the stuffy house and entering the chilly night lessened some of the weight. Something tugged, urging her toward the woods. She padded barefoot through the dewy grass, then entered the darkness where she moved blindly through the trees. Branches reached out and bushes grabbed at her. She was being scratched, but didn't register any pain. She was lighter now, hurrying along, narrowly avoiding a wizened maple that was slowly dying, being eaten alive by invisible pests that gnawed at its insides.

There was a flash of white lashing out just ahead of her. She ran, grabbing it, soon realizing it was a scarf billowing in the breeze. It was tied around the base of an ash, either mocking her for her troubles, or signing to her some much-needed encouragement. She yanked on it, wanting to tear it down. Her fingers groped until they felt the knotted bunch at one of its ends.

Using both hands, she loosened the knot and opened the pouch, revealing a soft fuzz center. She pulled at it, massaging it with her fingers, then stilled. She recoiled, dropping it, realizing it was fur or hair.

She started to turn away but stopped, hearing a voice. She couldn't discern whether it came from her thoughts or from someone lurking in the darkness. She was fairly certain it wasn't her kids. There was no childlike tone in those words.

Not safe. Not here.

They still think this is theirs.

She backed up, stumbling. Straightening, she sensed something swaying just beyond her line of sight. Slowly, she turned her head. A few trees ahead, mere feet in the choking woods, something thick and rounded, undulated with the wind. There was suddenly a hitch in the rhythm and Kara's eyes widened, zeroing in on it, a mallet, swinging at eye-level with her.

The voice hissed, *They didn't do it. It wasn't them.*

She pushed back her wind-whipped hair from her face.

It wasn't a mallet at all. Realization crept in as she registered what it was. There was no mistake, even there in the night. As if moonlight had caught it just right, she recognized the heel of a swinging human foot. It peeked out from the torn hem of a light-colored dress.

Kara gasped, unable to scream like she wanted to, and spun around, awkwardly stepping back. Hearing it—*her?*—creak in the death sway, Kara glanced back around, facing it through strands of hair that acted like a blindfold.

Don't look!

But she did look. She peeked through strands of dark hair hanging in front of her face.

It wasn't a human that swung, after all. Something small and, extended, a dark shape, hung from the limb, instead.

Kara gasped, tearing her eyes away and backing up.

Please don't be Blacky.

She didn't want to look, but had to. Intelligently, she knew it couldn't be Blacky. That had been years ago. Finding a human out there—that would've been surreal, but that would've made more sense.

Now you're telling yourself it makes sense to stumble upon human corpses in the woods!

Kara looked up again at the tree. The corpse was gone. She could just make out the outline of the tree in the darkness, but saw nothing hung from it. She glanced at the other trees, in case she had looked at the wrong one, but no one hung from the trees.

Kara backed up, tripped, and fell down. She was caught. She twisted, shifting her legs to free herself. Finding it was only a thick vine drooping from a tree over the ground and not a madman vying to string her up, she scrambled back to her feet. Her eyes darted over the trees, noticing the white scarves that whipped in the wind. The trees were spinning; Kara bent over, willing the sickness to come out, but it festered until it rolled further into the depths of her stomach. She finally staggered away from the waving scarves. A fog was rolling in, quickly edging around her and the encroaching trees. She spun around and around, stumbling over tree roots, wondering where she was, which way was out.

After a moment, she stopped, noticing yellow dots of light cutting through the mist. They came toward her, at least a dozen of them, rhythmically swinging right and left. She backed up until she struck. She pressed against it, waiting. As they neared, she realized the dots were actually lanterns. The cloaked figures holding them kept to the shadows. They made no sound and, moving as if they glided just above the ground, they circled her and the tree she leaned against, the glow of their lanterns shining on her. She held up her arms, shielding herself, as if she could hide. Finally, the lights turned away and the shadowed figures passed by. She lowered her arms, watching them slip by. Just as quickly as they had come, the lights and the strangers had disappeared into the fog.

In her stupor, she was on the search again.

She didn't call out for her children this time, not with them wandering through the woods. Her eyes were alert as she combed over the ground and trees. Then the fog broke just enough, so she could make out Diane's form.

Kara hung back, ducking behind oaks, and watched. Her neighbor was in her garden, doubled over, rocking back and forth. Kara was at least thirty yards away, but she could see the old woman sobbed, a hand at her throat.

She started toward Diane, to offer comfort, but the strangers reappeared, sweeping closer, blocking her. They formed a line that separated them. However, Diane seemed oblivious to them.

With a pang of guilt, Kara turned in the opposite direction and trudged away, Diane's sobs fading until they were no longer heard. An animal screeched; something scampered near Kara, smacking against saplings and brush. Kara moved faster until she found the exit and escaped into her backyard. The crisp night air wrapped around her.

"Jack!" she screamed. "Lilah!" Wildly, she raced to the front yard and down the hill to the road. It was empty and not a soul was outside. She stopped abruptly, breathing so hard it rocked her.

Where were they? Had someone taken them?

A scream, high-pitched and short, pierced the air. If she hadn't been outside and hadn't been straining to hear, she would've missed it. It had come from down the road.

She took off with a jolt.

The soles of her feet slapped against rough pavement. She nearly fell three times as she raced down the center of the road. Fog gathered ahead of her. Adrenaline pumped wolfishly through her, filling her until she was practically seeping with the stuff. Finally, she saw the sagging barn greet her like a deformed being, a monster. She loathed it now, but she couldn't discern if it was because of its ugly face or from what she would find inside.

Slowing down, she stepped onto the grass bordering the barn. She gritted her teeth, entering the building. "Jack!" she cried. "Lilah!" It was nearly pitch-black inside. She winced as decayed straw stabbed her feet. "Are you guys in here?"

"Mom! Over here!" Jack called from deeper inside.

She choked back a sob in relief. "Is Lilah with you?"

"Yeah! She's here."

"Mommy, Jack hurt his leg!" Lilah called from the darkness.

"His leg?" Kara, her arms stretched in front of her, slowly followed their voices. It was like playing Blind Man's Bluff in a stranger's basement. "Where are you guys?"

"Under the loft. I fell out of it. Mom, I think I broke it," Jack's voice was calm.

Taking one step at a time, each foot sliding ahead of the other, stirring up straw, it felt like it took forever for Kara to find them.

"Here I am," Jack said, his fingers finding her arm in the darkness.

"Do you think you can walk out of here?" she asked him.

"I can try."

She moved her arm blindly under his and gingerly helped him up. He groaned.

"Mommy, where are you?" Lilah called.

"Right here, baby. Can you feel for my hand?" Kara reached toward Lilah's voice. Invisible fingers plunged into her palm. "Is it one leg, Jack, that hurts?"

"Yeah."

"Okay, try to put all your weight on the other leg. Try to walk out of here."

"Okay."

She felt all of his weight push down on her as he pressed against her. Slowly, cautiously, Kara led her offspring out of the barn. The path was free of obstacles, which was an answered prayer. A three-person body, they kept in a straight line, sliding their feet along until they felt grass.

Kara hadn't realized her eyes had been closed. She opened them and collapsed onto the ground, pulling her kids down with her. Relief flooded her, the emotion raw and overwhelming. She cried, resting her wet face in her hands for a moment, willing herself to calm down and take control of the situation.

Composing herself, she asked Jack which leg it was and he pointed at the right, which was turned unnaturally. "It hurts." He gritted his teeth, tears welling in his eyes.

"Okay, we have a little ways to walk to get back to the house." She thought for a second. "I can hurry back to the house and bring the car down. Are you okay sitting here for a few minutes, or do you want to try to hike back? You can lean on me." She looked around, her eyes settling on the silhouette of the farmhouse next door, dark and still as always. Her eyes darted again and sought out the porch-lit house across the road.

"I don't think I can make it that far."

"Okay, that's okay." She turned to Lilah, who had been so good and quiet sitting there beside her brother. "I need you to sit here with Jack. I'll be right back with the car."

Lilah nodded and inched closer to him. He was now lying flat on his back, his legs extended in front of him, one perfectly straight and the other twisted. He rolled part-way onto his left side, yelping in agony.

"Mom, hurry," he pleaded. Tears trickled down his cheeks.

Kara didn't dally. Her head clearing, she set off, taking the shortcut through the woods. She didn't care what might lurk there. She didn't look back, running into low-hanging branches and thornbushes. On one especially strong bush, she got trapped, her tee-shirt tangled up in a mess of burr hell. She swore loudly, tugging away. She returned home, ran through the unlocked backdoor, grabbed her car keys and cellphone, and hurried into the garage.

Chapter Twenty-six

Holding Lilah's hand, Kara came through swinging doors, leaving Jack behind in the hospital emergency area. The waiting room was nearly empty with one woman sitting at the check-in counter, penciling in an adult coloring book. Kara's eyes drifted over the chairs and couches facing the TV that dipped from a stand secured to the far wall. To her dismay, her mother sat beside John.

"Hi," Kara said, approaching them. Lilah let go of her hand, the statue in the crook of her other arm, and scrambled onto John's lap.

"Is he okay?" John asked.

"His leg's broken," Kara replied, sitting down beside John, who was now sandwiched between the two women. "He fractured his tibia. He'll be in a cast for a few weeks and then a walking boot. Jack's handling it really well. The doctor will be done plastering soon."

Lilah said with reassurance, "Jack's not gonna be like Marvin." She rubbed the clay frog's head and looked more like she was talking to it than to any of the adults in the room. "He's gonna be OK."

John and Kara exchanged glances before John said, "That's right, Lilahbean. Jack's going to be alright."

Kara watched her daughter for a moment, the girl's focus seemingly only on the frog. She looked unaffected by the weight of the words she had just spoken. Kara didn't add any additional words of encouragement. It hadn't occurred to her until then that the hospital they were presently in was where Marvin had passed away. She wondered vaguely if his ghost hovered near.

She finally adjusted in her seat and folded her arms, brought back to the reality that her mother, quite in the flesh, sat only a handful of feet away from her. Kara folded her arms, her eyes on the TV screen. The news program went into a commercial, which started with a series of flashing bright images. The light made her head hurt, so she turned her eyes down to the strap of her purse. "I'm surprised you're here, Mom. You really didn't need to come."

Margaret leaned forward, looking at her. She said, matter-of-factly, "When you called me frantic, what do you expect?"

Kara scowled. "I called you? John, did you—"

Margaret's eyebrows shot up. "You don't remember?"

John replied, "She was here when I got here."

Kara glanced at her mother's incredulous face and turned away again.

She had called? When?

"I guess it's just been too upsetting to remember. It happened so fast." Kara racked her mind trying to remember dialing Margaret. She had no recollection of it; frankly, she hardly remembered calling John. She looked in her purse, knowing the pill Shannon had given her hours ago was no longer there. Kara had bought into the promise of peaceful sleep. How strong had it been?

She searched inwardly, trying to remember what had transpired. She had lain on the couch, had woken up…She had found the kids in the barn. And what had Jack said about the hayloft…?

He wanted to check something out, he'd said as they had waited for the doctor to exam him. He couldn't explain it any better. He just thought—had felt—there was something there. He just had to look.

Come and see.

When Kara had asked what was in the loft, her interest piqued, he had said simply, "Nothing. It was empty."

Now Margaret was claiming she had called her, implored her to come. But when had she contacted her?

John was shifting in his seat, stirring her from her thoughts. "It's the first traumatic experience we've had," he mumbled.

Kara flinched, whipping her head to look at him. His eyes were on the TV. A classic game show was on now, the volume too low to make sense of the host's jokes. The first traumatic experience they had had? *What about Sophie?* she wanted to ask. Had he completely blocked out *that* traumatic experience?

"I can think of another one," Margaret said quietly, speaking Kara's thoughts.

Lilah fidgeted and hopped off John's lap. Pressing the statue against her chest, she curled up on Kara's lap, propping her legs up on the empty chair beside her.

"So, how's my granddaughter? I'll bet you're ready for bed," Margaret chuckled, acting the part of doting grandmother, a farce. "Or maybe breakfast. The sun'll be up soon."

Lilah shifted, closing her eyes and turning away.

John stood, saying he was getting coffee. "Want anything?"

Kara said, "No," and Margaret didn't reply. Kara watched him leave, not noticing her mother had slid into his seat until she turned back.

A nurse walked up to them, smiling kindly. "Jack's being very brave. They're just about done. You can come back now."

"Thank you. We're waiting on my husband," Kara said.

They watched her leave and were silent for a few minutes, staring at the flickering screen until Margaret asked, "What happened? Were you sleeping?" Her eyes searched Kara's face.

Interpreting it as an accusation, Kara said nothing. She twisted her hand gently in Lilah's dark tresses. If anything had happened to Jack and Lilah, she never would've been able to forgive herself. She rubbed her aching temples.

262

"Kara, what happened tonight?" Margaret's tone had softened.

The hairs on the back of Kara's neck stood; *she's trying to manipulate me, trying to act the part of mother*. She steeled herself, but replied honestly, "The kids snuck out of bed." *Leave it at that*, she told herself. *She doesn't need to know anything else.*

Margaret's eyes narrowed. "Is that normal?" She softened again, though, explaining that, in her stupor, Kara had called her frantically, asking her to come to the hospital.

Impossible. Why would Kara do that?

Kara closed her eyes, resting her head back against the wall, and waited for John to return.

They invited Margaret to sleep at their house when they went home an hour later. It was too late for her to make the long drive to Cosgrove. It was a normal offer a daughter would make to her mother. They exchanged little more than goodnights as Margaret settled in Jack's bedroom. He took the couch, his casted leg propped up on pillows. Kara, John, and Lilah went to bed too. This time, as dawn neared, Kara had no difficulty falling asleep.

Late morning found John in the home office and Kara and Margaret at the kitchen table, eating breakfast. It wasn't difficult to keep quiet so as not to wake Jack, as the awkwardness alone would've kept them in that state under normal circumstances. Kara, the first to finish eating, thought a tour of the house would've made the moment less awkward, but she didn't bother offering and her mother didn't ask for one.

Margaret dabbed her mouth with a paper towel. Kara watched her until she caught her staring. Kara looked away, her eyes resting on a white, gauzy cloth poking out of Margaret's open purse. A snapshot of the scarves hanging in the woods flashed in her mind.

Not hiding her rising suspicion, Kara demanded, "What's this?" She pinched the material.

"Nothing." Margaret brushed her hand away and tucked in the gauzy material.

"What is it?" Kara reached into the purse.

"Kara!" Margaret tried to push her away, but the invading hand shot in, snatching the material.

"What's this?" Kara turned the rectangular patch in her hand.

"That's a handkerchief."

The ends of the cloth were embroidered with lilacs. Kara remembered it from her childhood. She felt a mix of embarrassment and disappointment.

With alarm, Margaret asked, "Are you alright?"

Kara didn't meet her gaze as she shoved it back into the purse. She didn't reply.

Margaret looked at her daughter and then finally stood up. "I'd better be going."

Kara followed her to the front door. Without emotion, she said, "Thanks for coming out." She opened the door and met Margaret's eyes. Seeing they were bloodshot, Kara reluctantly softened her tone, "I didn't mean to worry you."

"I'm glad you called me," Margaret replied, crisply.

"Are you able to find your way out of town?"

"Yes. It doesn't seem complicated."

"Goodbye, Margaret." John had appeared at the office doorway. He gave her a slight smile that she didn't return.

"Bye, John."

Kara walked her outside.

"Goodbye, Kara," Margaret said when they got to the edge of the driveway. "Take care."

As Margaret started to turn away, Kara blurted, "Have you heard anything more from David?"

"David?" Margaret turned around.

"Has he reached out to you again? You know, you could've returned my calls instead of playing games with me."

"I don't know what you mean, Kara. David? Jack's father?"

Kara cringed at the mention of the biological connection to Jack. "Yes! David! Has he reached out to you again?"

"…I don't know what you mean. He—"

"Has he contacted you again?" Why was her mother playing this game? Didn't she realize how cruel it was?

Margaret's voice now had a defensive edge to it as she said, "I haven't heard from David since you were in college. I don't know what you mean, 'he contacted me.' I never told you that."

"What do you mean?" Kara asked in exasperation. "You texted me about it." Kara pulled the cellphone out of her jeans pocket and switched to the texts she had received.

"I never texted about him. I haven't even spoken his name since…I don't know how long. Maybe you heard this from Tracy."

Kara scrolled through the text messages. The immediate ones were old, with no mention of David. There weren't many between Margaret and her, but she ran her thumb up and down the window, sliding the same texts back and forth, as if she had overlooked them. But no matter how many times she scanned through the messages, she found none about David.

Where had they gone? Had Kara deleted them by mistake? She turned to the texts from Tracy, even though she knew all the messages had come from Margaret.

As she checked her email, even though she knew their exchange had been through texts, Margaret asked with concern, "Has he contacted you?"

Kara gave up the search, wracking her brain why she couldn't find them.

"Kara? Have you heard from David?"

"I…No."

"But someone else has?"

"…I-I thought…" Had anyone heard from him? If Margaret hadn't told her that, then who had? How could this be? The texts were…gone? She finally said, "I thought you told me he reached out to you…I guess I misunderstood..?"

"That's an odd thing to misunderstand. Where would you ever get that idea?"

"I don't know." Kara turned her gaze to the lawn, then rolled her eyes downhill to the road.

"That doesn't make any sense. Are you not telling me something? Are you keeping David a secret from me?"

Her mother was now accusing her of withholding information. Kara pressed her free hand to her forehead. "Like I said, I heard wrong. I haven't heard from David. Everything's fine." What in the world was going on?

Margaret stared at her until finally saying, brusquely, "Alright. Tell me if you hear anything."

Kara clipped back, "I will. Have a safe drive."

"Tell the kids I said goodbye."

Kara sat on the porch swing, her eyes on her mother's car as it drove down the driveway and turned onto the road, but she didn't really see her. Her thoughts were scrambled. What had happened to the messages? She looked down at her phone and scrolled through the texts again. They were short and trivial, no mention of an ex-boyfriend showing up after ten years. But she couldn't have made it up, because she had read Shannon the messages. That was proof she hadn't imagined it. It hadn't been a dream…

She tapped Shannon's name on the screen. When Shannon answered, Kara jumped right in, asking, "Remember how I told you about my ex and the texts my mom sent me?"

"Yes."

"I read you the texts, right?"

"Yes."

"So, I didn't sit there and hallucinate it."

"Huh? What do you mean?"

"I just confronted my mom about David and she said she hadn't seen him and hadn't texted me. I don't get where they could've gone...Do you think there's a glitch with the phone carrier?"

Shannon said, slowly, "Okay, so let me understand this. Your mom's texts are gone?"

"Only the ones about David. Those are gone."

"How can that be? The other texts she sent you are still in your phone history?"

"Yeah."

There was a pause as Shannon thought it through. Finally, she said, "I don't know why those would be the only ones missing if there was some kind of issue with the phone carrier. That doesn't make sense."

"That would be weird." Kara sighed. "Well, they were the latest messages. Maybe it was just the most recent ones that glitched...You know they were there." She laughed lightly, trying to comfort herself. "It's not like I imagined it all."

But Shannon's reply wasn't encouraging when she said, "You read them to me, but I didn't see them."

Kara narrowed her eyes, looking at the yard. "What do you mean?"

"I think," Shannon began, choosing her words carefully, "you've been dealing with a lot lately. Lack of sleep, grief, stress...I think it's really easy for us to trick ourselves."

"I couldn't have imagined reading you texts!"

"I don't have any other explanation, Kara. If that's not what happened, then what do you think it could be?"

Kara didn't say anything, her memory of reading the texts to Shannon while they sat at the kitchen table flashing in her mind. She had read them to her...She couldn't have imagined that.

"Do you want me to come over? I know it's been rough..."

"No, I'm fine," Kara said quickly. "It's a glitch or something..."

"Did you check Tracy's texts? Could they have been from her?"

"No. Tracy didn't send them."

"Are you sure? Maybe David contacted her instead and you got her and your mom mixed up."

"She didn't know David."

"Oh…Well, you have said she and your mom are close. Maybe she's the one playing games with you."

Could Tracy have sent them? Tracy and her mother had seemed to have grown closer over the last few months, and Kara hadn't talked much to her since the move. Could Tracy be callous enough to make up a story about David returning? Why would she do that? Was she bitter about Kara moving away? Their friendship had dwindled, that was clear, and she had suggested she move back to Cosgrove…

"Then I don't know," Shannon said.

Realization came over Kara then. "Wait a second."

"What?"

Kara slapped the seat of the swing. "My mom must've deleted them!"

"What?"

"Wow. That's crazy." Kara shook her head. She explained Jack's accident and how Margaret had spent the night. She must've gotten a hold of Kara's cellphone sometime in the early morning and deleted the messages. Her mother had reached a new low. She had worried Kara just because she and the kids had moved away.

"Wait. Your mom texted you these things about your ex and then deleted them? And then she denied she knew anything about it?"

Kara gave a short laugh, swinging. "Apparently."

"That makes no sense."

"A little revenge I guess?"

"Why would that make you want to move back to Cosgrove?"

"I don't know."

"If anything, it'd make you want to stay away."

"I don't know. None of it makes any real sense." Kara groaned. "Maybe she deleted them because she realized how juvenile it was. And then when I asked about it, she didn't know what to say."

"So, what are you going to do now?"

"Eventually, I'll have to confront her again, I guess. But I'm not talking to her for a while."

"I'd still keep your guard up, though."

"Yeah."

"Seriously. You're still not sure about what's going on. Don't think you're out of the woods yet."

"Hey!" Kara chuckled. "Are you trying to scare me?"

Shannon's voice lightened, not sounding as foreboding, "Sorry, too many true crime shows. But just be careful. You know what I mean?"

"Yeah, I do." They said goodbye and Kara clicked off her phone. She looked out over the road, contemplating her mother's actions. There was no logical explanation other than Margaret having deleting the messages. Had her mother looked guilty when she had denied sending them? Kara must have zoned out her reaction due to her own confusion.

Well, Kara surmised, her eyes trailing to the lamppost on the driveway, it was good news David wasn't seeking her out. She just had to deal with her mother, and she wasn't afraid of her.

Kara got up and walked to the oak, looking over at the lemon house. A shadow hung over her as she recalled pieces of the night. Had Diane been in woods? The memory was fuzzy and she wasn't sure she could trust it.

Kara crossed the yard and approached the Foremans' house. The dirty men's sneakers lay lopsidedly on the stoop, as if just tossed there. She peered through the screen door and, seeing no one, knocked.

She waited, but no one came. She looked inside at the door to the house, then pulled the handle, but the screen door was locked. Perhaps, Diane had left town to grieve with family. Kara realized she didn't really know Diane at all.

Kara went home, stopping in the office doorway. John looked up from his desk, but neither said anything. She turned away and as she started down the hallway, she felt something bubble inside, rising from the pit of her belly. It urged her to go out the backdoor. She hurriedly crossed the backyard, not stopping until she was at the tree line. White flaps of material waved at her in the breeze.

Why were they tied to the trees?

She didn't want to see them anymore. She yanked on the lowest hanging scarf, knotted around a fat limb. The material ripped, a third of it coming off in her hand. She pulled on the remaining scrap, but it wouldn't come undone. She tried to untie the knot, but was unable to. She grabbed a place higher on the material and tugged harder, but it wouldn't tear.

"Kara!"

She spun around.

"What are you doing?" John came across the yard.

"I'm pulling these down!" she hollered back from the woods. She turned around, seeking another scarf.

"Why?"

She was already pulling at the next one. It tore in half. "Because I'm tired of them." She balled up the slip of fabric in her hand. "Can we get all of these down?"

He reached up, touching the knot of the first scarf she had attempted to untie. His fingers swiped over it. "They're really secure." He looked up. "Some are kinda high. I could get a ladder…"

"Why are they here?"

"I don't know. Maybe Diane knows. Have you seen her yet?"

Kara looked at the yellow house, peeking through the trees.

Yes, last night…I think.

She looked down, searching for footprints, but the ground looked undisturbed. Now in daylight the memory of the night was absurd.

"She's not home," Kara mumbled. "Let's get the ladder."

"Are you okay?"

"I'm fine." She led him to the garage and keyed in the door code. As the door rattled open, she made the excuse, "You know how it is when I talk to my mom." It was the easy way out. If she told him about her mother's prank, John would be done forever with Margaret. But maybe cutting her out completely would be wise. It was something Kara would have to consider.

"I was surprised to see her," he said, pulling the ladder off the wall.

"Yeah, well..." She had no idea how to explain why her mother had come to the hospital, why Kara had called her. "She's my mom," she finally said. An easy excuse.

He didn't press any further as she followed him as far as the driveway. She placed a hand on the lamppost, feeling the cool metal, and watched him disappear around the house to the backyard. Someone had stood there watching her, now a faraway memory. If not David, who had it been? Or had that been a dream?

When evening came, Kara crept into the garage. She opened the trash bin, finding the pile of dingy white scarves John had taken down. He had found five. They hadn't come any closer to solving the mystery of why they had been tied to trees.

She selected one, stretching it to arms' length. A pocket was sewn into one end. Easily, she picked apart the loose thread and unfolded the material. Inside was a mound of brown hair. From the look of it, it was human.

271

Chapter Twenty-seven

The cast on Jack's leg was a tomb. Stiff, hot, and itchy, it was a constant reminder his leg was broken. Grace Township had been graced with an Indian summer afternoon and the heat and humidity of the day were stifling. He had been in the cast for a couple weeks and he was miserable. Lying on the deck, his back propped up by two patio chair cushions, he played lazily with his action figures, using the surface of his belly as a play mat. He stayed away from the pool, but every so often, he glanced at its edge, unable to see the water inside.

After a while, he dropped the action figures on the floor and looked out at the trees. Sparkling metal caught his eye. He hadn't been to the camper for weeks. He had thought, briefly, of showing it to Alan the day he had come over, even though it was still a mess. Finding the blonde hair wrapped around him in the pool had changed his mind. He hadn't said anything to his friend; he had acted as if nothing had frightened him away from swimming for the day (for life). He wouldn't have known how much to divulge and how much he actually believed to have been real and not imagined. Truthfully, however, he believed it all to be real. He just tried not to think about it.

Jack heaved himself up and grabbed his crutches. He moved easily off the deck and over the grass. He passed through the bracken and trees, seeing the camper squatting in the grass, waiting. When he came to it, he was sweating. He wiped his face with his forearm.

The itch under the cast was now unbearable. Invisible fingers trailed up and down his leg to the point that it almost tickled. It reminded him of a game his dad played with him every once in a while. He would run his fingers slowly up and down Jack's arm, and in a sing-song voice, sing, "Can you keep a secret? Can you keep a secret? Up to your elbow and dowwwn. Up to your elbow and dowwwn. Up and dowwwwwn." The object of the game was not laugh and not pull your arm away. You kept a straight face and tried your best at keeping your mind elsewhere, because if you paid attention to it, you were doomed.

But this was different. It was like someone was running several long strands of thread up and down the underbelly of the cast, from the top of his ankle to just below his knee.

Up and down, up and down, up and down. Can you keep a secret? Up and dowwwn, up and dowwwn. Uppppp and dowwwwwwn.

He shuffled around the camper, squirming, twisting what he could of his right foot, trying to turn the muscle trapped underneath the plaster. He set his crutches against the side of the truck, and leaning against it, bent over and shoved his fingers inside the front of the cast. He was able to get them in up to his knuckles, but his fingers didn't have enough space to scratch where he needed to. What he did reach just made him tickle more.

Can you keep a secret? Can you keep a secrettttt?

He pulled out his hand and, desperate, searched the ground for something he could use. The broken tree branches were too wide and the thorny bramble would be too painful. He stamped his good foot, kicking as best he could with one leg at the wild overgrowth.

"Ugh!" He had kicked free a discarded tree limb on the ground, which had been sheltering about a hundred ants and a handful of worms. He couldn't tell which creature was feasting on which. He moved his foot to slide the limb back into place, hiding them again.

As the sun beat down from directly overhead, the top of his head started to burn. Not only did his protected leg feel like it was being nibbled by insects racing up and down it, he needed to scratch his sweaty head and back.

He wanted to return to the house and forget the camper, but he would never make it back if he didn't take care of the burning, stabbing sensation pulsing up and down his leg.

Up and down, up and down, up and dowwwwn.

He pushed off from the camper, pressed his weight down on the crutches, and moved to the rear trailer hitch. He laid the crutches down on the bumper, leaning his left hip against it. Eyes scanning over the bramble, he knew there had to be something he could use. The perfect branch, long and spindly, was no more than three feet ahead of him. Using one of the crutches for support, he bent over and stretched out an arm as long as it would reach. He wrapped fingers around the skinny branch and moved back to lean against the bumper.

Not realizing he was smiling, Jack needled the tip of the branch inside the side of the cast. He moved it up and down, rubbing lightly before turning it toward the top of his leg. Ah, sweet relief! He rubbed firmly, moving it over his dry skin. He dug deeper, pressing into his hidden flesh, the madness of picturing hundreds of ants crawling up and down the length of his leg fueling his drive. He felt heady as a shadow draped over him. The bright white of the cast gradually dimmed. He wondered vaguely if he was going to faint.

"Jack! Are you out there?" his mother called. "It's dinnertime!"

He glimpsed part of her through the trees, swallowing a lump in his throat. "O-okay!" he managed to call back. His frenzied fist suddenly felt the snap and release of the branch. Stunned, he pulled it out of the cast, dragging it toward his naked knee. The bottom of it dangled by a few threads of bark, its broken end red.

Fascinated, he leaned against the rear bumper, the stifling heat filling him, drawing him to exhaustion. He ran his hand over the red. It was wet and coated his palm. It was blood, he realized.

Jack looked down at his cast, and although the shadow had lifted, it was now flecked with red at the top and bottom edges. Blood trickled down to his toes. He watched strands of red race slowly until they slid off the side of his foot, dripping onto the ground, getting lost in the grass.

The light-headedness and itchiness were gone and he felt cooler. Clouds rolled subtly over the sun, the breeze soothing. After a while, he grabbed his crutches, shoved off the camper, and carefully made his way through the tangled bramble back to the house.

When he came inside, Kara commented, "You're moving really good."

He sat at the table and looked down at his cast and toes. The blood had disappeared, and his cast and foot were quite unmarred. His brow furrowed, he straightened and looked out the window. A shadow passed over the glimpsing camper.

He jumped, then grabbed his crutches, ignoring Kara asking, "What do you see, Jack?"

He leaned against the window, nearly pressing his face against the pane.

"Jack?" Kara set a bowl of sauce on the table and moved to stand behind him.

"I'm hungry," Lilah announced, trekking into the kitchen, cradling the statue.

"Hung…" Kara stopped and blinked at her daughter. She realized Lilah had said the word correctly this time. Kara turned back to Jack. "What're you looking at, Jack?"

The shadow had lifted. Jack's eyes squinted over what he could see of the camper and just beyond.

"Jack?"

"Nothing," he replied, hurriedly. "I just thought I saw something."

Kara went back to the counter for a plate of bread, asking, "Was it a deer?"

"No. I don't think so," he mumbled. His eyes searched the area surrounding the camper. Nothing now. He returned to his seat, trying to push away the unnerving sensation.

Kara looked out the window over the sink. She glanced over the woods, not seeing what had captured Jack's attention, and turned back to the table. She smiled. "Hey, your field trip to the museum is tomorrow. I'm chaperoning."

"You are?" Still distracted, Jack started fixing his plate. He flinched when Lilah sat down across from him.

"Are you okay?" Kara asked.

"Yeah," he replied, not meeting her eyes.

Kara glanced out the window and then back at him. "And guess what else?"

"What?"

"The cast comes off tomorrow!"

"Already?"

"The doctor's moving you to a boot. We'll go to your appointment after."

Excitement didn't register on his face. "Can I skip the museum then?"

"No, but you're leaving school early."

His thoughts returned to the woods; could it get in the house? "Is dad coming home soon?"

She sighed, sitting down. "He should be home soon. I'll call him after dinner."

"Why don't you call him now?" Jack was looking out the window again, making the hairs on the back of her neck stand.

"Are you alright? Jack?"

He glanced at her, then looked down at his plate. "Yeah."

"Is there someone out there?" *The figure who watches me?*

"No. Just…I didn't see anything. I just want Dad home."

"Me too."

"What time's the field trip?"

"We meet at the museum at nine. Your class is walking, but we're driving."

"I don't take a bus," Lilah said, matter-of-factly.

"Nope, you don't." Kara smiled at her before returning her attention to Jack. "Sound like a plan, Jack?"

Chewing a forkful of pasta, he nodded.

Chapter Twenty-eight

The SUV following Kara honked, a light tap on the horn, but she didn't hear it. Nor did she notice the look Jack gave her from the passenger seat of the sedan as she slowed on Main Street. The For Sale sign was gone, no longer marring the front lawn of the Collumber house. She felt a pang of disappointment. Had it been sold? Her eyes drew in the double front doors, shuttered to the town.

"Mom?"

A lace curtain on the second floor wiggled. Kara inhaled sharply, pressing firmly on the brake. The SUV behind came to a screeching halt and laid on the horn.

"Mom, why are you stopping?" Jack asked with alarm at the same moment Kara realized her reckless action.

She glanced in the rearview mirror, seeing the driver's arms wave in agitation. She peeled her eyes away, pressing on the gas until she was down the street. She maneuvered into a parking spot in front of the single-story Grace Township Museum. Neither Jack nor she said a word as she helped him out of the car.

Two white-haired ladies and a middle-aged brunette greeted Jack's class just inside the door. Kara smiled at a few chaperones and Jack's teacher, Mrs. Haley, as she and Jack joined the fringes of the group. The brunette announced she'd be their tour guide and jumped right into her presentation. She started on what Ohio was like when Native Americans called the area home before settlers arrived. Kara followed behind as the group moved to a display case of artifacts.

Kara glanced around the thread-bare, carpeted house-converted museum. It wasn't difficult to visualize the living room they stood in, see the kitchen that used to be down the hall and the bedrooms beyond. The rooms were dim, as there were few windows, but floor lamps were on throughout.

"Now, does anyone here know the significance of arrowheads?" the tour guide asked the class. She held one up, looking around expectantly.

"Kara."

Kara raised her eyebrows, but saw it wasn't the guide who had said her name. As a student responded to the guide's question, Kara glanced around. She turned to her right, looking expectantly at the woman beside her, but the chaperone gave her a confused look and turned away.

"Kara."

Kara jerked around, making eye contact with the woman behind her. The lady leaned away, scowling.

"Kara."

This time it came from somewhere on her right. Kara glanced over the rest of the pack again. No one was looking in her direction. Had it been a man's voice? She wasn't sure.

"Kara."

Her eyes darted ahead at the guide.

"Er, ahem, *care of*, that is." The guide cleared her throat. "Excuse me. Settlers and Revolutionary War veterans found the land here satisfactory. Part of the compensation soldiers earned was acreage, something many took advantage of." The brunette led the group to a tall, glass-encased display where a manikin was dressed in full regular's uniform, brandishing a calf-skin canteen. She droned on about the attire of the day worn by patriots who strategized and fought invading redcoats.

Kara's head had started throbbing. She glanced around, but didn't immediately see Jack. Her vision was darkening and the guide was rambling. When the brunette moved again, her captive audience following to a display sitting on top of a sideboard, Kara didn't budge.

Something touched her shoulder, making her spin around.

"Are you alright?" one of the white-haired guides asked.

To Kara, the woman's face was too close and her features distinct, whereas her surroundings tilted and blurred in contrast.

"You look a bit peaked. Would you like some water?"

Kara swallowed the lump in her throat and blinked. "I-I think I'll go outside for s-some air."

"Would you like me to come with you?"

Kara shook her head and walked to the door, feeling dizzy, but moving surprisingly sure-footed. She made her way to a sidewalk bench, hearing the door close behind her once she was seated.

She tugged on her purse zipper, her eyes resting on a group of women across the street. One leisurely pushed and pulled a baby stroller as they chatted. Kara wondered if they had any real worries or drama snaking into their lives. Did they catch glimpses of their exes in grocery stores, in town, on their very own street? Did they have vindictive mothers who played cruel pranks she denied so as to increase paranoia in them?

She shielded her eyes, looking down the sidewalk, watching a cardinal land on the stop of a stop sign.

Did they have nightmares?

She tried to remember her dream from the night before, but she couldn't think. She was so tired, nothing made sense anymore.

I think someone watches me from the shadows.

And maybe Jack sees shadows too, she thought, suddenly remembering his question about ghosts. Had that been the night he had broken his leg?

Clouds shifted and she was bathed in sunlight. The women she had been watching had wandered away. Three old men sat on a bench across the road. One of them said something she couldn't make out and they chortled, their laughter rolling. It was a storybook town, and she wished she was a more active member in that story.

A woman darted past her then, startling Kara. Her brown shoulder-length hair flapped from side-to-side against her back. Kara watched her run across the nearly-deserted street, finding her resemblance to Tracy strong. If Kara hadn't known better, she could have mistaken her for Tracy. From the distance, as the brunette hopped up the curb and onto the sidewalk, joined now by a brown-haired man in a suit, she did look very similar to Tracy. But Tracy wouldn't be in Gracie Town without telling Kara. Kara wasn't happy with her as of late, but they weren't out and out quarreling. There'd be no reason for her to be there. The woman was just a lookalike; most likely, she didn't look at all like Tracy up-close. And now, focusing on the man, Kara's breath caught involuntarily. Positive she recognized him, she saw the woman step into a restaurant with Desmond Howard.

"Are you feeling better?" the white-haired tour guide called from behind her.

Kara turned around to look at the woman, who was standing at the museum entrance. She called she was feeling better, which was true. Her headache had eased, but now she realized her arms were cold. As Desmond and Tracy's doppelganger had disappeared inside the restaurant, Kara returned to the museum.

The guide clucked, letting her pass by. "Flu season will be here before we know it. I hope you aren't catching anything." She gestured with her chin toward the back of the building. "They've gone to the basement. That's where we keep the modern Gracie Town models and maps. We have a nice section on commerce down there too. I can show you where the stairs are."

They spotted Jack sitting on an olive green vinyl chair between the 1960's and 1970's displays, his crutches leaning against the wall beside him.

"There's no elevator and Mrs. Haley said I should stay here," he explained, looking bored.

The guide shook her head sympathetically. "I'm afraid we don't have the budget to install an elevator."

"You use the stairs all the time at home," Kara told him.

"We'd rather keep our...injured visitors up here. Just a precaution." She said to Jack, "The cool things are up here anyway." She winked and, before walking away, told them to feel free to look over the floor again.

"Mom, I'm bored. Can we go?"

"We can't leave without your class." Kara moved through the rooms, stopping in the area devoted to the nineteenth century. "Let's look at this stuff again."

He groaned, but leaned on his crutches and came over.

She tilted her head, saying quietly, "I prefer to look at this stuff on my own. This way we can take our time."

Next to the walnut bureau was a secretary desk. Kara ignored the folded cardstock paper positioned on its closed lid that read, "Don't touch, please," and slid her finger over the smooth, polished wood.

"Mom, it says 'don't touch'," Jack hissed.

She stopped touching it and gave him with a mischievous smile. She looked up and was drawn to the painted portrait hanging on the wall behind the desk. It was of a brown-haired man with piercing blue eyes. He was handsome, dressed in an old-fashioned suit, and wearing a beard that was fuller than most would wear in the twenty-first century.

"Who's that?" Jack asked, noticing it too.

"I don't know."

"Ah, I see you've found something of interest." The guide from the door returned.

"Who's this?" Kara asked, pointing at the portrait. The artist's brushstrokes were so detailed and precise that she felt like the subject watched her.

"Ah, you found the most eligible man in all of Gracie Town." The woman sighed, crossing her arms over her chest.

" 'Most eligible'?" Kara asked.

"Come, follow me. We need to go back to the eighteenth century for that story." Excited now, the guide led them to the next exhibit, closer to the door.

Kara glanced over a dozen miniature paintings set in silver frames, gracing the top of a harpsichord. They were mostly of children. "Which one is he?"

"Oh, none of those. He's in the painting on the easel behind the harpsichord." The guide moved around the instrument and tapped the top of the canvas, stretched four feet by three-and-a-half feet.

Kara slipped past Jack, and stopped, her breath catching.

The guide admired the painting. "Robert Collumber, our unofficial patriarch, died alone and heart-broken." The man in the portrait was obviously the bearded man, but in this painting, he was much younger and clean-shaven with chiseled features.

And Kara recognized him.

She digested the name. "Collumber? As in the Collumber house?"

"The very one. The Collumbers were wealthy Virginians. Shockingly to his family and social circles, Robert enlisted in the American Revolutionary War at its start. After the war, he settled here in Grace Township on a land grant. Even from a portrait painted over two hundred years ago, you can see how handsome he was."

"Wow..." Kara didn't sigh because she finally had put a face to the namesake of the estate. She was in awe because Robert Collumber was the man from her dreams...her nightmares! She knew it was absurd. How could she have dreamed of him?

"Mom, can we go now?" Jack asked, turning away.

"Jack," Kara said, distractedly, "your class will be up any minute."

"Oh, yes," the guide nodded. "I can hear them coming up the stairs."

"He lived in the Collumber house down the street?" Kara asked.

"Yes. Soon after the war ended, Collumber decided to set roots down here in virtually uncharted territory. In fact..." The guide pointed at a framed map hanging on the wall across the room before leading Kara to the brown creased paper, crudely drawn by hand. "His land was from here to here." She traced a finger that lapsed nearly five hundred acres.

Kara peered closer at the small handwriting. "Is that...Oh, Jerome Point." She frowned. She had thought the map covered—

"It used to be Jerome Point. Now it's Seter Lane. Right there." The guide tapped the glass at the center of a crooked rhombus.

Kara's heartbeat quickened, recognizing the plot of land the guide indicated was where her house was located. Robert Collumber had walked on her property two centuries ago. It was incredible, the idea that this man had actually lived where she lived...this man from her dreams.

Sensing Jack approach her from behind as the rest of the class tromped into the room, Kara composed herself and said, "See Jack, that's where our house is."

"It is?"

The older guide asked, "You live on Seter Lane?"

Kara nodded. "Yes. Right there."

"Then you're within the boundaries of Collumber's property."

The classroom's guide asked the older one, "Did you tell them his story?"

The white-haired woman crossed the room to Collumber's portrait. Everyone gathered around. "After the war, Collumber was paid for his services, as well as granted land in Ohio, more specifically, in Gracie Town. He never returned to Virginia, settling here instead. Actually, he had a hand in building some of the buildings on his estate. He was a hard worker and loyal to a fault, as the saying goes.

"One day as he was cutting timber for his home, his stables, a barn..."

Kara's thoughts fluttered to the gray barn. If that wasn't the same structure (it couldn't be that old, could it?), then it was possible Collumber's barn had been built in the same spot years before. She had dreamed of it and she had felt it.

The guide continued her tale, "After cutting wood all day, Robert ventured one last time into the woods. But instead of gathering more wood, he discovered he wasn't alone. There, surrounded by trees, he found a woman, lying unconscious.

"He nursed her back to health, finding she was pregnant and had run away from home. We have no record of the baby's father, but it's believed she had been forced into an unwanted betrothal to him, or he had died and left her a pregnant widow. Unfortunately, we only have stories passed down from generations to rely on. Collumber, being the loyal man he was, vowed to take care of Elizabeth and the child. Her family sent out a search party, but she never returned to them. It is unknown if they ever heard from her again. Romantics like me like to think her family had been cruel to her, which had been the cause for running away, and Robert rescued her from a life of misery.

"But still...the new family was content, but not for long. Collumber, a quiet man, prevented most details from leaking to the newspapers. It is believed he didn't want Elizabeth's family gaining insight on where she was. But soon, tragedy struck and, as a result of his secrecy, no records exist of what happened to Elizabeth, or the infant, for that matter." The guide sighed. "Legend has it that Robert refused to give a clear explanation to the authorities on how they died. Was it disease? Most likely. But we don't exactly know, which is strange. Possibly, it was murder; maybe he realized he wasn't prepared to care for this ready-made family. But that's a far-fetched theory and one I don't like to entertain. It remains a mystery. Historians know so little. It is believed Collumber destroyed their belongings, as if he was ridding himself of their memory. Two portraits of mother and baby, however, remain."

The guide ushered the crowd to the opposite side of the room, Jack hobbling near the front. With an over-dramatic flourish, she gestured to the wall. "Elizabeth!"

Jack looked past a display case, seeing a portrait of Collumber in uniform, then a painting of a frail-looking baby dressed in a christening gown, before straying to the one of Elizabeth. He froze.

The blonde woman in the portrait was seated, wearing a blue dress and pearl necklace, with long, wavy hair spilling over her shoulders. Wisps of the yellow hair needled their way here and there, as if the artist had caught them in a breeze. The streaks of yellow took Jack back to his swimming pool, to blonde strands in the water, tangled between his toes, knotted in the ladder, the ghostly shoulder he had touched…

His heart beat faster; his breathing grew shallow. As the crowd encircled him, he broke away, needing air.

Kara, at the back of the crowd, craned her neck to see. Catching sight of the yellow hair and curve of the head, she suddenly felt sick, her face growing warm. The painted face blurred for a moment and then cleared again, giving credence to the woman's distinct features. The woman in the painting was beautiful: large blue eyes, smallish nose, full lips, fine cheekbones. But to Kara, the portrait had split in two: one of lovely Elizabeth, the other of the blurred monster, who haunted her dreams.

How could it be? It wasn't plausible that Kara knew this couple. She looked away, her eyes landing on the portrait of the baby. Even in its portrait, the infant appeared sickly. Her stomach twisting, Kara backed up, mentally filling in the tour guide's missing details.

I know Elizabeth drowned. The image of the woman being carried out of the pond buzzed behind Kara's eyelids, urging her to shut them so she could replay the scene.

"...Poem written about Elizabeth," the tour guide was saying at the back of Kara's mind. " 'Yellow hair, gold hair, dressed in bands, met a fair man on unfound lands...' "

Fighting to remain alert, Kara stepped aside. She spotted Jack hunched over at the door. His expression looked as strange as she felt.

"Are you alright?" she asked.

"Can we go?"

"Yes." The room was suffocating.

"Did you guys see the Collumber house finally sold?" The third tour guide appeared beside them. "I'm so glad it did. That house has been empty for years. Historical landmarks need caretakers."

Kara stared at her. "It was empty for years? But there were fresh flowers on the porch a couple months ago," Kara said, remembering the pink roses spilling out of them the day they arrived in Gracie Town.

"The town council maintained the house. Every so often they list the house for sale and then pull it off the market after lack of interest. For a time, they were going to make it a museum, but it never panned out. I'm happy it's finally sold, though."

"Who bought it?"

"I heard it was someone from out of state. I'm sure the township will be on them to keep the integrity of the estate intact."

Kara's legs felt weak and her throat burned. She excused Jack and herself, explaining to the guide he had a doctor appointment to get to. Jack was quiet, going outside ahead of Kara, instantly finding relief in the cool autumn air.

Kara drove to Grace School to pick up Lilah before the appointment. She glanced at the Collumber house as she passed by, seeing it in a new light now that she had faces to go with the property. Her perception of it had been altered. She couldn't quite understand her feelings about it now; she just felt different, almost detached. She parked in the lot and told Jack she'd be right back. She crossed over the pavement and opened the front door of Grace School. It took her a moment to adjust to the dim foyer. Piano music and children singing drifted from the back of the building.

"Oh! Hello, Mrs. Tameson."

Kara turned, finding a teacher rounding the corner, balancing a tray of snacks in her hands, an oversized tote bag pulling on her shoulder. "I would've called," Kara explained, feeling oddly nervous, "but I was in town on a field trip that just ended. Is it alright if I pick up Lilah now?"

"No problem!" The teacher shifted sideways, fighting back the tote bag that lurched forward. Kara pushed it back for her. "Thanks! If you don't mind, Lilah's using the staff restroom on the second floor. The one down here was in use so I had her use that one…"

"Sure, no problem. I'll get her."

"It's just upstairs."

Kara turned around and, stepping over the chained "Staff Only" sign draped across the bottom staircase step, climbed up the worn, carpeted stairs to the landing. To her immediate right was a closed door with another "Staff Only" sign posted. She looked to the left and saw only one of the other four doors on the floor was open.

She looked in, finding the office empty. She glanced back at the empty hallway, her eyes rolling over the staircase leading to the third floor. She turned back to the open room, calling, "Lilah?" She entered, her footsteps loud on the aged, floorboards. She moved to the closed door on the left-side of the room. "Lilah, are you in there?" She heard water running on the opposite side.

Kara hovered at the door for a few seconds before turning around. A fireplace was centered against the wall. Overlarge for the room, the hearth was wrapped in smoke-stained stone, its gaping hole covered with an iron grate. Her eyes wandered to the desk on the far side of the room, topped with a computer and picture frames. With interest, she noticed the desk and chair were on a dais, a few steps higher than the rest of the room.

She admired the ornate crown molding and then wondered again if she was in the right room. She started for the closed door. "Li—" but she faltered, catching sight of her vantage point outside.

Through the bubbled glass window between the fireplace and closed door, Kara saw she was level with the Collumber house. She ignored the squeak of the faucet being turned off, focusing instead on the second-floor windows across the parking lot. Lace curtains, like the ones in the room she was in, were drawn back, open to the Federalist period house's shadowed interior.

Time had stopped. Kara blinked, her eyes boring into one of the open windows. She waited for movement, a face, a hand, something to move on the other side of that window.

"Mommy?" Kara barely heard Lilah's voice as her daughter approached her. It took Lilah repeating her name for Kara to drag her gaze away from the house across the way.

"All set? I'm taking you home early." She took Lilah's damp hand and started to leave, but stopped, her eyes resting on the windows on the far side of the room to the right of the desk sitting on the dais.

She released the hand. Rapidly, her body knowing before her mind did, her eyes moved from the platform to the enormous fireplace, and back to the window. Déjà vu coursed through her. She knew this room; she had dreamed of this room, and in her dream, the bonus room had been on the other side.

With a quick stride out of her control, her face hot, her palms sweaty, Kara passed the dais and went to the window. She didn't want to look, didn't want to see into her own house, tucked away on Seter Lane, but she had to. She pulled back the dainty curtain and looked out. But…it was Main Street, not her house on the other side. SUVs and cars passed by below.

She turned toward the dais, ignoring Lilah's whines. Instead of the desk, Kara saw the grand bed that had been there before. In that bed was the hideous woman with no face, wrenching her body, reaching for her baby. Elizabeth.

Jumping back, Kara's fingers brushed the side of the desk, breaking the vision. Blinking, she looked at the desktop, seeing in the framed photograph the image of Mrs. Chandler, the principal of Grace School. This was her desk, her office. Near the computer keyboard, Kara noticed a shot glass. Something small was inside. She picked up the glass and turned it over. A heavy ball of lead rolled into her palm. The marble she had found at home.

It looked like a musket ball.

And she knew that's what it was.

Afraid, she set the ball back into the shot glass and backed away. Avoiding the fireplace, she gripped onto Lilah's hand and steered her out into the hallway. Kara turned to look back, her eyes fluttering over the fireplace, platform, and window again.

It was just an office.

Chapter Twenty-nine

The ride home from the doctor's was quiet; no one asked to turn on the radio, nobody spoke. Lilah fidgeted in the backseat and Jack, who was in the front, stared out the passenger side window. Kara gripped the steering wheel, making the turn onto Seter Lane.

Jerome's Point, this was Jerome's Point, she thought, her eyes twitching, as she waited for the gray barn to come into view through the trees. And then it *was* in full view.

A voice that sounded like the breeze, whispered, "It's not yours."

Kara pressed hard on the brake.

"Hey!" Lilah exclaimed, the statue slipping from her lap. It fell with a thump onto the floor below her feet.

"Did you hear that?" Kara asked, staring at the barn they sat in front of.

Jack looked up and cried, "Ew!" when he saw a swarm of turkey vultures covering an animal carcass on the road in front of them.

Not hearing him, Kara steered the car into the front grass of the barn and parked.

Jack dragged his eyes away from the birds when he heard a door click shut. "Mom!" he called when he saw her already advancing on the barn.

She didn't hear him, because the urgent "Come and see!" whispering from inside the dilapidated barn was stronger. She stepped into a sliver of sunlight shining from inside and continued under it, going in the structure.

Kara paused, looking up at the window above the hayloft. That was from where most of the light poured in. Additional light seeped in through cracks in the wooden slats all around the building. She lowered her eyes on the loft below the window and started walking again, surefooted, across the straw-covered floor to the wood ladder. This time, it wouldn't be like her dream.

She climbed, without fear she'd slide down. Up she went until her head cleared the floor of the hayloft. The loft, caked in dirt and animal droppings, was empty, except for a tousled pile of straw at the far end.

"It's mine!" a woman's voice cried out, the sound bouncing off the walls around her.

Kara jumped, nearly letting go of the ladder rung.

"Give it back!" the voice demanded.

"I…what..?" Kara climbed up all the way to the safety of the loft and backed away from the ladder. Her eyes darted around the barn, exposed as it now lay spread out for her. There was no movement below and, flicking her eyes around upstairs, she saw she was alone. "Hello?" Kara called cautiously.

When the voice had been stilled for a long moment, Kara turned her attention to the pile of straw. She slid her feet around in the sticks that had broken loose, searching. She felt something was there, as if St. Anthony was guiding her to a Lost and Found stand. She dropped to her knees and pushed her hands into the pile, not feeling the sharp sticks poke her and snap against her hands and arms. She pressed on, scattering the pile, lessening its height as she quickly made a mess.

She pressed on, leaning her whole body so that she was now in the straw. *Where is it?* She moved quicker, and was nearly frantic as she leveled out the sticks until there was no longer the hint of a pile. She crawled over the debris, feeling around until a toad hopped out. Kara cried out, falling back on her knees. She watched it turn a 90-degree angle and hop a few paces away before it stopped. It watched her, waiting for her next move.

She blinked, forgetting it, looking instead at the mess she had made. Her eyes did the searching now, hoping to glimpse a bulge, a hint of color, a secret. Finally, she got to her feet and turned away. Starting for the window, she stepped down on the last bit of kicked straw, and heard a crunch that sounded like broken glass. She stopped, looked down, and raised her foot. The edge of a four-inch piece of beige slate had broken away.

She squatted down and picked up the larger piece. It was dirty, but it looked to her to be natural rock, like limestone or clay. That wasn't what she wanted to find, was it? She glanced over the straw, seeking something, anything, but found nothing else. She dropped the slate onto the floor. She stood up, dusting off her jeans, and went to the window. She looked out, seeing the silo and then the trees beyond. The pond was hidden behind evergreens. She turned her gaze to the right, onto the backyard of the farmhouse next door.

She inhaled sharply.

A pick-up truck was parked in the driveway.

"Get out!" The male voice was inside her head. She obeyed, twisting away from the window and hurrying to the ladder. Down she went, nearly missing the bottom rungs, and jumped to the ground. She sped-walked to her car and got in behind the steering wheel, unaware both of her children hadn't moved from their seats, nor spoken a word while she was gone.

Kara reversed and pulled out onto the road, nearly striking a feasting vulture that begrudgingly took to flight a moment later than its cohorts. The car thumped over the remains of the now-unrecognizable animal carcass as it slowly passed the farmhouse. A man walked out the front door of the house and start crossing the front lawn toward the barn. Kara passed the house glimpsing him in the rearview mirror, glancing until the road eased to the left and he disappeared from view behind bowing trees.

When they arrived home, Kara helped Jack, fitted in his new boot, out of the car and to bed. He went willingly. She paced around in the foyer, fighting the urge to return to the barn. Questions ran through her mind: should she ask the man about the barn? Should she watch for him to leave and then explore some more?

Lilah broke into her racing thoughts, "I wanna go outside."

Kara looked over her arms, finding goosebumps. She rubbed one of them.

"*Mommy!*" Lilah whined.

"Lilah." Kara followed her to the backdoor and halted. The terrible statue was in Lilah's hands, the mocking clay girl and frog.

"Oh, I know!" Lilah shot up a finger, her other hand holding the statue now solely by the girl's head. "Lemme show you something!"

Kara looked down at the floor, steadying herself. Why was her heart racing?

"C'mon, mommy. It's a surprise!" Lilah unlocked and flung open the backdoor

"Lilah…" Kara followed, closing the door behind her.

Lilah punched a fist toward the woods on the west side. "It's over there." She clasped her hands together, sandwiching the statue between them. "In the woods!"

Kara rubbed her temple. "How far are we going?"

Lilah didn't reply, already running through the yard.

Kara glanced at the trees the opposite way. A canvas tent flickered in her mind…

She now had names and faces for who had owned the grounds. Had she known them from her dreams? Was that even possible?

She heard fluttering and looked up just in time to watch a hawk take off from a treetop and fly away.

"Mommy! See the truck?"

Kara shifted her attention and followed Lilah to the tree-line.

Lilah went into the woods. "It's right here, Mommy. Isn't it cool?"

Kara stepped around a thornbush, then stopped. She was looking at a pop-up camper. Astonished, she asked, "Where did that come from?"

"Me and Jack found it." Lilah bounced around.

Kara peered into a grimy window, making out a countertop.

Lilah urged, "Go inside!"

Kara moved to the door, cautiously opening it. It gave, squeaking on its hinges. The stench hit her. She looked in, seeing a large pile of debris to the side. She backed away, letting the door slam shut.

Lilah said, "Let's play house." She held up the statue. "My doll wants to play."

Kara backed up, confusion roiling in her. "No. Not here. This isn't ours. We have to play somewhere else until I find out whose it is."

"It's not Jack's!"

"Jack's seen this?"

Lilah nodded vigorously. "Uh-huh."

"Why didn't you tell me about it?"

"I dunno. It's a surprise."

Kara's glanced at the mocking frog before steering Lilah around by the shoulders. "Daddy and I will discuss it. For now, let's go back to the house. We can play on the deck."

There was a reluctant "Okay" from Lilah, who walked ahead.

Kara held back, taking in the pop-up camper, noticing for the first time orange letters painted on its side. An "L," "P," and a "U." Moving to the rear of the vehicle, she saw an "H" and an "E." At the front bumper was an "S" and a vertical splash of paint beside it. The end of the word or phrase.

She stepped over saplings, seeing no other letters. Starting again with the "H," as that was the next letter after the vertical splash, she rounded the camper again, stringing the letters together. She realized the vertical line was actually an exclamation point. The phrase was unnerving.

Lilah called from the deck, but Kara didn't reply as she slowly exited the woods.

"Help us!" was written in large, sloppy orange letters.

Help us!

Had the camper always been there? Who had painted the unsettling phrase? Was it another prank?

"Mommy, somebody's here," Lilah whispered when Kara had crossed the lawn.

"Where?" Kara spun, her eyes on the trees. From the bottom of the deck, the camper was perfectly hidden.

"Somebody rang the doorbell."

Ding-dong ditch.

Kara listened, hearing a motor rumbling. Someone was there; they had stayed to be found.

Not ding-dong ditch.

Kara and Lilah crossed through the house. Kara peeked out the sidelight. Desmond blinked back at her.

"Hi there!" He greeted when she opened the door.

Kara frowned. "Hi."

He glanced at the road and then back at her. "How is everything?"

"Fine."

"Good. Ahem! I was just driving by and—" He glanced at the yard. "Thought I'd stop and check in on you."

Her stomach flip-flopped. It was the watchfulness in his eyes, how he glanced behind her into the house, and the fact he had dropped in already to check on them that made her uneasy. "We're fine." She didn't mention the RV, didn't ask if he knew anything about it.

"Mind if I come in?" he asked. "For a chat." His smile didn't reach his eyes.

"I don't think now's a good..." her words drifted when a jeep pulled into the driveway. She recognized it was Shannon and immediately felt a sense of relief.

Desmond squinted at the jeep, taking a few steps down the sidewalk toward the driveway. "Alright, let me know if there's anything you need."

He hurried to his sedan and backed out, letting Shannon into the turnaround before he went down the driveway.

Lilah stayed in the house, and Kara met Shannon on the driveway.

"Hey," Shannon said, stepping out of the jeep. She slung a tote bag over her shoulder and waved a two-foot, stuffed scuba diver toy. "Thought I'd swing by and see how Jack is. He got the boot put on today, right?"

"Yeah. That was nice of you! You just missed my real estate agent."

"Oh?"

"He's getting creepier the more I see him."

"What happened?"

Kara forced a laugh. "Nothing. Let's go in." She hung back under the lamppost as Shannon walked ahead. Her lips twitching, Kara's eyes drifted up to her curtained bathroom window. She looked for a moment before following Shannon into the house.

They found Lilah sitting on the floor in the great room watching TV, her desire to play forgotten. The statue was on her lap, near as always.

"Jack's napping right now. Want a drink in the meantime?" Kara asked, moving to the kitchen cabinets.

"Sit. I'll get it. Water, tea...wine?" Taking a look at the circles under Kara's eyes, Shannon headed to the refrigerator. "Wine it is. Kara, sit."

Kara obeyed, sinking into a chair at the dining table. She watched Shannon set her tote bag on the floor, then expertly move around the fridge and cabinets.

"Will John be home soon? What time is it?" Shannon glanced at the microwave clock.

"I haven't heard from him yet." Kara sighed, resting elbows on the table and sliding her chin into her palm.

"Wine'll probably put me right to sleep," she said when Shannon set the glass in front of her.

"I'll start dinner in a few. I brought my overnight bag in case he's out all night."

Kara laughed. "I'm okay. I'm so tired, I'd probably sleep through a haunting."

"It's fine. Tom already knows I might be staying over. Oh, he's coming over to put up your chandelier."

"Didn't you see it? We installed it."

"You did? How did I miss that?" Shannon returned to the foyer and called, "Wow, I totally missed that!" She came back to the kitchen and sat across from Kara. "I'm glad you did. It would've been a constant reminder…" Shannon's words trailed and for a moment they sat wordlessly, cartoon noises filling the awkward quiet. Kara straightened in her seat at the memory of Marvin, lying crumpled in the foyer.

Kara's cellphone dinged. She pulled it from her pocket and looked at it. The text was from John.

Working late. Deadline is today. I'll try not to stay out too late.

"John's working late." She clicked off the phone and set it on the table.

Shannon clapped her hands together, the enthusiasm for Kara's benefit, Kara was sure. "I saw a pizza in the fridge. Does that sound good?"

Chapter Thirty

Jack woke up in time for dinner. He wasn't smiling when he thanked Shannon for the stuffed scuba diver toy, but Kara blamed his docile response on his sleepiness. She watched him slip the toy behind the couch, but made no comment, nor brought any attention to the action. After they ate, Jack and Lilah took to the TV, while Kara and Shannon remained in the kitchen. Seated, Kara leaned back, propping her feet on the chair opposite.

Shannon nodded at the great room. "I didn't watch much TV growing up."

"Oh? I lived on TV. You can sing any TV theme song and I can probably guess what show it is."

"Tempting. Too bad I can't quiz you. If only I had known twenty years ago to watch and take notes!" They laughed.

"Shoulda, coulda, woulda," murmured Kara. She gazed out the window, noticing some of the leaves had already changed colors as the last of the twilight faded into night. She sipped her wine. The light over the sink was on, filling the room with a homey glow, although the dining room beyond had darkened. Night was quickly growing longer than day, the sun and the moon, nature's changing of the guards.

Shannon selected a glass bottle of cola and returned to the table.

"Do I need a bottle opener for this?"

"No, it's an unscrew," Kara replied. She sipped her wine. "John's deadline to finish the project is today."

"Is everyone staying?"

"In the office?"

Shannon nodded, drinking from the bottle.

"It's him and, I think, the other three guys in I.T. that're still working."

"No lady I.T. staff?"

Kara swallowed wine, ignoring Shannon's sobering look. "He's supposed to be done tonight."

But what if he wasn't working..? What if he stayed away because of Kara's...obsession? Was Sophie an obsession? Was it important to keep Sophie shut away? Is that what other mothers did as time went on?

She swirled the wine in the half-full wine bottle. "Let's refrigerate the bottle. I don't like it warm."

"I'll do it." Shannon tucked it in the refrigerator.

"Mom, Lilah's asleep."

Kara and Shannon looked at Jack. He partly leaned on a crutch while leaning his opposite hip against the wall.

"Hey!" Shannon jumped up. "Don't lean on the wall. You'll make scuff marks!"

"Shannon!" Kara stood up.

"You've gotta be more careful, Jack. This is flat paint. It gets marked up easily."

He straightened, moving away.

"It's not a big deal," Kara told her.

"You don't want to ruin the paint."

Kara sighed, glancing at Jack, who had returned to the couch. "I'm going to put Lilah to bed." She went into the great room and asked if he was okay.

"Uh-huh," he mumbled.

"She didn't mean it. She was just worried about scuffing up the wall. Her boyfriend's helping with the house and she just wants to keep everything nice. She won't do that again."

"Okay."

"Do you have homework?"

He shook his head, then revealed the hint of a smile. "No."

Kara smiled back. "Okay, I'm taking your sister to bed." She picked up Lilah, conked out in her arms.

"Are we sleeping in your room?" His eyes darted to hers.

"For now, I'm going to have her in your room. Daddy's supposed to come home tonight, but if he doesn't, Shannon will sleep in Lilah's room. Is that alright?"

He turned back to the TV, his shoulders relaxing. "Yeah."

"Good. Okay, see ya in a bit." She carried Lilah up the dark staircase and nudged Jack's open door with her elbow, opening it the rest of the way. She arranged a pile of blankets on the floor beside his bed and set up two pillows at the head. She laid Lilah on top of the blankets and draped a sheet and a comforter over her. Lilah sighed heavily in her sleep and turned to her side, facing the dark space below Jack's bed.

Kara crossed the downstairs foyer just as the doorbell chimed, startling her. She opened the door to find a plump, middle-aged woman with fire-red hair smirking.

"Hello," Kara said, not recognizing her.

"Hi."

"Jane!" Shannon called from the kitchen. "Come on in!"

Kara looked down the hallway at Shannon. She was drying off a glass with a hand towel.

Jane stepped inside, brushing past Kara.

Eyes narrowed, Kara closed the door and followed the woman—Jane—into the kitchen.

Shannon told Jane, "Tom's coming."

Jane nodded.

"Hi, um…" Kara eyed Shannon, waiting for her to look at her, but Shannon turned her back on her. She poured orange juice a quarter of the way into the glass she had just dried.

Kara was going to introduce herself when they heard the front door open and close.

"Tom?" Shannon called. "Is that you?"

"Yeah!" he called back. He said hi to Kara before stepping past her. She watched as he poured himself a glass of orange juice too. To Shannon he asked, "This is all we have? Nothing stronger? I thought you were a wino."

Jane snorted.

"There's wine in the fridge." Shannon finally glanced at Kara. "It wasn't chilled, so we had to put it in the fridge."

Tom opened the refrigerator, grabbing the wine bottle.

Kara forced a smile on the redhead. "I'm sorry. I'm Kara."

They met eyes briefly before Jane looked her over and muttered something, looking away.

Kara turned to Shannon. "Shannon?" Who was this stranger and why were Shannon and Tom suddenly oblivious?

Tom nudged Shannon, the gesture so rough that she said, "Hey!" Rubbing her arm and scowling, Shannon said, "Kara, this is Jane. Jane, Kara."

Kara crossed her arms over her chest, turning back to Jane. "So, how do you know Shannon?"

Jane cackled.

Kara uncrossed her arms, turning to watch Tom pour wine into a third glass of orange juice.

Shannon sliced an orange into wedges, saying to Tom, "I thought I'd add a little finesse to my beverage."

"Finesse?" Tom chuckled. "Fancy."

Shannon carried her glass and a plate of the orange slices to the kitchen table. Sitting down across from Jane, she finally made proper introductions. "Jane, this is Kara Tameson, the homeowner."

"Ha!" Jane scoffed. "Owner."

Kara noticed Tom's head jerk up, meeting Jane's eyes across the room. Still gripping onto politeness, Kara asked again, "How do you know Shannon?"

"Oh, we go back a ways."

"Oh? Are you related?"

Jane mulled it over for a moment and then shrugged. "I guess you could say that."

Kara glanced at her friends, but they were silent, drinking from their glasses. "So—" She started again, but Tom set his glass down and stood close to her.

302

"I'm ready to install the chandelier. Where'd you put it?"

"Really, Tom?" Shannon raised her eyebrows.

He gave Shannon a look Kara couldn't define before heading down the hallway. Kara followed. She didn't understand the vibe in the kitchen, so she figured she might as well follow something she did understand.

"John and I already replaced the light." She noticed a black duffel bag by the front door. "I couldn't stand not having a light in here."

He glanced in the office, and then stopped by the door.

"John's not home," she said. "I told Shannon we already installed it. She probably should've called you. It would've saved you a trip."

"Is he out all night?"

"Probably. Call him tomorrow. I think we're ready to start on another project."

"Where are the kids?"

"Jack's watching TV and Lilah's in bed."

He nodded and then heaved the duffel bag over his shoulder before returning to the kitchen. Kara followed him, finding the ladies standing in front of the counter, their expressions blank.

Something was off. Kara's pulse quickened. She looked at Jack, seeing he had turned the TV volume low. He sat on the couch, watching them.

"What's going on?" Kara asked.

The adults exchanged looks, silently communicating.

Kara took an instinctive step back to the edge of the hallway. She tried to smile, act nonchalant, but faltered.

Tom dropped the duffel bag with a dead thump onto the kitchen table. "John's out tonight."

Kara's face grew warm. Why were they making her uncomfortable?

Shannon spoke up, "He's always working overnights. It's just Kara and the kids. That's fine."

He looked at Jane. "How are we doing this? Are you sure?"

Jane scoffed, "Hell, yes. It ain't right."

" 'Tain't right," Shannon said with an overexaggerated twang. "Classy, Jane."

"You!" Jane yelled, making Kara and Jack jump. "Have no business being here!"

"Hold it!" Tom hollered. He moved his hand to his bag, catching Kara's attention. She watched him unzip it.

"If I weren't here, we wouldn't have this chance," Shannon spat back.

Tom smacked her on the side of the head. "Shut up!"

Kara flinched, her heart thundering in her ears. She went to Jack, handed him a crutch, and led him out of the room.

"Hold on there, Kara," Tom said, softly.

She saw he had taken a slender rope out of the bag. Her eyes widened. The wind howled, long and loud, making all of them, just for a moment, turn their eyes to the windows where darkness lay on the other side. Kara swallowed, tightening her grip on Jack's free hand.

"I'm sorry about this," Tom said, sympathetically, "but I'm going to have to make you a little uncomfortable."

"What's going on?" Kara asked.

He crossed the room, two lengths of rope in his hand and, taking Kara's and Jack's hands, led them to the couch. He pushed them down gently. He looked at Shannon, who nodded, then turned back to Jack.

Jack looked at his mom for an explanation, but Kara could give none. As he shifted, something in his hands caught the light, catching Tom's attention. A metal medallion.

"What do you have there?" Tom asked.

All eyes were on Jack's hand. He opened his palm, revealing the toy sheriff's star her had found in the pop-up camper.

Tom's expression softened. "Where did you get that?"

Jack's eyes darted to Tom's. He swallowed, closing his fist around the star. "In the grass," he lied.

Tom locked eyes with him. "In the grass? In the backyard?"

Jack glanced at his mom and then at the two women in the kitchen, who watched in rapt attention. He glanced down at his buckled hand before meeting Tom's eyes. "Yeah."

"You know," Tom said, squatting down. "I had a star just like that when I was a kid. My friends and I played cops and robbers. D'you ever play that?"

"No."

Tom stood. They were quiet for a minute until he asked, "Do you have homework, Jack?"

"No."

"Why don't you go up to bed?"

Jack looked questioningly at Kara.

"Tom, what—" Kara stopped, seeing the warning in Tom's eyes.

Sternly, Tom said, "Jack, I think your mom would like you to go to bed."

Kara nodded. "It's a school night. Go to bed." As he started to get up, she whispered, "We'll be okay."

Jack, still clutching the star, hurried out of the room. The adults were silent, listening to him climb the stairs and shut his bedroom door.

Tom turned his attention to Kara. He was tugging on the rope, as if contemplating his next move. She hoped he would realize that whatever he had in mind was wrong and they would go on their way.

"I don't want to hurt you," he said, glancing at her.

"Get on with it already, Tom!" Shannon cried.

Kara's eyes darted to look at the woman who had been her closest friend over the last couple months. Shannon looked so different now, almost feral.

"What do you want?" Kara asked.

"Not many things. Just one really." Tom took Kara's wrists and knotted the rope around them.

Chapter Thirty-one

"Thanks for everything, John." Lance Thurston, the director of Severs, Ltd., slapped him on the back.

"We shouldn't see any more of those errors." John slid behind the steering wheel. He had parked close to a lamppost in Sever's nearly empty parking lot. The bright beam lit up Thurston's smiling face.

"You did a great job, John."

"Thanks. The team worked long hours to—" His cellphone rang. Glancing at it, he didn't recognize the phone number. Whoever it was had called him earlier that day without leaving a message. He sent it to voicemail. "...get the server going. Now onto the next thing."

"Isn't that right? You and your team did well. Keep an eye out. There's a bonus coming your way."

"I'm relieved it worked out, to be honest." That was the truth. His team had saved the company hundreds of thousands of dollars in potentially lost revenue with the software they had designed and had struggled to bring to fruition.

Thurston nodded. " 'Relieved' is the correct word for all of us. See you tomorrow. You have a hell of a long drive ahead of you, don't you?"

John started the engine. "About an hour. Not too bad."

"We'll see you tomorrow."

John steered the car out of the parking lot and headed for home, driving above the speed limit. Kara would be upset he had worked again through the evening. As he pulled onto the highway, he flipped to his voicemail, and played the new message.

"Hi, John. Ahem! This is Desmond Howard from City Realty. Um...I have some concerns about your, uh, your house..."

Chapter Thirty-two

"Keep your voice down," Shannon warned Kara. "I don't see the kids waking up, not after that pill I slipped them at dinner." Shannon's lips curled, cruelly. "Not as heavy as the pill I gave you a couple weeks ago, but something to keep them down. Still, we don't need you making any noise."

Kara's eyes blazed. "What did you give them?"

Shannon pulled a gray hoodie out of her tote bag and put it on. "Nothing too strong. Don't worry about it."

Kara turned her eyes on Tom, pleading, "I wish you would tell me what you want." She was afraid of the answer.

He was in the kitchen, rifling in his duffel bag. Kara didn't want to see what he would pull next out of his bag of tricks. It was insane. She was tied up, for God's sake!

Shannon went to the far side of the great room. "I can't believe I was so dumb. I actually thought we could be friends. Can you believe how dense I was?" Laughing, she pulled a serrated knife from her pocket.

Kara inhaled sharply. She watched the blade as Shannon moved it from hand to hand. She didn't say anything for a time. No one did.

The silence was finally broken when the wind howled outside, a low, lengthy moan. Kara's eyes flicked toward the backdoor. Someone passed by on the other side of the glass panes. Excited (was it help, or was it another of Shannon's cohorts not yet announced?), Kara leaned forward. The wind howled again. Her eyes flicked to Jane and Tom, seated at the kitchen table, their expressions unreadable.

Shannon moved to the center of the room, drawing back Kara's attention. "You told me all about your baby girl. Sophie." She paused, tilting her head to the side. "Hell, you even dragged me to the cemetery to check out her grave. Now, I thought that was a bit morbid. Maybe even a bit self-centered if you think about it. 'Let me tell you all about my baby, the one I confuse with my living kid, boohoo.' Such tragedy, Kara. Tsk, tsk."

Shannon stepped forward and Kara stood. She moved away from the couch, angling her bounded wrists ahead of her, turning. Shannon moved forward and Kara moved back until her back bumped against the playroom door, a dead end.

"I can tell you all about tragedy, Kara. It happens all the time, even to rich people like you. Sucks doesn't it, that not even money could keep your baby alive? No money in the world could bring your daughter back. But then, you were able to have another daughter, weren't you? Speaking of which..." Shannon spun around and headed toward the hallway. She turned sideways and smiled cruelly. "Maybe we need to bring out the kiddos."

"No!" Kara shouted. "Leave them alone!"

Shannon turned her back on her and sprinted down the hallway, the knife lowered at her side, running like a woman possessed.

"No!" Kara screamed, crying. She ran after to stop her, but Tom blocked her in the kitchen.

"Shannon!" he yelled. "We're not involving kids in this! You touch them and I walk."

The three in the kitchen looked down the empty hallway. Seconds later, Shannon reappeared.

The sudden movement made Kara jump. "Please, Shannon." Tears glided down Kara's cheeks. "I don't know what's going on, but please don't hurt Lilah and Jack."

Shannon marched up to Kara, their faces inches apart. Kara flinched, pulling back. Shannon hissed, "Don't worry, Kara, they'll be fine." She moved away, plopping down on the couch, and crossed her legs.

"Oh, look at this," Shannon said, picking up Lilah's clay statue by the neck. Fixing her eyes on it, she said, "This thing is cursed!" She pulled her arm back, ready to hurl it across the room.

But Kara's outburst stopped her. "No, please! You know Lilah loves her doll." After all this was over, Lilah would need it for comfort. Kara might not make it through the night, but Lilah would. She had to believe that anyway.

Shannon turned blazing eyes on Kara. "Lilah's doll?" She lowered the statue and slid her fingers, almost lovingly, over its taped body. "Do you know what this is?"

"Shannon," Tom growled. "That's enough!"

She ignored him. It was now only her and Kara in the world. "I can't believe you gave a chipped, fragile statue to a child as a toy."

Kara tried to back into the hallway, but Tom rested a heavy hand on her shoulder and steered her into the great room. He gave her a push, making her drop onto the armchair, catty-corner to the couch where Shannon sat.

Shannon waved the statue at her. "You dug this up, didn't you?"

Kara nodded and replied, "John found it, landscaping."

Shannon laughed loud and hard. "You're both idiots. Nothing pleases me more than to finally be able to tell you that to your face. I only wish John were here so I could tell him too."

John. He hadn't texted Kara again. Would he be coming home soon? She strained to listen for his car, but she heard nothing besides the howling wind.

Shannon stood up and backed up to the fireplace, holding up the statue like she was performing a classroom show-and-tell. "This is a St. Joseph's statue."

"St. Joseph?" Kara looked at her blankly.

"Well, alright, I didn't have an actual statue of St. Joseph." Shannon peered into the clay faces of the girl and frog. "I'm curious, Kara. Do you know who you bought this house from?"

Kara blinked away tears, glancing at the pair who kept silent in the kitchen. "The bank. It was bank-owned when we bought it."

"Do you know who the bank stole it from? Who the builder was, the actual homeowner? The one who drew up the plans for the property?"

Kara swallowed, shaking her head.

"You never cared to find out, did you? Well, how kind of you," Shannon scoffed. "Jimmy Howard. You didn't get any mail for him? Any past-due bills?"

Kara shook her head. The name rang no bells.

"Uncle Jimmy, Tom's uncle. Tom was more like a son to him. This was Jimmy's house. You know, we tried to get the house back. We tried to scare you out."

Kara's eyes widened.

Shannon continued, "They were subtle things, too subtle, but we tried to get you out. Little things like taping a note to your front door. 'Leave!' Boooo..." Shannon laughed.

"That was you?" Kara was aghast.

"There were other things too...things that go bump in the night." Shannon's lips curled.

It was impossible the nightmares were courtesy of Shannon, but it's where Kara's mind went. The dreams were because of...what, a ghost? Caused by the tragic Collumber family? Goosebumps ran along skin as she glanced about the room. Hearing the howling wind added to her unease. Was it the boogeyman haunting her on the other side of the backdoor? But who cared about the boogeyman when reality had turned to horror?

"Tom helped Uncle Jimmy design and build this house. The plan was for me and Tom to move in with Uncle Jimmy, because he didn't want to live alone anymore. Jimmy grew up here. They had a cabin in the woods then, dumpy, falling apart. I saw it when they tore it down. You wouldn't have believed the hard work that went into tearing down that cabin and hauling away trash. They burned most of it, but some of the pieces were too large, so they had someone take it away for scrap. Tom spent so many days and nights with Uncle Jimmy making the final changes to the house plans.

"Uncle Jimmy lived with us in town and they worked on this house every day. The house wasn't finished, but it was good enough to live in…as you know. It was time for Uncle Jimmy to move into his dream home. This home. But, oh no, he couldn't, Kara. The bank wanted it. Uncle Jimmy missed a couple payments and then the next thing we knew, the bank had foreclosed. They swooped in and grabbed his dream home and the land his family had owned for generations. It was the bank's, just like that." Shannon snapped her fingers.

Tears rolled down her cheeks, but she made no move to wipe them away. "Uncle Jimmy never got the chance to move his bed in. He used to sleep in that nasty camper parked in the woods. Have you seen it? Some nights he'd sleep in the house, though, curl up with a blanket in his dream home…And then you asked John's friend at your party if that nasty blanket you found was his!" She cackled obscenely. "I bet it was Jimmy's!"

Kara exhaled, remembering the paint-spattered woolen blanket she'd found in her bedroom closet. She asked, "Why did he write 'help us' on the camper?"

Shannon laughed, "Did he?" She waved Lilah's statue around and rolled her eyes upward. Mockingly, she said, " 'St. Joseph, please help us keep our dream home'…"

"I'm sorry he lost the house," Kara said, sympathetically. "We didn't know anyone had owned it."

"Of course, someone owned it!"

"We really didn't know. We figured the bank had been the only owner before. I didn't know it had been foreclosed on."

"You gave no thought to who had it ripped from their hands." Shannon held up the statue again. "St. Joseph is the patron saint of house sellers. I got this from Buried

Treasures. I buried it the day the bank listed the house for sale. Legend says it causes a quick sale. You bury a statue of St. Joseph upside-down in the yard and you're supposed to sell the house fast. Me and Tom were going to buy the house from the bank. We were scraping together what we had when that damn real estate agent—your agent—swooped in and sold it even before it was listed for sale!"

She sat up and pounded the statue against her leg. "But I guess the joke was on me, because I didn't even get a statue of St. Joseph! I messed that up, huh?"

Shannon was silent for a while before continuing, "Do you know I used to own Buried Treasures?" When Kara's eyebrows raised, she laughed. "Yep. Imagine that! It was a long time ago and I only had it for a year before the bank took that away too. When you realized the statue resembled the shop sign, I told you I took Lilah there to ask about the statue, which thank God, you believed. We never went. You are just dumb sometimes, Kara. Tsk, tsk.

"That damn real estate agent!" Shannon hollered. "When we heard you guys had moved in, we started contacting him, letting him know he made a horrible mistake. Yes, I admit, we panicked. He's so pigheaded, he didn't do anything to back out of the transaction." Shannon pounded her free fist into her thigh.

Kara's thoughts fluttered to Desmond, how he had told them about the pocket listing. As far as she had known there had been no competition on purchasing the house. Had he known Tom and Shannon had wanted to buy it? And he had been around several times since they had moved in. In fact, he had wanted to come inside that day. Was he going to warn her?

Shannon whipped her head to glare at Tom. "Did you take care of him?"

Tom nodded. "Just before I came here."

A tiny cry escaped from Kara's lips. What did that mean? What had he done to Desmond?

313

She started to say she was sorry when her cellphone rang, surprising the room. She whipped her head, her eyes locating it on the kitchen counter.

Tom scooped it up. Kara waited for him to say who it was, but he didn't. He sent the call to voicemail and returned to the table with it.

The front door opened and closed then.

Kara sat up, hoping to see John.

"Hello?" Shannon called.

Tom said, "It's Matthew."

A guy wearing a black hoodie and jeans shuffled into the kitchen. He had a round, youthful face and shaggy black hair. He slouched, looking uncomfortable.

"It's about time," Jane said.

"Surprised to see Matthew?" Shannon asked Kara.

Kara glanced at the disheveled guy and started to shake her head no.

Shannon said, incredulously, "He's your neighbor's son!"

Diane's Matthew? Kara looked, but his head hung down, hiding his face.

Shannon seethed, "I'm so glad we got rid of that old man. Tom was so ticked off with him—Marvin—about that stupid chandelier. That was Tom's job! I'm glad he's gone. D'you think the ladder was stable? Hmm, whaddya think, Kara? Think it'd be hard to loosen the locks?

"And to think this miscreant could keep an eye on you." Shannon moved to the breakfast nook and grabbed Matthew's earlobe. He moaned and squeezed his eyes tight. "He was practically useless!" She stooped down, trying to force him to look up at her.

Tom growled, "Shannon, leave him alone."

She let him go. "Did you even do anything to help us?"

Matthew glanced up at her before lowering his eyes again. "I watched her a few times at night," he replied, his deep voice quiet. "She saw me."

Watched her at night? Kara's arms went to her chest. Matthew was the figure in the shadows? It was confirmation she hadn't imagined it, but hearing he had watched her more than once made her feel sick.

"The dead animals were a nice touch," Shannon said. "Shoving nails into one of them. Nice." She looked at Kara and said, "You never mentioned those to me."

The dead opossum and raccoon she had discovered on the porch and deck! John had assumed the nails in the raccoon's body had been from the driveway. That meant Matthew had driven them into the animal and planted it in their fire pit? And how had he killed the opossum—strangled it?

Matthew sputtered, then said, "I started right when they moved in. I rang the doorbell. They couldn't figure out who or what it was." Kara remembered very well: someone playing Ding-dong Ditch.

Shannon shoved him, making him lose balance. "You were supposed to scare them! How's that scaring somebody?"

Oh, but Kara had been scared, uneasy from the start.

"So," Kara spoke up. All eyes leveled on her. "Were Marvin and Diane behind this too?" She had felt hostility from Diane, but Marvin had been in her home several times; he had befriended them. His involvement would've added to her shock.

"No," Jane replied. "They had no clue."

Tom ran his hands along the duffel bag. "Matthew'd stay with his parents he was having…an episode. He's a good kid. He helped my uncle and me sometimes on the house. He was here when we found out about the foreclosure. He saw how much living here meant to us. He wanted us to get the house back and he was willing to help anyway he could."

"He did things, we did things," Shannon said. "Drugging you with my sleeping pill didn't really do anything, I guess. I don't know what I really wanted to accomplish with that. I guess you could say we were desperate, trying whatever we could. 'Death by a thousand papercuts'."

Kara recalled the hallucinations from that night, the night Jack had broken his leg: the figures in the woods and finding Diane out there…

She shivered, asking, "Did you tie those scarves around the trees?"

"Scarves?" Shannon double-blinked. "What are you talking about?"

Matthew knew, however. He smiled shyly, glancing at Kara and then back at his feet.

Shannon nudged him. "What scarves?"

His voice was barely audible as he explained, "Mom tied those up to keep away the deer. They were eating her garden."

Kara asked, "Why was there hair in them?"

"Deer hate the scent of human hair. We put lots of scarves with hair in the woods."

"What about Blacky?"

Matthew scowled. "He was a dumb dog. He was getting into the garden, so I tied him to a tree to keep him out. He jerked around, though. Killed himself. Dumb dog."

So, Kara thought, swallowing, that's how the dog had died. She refrained from asking for the location. She never wanted to know that.

Shannon glared at Matthew. "Nobody pays any attention to Matthew, which should've made him perfect for our plan. He was supposed to scare you, Kara. But he failed."

But he *had* scared her; everyone in the room scared her.

Shannon continued, "So I had to take matters further. You telling me about Jack's estranged father was perfect. Have him stalk you a bit, creep you out."

Kara was stunned. "David was working with you guys?"

"No! We never met him. You're the one who told me about him. You gave me the idea. Remember those texts you got about him? That was me and Tom."

"Those texts came from my mom…"

Shannon smiled. "Pretty ingenious, huh? I put Tom's number in your cellphone and labeled him, 'Mom'. Hahaha! That wasn't your mom texting! I'm kinda proud of that idea."

"It was you? My mom never heard from David?"

"Nope. We just had to be careful not to say anything too threatening, so you wouldn't call the police. I finally had to delete the message history. I don't know, what do you think, Tom? Maybe one more text would've pushed Kara over the edge."

"It doesn't matter," Tom said. "Let's get on with this." He stood up, but hesitated when they all heard shuffling.

"Is there a party going on?" John appeared in the hallway, his laptop bag slung over his shoulder.

Chapter Thirty-three

Tom lunged at John, but John jumped back. As Tom reached for him again, John whipped his laptop bag at him. It connected with Tom's jaw, pushing him backward. Tom wobbled, but quickly regained his balance.

John's eyes tore around the room, locating Kara, who was at the edge of the great room. "What the hell is going on?" Noticing her bound wrists, he side-stepped over to her, his laptop bag in front of him like a shield.

"I don't know," Kara confessed.

He glanced at the people in the kitchen—friends—before stooping to unzip the bag.

"Drop it, John," Tom warned, moving to Kara's other side, an arm behind his back.

John ignored him, reaching his hand inside the bag.

Tom's fist shot out, smashing a wine bottle into the side of John's head. John dropped the bag and staggered toward him, but Tom struck him again above his ear. John crumpled to the floor.

Kara screamed.

"Sit down!" Shannon ordered, charging toward Kara.

Kara ignored her, hopping over John's legs and sprinting toward the hallway. Tom came up behind, yanked on her shoulder, and pulled her down. He dragged her across the floor to lie beside her unconscious husband.

Kara grabbed Tom's ankle, digging her fingernails in. He kicked her shoulder, making her let go. She rolled to her side so the wounded shoulder was off the floor. She inhaled deeply, then got to her knees and shimmied to the other side of the room. They watched her move away until she stopped at the bonus room door. She sprang to her feet, ignored the pain throbbing in her shoulder, and opened the door. She slipped in, and closed it to the sound of Tom's reacting feet.

It was difficult to move, her balance off-center because of the rope cutting into her wrists. Ignoring the pain, she pushed the loose wood planks against the door. It wasn't hard to push the pile that had been leaning against the near wall, but she knew there was no time to build a decent barricade. She knocked a box of nails over, the metal slivers scattering over the floor, as she clambered for another exit. She yanked on a window, but it wouldn't budge, the abrupt stillness of the plastic sash against her fingers aggravating the pain burning in her shoulder.

Tom was pushing the door open, with Shannon close behind shouting obscenities. Their voices a faraway hum, Kara noticed a pale, wavering light in the backyard, near the tree line. She stared, watching it turn, firing into a streak of light until it twisted, and then suddenly, it raced right at her. She had no time to react. It drew near with a flash: a face appeared on the other side of the window. Its eyes were wide and its mouth was opening. Kara stared into that mouth, a black hole, opening wider. She was sinking into it, a drop of water vanishing into a pool of blackness. The face smacked into the window, opposite of Kara, the rattling of the pane startling her. Then the face was gone.

Kara looked out at the trees—thin, black stilts. Her head twitched, her heart raced. Ignoring the yells of her captors, she heaved her hands up and unlocked one of the locks in the top sash.

She didn't have time to unlock the second.

Tom grabbed her under the armpits, yanking her to her knees. She cried in agony as he dragged her out, her knees sliding over nails and a two-by-four. He dropped her in the great room and reached for the playroom doorknob. Before he slammed the door shut, Kara saw the fluttering of a white scarf outside. Or she imagined she did.

Chapter Thirty-four

Jack hovered in the upstairs half-landing. When the downstairs voices had raised the first time, he had departed his bedroom, trusting the sturdiness of his new boot and leaving his crutches behind. He didn't understand what was going on, but hearing his mom scream, he knew he had to do something.

He crept downstairs, holding onto the railing to balance as he wasn't sure he had it yet. He trained his ears to listen to the adults speaking, which was difficult to do over the loud thrumming of his heart. When he cleared the last step, he hobbled across the foyer, his boot tapping against the tile. Sounds of scuffling coming from the back of the house convinced him to hide in the most immediate room, which was the office. The chandelier in the foyer and the outside porch light kept the room from being completely cast in darkness. He ran his hands over the desktop, his fingers bumping into a notebook, a cup of pens, a stapler. Was there a phone?

His back on the doorway, he combed clumsy hands over a shelf. He struck a mug, catching it before it hit the floor.

"What are you doing, Jack?"

The voice, female and clear, made him stop. His heart leapt into his throat. Wild-eyed, he slowly turned around to see who had caught him.

He saw Lilah.

It took him a moment to realize no adults surrounded him; it was just his sister, pushing curls out of her eyes. He exhaled before managing to hiss, "What are you doing down here?"

"I couldn't sleep." She blinked heavy eyelids, fighting sleep.

Mom's scream woke you up, he thought.

"Go back to bed." He didn't understand what had been happening that evening, but he knew something bad was going down. He ushered her to the staircase. "Come on, let's go back to bed."

"Do I hear someone?" Shannon's voice shot through the house.

His breath caught. He tugged on Lilah's hand. Somehow, he was able to coax her to hurry back to her makeshift bed in his bedroom.

"Where's my dolly?" she asked, crawling under the pile of blankets on the floor. He glanced around the room for it, having no idea where that stupid statue was, but looking at Lilah again, he saw she had turned away from him and her eyes were closed.

He started to turn away when he heard footsteps on the stairs. Someone was coming. He dove under his bedcovers, not bothering to wrestle the blanket over his booted leg. He turned his back to the door and shut his eyes, willing his heartbeat to slow down. He heard the door push open seconds later. Someone stood there, eyes trained on his back, surely watching the rise and fall of what should be steady breaths. He kept his eyes closed. Nothing could get him to open them at that moment.

Not unless his mom screamed.

And then, she did scream.

It took all of his will not to move.

Shannon cursed under her breath. "Jack?" Shannon whispered. "You awake?..Lilah?"

He kept his eyes clamped shut, imagining her watching him, her face inches from the top of his head. He hoped Lilah stayed asleep.

It felt like forever, but a moment later, he heard Shannon back away and close the door. He didn't move. He was afraid that when he turned over, she'd be standing there, in the dark bedroom, watching him.

Shannon strode to the kitchen. "What happened?"

"She's just making noises again," Jane replied, scowling. She was leaning over the side of her kitchen chair, her eyes on Kara and Tom. Kara sat on the great room floor, her back against the couch Tom sat on. He had dragged John's unconscious body to the opposite side of the room.

Shannon snapped, "Kara, we don't need you waking the house, or the neighborhood, for that matter. Tom, let's get this over with. I'm losing my patience."

Tom squatted on the floor in front of Kara, looking like his old self. His face was open, kind, endearing even, as he explained something so bizarre, as if he were giving normal directions. "I brought the quit claim deed. All you need to do is sign it and all this will be over. We spend the night, with no harm to you and your family, and help you pack. You guys move out tomorrow. The property will then revert back to me." He glanced at John's prostrate body and said quietly, "I'll get John's signature later."

Shannon placed her hands on her hips asking, "But how are we gonna get them to shut up about tonight? Not go to the cops?"

"This was your idea." He shoved a hand through his hair.

"Are you kidding me right now?"

Jane muttered, "Typical."

Shannon spun around. "What does that mean?"

Before Jane could reply, they all heard it, faintly, but distinctly, the sound of a door shutting.

"Who's that?" Tom stood up and hurried toward the front of the house.

Kara stared at the empty hallway. Was somebody there to help her family? Or was someone else coming to team up against them?

The first floor waited in silence, all eyes on the hallway, listening to Tom move through the foyer, office, and mudroom. They heard the front door open slowly. There was a pause before it closed again. They listened to Tom take the stairs and move from room to room. A moment later he thumped downstairs, reappearing in the kitchen.

"The boy's gone."

Chapter Thirty-five

Jack had waited for a distraction, for the adults to speak in conversation before making his big move. If he stayed in the house, no one would know his family needed help. He thought about bringing Lilah, but realized quickly she'd be too slow, or worse yet, she'd whine, calling attention to them as they escaped.

He pressed weight down on his booted leg, testing its strength. He had done the stairs earlier without crutches. He had been slow, but he had been able to maneuver without them. He walked the length of his bedroom, not happy with his speed and limp, but he couldn't chance using crutches, not if he wanted to slip outside unnoticed.

Jack moved quietly but steadily, slinking along the wall as he hobbled downstairs. The adults were talking, but he couldn't decipher their words. He paused when he reached the foyer. He glanced around, making sure he went undetected. This was it.

Satisfied, he hobbled to the front door and turned the knob easily. As the door yawned open, the crisp night breeze rolled over his face, the sensation wonderful. He stepped out onto the porch, easing the door shut behind him. He made no haste scrambling down the porch steps and over the gravel driveway. The air was chilly and the wind howled in misery, but it washed over him like a baptismal fount, a welcome exchange in contrast to the stifling house. Jack moved fast. It was as if invisible arms dragged him, propelling him forward.

"Leave…leeeeaaaavvve…" the wind whispered; the command was so clear, it was as if someone breathed it in his ear.

Jack developed a rhythm, hobbling around the house and across the side yard. Already the grass was covered in a frosted glaze, crunching under his sneaker-covered foot and the oversized black boot. In the slumbering night, he was so loud, signaling where he was headed.

The moon was a sliver, a useless slip of light in the murky night sky; it did nothing to guide him, but he knew the way. The grass that should've been cut one last time before the first frost of the season prodded his ankles as he pushed through thornbushes.

"Jack!" The bellow was Shannon's.

He didn't turn around. He pictured her on the deck, searching for him in the darkness. If he had turned around he would've seen her, the house light illuminating her from behind. He may not have been able to make out her features, but seeing her would've frozen him.

The adrenaline he burned through like fuel protected him. He had made it to the beat-up camper and quickly—and quietly—he pulled open the door, stepped onto the stairs, and entered the blackness.

Kara hoped neither of her children had made the noise that had alerted Tom. She prayed they were fast asleep, oblivious to the goings-on of the first floor. Their best strategy was to stay out of sight. She glanced at Shannon and Jane, their bodies turned away from the great room, before rising to her feet. Tom's duffel bag had been moved to the top of the armchair that served as a divider between the breakfast nook and great room. She just needed to get to that bag, into his treasure trove.

Kara strode to the chair, her fingertips touching the bag. She halted when something grabbed her ankle. She gasped, looking down.

John was awake, his fingers wrapped around her. She stepped back, glancing at their captors. Shannon and Jane's attention was still on the hallway. John wobbled to his knees as Kara reached for the bag. Shannon looked over.

As Tom had come in then, telling them Jack was gone, Shannon yelled, "Tom!" She lunged for the bag, but Tom stepped in front of her, his sudden movement knocking her to the floor.

John's hands dipped into the bag as Kara stepped to the side. Tom grabbed a hold of the bag with one hand and started pummeling John with his free fist. John took the blows, his hands finding the cold metal inside. He withdrew the pistol just as Tom let the bag go.

Tom, ignoring the impending danger of the gun, hopped, throwing all of his body weight into the movement, and came crashing down on John. The men wrestled with the gun as Kara kicked Tom's back with blind fury. Shannon joined in, focusing her blows on Kara. She pounded Kara's back, quickly over-powering her. Kara and John dropped unconscious to the floor.

Tom punched John twice more in the forehead before getting to his feet. He brandished the gun in one hand and took unsteady steps, backing into the breakfast nook.

Shannon cussed, smacking Kara's ear before she stood up.

Jane, slouching in her kitchen chair, glanced down at Matthew, who was curled up under the table. Looking up, she asked, "What about the boy?"

Shannon stepped over Kara's limp body and flung open the backdoor.

The best places to hide in the camper were probably inside the under-counter cabinets or underneath the bed. Jack chose the latter, pressing his back against the wall. He squeezed his eyes shut. In his mind, he had vanished, but in reality, he was a scared boy lying on his side, feigning sleep.

"Jack, I know where you are!" Shannon wailed, her voice horribly near. She was closing in, hurrying toward him over the grass.

Jack was still, hearing the sound of her reckless steps growing louder.

"I hate this ugly thing," he heard her say, the thornbushes rasping as she pulled their branches apart to make an opening for herself. She had spotted the camper. "You're not hiding in there, are you, Jack?" The tone of her voice had suddenly changed; she had asked it lightly as if this was just his mom's friend talking to him conversationally.

He opened his eyes and rolled to the middle of the floor. She was shielded in darkness, but he realized, so was he. He heard her come closer, cautiously, toward the rear of the camper, but he thought that maybe he had the upper-hand. He knew the angle of the parked vehicle and he knew about the trail into town. It was possible Shannon was unaware of these things in the dark.

Her annoyance was back. "Jack, get out here!" She cried out, then swore, having walked into a thornbush. She struggled, forgetting him for a moment, her mind on the plethora of burrs sticking to her. She ripped some off, but there were too many and now her hair had been caught on the bush. Someone tugged on her shirt.

She turned around, but saw no one. She started forward again, but her leg was yanked. Was that a ring of branches pulling her back? Weaved, thorny wood wrapped around her leg, tugging her downward. It felt like a hand bent into a vice-like grip, pulling into the meat of her leg. She twisted her head to see what had a hold of her.

A mist crept toward her and in the fog that wrapped around her leg a man's angry face appeared. She screamed at the same time his hazy mouth opened and howled at her.

Jack paused, listening as Shannon tried desperately to untangle herself from the wiry branches. He opened the door of the camper. It squeaked—there was no avoiding that—and he slipped down to the ground. He hurried, taking long, awkward strides, moving away as swiftly as he could, further into the woods.

Chapter Thirty-six

"Tom!" Shannon hollered, rushing in through the backdoor.

Tom sat on a kitchen chair, holding the gun in his hands. "What happened to you?" he asked, noticing the burrs stuck in her hair and on her hoodie and jeans. Bloody scratches were etched across her cheeks and chin.

"Are they still out?" She took in the scene in the great room. Kara, eyes closed, lay on the floor on the far side of the couch, only the top of her head seen from Shannon's view. John was near the fireplace, on his side.

"Yes, dammit!" Tom hissed. "Did you get him?"

Shannon bristled, slamming the door shut behind her and rounding the table. "No!"

"You dumb bitch!" Jane rose from the table and lunged for Shannon.

"Don't call me that!" Shannon ducked slightly, so that the plump woman was forced toward her curved upper back instead of her face. They crumpled to the tiled floor, Jane on top of Shannon only briefly, before Jane fell over so that Shannon was on top.

"Stop it!" Tom jumped to his feet, standing over the women who pounded each other and pulled hair. Jane overpowered Shannon and was now on top, straddling her.

"Get off me, you fat beast!" Shannon gasped.

"People can probably hear from the road," Tom growled, his voice low. He bent down, yanking Jane away by the armpits. She fell ungracefully onto her side, shaking the kitchen floor and rattling the dishes encased in the cabinets.

Shannon struggled to her feet and moved ungainly toward the great room.

"This is a joke. One big disaster," Jane said sardonically. She stayed seated on the kitchen floor.

Shannon turned around, glaring at her, caught in a moment of indecision as she didn't know if she should return to beat up the older woman or obey her boyfriend's command for peace.

"Jimmy died heartbroken," Jane hissed at Shannon. "You might as well have murdered him, taking this house away from him like you did."

"What are you going on about?" Shannon looked down at the sneering redhead.

"I'm not dumb."

"That's funny. You're certainly not smart."

"Shannon." A warning from Tom.

"You're an idiot. You let these bastards take all that Jimmy had. This house," Shannon's voice was rising steadily. "was his retirement plan. All you had to do was make sure he didn't lose the house. That was it. Even the plan to have Tom in charge of the bills, in charge of the construction, was so easy to follow. A moron could've just sat back and done nothing. All you had to do, you fat moron, was let Tom handle it!"

"Shannon, shut up!" Tom yelled.

"No, Tom!" Shannon hollered back. Her eyes burned on Jane, whose blazed back as she scrambled to her feet. "You were always so greedy. Jane, who thought it was her right to live in the fancy house. The fat cow who Uncle Jimmy wasn't ever going to marry. He only kept you around because he felt sorry for you."

Jane shook her head, her husky voice low, but dangerous, "He was going to have you out of the picture. It was a matter of time. I wasn't going to say anything." She was directing her words to Tom now, who sat at the table, glaring. "She has no idea we had a plan. That proves how good it was, and it was my plan. Well, mine and Jimmy's."

Seeing Tom wasn't disputing, Shannon asked Tom, "What's she talking about?"

He was silent.

Shannon redirected her gaze on Jane. "You're pathetic."

Jane laughed. "I'm not the pathetic one. Oh, I knew what my place was. You were the sad, clueless one."

"Shut your mouth!" Shannon lunged at her. Her body shuddered in rage as she shoved her fingernails into the side of the woman's exposed neck. Jane screamed in surprise at the sudden burning pain as Shannon's nails combed steadily and deeply into her flesh, moving downward until her hand bumped off the start of Jane's rounded shoulders.

"I'm going to kill you!" Jane screeched, bending over and running head-first into Shannon's belly. The force was enough to shove the pair into the great room, but not enough to knock Shannon down.

"Do it!" Shannon screamed. She turned around and raced back to the kitchen, her hand moving instinctively for the butcher block of knives, as she had misplaced her knife somewhere. Her fingers moved deftly to the handle of one, but they were not quick enough to grasp. Jane was on her, knocking her away and shoving her back to the floor.

"Stop it!" Tom sprung back to life. Matthew, forgotten, cowered under the table as Tom yelled again, "Stop this now!" Tom rounded the table and in two strides had them pulled apart.

He grasped onto a chunk of Shannon's hair and she yelped as he dragged her across the floor. He let go and she stood up uneasily. "Sit down!"

"Tom!" Shannon cried out in surprise.

His glare made her look down at the tabletop. He said in a low voice, "Seeing as our plan was doomed from the start, we need to figure out a new one. We've been screwed and we know that. Now we have to fix it. So, Shannon, where's the boy?"

She stuck out her lower lip. "I couldn't find him."

His voice rose, "Didn't you just follow him outside? Is he outside?"

She shrugged; it was the easy way to avoid probing questions she inexplicably couldn't answer. How could she explain that just moments before something had tugged on her, keeping her away from the camper? Something had scratched her. She wanted to believe she had gotten tangled in thornbushes, but she wasn't sure that was true. "I followed him outside." She looked up at her boyfriend, softening. "It's pitch black out there."

Tom sighed heavily. "Why did you come back? If you don't know where he went, why the hell would you come back inside? He might be at a neighbor's now calling the cops."

"Dummy didn't think," Jane spat. "Jimmy's rolling over in his grave."

"Jimmy was a moron," Shannon said. "He was useless, the downfall to this family. He never would've built this house if it weren't for Tom. He had no plans for his inherited property. Jimmy was an idiot and I'm glad he's dead."

"Shannon!" Tom cut in.

"I don't care anymore, Tom. This is our house. Jimmy was nothing more than a guy who mowed lawns. He would've been happy living in his camper."

"You're clueless," Jane said, her back propped up against the lower cabinets. "You were never part of the plan. Jimmy and Tom were going to build this house and then Tom was going to dump you. He doesn't want you."

Shannon glowered. "Shut up."

The older woman sighed. "Tom, I'm over this. When are you going to tell her the truth?"

Shannon looked at him. "Tom? What is she talking about?"

A beat passed before he turned his eyes on Shannon and opened his mouth. But before he could reply, a shuffling came from the great room.

Tom jumped up and spun around. John's eyes were still closed and Kara's head hadn't moved. Cautiously, Tom nudged them with the toe of his boot. He wondered if John had shifted in his deep sleep, but wasn't certain. Kara appeared to be in the same senseless state as before.

Tom returned to the kitchen. "We've sat too long."

"How do we know the girl is still upstairs?" Jane asked.

Shannon ran from the room, thundering up the stairs. "Tom! She's gone!"

Chapter Thirty-seven

Kara opened her eyes to a solid, pale blue ceiling. It looked near, but reaching out an unbounded arm, she realized it wasn't close at all. She shifted, realizing she lay on a hard surface. Something tickled her neck. She turned her head, finding she was on grass. The wall above wasn't a wall, after all. It was the sky: clear, powder blue, without a cloud to mar it.

As she wondered how she had gotten outside, she heard lapping water and intermittent bubbling. She eased up onto her elbows and looked out. Seeing evergreens horrified her. She recognized this place.

She sat up all the way and pulled her knees to her chest, raking her eyes over the grassy shoreline, then looked ahead at the wavering water. She didn't want to see anyone in the murky water, struggling to breathe, struggling to live.

"Leeeeaaaaaave!"

The command was like a thousand leaves brushing against the wind, an urgent sound she felt more than heard. It wasn't a prank; it was a command. Get out and go.

And she would. It was the one thing she wanted to do more than anything. She wanted to go.

Something yanked on her hands, making her look down at them. Her wrists were tied together with rope again. Trying to understand what was going on, the wind howled, forcing her to look up. The powder blue sky had turned a sickening greenish-gray.

It was going to storm. The lapping of the water had intensified, turning choppy now, and a whirlpool had formed in its center. A head bobbed; someone was in the center of its eye, their arms waving frantically as the churning water tugged them down.

333

Chapter Thirty-eight

Shannon ran downstairs and flung open the front door, expecting to see Lilah tottering down the front lawn. Instead, blackness stretched for a great distance until it was interrupted by dotted lights coming from the neighbors' houses across the road. She slammed the door shut and barreled down the hallway.

Another door slammed.

Tom, Shannon, and Jane turned toward the great room. Beyond Kara and John's limp bodies, the playroom door had closed. Jane, with Tom close behind, skirted across the room and pulled it open. Something yanked her in, the door slamming shut in Tom's face.

Tom twisted the doorknob, but the door stayed closed. "Is it locked?" he asked incredulously, knowing there was no lock.

Shannon pounded on the door. "Jane! Open the door!"

Something gurgled on the other side of the door, startling them, making them back away. The gurgling turned into gagging before reverting back.

Tom shoved Shannon, knocking her to the floor. She rolled onto Kara's leg. Kara moaned, but her eyes stayed shut. Tom changed course and started kicking the door. After a few tries, the wood splintered just below the knob. He started to reach his hand into the hole to grab the interior handle when the door swung open. He stumbled.

From the shadows, Jane faced him, her back pressed against the wall between the windows. Her fingers were wrapped around her throat, her eyes bulging.

Shannon had followed Tom in. "Is she choking herself?"

He moved cautiously toward Jane. That was what it looked like; it was as if she were fighting herself from strangulation.

334

He yanked on her wrists. But her hands held tight. Shannon pulled on Jane's waist, moving her as Tom tugged at her hands. Finally, as Jane's eyes started to close, her hands let go, the force of her release knocking Tom and Shannon to the floor.

As Jane slid to the floor, her cough rocking her whole body, Shannon and Tom noticed the puddle of water she sat in. Their eyes followed its path, seeing water streamed in from the window sill.

Jane jerked suddenly, her cough worsening for a moment before she started spitting up water. Shannon watched her, horrified. The redhead's body trembled violently for a moment.

When the cough had finally settled and she had regained her normal breathing, Shannon asked delicately, "What happened?"

Jane cleared her throat and worked to stand. She turned blazing eyes on Shannon. "I was drowning!"

The statement baffled them, but neither Shannon nor Tom made any comment. What they had witnessed made no sense, but they still hadn't found Lilah and that was where they turned their attention back to.

Tom went to the backdoor and pulled it open. A strong gust of wind blew, striking him off-balance. He fought against it, going to the deck. His hair whipping, he looked out over the dark trees surrounding them on all sides. The kids were out there somewhere.

Both women stood beside him, heads barely reaching his chin line.

"What're we gonna do?" Shannon asked, her voice unsteady.

The sound of the closing door woke Kara. From where she lay on the great room floor, the kitchen looked empty.

Had they all gone outside?

She eased herself up to sit, feeling every bruise and scrape on her body. She was disheartened to find her wrists were still tied together, the remnants of her dream still hovering in her mind. She was still a prisoner.

She honed in on the backdoor, expecting it to open at any moment. Her heart galloped so hard she barely heard anything else; she only had her eyes to rely on to know if her kidnappers (friends) would reappear in the kitchen. She crawled awkwardly to her unconscious husband and grabbed a hold of his shoulder, shaking him. She tugged at his shirt, but he was senseless.

Her cellphone was on the kitchen table. She could see it from the great room where she had now risen to her knees. She thought about looking for John's phone—it was probably in his pocket—but that would take too long to find. What if it wasn't there?

Kara rose to her feet and moved in a semi-squatted position, praying those on the deck didn't hear her. She hesitated at the kitchen's threshold. The room was fully lit and the backdoor was made up of glass panels. There was no hiding now. Shannon's back was to her, but she couldn't see where Tom and Jane were. Kara glanced at the cellphone and then back at the door. She swallowed, pausing the hammering in her head for a brief moment. She had to move fast.

She stepped into the kitchen and then halted on shaky legs.

Matthew was sitting under the kitchen table. She had forgotten about him. He had been looking out the backdoor too, but he heard Kara and now his eyes were on her. Close-up, he looked like a frightened boy. *He won't hurt you*, she told herself, *he's scared too.*

She straightened, then ran around the table, snatching her cellphone with her clasped hands, and bolted toward the front of the house. She pressed 9-1-1 on her way upstairs, searching for Lilah.

Chapter Thirty-nine

"The girl could still be inside for all we know," Jane's tone was neutral, not a hint of what had just happened detected. She appeared oblivious to her soaked shirt.

Tom scratched his head, knowing the woman beside him had nearly drowned (where the water had come from, he would have to think about later), but pushed it aside. He made his decision. "Shannon, go inside and look under the beds, in closets, inside cabinets, wherever. There's a good chance she never went outside. She knows you. She'll come to you."

But Shannon's mind was on the authorities. They had made such a commotion that even here on the outskirts of town, someone could've heard something out of the ordinary and made a fateful phone call. "What if the cops show up?"

His eyes were blazing as he spun around. "We need to hope no one heard anything and play this out. There's nothing else we can do. We need to fight while we still can."

"This has gone so totally wrong," Shannon said in a small voice.

"You started this and now we have to finish it," Tom said, softly. "You didn't think this through, Shannon. It's a mess."

"But we had to do something. They were living in our dream home."

"It wouldn't have been our dream home anyway."

"What do you mean? We still can live here. There's a chance."

He shook his head, looking down at her with sympathy. "That was never the plan. It's been over for a long time. We're done. I was going to break up with you months ago before all this started."

"What?"

Jane barged in, saying, "I'm gonna go look for these brats out here."

Tom grabbed Jane's arm and said to Shannon, "Just find the girl."

"What do you mean, you were going to break up with me?" Shannon asked, alarmed. "When? After you helped the Tamesons fix up their nice, new home? It was me that got you lined up to be in the house, to have access to it."

"I didn't need you to get my house back!" he spat back, startling her.

She scoffed, "Then what plan did you have, because you never told me anything."

"That's why I didn't tell you anything. I wasn't going to be with you anymore!"

The words cut her. She tried to swallow.

"Tom, I'm going," Jane said, annoyed with the time they were wasting.

"Okay, go!" He relented. "Take the woods over there on the side closest to town. He's only a kid, but he could've sensed it was smart to get help in town."

She headed off down the deck steps, disappearing into the darkness.

Shannon asked him, finding her voice, "What was your plan then?"

"My uncle and I were going to finish building the house and then he was going to have Jane and me live here with him. He was sick. I don't know if you know that, but he wouldn't have lived very long. Then Jane was gonna get the boot and it was going to be all mine. That was the plan."

"Why did you stay with me?"

"You know how fast it all happened. One day I was helping him put in floors and then the next day he was telling me he had been evicted, and then the sheriff showed up and forced us off the property." He didn't see her anymore. He was recalling that day and the disgrace he and his uncle faced over the next month. Jimmy had stopped

338

making payments on his building loan, had been foreclosed on a few months later, and had been evicted a few months after that, all without Tom being in the know. The bitterness of losing the property that had been in his family since the early 1800's had not faded since the day the sheriff had flashed the eviction notice in his face, the sheet of paper his uncle had pretended didn't exist.

"But if it weren't for me, you would never have been able to own the property," Shannon told him.

"What are you talking about? I didn't need you to get it. I was just slow on breaking it off with you. I had other things on my mind, didn't I?"

"He'd never have let you live here," she said. "You're dense. What would your uncle, practically married to that cow, want with you living here? I don't care that you thought he was sick or terminal or whatever. There's no way they would've kept you around for more than a few weeks. Your uncle wasn't trustworthy. He would've used you until the house was finished and then he would've shown you the door. You had no claim to the property. He would've married the cow and then when he died, if she didn't have a heart attack first, she would've owned the house. You never would've gotten it. So, I did what I did for us."

"Becoming friends with the Tamesons wouldn't have given us the house."

"Your uncle died before the Tamesons moved in. Remember?"

Tom's eyes flickered. Not more than six months ago, Jimmy had died. He had padded his lawn mowing business with some extra contracting work as a painter. He'd been at one of his jobs, painting the exterior siding of a commercial building when a sudden heart attack had sent him falling off scaffolding and onto the parking lot below.

"So what?"

"So, let's just say I knew he had a weak heart and I loosened some screws on the scaffolding…If we had been quicker, we could've bought the house back."

He was trying to understand. "Are you saying you made it so the scaffolding would fall apart?"

She drew her lips back, exposing brilliant white teeth. She looked inhuman, her cruelty illuminated by the single deck light. "I just hoped the fall to the ground would've broken his neck, killing him in a freak work accident. The heart attack made it all neat and tidy."

He hated her in that moment. There was no turning back to how he had felt about her a year ago. Back then, he thought they would've been married by now. "You're telling me you killed my Uncle Jimmy? The man who raised me? My only family in this world. You did that?"

She nodded, stepping close to him. She smiled tenderly, thinking this was her saving grace. Surely, he'd fall back in love with her again for what she'd done for them. She had removed the unneeded uncle and was well on her way to removing the Tamesons. The plan was getting back on track. They'd dispose of a few people—somehow—and then they'd be living here in their dream home just like they had planned all along.

He stepped back, his face distorting with rage. He was raising his clenched fist when a powerful blow knocked him down to the deck floor. A quick, whip-like crack thundered in the night.

Chapter Forty

Tom looked down at his chest and then at his legs. He was covered in blood, but he didn't feel pain. He was numb.

I've been shot! he thought wildly.

Lying on his back, he reached down to touch his thigh. He pulled his hand back and looked at it, seeing his fingertips were red. It was blood. But why couldn't he feel any pain? Was he in shock?

Who had shot him? Had Shannon been holding a gun?

"I hate you!" someone screamed.

He jerked up his head and upper back to find Jane on the deck, holding his gun. He scrambled to his butt and bent his blood-smeared legs, scooting back. He saw with horror that Shannon lay on her back, her arms and legs slightly bent from the fall, but mostly due to the impact of the lone bullet that had struck her chest.

He looked down at his legs and wiggled them. He patted his hands over them and his chest, realizing he hadn't been shot. It wasn't his blood.

It was Shannon's.

He stood up on wobbly legs.

Jane wasn't looking at him. She kicked Shannon hard in the side. "Are you dead?" Jane asked, sardonically.

"What did you do?" Tom scooted to where his girlfriend lay and looked down at her unblinking eyes that stared at the night sky, then at the bloody sweat jacket that covered her. "You killed Shannon?"

The wind whipped Jane's hair around, her distorted face a beacon in the midst of a hurricane. She spat, "She killed Jimmy. I heard her confess it. I loved him more than anything." She looked at him coldly. "Why did you stay with her for so long?"

"I don't know. I should've ended it a long time ago."

"Yeah, you really should have."

He didn't have time to react. Jane raised the gun and pointed it at him, firing; a second shot clipped through the night.

As the third bang shot through the cold darkness, this one self-inflicted, sirens rose from the depths down the road. A boy and his younger sister, spotted on Seter Lane moments before, had alerted a driver who had been pulling up to his farmhouse.

The Tamesons' front yard was suddenly bright, flooded with blazing white floodlights.

Epilogue

Normally, an overcast October day would have made Kara lethargic. She wouldn't have wanted to get out of bed. But that day, she didn't notice the gray clouds that had gathered in the sky, blocking out the sun, nor the chilly air that added to the bleakness. Today was a happy day. At least that was what she had decided it would be.

She turned her back on the house at 110 Seter Lane and, taking Lilah's hand in hers, walked cautiously down the porch steps. Her sleep had improved (she hadn't had any nightmares anyway), but she still hadn't slept through the night. None of them had been sleeping very well in the hotel room they'd been staying in over the last week. The soreness from the hard, ultra-thin mattress hadn't done Kara's bruised body any favors.

"Mommy, will we have a big yard?" Lilah asked, letting go of Kara so she could clutch onto the statue with both hands.

"Big enough," Kara replied, following Lilah down the stepping stones that led them through the grass. Truthfully, she didn't think there was much lawn on the property of the apartment complex they were moving to in town. But she didn't add to her statement.

"Mom, can we get chicken tenders for lunch?" Jack called from the sedan.

"Yeah, that sounds good," Kara replied. She and John had spoken with the kids very little about the horrific night, but they knew the day would come when there'd be questions. Although they didn't press the subject, they had assured the them the bad guys were all gone.

Well, almost.

The police told her, and John tried to reassure her, that Matthew Foreman, the lone antagonist who had survived that night, was no threat; especially since he was tucked away in a psychiatric hospital. He had had a mental breakdown that night and apparently, hadn't come out of it. At least, that's what she was told. Nobody mentioned if they had reached out to Diane about her son. Kara assumed they had.

Kara gazed across the front lawn to the lemon house, peeking from behind the fall foliage. John didn't know she had gone over there earlier that morning. She had slipped in the screened porch and through the front door into the house, which had been, surprisingly, left unlocked. Kara had called for Diane, passing from room to room, not caring she was trespassing. Ultimately, it didn't matter: Diane wasn't there.

Kara looked around, seeing two framed photographs of Diane and Marvin propped up on the fireplace mantle in the living room: one of them from a decade or so before, and the other a faded shot of them as a young couple on their wedding day.

Kara was invading their privacy, she knew that, but the longer she was there, the more she wanted to see, wanted to know about her quirky neighbors. She returned to rooms she had breezed through earlier and even glanced into closets. She couldn't say she gleaned any information related to Diane's whereabouts and, really, her visit resulted in more questions than answers. Why, for example, did Marvin have more clothes than Diane hanging in the closet, and why didn't Diane have anything in any of the bedroom dressers? Marvin's belongings were everywhere: his slippers by the TV set in the living room, his dirty boots by the backdoor, a book on farming left open near the kitchen sink.

Where did Diane keep her things?

Kara didn't stay much longer, knowing she'd stayed too long and, frankly, she was unsettled by the questions that were growing. Diane was a mystery to her and it seemed she always would be.

Kara had packed Sophie's memory box in cardboard marked, "Sophie" in black ink. Even though Shannon hadn't said anything about putting the white box on her bedroom floor or moving the receiving blanket into the kitchen drawer, Kara told herself it had to have been Shannon that had done those things, because Kara couldn't cope with the blame. She had looked one last time at the box's contents, making sure the receiving blanket still smelled of baby powder, before packing it away. She wouldn't pull the box out until they had moved into their permanent home. She wouldn't keep it hidden like she had. She just needed to wait until the time was right to display it.

As Kara approached the sedan, there was a sudden crash that made all of them jump. She spun around, looking up at the French country house with the rounded, chocolate brown shutters and the creeping brick that edged around the first-floor windows, her heart beating wildly. But nothing stirred; the curtains stayed shut, sheltering all of the windows, blocking her out.

"Mommy!" Lilah cried.

Kara looked down. The statue had fallen, busted into tiny pieces. Kara stood over the mess and half-expected to see some hidden treasure, perhaps a slip of paper, a note. But the statue had been hollow inside all along.

"All set?" John called. He stood beside the rented moving truck, his hand resting on the driver's door handle. They were all packed.

Kara glanced up again at the house, the dream home. Her eyes scanned the trees that framed the picture-perfect house. She was glad she couldn't see the single, stray white scarf she knew was staying behind, the one she had seen when she had tried to make her escape that night through the playroom.

There was a mystery on the hill, one she had been hounded by in her dreams. She had some pieces of the story, or so she thought. She knew Robert Collumber and his beautiful Elizabeth had met there, just like she knew he had had a barn once at the end of the lane where the dilapidated gray structure now sat. The young couple had tried to raise their child at the fine estate in town, but all of their lives had ended in misery.

Kara wondered at the way the wind had blown that horrible night a week ago, and thought perhaps, something otherworldly had helped her family survive, perhaps the Collumbers, but that was too fantastical to think about at present. She hadn't told John about them, but maybe one day, far in the future, she would when the pieces made sense—if they ever made sense.

Eventually, after the house sold, they'd start looking for another home. Maybe a dream home, maybe not. She wasn't picky; she was looking for ordinary now.

"We're ready," Kara said. She led Lilah to the car, ignoring her cries. Kara didn't bother picking up the shattered clay pieces scattered over the stepping stones.

*** *** ***

Acknowledgments

Writing fiction can be a lonely activity. Basically, it's just you and the pretend people you've made up. Plotting, however, can be a family sport.

Thank you to Chris, Gwendolyn, and Daegan for thinking out loud with me when I've come across a plot hole, listening to me read you an excerpt for feedback, and for leaving me to my quiet workspace (i.e. make-believe world) when you've seen me typing. Your support has helped me immensely.

Also, a special, additional thank you to Chris for the cover art, formatting guidance, and steadfast encouragement. I've spent too many years on Seter Lane and I swear (this time for real), I have moved on to writing the next novel.